WILTED CROWNS

WILTED CROWNS

IRONFORGED • BOOK ONE

JT BALDWIN

ISBN-13: 978-1-968923-22-8

Cover design by: JT Baldwin
Printed in the **United States of America**

To Queen Aerin of House Gennom, Elsbeth Ellinon, and Peri Blackwood—
though the names have changed over the years, the inspiration has not.
To me, you will always be Meg.

"THEY GAVE US A CROWN OF DUTY – NOT OF GOLD, BUT OF OBLIGATION.

NOT TO RULE, BUT TO PRESERVE.

NOT TO COMMAND, BUT TO SERVE.

HISTORY TEACHES US THAT EMPIRES DO NOT FALL TO INVADERS ALONE. THEY ROT FROM WITHIN—WHEN CONTROL IS MISTAKEN FOR ORDER, AND SILENCE REPLACES TRUTH.

POWER DEMANDS SCRUTINY. AUTHORITY DEMANDS LIGHT."

– **Minister of War Renik Korvyn**
Address to the Continental Council, 2156

Book One | TABLE OF CONTENTS

Front Matter

Wilted Crowns

Back Matter

Book One | Map

CONTINENTAL GEOGRAPHIC SURVEY

Eastern & Central Territories

Commissioned under the Pendleton Infrastructure Act, 2155 A.E.

Revised Edition – 2191

⊙

The Bethshelm Canal predates the Continental Authority by two centuries—built to carry coal and ore from the Blackiron mines to the smelters at the water's edge.

Thirty-seven gates still control the flow.

LEGEND

- ◇ Town
- ◈ Township/Transfer Stations
- ● Minor Metropolitans
- ◉ Major Metropolitans
- ⚓ Port – Union Administrative District | **UAD**
- ⊛ Capital – Continental Authority District | **CAD**

a Basin
Halstrom Entry
Pinecrest
North
Port Adams
Braelocke Hollow
Margos
Greeley
Hammison
Authority
Kiron
Gate 20 - Hammison
Gate 12 - Breakwater
Bethshelm
Gul

UAD Port Franklin | Reed's Harb
Valcross Junction
The Chapi Loop
Millhaven
Eastrun Power Complex
Kijorh Dam
Belfast Mills
ate 31 - Kiron Hills Lock
Steps | Tiller's Gap
UAD Beltmoire | Beltmoire
Sarin Bay
Delvaine
Valdris Sea
Solstice Bay
CAD Hamilton
nta
UAD Port Madiso

Part 1

"Our northern territories have become dependent on failure. When infrastructure collapses, someone always fills the void—smugglers, thieves, opportunists who dress criminality in the language of community. They are not heroes. They are symptoms. And we do not treat disease by celebrating its symptoms. We treat it by restoring what should never have broken."

— **Chief Minister Shori Ashford**
Internal Policy Assessment, 2189

1 | Peri

Mid Spring | 2191.110 · 5:45 | Z2

Gate 31 | Kiron Hills Locks

Peri's eyes opened to riveted steel and the water stain she'd been watching spread since winter. Industrial windows letting in the first gray suggestion of dawn. The air held the damp chill of the canal, her breath misting white above the wool blanket.

Her hand found the nightstand, fingers closing around chrome before her mind caught up. Stopwatch.

She sat up. Her feet hit the floor, shock traveling through her ankles.

She dressed in darkness. Shirt. Pants. Boots—soles worn thin enough to feel gravel through them—laced with fingers that didn't need her. Jacket off the chair—mustard canvas soft at the elbows, oiled against the weather, smelling like every job she'd ever worked.

The stopwatch slid into her pocket, thumb lingering on its worn edge.

The door eased open, quiet against its hinges. The warehouse spread beneath her. Three stories of open dark, the kind that settled into concrete and stayed. Tarps over vehicles in the gloom, the bulk of the forge, tool racks along the far wall, every peg loaded, everything in its place. Windows blacked out on the lower floors, the glass painted over so long ago the paint had started to peel.

Overhead, the fluorescent tubes clicked on in sequence, humming to life one bank at a time. Cold light stuttering across steel.

Machine oil and concrete. Home.

The stairs rang beneath her, each step a quiet percussion that carried through the open space. Three flights down, her hand on the railing not because she needed it but because the metal was so cold it kept her sharp.

Light from the far corner. Kitt's workbench. A small sun in all that darkness.

Peri crossed the floor, weaving between tool chests and parts bins. Ahead, the workbench light pooled in a circle on the floor. Kitt sat inside it. Hunched forward, hands working.

She'd been there all night. Peri knew it from the set of her shoulders before she was close enough for anything else.

Kitt. The dark circles were worse—Peri clocked that first. The hair shoved into its usual chaos, the hoodie pulled against a chill she hadn't thought to fix. Seventeen, and running on nothing again. Her fingers moved between the iron and the wire strippers like they didn't know the rest of her was exhausted. Maybe they didn't. Smoke curled from the iron's tip, the sharp bite of hot solder cutting through all that oil and concrete.

Months of this.

"Frequency drift." Kitt's eyes stayed on the components. "The crystal oscillator keeps shifting." She exhaled through her nose. "Fucking tolerances."

Peri watched her work. The way her fingers moved, even now, even like this—still certain. Kitt touched the multimeter probes to the open guts of a field radio, Authority surplus, modified well past recognition, and watched the needle swing across the dial. Tapped the case with one knuckle. The needle drifted. Settled.

Peri stopped at the edge of the light.

"Three months." Kitt didn't look up. "Three months of chasing this. Sixteen relay stations across the territory. Every time I think it's stable, the drift compounds and the whole network drops." Her fingers made tiny adjustments with a pair of pliers. "The old crystal stocks are depleted. Nobody manufactures to these tolerances anymore. Everything we've built. Gone."

"Kataero have any ideas?"

"Dad taught me engines, not this." Kitt's mouth twitched. "He'd have put it through the wall by now."

Peri's gaze traveled across the workbench. Wire clippings. Handwritten notes. Schematics that looked more like maps than circuits, numbers crowding the margins in Kitt's cramped hand. A pencil sketch half-pinned under a coffee mug—something structural, concrete and water, lines too deliberate to be absent-minded. Her eyes moved past it. Tools laid out in cases with foam cutouts for each piece. The kind you couldn't buy, only inherit or trade favors for.

"Morning," Peri said.

Kitt glanced at her, then back to the oscillator. A nod. "You're early."

"Same time as always."

"Sun's not up yet." She touched the probes to another point, checked the dial. "That makes it early."

Peri stepped closer. The only warm spot in the whole place, heat coming off the lamp, the iron, Kitt herself. The radio pulled apart, wires spilling out of it. The iron still trailing smoke. Half-empty coffee cup balanced near the edge.

Her thumb found the stopwatch through the fabric of her pocket. She shifted her weight. Then again.

"You've been at this all night."

"Couldn't sleep." Kitt set the iron down. Her eyes found the copper tangle framing Peri's face. Her mouth twitched. "What's happening with your hair?"

"You're one to talk."

Kitt raked her fingers through her own cropped mess. "I've been working for hours."

Peri touched the side of her head. "Yeah. I just woke up."

"Sit." Kitt gestured to the stool.

"I need to—"

"Sit down. You can't run like that. You'll waste time stopping halfway through to fix it when it drives you insane."

Peri sat. The stool cold through her pants. She turned her back to Kitt, and her leg started bouncing before she'd settled. The warehouse door right there. Twenty steps. Less.

Kitt's hands slid into her hair. Fingers separating the tangled mess, working through knots with small, sure pulls. Peri's head tilted before Kitt asked it to—her neck already knowing the angle, the way it had since she was small enough for someone else's hands to do this. She couldn't remember whose.

For a moment, Peri stopped wanting to move.

Her eyes closed. The pull and weave, Kitt's callused fingertips brushing her neck. She could hear the soldering iron ticking as it cooled, metal settling in the roof beams, the low murmur of water cycling through the lock gates.

Her leg had stopped bouncing. She didn't know when.

Kitt wove the final section and secured it with the elastic from her wrist. One last tug drew the braid snug against Peri's spine.

"There. Done."

Before Peri could stand, Kitt's arms came around her from behind. Peri went still—and then her weight settled back against Kitt's chest. Kitt's chin on her shoulder, the hold sudden and tight despite the cold. Close enough to feel her breath, the coffee and solder smoke that clung to her.

"You okay?" Kitt asked.

Peri looked down at Kitt's forearm where it crossed her chest. Caught it. Held it. The difference in their coloring so plain up close—Kitt's darker skin against her own.

She squeezed once.

"Yeah. Just need to run."

Kitt stayed a moment longer, breath warm on Peri's neck. Then let go.

Peri stood. Scalp tingling from the tight braid. Already wanting the door.

Kitt picked up the soldering iron.

"Say hi to Emma for me."

Peri headed for the warehouse door. Cold morning air hit her face when she pushed through, carrying the smell of canal water and spring growth.

Behind her, the workbench still glowed. Kitt's small sun against the warehouse dark.

Peri pulled the stopwatch from her pocket.

⊙

The service road stretched east. Behind her the lock towers rose against the gray sky, rust bleeding down their faces in long orange streaks, the spillway dark and dripping.

Peri stopped at the edge. Rolled her right ankle, then her left. Swung each leg forward and back, feeling the hip flexors wake up. A lunge on each side, quads loading, the pull in her left shoulder when she reached—she rolled it once, twice, let it settle. Slapped both thighs hard enough to feel it.

She straightened. Shook out her arms.

Drew a slow breath in. Let it out.

A red curl dropped across her face. She blew it aside.

Let's do this.

Click.

Her legs slipped into rhythm at once. Not fast. Not yet. Just steady.

Ten miles. Five out, five back. Downhill on the way out, uphill coming home.

Each exhale ghosted white, heat building as her body found the gear it knew—the one between effort and ease where nothing hurt. Boots on wet pavement, the canal sliding past on her left, black water catching the first light. Her breath and her footfalls and nothing else.

The road unwound ahead of her, empty, the world not awake yet. Stride lengthening as the muscles warmed, the tightness in her calves loosening, her arms settling into their swing. She passed the first mile marker without checking the stopwatch.

Just this. Just the body in motion.

Mile three. The canal bending south. The road rising slightly, her legs adjusting without being told. Trees thinned along the bank and the hills opened up around her, wide and green and still holding the last of the morning fog in their hollows. Smoke from Belfast Mills hung low in the still air ahead.

Kitt's voice, bleeding through. *Three months. Nobody manufactures to these tolerances anymore.*

Nobody builds anything, anymore. Peri pushed harder.

Sky brightening. Streetlamps clicking off along the canal, photocells registering dawn.

Braid whipping against her back.

Mile four. Belfast Mills. Brick and timber houses climbing the hillside, chimneys trailing coal smoke into the pale sky. Doors opening. A dog tied outside the general store, watching her pass. The smell of bread from somewhere. The Chen bakery, ovens already going.

The lights were wrong.

Kitchen windows flickering. Brightening, dimming, clawing back. The grid straining under morning load, worse than last week, worse than the week before that. The whole settlement blinking.

Movement ahead.

A kid burst from one of the houses. Yellow coat stark against the gray. Emma Chen, dark hair streaming, legs pumping as she tried to cut Peri off.

Peri shortened her stride.

"Peri!" Emma windmilled both arms, managed a few stumbling strides alongside. All elbows, knees, more enthusiasm than coordination. "Mama says thank you for the medicine! My brother's fever broke!"

"That's good, Emma."

Emma was already falling back, legs too short to hold the pace. Still waving. "Thank you!"

"Say hi to your mama." Peri lifted a hand as the gap widened. The yellow coat getting smaller behind her. Three weeks ago they'd lifted those antibiotics, the job that almost got them caught. Emma's brother had come back from the edge.

She faced forward. Let the rhythm take her back.

Sixteen relay stations.

Mile five.

The road ended where pavement became dirt track. Kyjorh Dam rose against the brightening sky, two hundred feet of concrete climbing out of the valley. Even from here the rust-orange stains bled down its face where the rebar had gone through. Water pooling at the base where it shouldn't be. The western spillway casting a shadow that sat wrong against the valley floor.

Peri slowed, letting her heart rate come down in stages. Sweat dripping from her temples despite the morning chill.

The sun broke the horizon. Warmth on her flushed face. The dam's shadow pulling back from the valley floor.

Peri turned. Faced uphill.

Five miles. The grade she'd been saving.

She started running.

Gravity hit at once. Legs protesting. She drove harder.

Each breath scorched. Thighs screaming, calves knotting.

Sweat in her eyes. Salt sting.

Seven miles. Eight.

Legs shaking. Speed bleeding off.

She didn't stop.

Nine.

Breathing ragged. Gasps that never filled her lungs.

The last mile burned worse. Every stride an argument. Everything begging to stop.

She held the pace.

Gate 31 ahead.

Click.

Peri stepped off the road into wet grass. Her legs quit. Just refused. She went over backward. The impact soft. Cold seeping through cloth, shocking on overheated skin.

She lay there. Staring up at a sky gone bright and endless.

Her lungs heaved, each breath dragging back toward normal. Her heart hammered, pulse so strong she felt it in her temples, her wrists, her throat. Sweat ran from her hairline into the grass, the heat bleeding out of her in stages. Muscles twitching, calves, quads, the long muscles along her spine, firing at nothing, still running when the rest of her had stopped.

The clouds moved. Slow and enormous, pulling west. She felt herself go with them, the ground tilting under her back, the sky and the earth trading places. The wind pushed through the grass and she felt it on wet skin and she stopped knowing which direction was up. The world enormous and indifferent and real.

Then the stillness found her. The run was over and there was nothing between her and herself.

Her fingers found the stopwatch in her jacket pocket. Closed around chrome still warm from her body, pulling it free.

Her arm dropped to the grass. She wasn't ready to look. Not yet. The sky above her, bright and empty, the kind of sky that didn't care what the number said.

Her breathing slowed. She lifted the stopwatch. Held it above her, arm trembling from the run or from something else. The sun behind the watch, blue sky framed in the gap between her fingers.

Eighty-six minutes.

Three minutes slower than yesterday.

The number settled into her chest like something swallowed wrong. She kept her arm up, the watch trembling against the sky, as if holding it there long enough might change what it said. Eighty-six. Not the eighty-two she'd been chasing for weeks. Not the number that meant she was worth the space she took up.

She closed her eyes. Let the stopwatch rest on her thigh. Chrome going cold against her leg.

"Peri!" Kitt's voice, from down the hill. "I got a job!"

She didn't move. The number still there behind her closed eyes, white against dark, the way numbers stayed when she'd stared at them too long.

"Peri?" Closer now. More insistent.

The sky came back. The wet grass beneath her. Kitt's voice pulling her up from wherever she'd gone.

She let out a slow breath. A copper curl had worked free, brushing her cheek. She pushed it back.

She slipped the stopwatch inside her jacket pocket.

She stood. Muscles protesting. Legs shaking.

"Coming!" she called back. Brighter than she felt.

She started walking toward Kitt's voice.

2 | Peri

2191.110 · 7:24
Gate 31

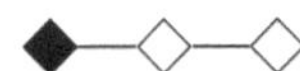

"Peri!"

Kitt came up the road at a jog, arms swinging, and pulled up short a few feet away. Rubbed her arms once. The hoodie wasn't built for standing still.

"Where have you been?"

Peri looked at her.

Kitt's mouth pressed shut. She fell in beside her without another word.

They walked back toward the warehouse together, gravel crunching underfoot, the morning cold between them. The door stood open. The shade hit Peri and she went still—just cold, just shadow, sweat cooling tight across her shoulders. Dust turned slow circles in the shaft of morning light behind her.

Her legs remembered every step of the climb.

Kitt drifted toward her workbench. Pulled out the chair and dropped into it the way she always did, one leg tucking under her. Her eyes moved over the scattered components, reorienting herself.

"How was the run?"

"Hard." Peri crossed the floor, boots scuffing concrete. Her right calf cramped mid-step. She caught herself on the edge of the workbench, waited it out. "Took longer than yesterday."

Kitt nodded once. Didn't push it. Her hand found the notepad.

"I got something." She looked up. "You're gonna hate it."

"Then start with the part that makes it worth hearing."

Peri dragged a chair over. The metal legs grated against the floor. Sitting hurt almost as much as standing.

"Tell me."

Kitt came alive.

"Okay. Here." She flipped back through the notepad, quick, practiced, someone who knew exactly where everything lived. "Three weeks ago. Chatter about generator assemblies. Confirmation requests for turbine components, industrial cabling." She turned more pages. "Then here. Switching assemblies. Someone asking about routing schedules through the northern corridor."

Peri nodded, eyes tracking the cramped handwriting. Diagrams she couldn't read. Columns of numbers with units she didn't recognize.

Kitt stopped. Watched her face.

"Still with me?"

"Keep going."

Kitt reached under the bench. Pulled out a second notebook, older, the cover soft at the corners. Then a third. She stacked them beside the first.

Peri looked at the stack.

A year. Maybe more. Kitt had been filling these, cycling through them, filing them away under her bench, saying nothing. Waiting until she had something real.

When did you start this?

She didn't ask.

Kitt was already moving, pulling the oldest notebook from the stack, flipping to a dog-eared page with the ease of someone navigating her own mind. "LAP-7. A year ago it was just noise—construction authorizations, procurement requests. Authority bureaucracy." She looked up. "Then the same designation started showing up in engineering consultations. Structural assessments. Reservoir capacity studies. Different departments entirely."

She reached under the bench and came up with a folded map, worn soft at the creases, spread it across everything. Northwestern region. Port Adams along the coast, rail corridors threading inland, and there—southeast of the city, up into the mountains—a red circle, hand-drawn, slightly uneven.

"Lake Alpine." Kitt's finger landed on it. "They finished the reservoir two years ago and nobody asked what comes next." She looked up. "I've been asking."

"And this morning?"

"Shipping manifest fragments. Same designation—procurement this time." She looked like someone who'd been sitting alone with a lit fuse. "They're not planning anymore. They're building."

Peri leaned in. "Building what?"

"Generator assemblies. Transformer units. Turbine components." Kitt's finger moved across the map. "You don't order turbine components to patch something. This is new infrastructure. Factory-fresh, moving north through a corridor that doesn't match standard Authority distribution routes."

"A train."

"A supply train. Northern route. Couple weeks out, maybe less." She shrugged the hoodie off and dropped it over the chair back. The shirt underneath read *Power Outage* across the chest. "I don't have the exact schedule yet. But I know the corridor and I know what's on it."

Peri leaned back. The chair creaked under her. She stared at Kitt's notes without reading them, letting the shape of it form.

"So right now we have a possible train hauling maybe-useful equipment, headed vaguely north, sometime in the next one to two weeks."

Kitt's expression flickered. "When you say it like that—"

"I'm not throwing it out." Peri motioned at the notebooks. "I'm sorting what we know from what we're filling in."

Kitt's jaw tightened. "I've been following LAP-7 for over a year. These people have been feeding me pieces the whole time—not all at once, not in a way that was useful until now. But every single fragment checked out. Every one." She looked at Peri. "They've never been wrong. Not once."

Peri let that sit. A year. Pieces. Every one.

"That's different from what came through this morning."

"Different how?"

"Because cargo manifests and routing data aren't fragments, Kitt. That's not someone passing along overheard chatter." Peri nodded at the notebooks. "Someone either got access they didn't have before, or they had it all along and never shared it." She let that land. "Either way, I want to know why they're giving it to us now."

Kitt's knuckles went white against the bench edge. "Does it matter if we can verify it?"

"Whether it is or not, we still need to know where it's coming from. We need that answer."

"It's the answer you're getting right now." Kitt pulled the notepad back an inch. "The information checks out. The cargo types make sense. The timing is solid. Do you want to explore this or keep cross-examining me?"

"I'm not cross-examining you. I'm asking what we're working with before we commit to chasing this."

Boots on concrete. Heavy, measured steps crossing the warehouse floor.

Connor came in first, two plates balanced easily in his broad hands. Steam curled from eggs, bread torn into rough chunks beside them. Kataero followed half a step behind, carrying mugs that clinked softly.

Kitt shot to her feet. "Dad. Tell them this is worth looking at."

Kataero's gaze moved from Kitt to Peri. He said nothing. Just set the mugs down.

Connor set a plate in front of Peri, then one in front of Kitt. He looked at her.

Peri pulled the stopwatch from her pocket and held it up.

Eighty-six minutes.

She watched his face work the math. Three minutes off pace. Three minutes she couldn't account for with terrain or weather or tired legs.

Connor's eyes narrowed a fraction. His hand came down on her shoulder. Stayed there. Weight without words.

Then he let go and stepped back.

"What job?" Kataero asked.

"Supply train. Northern route. Couple weeks out, maybe less." Kitt gestured at the notebooks, the map still spread across everything. "Generator assemblies. Turbine components. Infrastructure equipment—the real kind. Factory-fresh. LAP-7, the Lake Alpine project. Someone finished the reservoir and now they're moving the rest of the pieces into position." She looked at him. "This could actually fix something. Not patch it, not keep it limping another month. Fix it."

Kataero picked up the notepad. His eyes moved over Kitt's scrawl, the manifest fragments, the routing notes, the columns of cargo designations. Then they settled on the map beneath it.

He reached out and pulled it free from under the notebooks.

"This is my map."

Kitt's chin lifted slightly. "I borrowed it."

"Unborrow it back where you found it." He held it out.

Kitt took it, mouth pressed flat, and folded it with slightly more force than necessary.

Kataero looked at the notepad again. "Generator parts," he said quietly.

"Yes."

"And turbine components."

"Yes."

He set the notepad down the way he'd set the mugs—precisely, like each object had earned its place. His eyes moved to Kitt. "Where is this intelligence coming from?"

Kitt's fingers clenched. She looked at Kataero. Then at Peri. Then back.

"Gods." She flung her hands up. "You and Peri—" Irritation flared. She shook her head. "You're both asking the wrong question."

"No," Kataero said. "Because if someone has access to Continental Authority manifests, they're either inside the system or stealing from it. Either way, there are risks we need to understand before we move."

Kitt snatched the notepad back.

Connor put his mug down. Not loud. Just enough.

The room stilled around it.

He reached for the notepad, waited just long enough for Kitt to let it go. His eyes moved through the routes and cargo codes the way they moved through everything. No hurry. No reaction. When he looked up, his gaze settled on Kitt.

"Can you get more?" Quiet. Direct.

Her grip loosened a fraction. "Yes."

Connor glanced at Kataero.

Kataero nodded once. "Timeline?"

"Two weeks. Maybe less."

"Then get us what we need." His tone stayed even. "Then we decide."

Connor's hand closed on Peri's arm, a single measured squeeze. Then he headed for the door.

Kataero lingered. His gaze moved between Kitt and Peri.

"Eat," he said. "Both of you."

Then he followed Connor out.

Kitt set her fork down before she'd picked it up. "You could have backed me up. Just a little."

Peri's elbow found Kitt's ribs. Not hard.

Kitt's head jerked up, startled.

"Hey." Peri waited until Kitt looked at her. "You held your ground in there with something real and you didn't back down. That's not nothing."

She nudged her again, lighter. "Even if you did yell at Kataero."

"Doesn't feel like I did much."

"Yeah, well." Peri flicked her fingers toward the scattered notebooks. "Get your source to cough up the rest. Then we'll have something to really fight about."

Kitt glanced down at her plate. "You think this is worth chasing?"

"I think you found something." Peri met her eyes. "So prove me right."

Kitt picked up her fork. After a moment she edged closer and let her head tip against Peri's shoulder.

Peri kept eating, letting Kitt's weight settle there. The smell of solder smoke still in her hair. Her own legs throbbed, exhaustion buried deep in the bone.

"If this lands," Kitt murmured, "there could be more." She speared a bite of egg, then used the fork to trace invisible routes in the air between them. "I've been tracking patterns. Infrastructure loads moving through corridors that don't add up. Feels like somebody's rebuilding things where no one's looking."

She bit down on the fork. Chewed. Her eyes still connecting lines only she could see.

Not just a one-off haul. A line of jobs Kitt had been mapping while the rest of them kept their eyes on next week's survival.

"One step at a time," Peri said.

Kitt lifted her head. "I need you to trust me on this."

Peri met her gaze. Dark brown. Steady.

"I do trust you." She didn't look away. "That's why I'm asking questions."

Kitt searched her face, weighing that. Then she nodded.

The light in the warehouse shifted as a cloud crossed the sun. They sat working through lukewarm eggs.

⊙

Crossing the warehouse floor, she caught the end of her braid—Kitt's work from this morning, still holding. She worked the elastic free.

The metal stairs rang under her boots. Her calves burned on every lift, her thighs trembling just enough that she caught the railing harder than she needed to.

She'd made it three steps up when Kataero's voice cut across the warehouse.

"Peri."

He never raised it. He didn't need to.

Her grip tightened on the railing, knuckles pale against the metal. She glanced back toward the corner office where yellow light spilled from the open doorway.

Three more seconds and she could have claimed she hadn't heard.

She turned and came back down, boots ringing on every step. Her fingers went back to the braid, working the next section loose.

Kataero sat at his desk, papers spread across every surface—maps of the northern territories marked in pencil, shipping manifests stacked by priority, Connor's handwritten notes on patrol patterns. Morning sun slanted through the window behind him, amber light catching the edges of everything.

Connor leaned against the window frame, arms crossed, eyes on the warehouse floor.

"Close the door."

She stepped in and pulled it shut.

She took the seat opposite the desk—wood, hard-backed. Her hands kept working the braid. Unwinding what Kitt had wound. Half of it still held, the other half loose and curling against her shoulder.

Kataero set his pen down. "What's your take on this?"

"The job?" She worked another section free. "Can't give much of an opinion on something we know so little about. But Kitt's passionate about it. That alone makes it worth exploring."

"And the source?"

"What about it?"

"What do you know about them?"

Her fingers slowed. "What Kitt told us. She's been working with them for three years. She trusts them."

"That's Kitt's assessment. I'm asking for yours."

She pulled the next section loose. "Kitt doesn't talk about her contacts. I know what she shares and nothing more."

She kept her eyes on the braid. Both of them knowing that wasn't an answer either.

Kataero's eyes stayed on her. "That doesn't concern you?"

"Should it?" She shrugged. "It's her world. She knows what she's doing."

"So none of us have met this source. None of us know who's feeding her Union logistics data or why."

"If the intel verifies, does it matter?"

Kataero leaned back. He turned the notepad square on the desk.

"It matters because Kitt is the only one vouching for it. Everything we'd be risking rides on her read of people none of us have properly vetted." He looked at her. "Do you think she's mature enough to carry that?"

Peri tilted her head slightly. "What does that mean?"

"She's seventeen."

"So?"

"So this isn't a supply lift. This isn't skimming food off Union convoys. This is infrastructure equipment. The kind of operation where one mistake gets people killed."

She tugged at the braid, harder than she needed to. "She did good work. She found something worth pursuing and she brought it forward. What more do you want?"

"I want to be certain she's ready for this."

"She's ready." Peri heard her own voice come out wrong—too fast, too loud.

Kataero's face didn't move.

"You heard what she had. You saw her stand her ground. What else does she have to prove?"

"I'm not questioning her planning. I'm asking whether this is the right job to learn on."

"Learn on." Her fingers found the last section, the tight one, the knot Kitt always tied at the base of her skull. She worked at it, nails catching, the knot refusing to give.

"How old was I when I started running my own jobs? Fifteen? Sixteen?"

"That was different."

"How?" She pulled harder. The knot held. "How is it different?"

"Because you were ready."

"And she's not?"

"I'm saying she hasn't run anything at this scale before." Kataero's tone stayed level. "Neither have you, for that matter. This is new ground for both of you."

Her fingers dug into the knot. Pulling. Twisting. It wouldn't give.

"Dammit, Kitt." She pulled harder. "Why are you so good at this?"

She tore at it.

The knot gave. The last of the braid unraveled, copper hair spilling wild around her shoulders.

She turned on Kataero. Her fist came down on the desk. Papers jumped.

"You're saying she's not there yet." The words came out flat, like she'd been waiting for him to say it. "That's what this is."

"I was fifteen the first time you sent me out alone. Nobody pulled me into an office. Nobody asked if I was ready or whether it was the right job to learn on." She pressed her knuckles into the desk. "I just went. Because that's what you needed."

"That isn't what I'm saying."

"Then what are you saying?" The heat climbing now, each word finding the next faster than she could weigh them. "You never questioned me. Never once. You just pointed and I ran." She pressed harder against the desk. "Because nobody told me I could stop."

"Peri... slow down."

"But Kitt gets the worry. The questions. Someone in her corner asking whether she's ready." Her jaw tightened. "Everything I never got. Because nobody ever—"

"That isn't—"

"Because she's your—"

Connor coughed.

Peri snapped in his direction. "What?!"

He hadn't shifted an inch. His storm-gray eyes were on her now, steady and unblinking, and she understood immediately that the cough had been a choice.

The blood left her face.

She stood there with her hands braced against the desk and nowhere to put what she'd almost said.

"Peregrine."

The anger went out of her the way heat leaves metal.

"I'm sorry." It scraped out small, uneven. She couldn't lift her eyes from the desk. "I'm sorry, Dad."

Kataero came around the desk, slow, each step measured. He stopped in front of her, close enough that she caught machine oil and clean soap.

His hand settled on her shoulder.

She made herself look up. Kataero's eyes, dark brown, steady. Whatever she was looking for wasn't there. It never was.

"What's happening?"

Her eyes settled to the floor. The scuffed boards. Her own boots, dusted white from the morning run.

"I keep—" She shook her head. Copper hair swung forward, curtaining her face. "I don't know. I just keep running and nothing changes."

Kataero said nothing.

"I'm not comparing you to Kitt," he said at last. "I'm evaluating an operation. Same as I would with anyone on this crew."

His hand lifted and settled again, heavier than before.

"Your sister looks up to you, Peri. Don't let her down."

He let go. Crossed to the door without looking back.

Connor pushed off the window frame. He crossed toward the door, then paused as he drew level with her. His hand closed briefly on the back of her neck, rough, the grip gone almost before she felt it. Tobacco and canvas and gun oil.

Then he was gone, following Kataero out. The door left standing open.

Peri stood alone in the amber light.

Her legs went first. The tremor she'd been holding back since the canal road, the morning run finally collecting its debt. She gripped the edge of the desk until the shaking passed, then let go.

She came around the desk and lowered herself into Kataero's chair. Deeper than the one across from it. The leather still warm from his body. Her elbows found the desk and she let her weight go into it.

She pulled the stopwatch from her pocket. Chrome caught the light, the face scratched from years of use. The hands frozen where she'd left them.

Eighty-six minutes.

She turned it over. The back worn smooth from being thumbed and worried through a hundred briefings and runs. The engraving faint now, almost invisible: *For Peri. —K.*

Kataero had pressed it into her palm when she turned seventeen, in his workroom at the locks. *For your work. You've earned it.*

For a moment she caught her own reflection in the chrome. Blue eyes—her father's, or so she remembered being told.

She looked for him.

A stranger looked back.

Her thumb found the crown.

Click.

The second hand jumped, then began its slow retreat. One hour winding back to fifty minutes. Thirty. Twenty. Ten.

Until both hands came to rest at twelve. Side by side.

She set the stopwatch on the desk. Centered it in a bare patch between the maps.

Movement at the edge of her vision, beyond the office window.

Her sister stood at her workbench on the far side of the warehouse. Twenty feet and a wall of glass between them.

Their eyes met across the distance.

Kitt turned back to her work. To the soldering iron that had probably gone cold. Her fingers moved over the scattered parts with that tight, precise care she used when she was upset.

Kitt's hands were shaking.

3 | Wynne

Early Spring | 2191.089 · 10:00 | Z1
The Monastery | UAD Port Madison

The doors rose above her. Oak darkened by decades of salt air. Iron banding green with age. The center panels worn smooth where generations of hands had pushed them open. Nineteen years behind these walls, and these doors had remained shut.

Warmth bled through the seams where the wood had shrunk from the frame, carrying grass and salt and the faint mineral edge of the Valdris Sea. Light from the gaps fell across her hands in thin bright lines.

The horn sounded from the inner courtyard, a single low note that rolled through the stone corridors and settled in her chest. The summons.

She turned from the doors and moved. The corridor cool beneath her bare feet, stone worn to a dull shine. The slight upward grade where the foundation followed the hillside. The damp patch near the western turn where salt air leaked through old mortar. Morning light fell through the arched windows in long bars, but she didn't slow down.

The inner chamber doors were modest by comparison. Heavy, dark wood, banded but unadorned. She drew a breath. Four counts in through the nose, held for four, released for six through the mouth. Her heartbeat settled into rhythm. Her fingers brushed her scalp, platinum stubble shorn close as the Order required.

She knocked once. Firm. Clear.

"Enter."

Master Kaelen Rev's voice carried through the thick wood. Unmistakable.

Wynne pushed the doors. They swung inward with a low groan, old wood flexing in the frame. Pressure from her shoulders, not brute force.

The chamber opened before her.

Cool air rolled out, ten degrees colder than the humid morning, the walls holding the chill even as spring warmed the coast. Sandalwood and old stone.

Seven. Seated in a ring, gray-robed, utterly still. She knew them the way her body knew their teaching—each voice, each method, the particular way each held silence.

The walls climbed into shadow around them, built from blocks quarried before the Collapse. Light knifed down through high windows in narrow beams, catching the slow drift of dust. Seven chairs. Seven Masters. Wynne the only one standing.

She walked to the center of the circle. Her bare toes drew an arc in the sand as she settled into position. Hands resting at her sides, weight evenly set, the quarterstaff a steady line along her spine.

Master Kaelen Rev sat directly before her. White hair drawn back in the traditional knot, weathered hands folded loosely in his lap. The deep brown eyes that had watched her from childhood to this morning. He inclined his head once.

The trial began.

Master Elyra Cowe spoke first from Wynne's left. Silver hair bound without a strand astray, posture uncompromising. When she leaned forward, her fingers struck the arm of her chair once, a single tap that carried more force than raised voices.

"You'll be exposed the moment you act." Cowe's voice carried years of hard lessons. "People will ask questions. Where did you learn? Who shaped you? What Order forged someone like you?" Her dark gaze narrowed. "And when they come hunting for answers, they'll find us. They'll drag their wars here. Their grudges. Their enemies. All the chaos we stepped away from long ago."

She leaned in further, fingers going still. "The children sleeping in our dormitories, safe behind these walls. Will they balance against the strangers you save? Can you measure fifteen lives here against fifty outside? A hundred?"

Wynne turned to face her directly, sand shifting under her feet with the pivot.

"No." The word came out quieter than she intended. "I can't measure them. I've watched those children grow. I know their names, their nightmares, which ones can't sleep through storms." She held Cowe's gaze. "But you're asking me to weigh lives I love against lives I haven't met, and call it wisdom. I don't think that math works the way you want it to. The moment we decide some people matter less because we haven't seen their faces, we've already failed what we teach."

"A noble sentiment." Cowe didn't blink. "And when they wrench our location out of you under torture, will nobility matter to the children who burn because you needed purpose?"

The image landed. She felt it in her stomach—the dormitory hall, the small beds in rows, the sound of breathing in the dark. She'd walked that hall a thousand nights.

"You trained me to resist interrogation for a reason," Wynne said. "If you believed those techniques were insufficient, you wouldn't teach them. But I won't pretend I can guarantee silence under every circumstance." She let that sit. "What I can tell you is that the risk of one student being captured is real. And the certainty of an Order that teaches protection while protecting no one—that's real too. I'm not choosing between safety and danger. I'm choosing between two kinds of failure."

"What's the point of these walls if one student tears them down? You mistake training for readiness. Your need to look for a fight is the most dangerous thing here." That single tap again, sharp on wood.

She settled back. Her eyes held Wynne's, flat, unimpressed, utterly certain.

"You'd risk everything we've built, every child behind these walls, because stillness bores you."

Her hand flicked once.

"Continue."

Master Thessa Mar rose from the chair at Wynne's right. Ancient, ninety perhaps, hands mapped with old burns and blade scars. In all Wynne's years, Mar had spoken perhaps a hundred words to her. Never more than five at once.

She moved to the center, each step deliberate, weight carried low. She halted three paces from Wynne. Near enough to engage, far enough to honor space.

"Show me."

Wynne shifted and reached back, fingers closing on the staff's grip without needing to look. She drew the quarterstaff in one fluid motion, wood whispering through the leather loop and settling into her hands at the balance points. Six feet of ironwood, the grain worn smooth against her palms.

Mar's eyes caught the light. She raised no weapon and took no formal guard, only stood with her weight evenly placed, hands loose at her sides.

Then she moved.

Fast. Crossing the gap in a single step, right hand darting for Wynne's staff.

Wynne brought the staff up. Wood met bone with a sharp crack, turning the reaching hand aside. Her hips turned, weight shifting through her core, the rotation flowing up from the ground.

The staff spun in her grip, wood sliding clean through her palms. Low sweep toward Mar's leading leg.

Mar stepped over it as if it were nothing and came on, inside Wynne's guard.

Her breath held to its rhythm. Bare feet gripping sand, toes finding purchase as she gave ground, angling away. Three strikes in sequence.

High at the shoulder.

Middle at the ribs.

Low at the knee—and when Mar's weight shifted to answer it, Wynne reversed the arc. The staff swept up through the line the first two strikes had opened, momentum unbroken, the wood tracing a clean vertical from low guard to high.

The staff halted a finger's breadth from Mar's throat.

The sequence was still alive in her body: arms, core, the follow-through coiled and ready. She held it there.

She met Mar's gaze.

Mar's eyes widened, just a fraction.

Then Mar smiled. Small. Unguarded. The first smile Wynne had ever seen from her.

"Mastery of body follows mastery of mind," Mar said, the rasp carrying through her voice. The First Tenet. The words carved above the training hall doors, spoken over every student on their first morning. "You know that. Not as a lesson. As lived truth."

Wynne let the staff fall away and stepped back. She bowed from the waist, staff laid across her body in formal salute.

She'd recited those words a thousand times. Heard them spoken over her as a child, repeated them until they lived in her hands, her feet, the rhythm of her breathing. Mar wasn't teaching. She was certifying.

"You taught me that, Master Mar."

Mar grunted and went back to her chair. She sat and addressed the circle, not glancing at Wynne again.

"She walks."

Wynne turned to the center once more and strapped the staff across her back with practiced ease.

Master Serrin Vale leaned forward in his chair opposite the doors. Gray threaded through his dark hair, pulled back tight, knuckles scarred from decades of training without gloves. When he spoke, he didn't blink.

Wynne didn't look away.

"A village militia captures a raider," Vale said without preamble, his voice flat. "They plan to execute him at dawn. You arrive the night before. He's guilty. You've seen the evidence yourself. Burned homes. Murdered families. Children among the dead."

He paused, still holding that unblinking stare. "The execution will start a blood feud. The raider's community will retaliate. The village will respond. Both communities will destroy each other over years. Hundreds dead." He let that settle. "Do you stop the execution?"

"Yes." She said it without hesitation. "I find another way."

"There is no other way." Vale's voice stayed even. "The militia won't listen. The raider won't surrender. So you fight the militia to save the raider. You injure good people protecting their homes. The raider escapes." He leaned back. "Six months later, he kills again. Different village. Different families."

"How many deaths can you justify to maintain your principles?"

The staff pressed against her spine where it crossed between her shoulder blades. She felt the weight of it there, the ironwood holding the shape of every hour that had brought her to this circle. The sand was cool and fine between her toes.

"Then I carry those deaths," Wynne said. "The ones from the feud if I don't act. The ones from the raider if I do. Either way, people die and I'm standing in the middle of it."

She looked at Vale directly. "You're telling me there's no clean answer. I believe you. But the version of me who stands aside and watches an execution—who learns to make peace with that—she's not someone I want to become. Even if she sleeps better."

"The world will force you to choose," Vale said. "And when it does, your principles will feel like luxuries you can't afford."

I know what I believe. I don't know if it's enough.

"Maybe," she said. "I'd rather find that out than never leave this room."

Vale sat back without another word.

The chamber went still.

Master Kaelen Rev rose. He crossed the floor to Wynne and stopped before her, close enough for her to see the fine lines at the corners of his eyes, the faint tremor in his hands.

"Three have spoken," he said, voice low yet carrying. "The vote."

He gestured toward the great doors. "Face your path."

Wynne turned. The oak-and-iron doors filled her vision, the seams of light still burning at their edges. Behind her, the circle, the Masters, the bowl she knew sat on the stone pedestal at the room's center. Two stones before each chair—one white, one black. White to release. Black to hold.

She heard Rev's robes settle as he stepped back into the circle.

Then footsteps. The first Master approaching the bowl.

A stone dropped. The sound clean and hard against fired clay, a small definitive thing in all that silence.

More footsteps. A second stone. A third.

The fourth landed and a voice followed it—Mar's roughened rasp cutting through the ritual's silence. "She earned it."

A murmur from somewhere in the circle. Protocol. Masters didn't speak during the count. But no one corrected her. No one would.

The fifth stone dropped. Footsteps back to a chair.

The sixth. Quiet steps forward, the stone placed without ceremony, quiet steps back. No pause. No words.

The seventh.

Silence held. Then Rev's voice.

"Six white. One black." A pause. "You may go, Wynne Kaede. The Order releases you to walk your own path."

His hand settled on her shoulder. She felt the tremor in it.

"The world is not what we told you it would be. You'll see the reasons we withdrew. The no-win choices, the failures that break people. When you do, remember: we didn't fail. We chose a different path than the one you're choosing now."

His grip tightened. "The troubles of that world stay outside these walls. There are promises this Order made long before you were born. We intend to keep them. Understood?"

"Understood," Wynne said. *The troubles will stay outside these walls. Outside with me.*

Rev stepped back, hand lifting with measured care. He gestured toward the great doors.

"Then go. Better the world if you can. Honor us by trying."

Wynne turned and walked toward the oak-and-iron doors. Bare feet sounding softly against worn stone. The staff settling across her back into the groove it had worn into her robes over years of carry.

Two attendants stepped from the shadows. They took hold of the iron handles, braced themselves, and pulled.

The doors swung outward. Decades of stillness broke with a raw scream of iron, rust giving way, the sound climbing into the rafters, swallowed by stone.

And the world came in.

Sunlight spilled through the growing gap, coastal sun, generous, striking her face. She closed her eyes against it for half a breath before letting it flood in. Heat poured through the white fabric of her robes, across her bare arms, the tops of her feet. The air heavy and alive in ways the thin warmth through the door seams had never promised.

A bird called from somewhere she couldn't see. A bright, tumbling phrase she'd never heard inside these walls, repeating once before the wind took it.

She stopped at the threshold. One foot still on stone worn smooth by centuries. The other poised over packed earth warmed by morning sun.

She looked back once. Seven Masters in seven chairs, watching. Shadows and stone and the quiet discipline of the only world she'd known. Master Kaelen Rev lifted his hand.

Nineteen years of stone beneath her feet. She knew every corridor, every worn step, every draft that meant the western windows had been left unlatched. Out there she knew nothing. Not the roads, not the customs, not what people did when they weren't bound by an Order's rules. Cowe's voice was still in her chest. *The children who burn because you needed purpose.*

She didn't have an answer for that. Not a real one.

Wynne turned forward.

Beyond the gates, the path dropped through a grove of live oaks twisted silver-green by the coastal wind, and past them, color. Wildflowers had taken a hillside in a wash of orange and violet she had no names for.

Her shoulders settled. The staff across her back felt lighter than it ever had, and the ground beneath her feet was solid and real.

Below the hill, past the tree line, the faint sound of a town waking. Carts on cobblestone. A harbor bell. The world she'd trained for, waiting.

She stepped forward.

The doors closed behind her.

4 | Kitt

2191.111 · 07:32

Gate 31 | Kiron Hills Locks

Overhead fixtures ticked out one by one, light-sensitive relays surrendering to daylight. Mechanical decisions going on without her.

Kitt stood at the charging rack.

Twenty-three glass cells stood upright in their wooden frame, hand-blown. Some burned with clean phosphor-blue, the glow steady and cold. Some fainter. Three dead black. The rectifier in the corner gave its low hum, working while she'd slept.

She reached past the bright ones at the front, too recently charged to trust, and drew one from the back. Lifted it to the light. Strong glow, even all the way through. The glass was cool in her palm, perfectly smooth except for the seam. She checked where glass met brass cap. No hairline fractures. Set it aside.

Took another. Same brightness.

The next showed a faint dulling at the base. She rolled it forward in the rack. Not ready yet.

She found a third that matched. Three cells, uniform glow, no visible faults. Those went into the padded pouch at her hip.

Yesterday's spent cells slid into the empty slots. The rectifier would handle the rest. By tomorrow, they'd be shining again.

She crossed to her workbench.

Overalls worn soft at the knees. The shirt underneath read *Measure This* across the chest, yellow tape measure stripes running down each sleeve like a logo. Sleeves pushed up past her elbows. Hands bare.

The warehouse ran quiet. No footsteps echoing off the concrete. No boots scuffing between the door and the stairs. No mug appearing at the edge of her bench.

Just Kitt and the radio equipment spread across every surface, oscillators and frequency meters, wire strippers and soldering irons, components laid out in patterns that made sense only to her.

The oscillator in front of her still drifted.

She'd been up since before dawn with it. She touched the probe to the test point. The multimeter's needle settled, point-zero-zero-three kilohertz off center frequency. Acceptable for consumer units. Not for relay work. Relay stations needed stability measured in fractions, signals that held their shape across miles of atmosphere and terrain.

She adjusted the bias resistor. Quarter turn. Checked the reading. Point-zero-zero-two. Better. She held her breath, watching the needle. It crept back. *Point-zero-zero-three.*

The soldering iron was already hot. She touched it to the joint, quick and precise, just enough heat to reflow without bridging to the adjacent trace. The smell of rosin cut through the air. She set the iron back in its cradle and checked again.

Point-zero-zero-three.

Something in the thermal compensation. She could feel it—not see it yet, but sense it in the way the reading drifted back to the same value every time, like a current finding its level. The fault was consistent, which meant it was findable.

She reached for the component tray.

Yesterday sat behind her eyes like noise on a clean signal.

Peri's voice through the office walls, not words, not from that distance, just the shape of them. The cadence of anger. Sharp syllables punching through insulation and concrete. Then Kataero's responses, low registers only. Measured. Even. The bass notes of a conversation Kitt could hear the edges of but couldn't reconstruct.

Then something louder. A sound that could have been a fist hitting wood.

Then silence.

She'd kept her hands on the oscillator through all of it. Adjusted the bias point. Checked the reading. *Point-zero-zero-three.* Stared at it without seeing it.

Boots on the stairs afterward, Kataero's pace, then Connor's heavier tread. She'd tracked the sound across the warehouse floor and out. The door. Gone.

Not Peri's boots. Peri hadn't left.

Kitt hadn't wanted to look. Had kept her eyes on the workbench, on the frequency meter, on anything with a reading she could interpret.

She'd looked.

Through the office window. Twenty feet and a wall of glass. Peri in Kataero's chair, not the one across from it, *his* chair, behind the desk. Hair loose around her shoulders, copper in the amber light. The braid Kitt had tied that morning, gone. Something small and bright in her other hand.

She'd spent seventeen years learning that face. Even at that distance, even through glass, she could read it. Not a smile, not exactly. Something carried entirely in her eyes. But yesterday wasn't the inverter memory, wasn't the midnight doorway, wasn't anything she had a reference for. Her sister, sitting alone in their father's chair, looking at her across a distance neither of them closed.

Peri turned away. Controlled. The kind of turn that said *don't.*

Kitt had looked back down at the oscillator.

Point-zero-zero-three.

That was yesterday.

Her shoulders were still locked high, muscles across her upper back carrying tension like corrosion on a junction.

She picked up the soldering iron again.

⊙

Static hissed through the speaker. A tone cut in. Three short pulses. Two long. One short.

Kitt pushed off from the workbench, chair gliding to the comms station. Her hand closed around the microphone. On the wall, the meter snapped from zero into green.

She keyed the switch. "Tabby. Reading you. Go ahead."

His voice came through, thinned by distance but clean. Readable.

"Good morning, Tabitha. I trust the overnight diagnostics completed without incident?"

She shook her head. Of course Cipher would formalize a callsign.

"Affirmative. Local systems nominal. Northern repeater showing intermittent degradation, still within tolerances but trending negative."

"Noted. We will return to that." The faint crackle of carrier signal holding steady. "First, the matter you raised yesterday. The intelligence package. How was it received?"

Kitt's hand tightened on the mic.

"Mixed."

"Mixed," he repeated. Neutral. Patient. Like he was cataloguing the word rather than reacting to it.

"Peri asked about the source. So did Kataero." She kept her tone level, the voice she used when people moved slower than the problem required. "They want verification before they commit."

"A reasonable position."

"It didn't feel reasonable. It felt like they didn't trust the work."

Silence on the line. The carrier still holding, the faint hiss of distance.

"They asked the same question," she said. "Both of them. Where's this coming from. Who has access to Continental Authority logistics data."

"And your response?"

"That the source has been reliable for three years. That the cargo types check out."

"Also reasonable." The carrier crackled softly. "Tabitha. May I offer an observation?"

She leaned back in the chair. "Go ahead."

"The questions they are asking, source credibility, verification, motive, these are operational questions. They indicate engagement, not rejection."

Each word placed like a component on a board.

She turned that over. "It didn't feel like engagement."

"No. It rarely does from your position." Something in his tone, not warmth exactly. Recognition. "You built the network. You identified the opportunity. That work stands regardless of the presentation."

Her hand loosened on the mic. She hadn't noticed how hard she'd been gripping it.

The carrier hissed softly between them. Static filling the space where words had been.

"The question now is whether you intend to pursue verification."

"Kataero told me to get more. Confirmation. Details."

"And will you?"

She frowned. "Of course I will."

"Good." Simple. Final. "That is forward motion, Tabitha. Not rejection."

The meter crackled. Not the steady gain she expected, erratic jumps. Needle twitching up, settling, jolting higher.

"Cipher, hold. I'm seeing anomalous readings on the northern relay."

"Describe."

"Erratic gain. Needle jumping past normal range." She watched it spike into amber. "Intermittent. Not consistent with local fault."

"The degradation you mentioned earlier."

"Worse. Significantly worse."

Kitt eased the microphone back into its cradle and stepped to the equipment rack. Her hands moved by habit, checking each cable junction for heat, play, corrosion. Antenna feed firm. No oxidation. No wobble. Everything seated. Everything clean.

She lifted the mic again. "Local systems nominal. Source is external. Repeater network fault."

"Estimated resolution time?"

Kitt slid the notepad closer, pencil already moving. Northern repeater chain in quick strokes. Three sites. Seven, Nine, Eleven.

"Depends what failed. If it's isolated to one repeater, I can reroute through the eastern backup chain. Adds latency, but we stay operational."

"And if it is not isolated?"

"Field inspection. Replace corroded components. Junction boxes at wire entries, water bypasses gaskets, pools inside, eats connections."

She circled each location. She should have checked them two weeks ago.

"Time required?"

"Six hours minimum if it's one station. Eight to twelve if multiple are compromised."

A pause. "And the verification work, the intelligence confirmation, that requires the network to be functional, yes?"

Kitt's pencil stopped.

Without the network, she couldn't contact the source. Couldn't get Kataero his verification. Couldn't move the job forward.

"Yes," she said. "It does."

"Then the repairs are not merely maintenance. They are operational priority."

The meter spiked. Red, amber, green. Unstable.

"Spring transition," she said. "Always hard on equipment."

"Indeed. But equipment can be repaired." He paused. "You have managed more difficult problems than corroded junction boxes, Tabitha."

"I'll take care of it," she said.

"I have no doubt. Contact me when repairs are complete, and be cautious. That terrain is unforgiving in spring melt."

The signal thinned as he spoke, voice smearing into hiss. "—careful... repairs..."

Then nothing.

The needle dropped to zero and stayed there.

Kitt stood in the empty warehouse, staring at the gauge.

She set the microphone aside and crossed to the workbench where her maps lay. Shoved aside oscillators and wire, tools and half-finished builds. The topographical spread covered the surface, northern territories shaded in browns and greens. Sixteen red dots scattered across the landscape.

The northern chain arced along the highest elevations. Stations Seven, Nine, Eleven.

She ran a fingertip along the signal path. Three years on this map. Every station a problem she'd solved with salvage, engineering texts, and stubbornness. The network carried every transmission the operation depended on.

Nobody talked about that. It just worked. That was supposed to be enough.

Break that chain anywhere and the whole northern sector went dark.

Spring melt. She'd known it was coming. Planned for it, marine-grade sealant, IP67 enclosures. But spring hit early this year. Variables she didn't control.

Static hissed behind her. No voice cutting through. Just noise.

She caught up her pencil and began marking. Northern chain. Stations Seven, Nine, Eleven. Somewhere along that arc.

Three repeaters. Ten to twelve hours of field work. Rough terrain.

She could handle the electrical work alone. That wasn't the problem. The problem was the terrain, steep approaches, unstable footing in spring melt, equipment loads that needed two sets of hands at minimum. She couldn't hold a junction box steady and solder a connection at the same time. Not on a slope. Not in mud.

She straightened. Her back cracked.

Connor for navigation. He'd know the safe crossings after melt, the fastest routes to each station. But Connor couldn't test signal paths or diagnose a fault by the sound of the static.

She needed someone who could work alongside her at the stations. Someone who'd learned enough from years of handing her tools and holding components steady while she soldered.

The pencil stopped.

Peri.

Last month, the inverter. Kitt had spent three days calibrating a voltage inverter for the medical wing, and Peri had knocked it off the bench reaching for a coffee mug. Three days of work in a thousand pieces on the concrete floor. Kitt hadn't spoken to her for the rest of the afternoon. Hadn't looked at her through dinner. Had gone to bed with her jaw wired shut around words that would have made things worse.

Peri had found her at the workbench after midnight. Hadn't apologized. Hadn't explained. Just stood there in the doorway in bare feet and an oversized shirt, hair loose around her shoulders, and waited until Kitt looked up.

Then she'd made that face.

Not a smile, not exactly. Something carried entirely in her eyes. Brows lifting a fraction, mouth barely curving, the whole expression saying *I know. I'm sorry. I'm ridiculous. You love me anyway.* All of it landing in a single look that had no right to work as well as it did.

Kitt had lasted maybe four seconds.

"I hate you," she'd said.

Peri's mouth had twitched wider. "No you don't."

"I really do."

"Come to bed. I'll help you rebuild it tomorrow."

She had. And Peri had. And by noon the next day the inverter was recalibrated and Kitt couldn't remember why she'd been so angry.

But yesterday wasn't a knocked inverter.

Yesterday was something past anger, a frequency in her sister's voice that Kitt didn't have instruments for.

She pulled a clean sheet of paper toward her.

Problems had solutions. The network had to work.

Her pencil touched paper. Started drawing with sharp, precise lines. Access routes marked in red. Equipment requirements listed in the margin. Time estimates broken down by travel and repair work.

Route planned. Equipment gathered. Technical procedures documented. Professional. Complete. Nothing Peri could criticize.

She bent over the paper, both hands braced against the bench edge.

Junction box requirements, IP67 rated minimum. Gasket material: neoprene, sixty-durometer shore A hardness. Screw torque: hand-tight plus quarter turn. Wire gauge, fourteen AWG copper, stranded not solid, stranded for flexibility at junction entry points. Marine-grade sealant at all penetrations. Application: bead around wire entry, smooth with fingertip, allow four hours cure time before energizing.

She kept writing.

Tools, full electrical kit. Soldering iron, battery-powered, with field tips. Multimeter. Wire strippers, flush-cut. Crimping tool. Heat shrink, assorted gauges. Electrical tape, two rolls minimum. Field radio for testing. Three charged cells. Spare fuses. Contact cleaner. Isopropyl alcohol. Clean rags.

She listed the rags.

Pencil moved across paper with soft scratching sounds. The warehouse stretched empty around her. Morning light climbing the walls now, the angle steeper, warmer. Relays clicking, the rectifier humming, but no boots scuffing concrete. No interruptions.

The radio stayed silent. Meter needle pinned at zero.

Her letters perfectly straight. Her lines exactly parallel.

The wood grain pressed into her palms.

She hadn't let go.

5 | Wynne

2191.089 · 11:22

Bay Markets | UAD Port Madison

Her feet found the change before she did.

Packed earth at the monastery gates, then worn flagstone where the trail switchbacked through the live oaks, then cobblestones — sun-baked, uneven, their edges pressing into her soles in ways the monastery floors never had. Buildings climbed on either side. Stucco fronts washed to pale yellow and coral. Laundry snapped between balconies in colors she'd never seen: deep reds, bright yellows, a blue that caught the sky and held it.

Then the market, and the world stopped making sense.

More people than she'd seen in her life combined. Hundreds, pressing through aisles of stalls, heat rising from the mass of bodies. Sound from everywhere — voices, cart wheels, a child's laugh breaking high and startled before the noise swallowed it. Her training reached for the crowd the way it reached for any room. Seeking stance. Center of gravity. The geometry of a single opponent.

A crowd had none. Just shifting mass.

A woman turned, her basket swinging wide. Wynne stepped back and clipped someone's shoulder. The man steadied his crate of fish with a grunt, his gaze going to the staff, the shorn hair, the white robes.

"Watch your left, sister."

"Thank you," Wynne said. The words came out formal. She'd spoken to the same forty people her entire life.

By the fifth or sixth near-collision, her training found purchase in new terrain. Seeing a vendor's shoulder dip before he bent to lift. Catching a woman's weight shift just before she stepped. Slipping through gaps a breath before they closed.

She felt herself smiling. Couldn't say exactly when it started.

People noticed her as she moved. A child tugged her mother's hand, pointing. Two women at a bolt-of-cloth stall watched her pass. One leaned toward the other. "Don't see them out often."

An old man on a stool outside a spice shop raised his hand. Someone who remembered when monks walked these streets freely. Wynne returned it, palm open, the way Rev had taught her. The old man's eyes creased. He looked away.

⚙

Fish and salt and melting ice, then something else. Bread. Fresh. Heat rolling out of a shop front in a low wave that found her face before the smell fully arrived.

She stopped. Nothing like the monastery's bread: dense, dark loaves baked in batches, fuel-efficient, nourishing without pretense.

Her stomach answered before her discipline could intervene—a clean, sharp ache. She'd left before breakfast, and dinner already felt like it belonged to another life.

A woman stood behind the counter, dusted to the elbows in flour, pulling a tray from the oven with bare hands toughened by years of repetition. She looked up. Her gaze had the weight of someone who'd lived a full life next to a closed door.

"Well," she said. "Been a long time."

"I'm sorry?"

"Since one of yours came down." The woman set the tray on the counter. "I was a girl. Used to watch your people come through on market days. My mother traded with the Order." She studied Wynne. "You're young for it."

"For leaving?"

"For all of it."

The woman pulled a loaf from the tray, tore it cleanly in two, and held out the larger half.

Wynne's hand went to the pouch at her belt. "I have coin—"

"Order's mark." The woman glanced at the pouch without reaching for it. "I know what it looks like. My mother kept one on a cord around her neck until she died." She pushed the bread closer. "This isn't trade. This is a woman feeding a girl who left without breakfast. Take it."

Wynne took the bread. The crust cracked under her fingers, warm through, the inside soft and steaming faintly in the morning air. She bit into it and the taste flooded in: salt and grain and something almost sweet, a richness that coated her tongue and made the second bite involuntary.

She ate standing in the street. The bread was the best thing she'd ever tasted. She knew hunger was doing the work. It didn't change the taste.

"Thank you," she said when it was gone.

The woman waved her off. "You tell that mountain of yours I said hello." A pause. "And that some of us are still down here. Waiting."

Wynne held the words longer than she expected to. *Some of us are still down here. Waiting.*

She bowed, the formal salute, staff across her body, and the woman laughed. Short, surprised. "Go on," she said. "Whatever you're looking for, it isn't in my shop."

⚙

The market thinned as the stalls gave way to shop fronts, permanent buildings, doors propped open against the heat. The crowd loosened. Her feet found shade where awnings threw it, skirting the worst of the sun-baked stone.

Music reached her first. Strings and brass, structured and purposeful, coming from somewhere she couldn't place—not a musician, not an instrument she recognized. She followed it the way she'd follow a voice through the monastery corridors.

A shop front opened onto the street, its interior dim against the bright glare. On a counter inside, something waited.

Wynne stopped.

The light was wrong. Not flame—it didn't breathe. Not sun—it moved, shifted color, ran cold and alive behind glass simultaneously. Something trapped and restless she had no name for.

She stepped closer. The light resolved into a person. A woman, seated behind a desk, hands moving as she spoke. Her voice came not from her mouth but from metal grilles on either side—sound separated from its source, fastened into the air.

The image changed. A harbor. Ships with metal hulls larger than anything Wynne had believed could stay afloat. Then back to the woman, mid-gesture, finishing a sentence as though the distance meant nothing.

How.

"First time seeing a television?"

She turned. A young man leaned in the doorway. Perhaps her age, perhaps a year older. Half a smile, arms crossed.

"Television," Wynne said. Tasting the word.

"That woman's in a studio right now. Hundreds of miles north." He nodded toward the screen. "The television carries it here. Live. Happening while we stand here."

"How does it work?"

He unfolded his arms. "Radio waves, mostly. Broadcast from towers, picked up by the receiver." He tapped the side of the box. "This just translates it into something you can see and hear."

"The woman," Wynne said. "Is she aware we're watching?"

"She's broadcasting. She knows someone is. Just not you specifically." He leaned against the doorframe. "She's in a studio. You're here. The television is just a window between the two."

"So her image is here, but she remains there."

"Exactly." He studied her face. Whatever he found there softened the amusement into actual interest. "You really are seeing this for the first time."

"I'm seeing most things for the first time today."

He laughed. Brief, genuine.

On the screen, the image shifted. The woman gestured toward something beyond the frame, and the view opened: buildings climbing upward. Ten stories. Twenty. Glass and steel throwing back the light in sheets.

"Where is that?" she asked.

"CAD Hamilton. The capital." He looked at her more carefully. "Far north. Long journey."

Hamilton.

The word landed behind her ribs where breath began.

"How do people travel that distance?"

"Train, mostly. Station's on the east end of town. Runs two a day, about ten hours with stops." His gaze dropped briefly to her bare feet, then back. "Ticket costs currency. Not cheap."

"And if you don't have currency?"

He considered her for a moment.

"Then it gets harder," he said. "But people find ways. They always do." A pause. "The Order's mark won't spend at the station. But there's work on the docks if you need to earn passage. They don't care what you wear or where you're from, just whether you can lift."

He pushed off the doorframe and extended his hand. "Billy. Well, William. But everyone calls me Billy."

Wynne looked at the hand. At the monastery, you bowed. She took it. His grip was firm, calloused, brief.

"Wynne."

"Good fortune, Wynne." He said it easily, the phrase worn smooth by use. But he held her eyes when he said it.

He disappeared back into the shop. The television still glowing, still showing distant Hamilton.

She drew a breath. Four counts in. Held for four. Released for six. The rhythm was hers, and she needed to know it still worked here.

Wynne turned and walked.

6 | Peri

2191.111 · 08:17
Gate 31

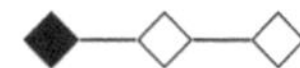

Fifty yards out, already easing down. Peri rounded the last corner on legs that had stopped cooperating somewhere around mile eight. The warehouse door stood open, morning light hard through the gap.

She stopped at the threshold, one hand on the frame. Breath not caught up yet.

Kitt was at the workbench. Hunched into it the way she got when she hadn't slept.

She looked up. Straight to Peri's hair.

Peri touched the back of her head. The ponytail had been losing since mile three and she knew it, elastic sitting wrong, strands loose at her neck.

Kitt's mouth flattened.

"Network's failing. Three repeaters down. I need you and Connor."

Peri pushed off the frame and crossed the floor, legs settling into the heavy ache of muscles that knew they were done.

The CB mic sat at the near end of the bench, coiled cord trailing to the wall box. She keyed it.

"Connor—"

Feedback screamed through the warehouse. She yanked her thumb off the button and stepped back, ears ringing.

Kitt didn't look up. "You have to move away from the bench."

"Ever think about upgrading things inside the warehouse?"

"Ever think about not standing next to the transmitter?"

Peri stepped back two paces and keyed the mic again.

"Connor. Peri. Need you at the workbench."

Static. Then his voice, thinned by distance and concrete: "Copy. Two minutes."

Peri clicked the button twice before returning it on its hook.

Kitt was already moving toward her, hands coming up—the automatic reach, the same hands that braided her hair every morning before a run.

Peri stepped back, both palms up. "I'm showering. My hair's soaked with sweat, there's no point."

Kitt's hands slowed. Her fingers curled closed. Her arms dropped. She turned back to the maps.

Somewhere behind the storage rows the loading dock door rattled up, metal grinding on metal. Footsteps followed. Unhurried.

Connor's walk.

He came through the gap between the rows, wiping his hands on a rag, tool belt low on his hips. He tucked the rag into his back pocket as he reached the workbench. Looked at Kitt. Looked at Peri. Said nothing.

Just waited.

Kitt spread the map across the bench.

Peri glanced at it. "Is that one of Kataero's maps?"

Kitt smoothed a corner down without looking up. "Maybe. Keep your trap shut."

Her finger traced the northern route—a rough triangle cutting through the high terrain. "Repeaters Seven, Nine, and Eleven. Spring melt's gotten into the junction boxes. We're seeing signal degradation across the whole northern chain and I've got a storm system moving in inside four days." She tapped each station in turn. "Six hours if it's surface corrosion. Eight if water got past the gaskets into the wiring."

She kept going. IP67 enclosure ratings. Neoprene gasket tolerances. Wire gauge requirements at high-elevation junction points, stranded not solid, flexibility at the entry point, marine-grade sealant application, cure time before re-energizing.

Peri tracked the first two minutes of it. Then the words stopped resolving into meaning.

Kitt glanced at her once. Then turned to Connor.

"The seal fails at the wire entry first. You'll see green oxidation around the housing seam—that's your tell." Connor leaned in, his finger following the route on the map. "If it's just surface corrosion we clean it, reseal, and test. If water's inside the housing—"

"We replace the assembly," Connor said.

"We replace the assembly."

Peri pushed back from the bench. "You two nerds figure it out. I'll be back in fifteen."

Neither of them looked up.

She climbed the stairs, Kitt's voice fading into the warehouse below. Technical. Precise. Not missing her.

The hall ran short and narrow, three doors off it. Hers was the last.

She pushed it open.

The room was lived-in without being comfortable. A bed with an iron frame, wool blanket pulled roughly flat. She'd stopped making it properly years ago, just smoothed it enough to sleep again. A chest of drawers, scarred from being moved too many times. On the far wall, the canal window, glass fogged at the lower corners where the seal had gone soft, morning light coming through gray and flat.

The weapons rack stood beside the door. Her defensive blade and its spine harness, the leather worn to her shape. Below it, the training sword Kataero had given her when she was nine—wood, wrapped grip, the blade edge nicked from ten years of use. She'd never taken it down. Never gotten rid of it either.

On the small shelf below that, a glass cell she'd pulled from Kitt's charging rack three months ago, trying to understand how it worked. She still didn't. The glass sat there quietly, holding its charge, waiting for someone who understood what it was for.

She stripped as she crossed the room. Shirt first—the fabric had bonded to her skin, sweat gone cold and tacky. It pulled free in one long unstick. Pants followed. She left them where they fell.

The shared bathroom door was open. She pushed through into it.

Kitt's side of the vanity: organized, labeled, everything where it belonged. Small mirror above it, clean.

Peri's side: a few things, shoved to the back. Her mirror had one addition.

A strip of tape across the lower corner. Her own handwriting, cramped and decisive.

What's the point?

She looked at it. The way she always looked at it—straight on, no flinching.

It still landed. Every morning.

The pipes knocked twice before the water came. She stepped in while it was still cold.

The shock hit her scalp, her shoulders, ran straight down her spine. She stood into it. Waited.

When the heat came it came hard, water pressure hammering the back of her skull, her neck, the tight muscles across her shoulders.

Eighty-six minutes, thirty-two seconds.

Thirty-two seconds slower than yesterday.

She tipped her face into the spray and closed her eyes. Let the heat work through her scalp, down through the layers of effort and cold and morning.

The scar found her first.

Left shoulder, the narrow ridge arcing from blade toward collarbone—hot water always pulled at it, the skin puckering differently from everything around it. She reached up without deciding to. Fingers on the ridge. Pressing lightly.

She'd been fifteen. A man who hadn't appreciated being taken for a fool.

Steel punching through skin. Clean. Deep. The heat of blood down her back. The sound she'd made—not a scream, just a hard exhale, like being winded. The ground tilting.

"Peri?!"

Kataero's voice. Fear in it—raw, unguarded, nothing like his usual register.

His palms over the wound. Warm. Solid. Blood between his fingers and hers. *"I've got you. I've got you."*

She reached back further.

Seven years old and airborne—his hands under her arms, spinning her. The warehouse ceiling wheeling overhead. Her own shriek bouncing off the concrete. His face at the center of everything, grinning.

"I've got you!" Laughing.

He set her down and straightened up. Pepper's hand found his shoulder as he rose.

She stood in the kitchen doorway. Apron over her dress, flour along the hem—the permanent kind, the kind that didn't wash out anymore.

Hair tied back, copper going loose at the temples, the same curl Peri saw in every mirror. Green eyes moving over the warehouse floor.

"If you two are finished, the table needs setting. Where's Kitt?"

No. You need to go.

Her gaze found Peri's. Steady.

"I can see the worry on your face. She didn't go far."

You aren't allowed here.

She pushed off the doorframe. Crossed the floor without hurry. Crouched to Peri's height and brushed the copper loose from her face with two fingers.

"Go find Kitiara, Peregrine. Make sure she washes her hands."

Get out.

She smiled. Small. Like she'd heard this before and wasn't troubled by it.

"My brave girl."

Stay the fuck out.

The vision held a moment too long.

She opened her eyes.

Water ran down her face, her lashes, her throat. Steam thick around her. And in the fogged glass of the shower door—her own reflection looking back. Copper hair dark and plastered flat. Blue eyes where the green had been.

Her hand fell from the scar. Water beat against her face, scalding now. She reached up and twisted the tap.

Cold hit like a fist. She stood into it.

Then she reached for the soap and scrubbed.

Clean up. Clothes on. Back downstairs. Fifteen minutes. Move.

She came down the stairs ten minutes later. Boots laced hard. Long sleeves despite the morning warmth. Hair still wet, dragged back into the same loose ponytail.

Connor was already at the loading dock, truck backed in tight, tailgate down, ramp extended. Tool boxes lashed in the bed. Water and emergency kit where they always went.

She stopped at the top of the ramp.

He packed for two.

The bed of the truck was half-loaded. She stepped up and started on the tie-downs. Thread the strap, haul it tight, lock the buckle, yank twice to be sure.

Connor held out the field radio. "Cells are dead."

Peri crossed to the charging rack. Twenty-three glass cells in their wooden frame, some burning clean phosphor-blue, some faded. Three dead black.

She reached for one of the brightest.

"Peri." Kitt didn't look up from the map. "How many times?"

Kitt crossed the floor, plucked the cell from Peri's hand and set it back. "Too fresh. Charge hasn't stabilized." Her fingers moved past the front row and drew three from the back—glowing even, softer. "These. Yesterday's. Proven."

"Right." Peri took them. "I forgot."

"You always forget."

"Maybe that's why Kataero only has me fetching things."

Kitt didn't look up from the radio case. "Install the cells, Peri."

Peri knelt. Three empty brass housings exposed. She slid the first cell home, glass seating with a soft click. Blue light spilled through the tiny window. Second cell. Third.

The radio answered with a low hum, faint vibration under her palm. All three windows glowed steady.

Kitt dropped three velcro patches into Peri's hand. "Cover them. Save the charge. When you test signal strength, pull the patches. Blue means good. Cells dim, move to higher ground."

Peri pressed each patch over its window. The light vanished. She shut the lid. Snapped the latches.

Kitt glanced at the case. "This time, try not to lose the radio."

A strap went over the radio case. She cinched the last of the gear.

"Peri."

Kitt stood at the tailgate, hands lifted.

"Your hair."

Peri glanced at Connor. Already at the driver's side, back to them.

She sat on the tailgate and turned her back to Kitt.

Kitt's fingers found the elastic and slid it free. The pull and weave started. Wet hair, tight sections, the familiar pressure against her scalp.

Silence. Just Kitt's hands working.

"There. Done."

Peri reached up, fingers following the line of the braid. Tight. Secure. Flat to her skull.

Not yesterday's weave. Getting it done.

She turned. Kitt was already stepping back—something locked down behind her eyes that she was carrying alone.

Peri knew that look. Had worn it herself often enough.

Before Kitt could clear the tailgate she caught her wrist. Drew her in—gentle, but not optional.

Kitt pulled back. "No."

Peri held on.

"Peri—"

"Kitt."

Kitt went still.

Peri leaned forward until their foreheads touched. Held there. The world reduced to that small pressure—bone to bone, her sister's breath uneven against her cheek, the morning cold around them and this one point of warmth.

Then Kitt's breath caught—and her arms came up and wrapped around Peri.

Solder and coffee and Kitt.

Peri stayed until she felt the tension go out of her sister's shoulders.

Then she eased back. "Thanks."

Kitt's hands lingered before falling away. Her eyes wet at the corners, jaw set.

"Six hours. Field radio checks every two—nine, eleven, one." A beat. "You miss one, I send Dad after you."

Peri swung off the tailgate. "You'd like that."

Connor slid behind the wheel. The engine caught, idled, then dropped into gear. Peri pulled herself into the passenger seat, shut the door—it closed with a solid, final thunk.

The truck eased forward. Out through the loading dock doors into morning. She gripped the door frame, fingers braced.

They drove in silence. Engine noise and the rattle of gear in the bed. Road unwinding ahead. The warehouse falling away behind them, the canal glinting flat and silver through the trees.

Peri settled into the seat. Her legs throbbing, finally allowed to be still. The hills rolling out green and gray, fence posts ticking past.

"You know... if you were more aware of your sister, you wouldn't have to apologize so much."

Peri watched the road. "But then we wouldn't get to make up." She glanced at him. "That's the important part."

Connor said nothing. But the corner of his mouth moved—not quite a smile. Something closer to a concession.

Her hand found the stopwatch in her pocket. Still there. Still zeroed.

She left it where it was.

Her eyes went to the side mirror. Kitt stood in the loading bay. Small. Unmoving. Peri watched until the road curved and the warehouse slid out of frame.

7 | Peri

2191.111 · 11:51

Old Logging Road | 3 Hours North of Gate 31

The logging road hadn't been used in years. Decades, maybe. Ruts carved into hardened earth, brush scraping the undercarriage as they climbed. Engine strain traveled through the seat, through the floorboard under her boots. A low, determined growl.

Air grew colder as the trees closed in. Peri's breath fogged in the cramped cab, thin clouds that vanished before they formed.

Connor drove without speaking. Hands easy on the wheel, reading the ruts and the grade and the soft shoulders the way he read everything. Quiet, patient, choosing the path that would break them least.

The road ended at a clearing. A metal tower rose above the tree line—thirty feet, angular against open sky. Radio equipment near the top, solar panels below, a weatherproof housing at the base.

Connor killed the engine. Silence rushed in—wind through the trees, water dripping somewhere out of sight.

Peri climbed out. Cold hit her face, sharp and clean. But the sun was warm where it touched—her arms, the back of her neck.

Connor moved to the truck bed, boots crunching on gravel and dead needles. Tool box first, then radio equipment, then testing meters wrapped in protective cloth.

Peri grabbed her jacket from where she'd left it crumpled in the bed. Tied it around her waist for now.

They approached the tower together, Connor moving slightly ahead, already scanning. He set the tool box down with a dull thunk. Opened the access panel—the junction box inside already visible, green corrosion creeping across the connections.

"There it is," Connor said. Unsurprised.

Peri moved to the edge of the clearing, where the ground dropped away.

The locks below. Gate 31. The warehouse, a rectangle of corrugated metal beside the canal. Water catching sunlight, throwing it back in pieces. Belfast Mills in the distance, small and quiet from this height.

Wind found her face, cooler up here. She closed her eyes. Let it move through her hair.

Behind her, Connor went to work. The soft scrape of metal, the quiet clink of tools.

Peri opened her eyes. Walked back. Lowered herself onto a flat rock near the tower base—close enough to be useful without being in the way.

She shoved her sleeves higher. Sun soaked into bare skin, warm against the cold air.

Connor stripped corroded connections, checked wire integrity with instruments that clicked and hummed.

Wire strippers, held out at the exact moment he reached for them.

Connor took them without a word. Without looking.

Multimeter next. Then pliers. Each tool sliding into his reach exactly when he needed it, her gaze on the view below while her hands tracked his rhythm.

Connor pulled his pant leg up, drew a slim knife from his boot strap, and trimmed a corroded lead clean. Blade back, pant leg down, hands already reaching for the next connection.

Peri raised an eyebrow. Passed him the solder.

"How many more of these?" Her voice too loud in the open space.

"Two."

"I'm already tired."

Connor kept working.

"Yesterday sucked."

He kept testing connections, but he was listening.

Peri drew her knees up tight. Wrapped her arms around them. Stared down at the locks below, at the layout she knew by heart.

"Every day. Every week. Every month." She leaned forward. "We go out and pull supplies. Slip into Hammison. Break into Margos. Cheat some merchant in Bethshelm. Come back. Hand everything out. Do it again. I've robbed that same merchant five times this winter. And every time I start thinking... what's the point?"

Wind moved through the trees. Below, the steady rush of water.

"I know what you're going to say." Her voice dropped, went low and rough, slipping into Connor's gravel. "'People depend on us.'"

"I know that. I do. But I can't shake the feeling we're slapping a bandage on something rotten underneath. That all we're doing is... stalling."

Metal clicked as Connor set a tool down. Peri passed him the wire cutters without looking.

"And Kataero." She let out a breath through her nose. "His whole 'Your sister looks up to you. Don't disappoint her.' What am I supposed to do with that? Really helpful timing, Dad. Exactly what I needed. Just pile that on top of everything else."

She picked up a pebble beside her boot. Rolled it between her fingers.

"First off, Kitt's old enough to figure her own life out. I'm not her keeper. I'm barely keeping myself vertical." She hesitated. "Second, since when am I qualified for anything? I'm a thief. I thief things. There's nothing noble in that. No banner to march under. No real purpose."

She flung the stone, putting shoulder and spine into it. Watched it arc out over the drop and vanish into the trees. No impact sound—just gone, swallowed by leaves and distance.

"What kind of leader makes a living stealing?"

Only the wind answered. The water. Connor working.

He kept at it. Testing connections, watching the meter, giving small nods at each reading.

"Good," he murmured, more to the equipment than to her.

He picked up the sealant and laid a precise bead along the junction box. Closing every gap.

Peri pushed to her feet. Brushed at her pants. Walked over to where the field radio sat on its tarp. Lifted the handset. Thumbed the transmit.

"Tabby, Falcon. Radio check. Over."

Static came back. Empty channel, waiting.

Connor finished the line of sealant. Capped the tube. Returned it to the toolbox.

Then he stretched—arms up, back arching, joints popping. Sunlight caught the gray threading through his beard.

"What were you going to say to Kataero yesterday?" Connor asked. Quiet, almost gentle. "Before I stopped you?"

Peri kept her gaze on the radio. The small green power light burning steady.

"I'm just a brat he inherited."

Connor watched her. Patient as stone.

“Is that what you think?” he asked at last.

“Yes.” The word faltered. “No.” She swallowed. “I don't know. I don't know what I think anymore.”

The radio crackled—static shifting, still no voice.

“I know he loves me. Gods, I love him. But we never... talk. Not really. It's always about the next thing. The Locks needs this. The town's running out of that. Every day it's more he hands off to me. More responsibility, more weight. Like he's getting me ready for something and won't say what it is.”

“He trusts you,” Connor said. Flat, sure. “He knows you can do it.”

“I'm a kid.” The words snapped out harder than she meant. “He started leaning on me when I was thirteen. I started leaving for jobs at fifteen. Fifteen, Connor. And there was no speech about me 'not being ready.' Just—go. Out of sight, out of mind. Keep me occupied so he can focus on his real child while I'm trying to deal with Mom leaving and being sent away from home by the man who's supposed to be my father.”

The handset plastic dug into her palm. “Nobody wants me around. Nobody wants to handle me. So they just... ship me off. Hand me jobs. Keep me moving so I don't get time to notice how alone I am.”

She exhaled hard. Straightened her shoulders.

Connor cleared his throat.

“Well, you're just a glutton for punishment, darling.” Hand to chest, mock-wounded. “All noble and long-suffering. Watching over the Blackwood brat after her fearless, heroic father died in a pointless war. Such sacrifice.”

The radio came alive before Connor could answer.

“Falcon, Tabby. Reading you clear. Signal strength is solid. Repeater Seven is operational. Nice work. Over.”

Kitt. All technical satisfaction, that particular edge she got when machines behaved.

Peri keyed the mic again, forcing her tone level. "Copy, Tabby. Moving on to Repeater Nine. Falcon out."

She set the handset down harder than she needed to.

Connor swung the junction box shut. Started putting tools away.

"Lin and I enlisted together," he said. Not looking over. Eyes on the tools, on the work of his hands. "Sixteen years old. Thought we knew something about the world."

His hands paused on the wire strippers. Just for a moment.

"We didn't know anything. Two stupid kids playing soldier." The corner of his mouth twitched—not quite a smile, not quite pain. "The trouble we got into. The places we went. Lin always three steps ahead, dragging me along, making me laugh when I wanted to quit."

He set the strippers in their slot. Reached for the pliers.

"Twenty years I've been carrying him. Twenty years of seeing his ghost in every kid that moved too fast, laughed too loud, couldn't sit still." He looked at her then. Really looked. "And then you grew up. And it wasn't ghosts anymore."

Peri looked away. Found the radio's green light and fixed on it.

"You move like him. That restless energy—can't sit still, can't stop pushing, always has to be doing something." Connor's voice dropped, rougher now. "You've got his eyes. His laugh. That way of dragging people into whatever you're doing and making them glad they came."

He closed the toolbox. Latched it with a soft click.

"Kataero stepped into the space Lin left. Gave you a father when you needed one. Trained you. Raised you." He straightened, toolbox in hand. "And I'm here because Lin was my best friend. And his kid deserves someone who remembers him."

Connor headed for the truck, boots crunching on gravel.

But he paused at the tailgate. Half-turned.

"Lin was a great man who found his purpose. What made him who he was—it's in you." He looked at her. "You'll find yours."

He turned back to the truck bed, setting the toolbox down with care.

Peri stayed where she was. The radio hummed behind her.

She stood there long enough that the silence stopped mattering.

"I don't remember him," she said. Almost a whisper. "I don't remember anything."

"I know." Connor's voice was gentle. "That's why I do."

The wind cut under the jacket knotted at her waist.

She shrugged into it. Let its weight settle across her shoulders.

She took one last look—the Locks below, the warehouse, the canal running south. Home. Whatever that meant.

Connor turned the key. The engine caught—too loud after so much quiet.

The truck jolted, caught, and started down.

Two repeaters left before the light ran out.

8 | Kitt

2191.111 · 14:18

Kyjorh Dam | 8 Miles east of Gate 31

Water where water shouldn't be.

Kitt stood at the edge of the flooded basin. The concrete apron—designed to be dry, built to channel overflow through proper spillways—sat under six inches of murky water that stretched to the dam's base. Her boots were already soaked. She'd walked through it without noticing, focused on the dam itself.

She followed the water back toward the drainage channel. There—the culvert grate, half-visible beneath the surface. Clogged. Debris and sediment packed tight, water backing up with nowhere to go. Drainage system intact but unmaintained. The water wasn't a structural failure. It was neglect.

She pulled out her notebook. Started sketching the water line, marking where it met the intake structure, where it pooled against the access doors. The rust told the rest—orange and granular where flooding was recent, deeper brown scaling where moisture had been sitting for months. The scaling along the access door hinges had started to pit the metal underneath.

She could fix the drainage. A day's labor. The water would drain. The apron would dry. The concrete underneath was sound.

That was the pattern she kept finding. The bones were good. Everything laid on top of them was failing.

"You're sure this is where we'd bring the equipment?"

Marcus stood beside her, arms crossed, studying the flooded basin. Baker's hands, broad and scarred from oven work. He'd carried equipment on every job she'd run this year. Followed instructions precisely. Didn't ask unnecessary questions.

"The maintenance road comes in from the south." Kitt pointed without looking up from her sketch. "Through the access tunnel. That's how the original equipment was installed."

Seth splashed toward them from the basin's perimeter, sandy curls dark with moisture at the ends. He'd been checking the secondary access points Kitt had marked on her map—sent him out an hour ago, and he'd covered all three without needing to ask what he was looking for.

"South access is passable," he reported. "Tunnel lights are dead, but the path is mostly clear. Some debris about halfway through—looks like a ceiling panel came down. Day's work to clear it, maybe less with the right tools. We can get a truck through."

"Good." Kitt marked the tunnel route on her sketch.

"Kitt! Look!"

Emma Chen splashed past all three of them, yellow coat bright against the gray morning.

She'd showed up at the warehouse an hour after Peri and Connor left—eight years old, rubber boots too big for her, asking if she could come along for "science stuff." Marcus had looked at Kitt. Not asking permission exactly, but weighing it—could he come if Emma came, or did he need to stay behind with her.

Kitt had done the math. She needed Marcus at the dam. There was no one at the warehouse to watch Emma. One of those problems had a solution.

Small nod. That had settled it.

Now Emma crouched at the water's edge, poking at something with a stick. "There's fish! Little ones!"

"Emma." Kitt's voice came out sharper than intended. "Don't wander off."

The girl looked up, stick frozen mid-poke. Something in Kitt's tone must have landed because she straightened immediately, sloshing back toward her father.

Settle down. You'll fall and crack your head open.

The words rose unbidden. Not her voice—her mother's. The exact tone Pepper had used with Peri a thousand times.

Kitt's hand lifted—half a gesture.

She let it fall.

"Stay close," she said, softer now. "The footing's bad and I need to concentrate."

Emma nodded solemnly. Fell into step beside Marcus, who rested a hand on her shoulder.

"She gets bored easy," Marcus said quietly. Half apology, half explanation. "Her mother is the same way."

"It's fine." She gathered her pack, adjusting the field radio's strap across her shoulder. The glass cells glowed blue through the viewing window. "Let's see what we're actually working with."

The access door fought them. Seth put his shoulder into it and the hinges screamed—seized metal grinding against seized metal, a sound that told Kitt everything she needed about the maintenance schedule. Rust broke away in orange sheets that scattered across the water's surface and floated there.

Inside, the powerhouse stretched into darkness. Kitt's flashlight cut a pale cone through the gloom, catching dust motes suspended in still air and the hulking shapes of machinery beyond.

The smell hit first. Machine oil gone rancid—failed seals, lubricant stagnant in sumps that hadn't been drained in years. Damp concrete—moisture intrusion well beyond the flooded apron. And underneath both, sharper, the copper tang of active corrosion.

Three different failures. Three different timelines. None of them recent.

"It's dark," Emma whispered.

"Stay behind your father."

⚙

The turbine hall opened around them.

Sixty-two feet to the ceiling, a hundred and forty long. The space swallowed her flashlight beam, gave back only glimpses. Steel catwalks overhead, rust bleeding down their supports in long brown stains. The air colder here, still, carrying the mineral tang of water pooled somewhere she couldn't see.

Three turbine-generator units dominated the floor. Each one massive—cylindrical housings painted industrial green that had faded to something closer to moss, bolted to concrete pads that ran deep into the foundation. Two megawatts rated capacity per unit. Six megawatts total. Enough to power Belfast Mills and every settlement within twenty miles.

That was the design. That was what this place was built to do.

"What are those?" Emma's voice came back to her twice, bounced off concrete and steel.

"Turbines." Kitt crouched beside the nearest unit, pulling a wrench from her pack. "Water comes in through pipes—penstocks—and spins these. The spinning drives a generator that makes electricity. Like a waterwheel, but enclosed. Much more powerful."

She started with Unit One. The operating unit—the only one still connected, still turning, still producing anything at all.

She felt it through the wrench before she heard it. Vibration that should have been smooth running ragged—something rough, uneven. A machine working harder than it should to produce less than it could. She pressed her palm flat against the housing. The tremor traveled through her hand, up her wrist. Bearing wear. The kind of deep-seated degradation you couldn't see, only feel.

Seth and Marcus held lights where she pointed them. She worked her way around the unit, hands finding each component the way she'd find connections on a circuit board. Wicket gates first. Three of the twelve seized, locked at angles that throttled intake and forced the remaining nine to compensate. The mechanical governor held together with wire patches—layers of them, different gauges, different hands, different years. Someone had kept this running through sheer stubbornness, replacing failed components with whatever was available, rerouting around faults instead of fixing them.

The voltage regulator was worse. Burned out and jury-rigged so many times she had to trace each wire individually to understand what it was doing. At least one connection ran from a dead terminal to another dead terminal, left in place because no one knew if removing it would bring down something else.

The whole system was eating itself—every upstream failure compounding into the next, the machinery fighting its own damage at every stage. She checked the output meter on the switchgear panel.

Roughly four hundred kilowatts. Twenty percent of a single unit's capacity. Three percent of what this plant was designed to produce.

She pressed her palm to the housing one more time. The tremor still there. Patient. Persistent. A machine that hadn't stopped trying.

She moved to Unit Two.

Different story. Access panels closed, bolts corroded but intact. No oil stains. The penstock valve upstream shut—deliberately positioned. Someone had shut this unit down properly. Drained the systems, closed the valves, sealed it up. A controlled decommission, done with care.

She put her hand on the housing. Cold. Still. But the metal was sound—less corrosion than Unit One, protected by the shutdown. The bearings, the runner, the generator windings—all sitting in a dry, sealed environment instead of grinding to pieces under load.

This one might come back.

Unit Three turned her stomach.

Access panels open. Tools on the floor—a wrench, a pry bar, a wire brush, all corroded past use. Someone had been working on this unit and stopped. Mid-repair. Components pulled and never replaced, the generator housing open to the air. She could see the stator windings inside—copper gone green with verdigris, insulation cracked and peeling from conductors.

She didn't need to test it. Whatever had happened—whoever had been working here and walked away—Unit Three had been dying in the open ever since.

This one would need everything. New generator windings. New control systems. New switchgear. Precision-manufactured equipment that couldn't be fabricated from salvage.

The kind of equipment listed in the cargo data Cipher had flagged three days ago.

She stood between the three units. One limping. One sealed and waiting. One gutted and exposed.

"This place could power Belfast Mills for decades," she said quietly. "All of it. Every house, every workshop. The clinic. The water pumps. Everything."

"If it worked," Marcus said.

"If it worked." She looked at the output meter. Four hundred kilowatts where six megawatts should be. "Two units running at full capacity with the third in maintenance rotation. That's the design."

She turned back to Unit Two. The sealed housing. The cold metal under her palm.

"What's failed are the electrical systems. Generator windings. Transformers. Voltage regulation. Control circuits." She looked at Marcus, then Seth. "Those are the components you can't build from scrap. You need precision manufacturing."

She let that sit.

"The water's still here. The dam's still here. The turbines still turn." She closed her notebook. "What's missing is what makes the turning into electricity."

⊙

An hour into the assessment, the radio crackled to life.

The cells in the viewing window flared brighter—blue intensifying as the signal came through.

"Falcon to Tabby." Peri. Slightly breathless. "Radio check. Repeater Eleven is operational. That's all three. Network's back online."

All three.

Kitt stood near the dead turbines, notebook in one hand, light tucked under her arm. Three repeater stations across the northern chain—every junction box she'd worried about, every corroded connection she'd mapped on the workbench yesterday morning. Operational. Her network, carrying signal again.

She keyed the mic. "Tabby copies. Reading you five by five." The signal was clean. Strong. No crackle, no drift—the kind of clarity she hadn't heard on the northern band in weeks. "Nice work, Falcon."

"We're packing up now, should be at base by nightfall." A pause. Static shifting. "How's the dam?"

Kitt looked around the powerhouse. The one struggling turbine. The sealed unit waiting. The gutted one with its tools on the floor.

"Worse than I thought. And better than I feared."

A pause.

"Copy that. We'll debrief when I'm back. Falcon out."

The signal cut. The cells dimmed back to their glow.

Kitt held the radio a moment longer. The powerhouse sounds filled back in—the struggling hum of Unit One, water dripping somewhere in the dark, the small shuffling sounds of Marcus and Seth and Emma waiting for her to come back to the work.

She clipped the radio to her belt.

Emma was staring at the radio. At the viewing window where the blue light had pulsed.

"Why did they get brighter?" she asked. "When your sister called?"

Kitt looked at the cells. At Emma's face—open, waiting.

"The phosphor cells store electrical charge," she said. "Chemical energy converted from light—that's how we charge them in the racks back home. When a radio signal comes in, the receiver circuit draws current to amplify it. That current passes through the cells. The increased load causes a temporary spike in their luminescence as electrons move through the phosphor matrix at a higher rate."

Emma blinked. Her face went carefully blank.

Kitt recognized that expression. She'd seen it on Peri, on Kataero, on Connor.

"The chemical reaction that makes them glow gets stronger when more electricity moves through them." She reached for something concrete. "Like... like how a fire gets brighter when you add more wood. More energy in, more light out."

The analogy was wrong, technically. Fire was combustion. The cells were phosphorescence. Different mechanisms entirely.

She hoped it was close enough.

Emma nodded slowly. "Okay."

She glanced at Seth and Marcus.

Both men wore the exact same expression Emma had.

Seth raised his hands slightly. "I just move things, Kitt."

"I bake bread," Marcus added. But he was smiling.

Kitt turned back to her work.

Twenty minutes later, the radio crackled again.

"Panther to Tabby."

Kataero's voice, carrying that particular edge of frustration she knew too well.

"Tabby here. Go ahead, Panther."

"Where did you put the secondary frequency charts? The ones with the repeater calibration data."

"Filing cabinet. Second drawer from the top, left side."

Static. Shuffling sounds. A muttered curse.

"It's not here."

"It is. Left side of the cabinet."

"I'm looking at the left side. There's nothing but old manifests."

Kitt closed her eyes. Held her breath until the impulse to say something regrettable passed.

"Dad. Your other left."

More shuffling. A drawer sliding open.

"...Found it."

A pause. Then, gruff but warm: "Thank you."

"Love you too. Tabby out."

She lowered the radio. Found everyone staring at her.

Seth caught Marcus's eye. Marcus shook his head slowly, shoulders shaking.

"What?" Kitt demanded.

"Nothing," Seth said, fighting a smile. "Just... 'your other left.'"

"He does this every time."

"Sure he does."

Emma giggled. The sound echoed in the vast space, incongruously bright.

Kitt turned back to the turbine with more force than necessary. "Can we focus, please?"

⚙

Emma edged closer as Kitt finished her last round of notes. Voice low, careful—the way she'd approached the water's edge earlier, testing whether the ground would hold.

"Kitt? If you had the right parts... the ones it's supposed to have... could you fix it?"

Kitt's pencil stopped.

She looked at Emma. Then at the three units behind her—the one grinding itself apart, the one sealed and waiting, the one gutted and open.

Could she do this.

Rewire control systems. Rebuild switchgear. Install new generator assemblies and integrate them with fifty-year-old mechanical infrastructure. Commission units that hadn't run in decades. Bring six megawatts back online with a crew of people who baked bread and moved things and held flashlights at the wrong angle.

"I don't know," she said. Then, quieter: "Maybe."

Emma nodded. As though maybe was enough.

"So the maintenance road comes through the south tunnel," Seth said, studying the map Kitt had sketched. "We clear the debris—day's work. Then we can get vehicles all the way to the powerhouse floor."

"In theory." Kitt traced the route with her finger. "The tunnel slopes down. If the water level rises much more, we'll be driving through it."

"Can we pump it out?"

"With what? The dam's generators are what we're trying to fix. We'd need external power to run pumps big enough to matter." She shook her head. "You need power to fix power. You need equipment to get equipment."

She thought of the equipment list on her notepad. Generator assemblies. Transformer units.

"There might be another way," she said quietly.

Seth and Marcus looked at her. Waited. Neither pushed.

"When you're ready to talk about it," Seth said, "we're listening."

They emerged from the powerhouse into afternoon light that hit too bright after hours in the gloom. Kitt blinked against it, eyes slow to adjust.

Marcus lifted Emma onto his shoulders, her yellow coat catching the sun.

"I need to head back," Marcus said. "Got to start prepping the dough for tomorrow."

"Go." Kitt waved them off. "I've got what I need for now."

Seth lingered as Marcus and Emma started down the path, their voices carrying back—*Daddy, why is the water green?* and *Algae, sweetheart, tiny plants that grow in standing water*—growing fainter as distance stole the words.

"You're going to do something about this," Seth said. Not a question.

"Yes."

"Good." He held her gaze for a beat. Then turned and followed the path down.

⊙

Kitt stood alone at the edge of the flooded basin.

The water lapped softly against concrete. Somewhere inside the powerhouse, Unit One hummed—that same rough vibration. Still running. Four hundred kilowatts where six megawatts should be.

Could you fix it?

"I can fix this."

She turned and started walking home.

9 | Wynne

2191.089 · 12:24

Pede-Meyers Madison Yard | UAD Port Madison

The noise found her first. A deep, mechanical grinding that climbed through the soles of her bare feet before it reached her ears—diesel engines turning over, the shriek of metal wheels braking against rail, the percussive bang of coupling cars connecting down the line. A chain of fists striking in sequence.

Then the warehouses parted and the yard opened before her.

A locomotive sat idling on the nearest track, heat shimmer rising from its hood in waves she could feel twenty paces out. Beyond it, flatcars and boxcars in loose formation, some sealed, some open to crews working their interiors. Forklifts shuttled between warehouse doors and the rail line, engines coughing at each turn.

She'd read about trains. Seen drawings. None of it had prepared her for the scale, or for the way the entire yard moved at once—men, machines, cargo flowing in patterns she couldn't yet read but could feel had structure.

A squat building sat off to one side, ticket office by the look of the painted sign and barred window. She joined the short queue. Three people ahead. Then two. Then one.

When she reached the window, the clerk glanced up from his ledger. Paused. Took in the platinum hair, the bare feet, the staff strapped across her back.

"Passage to Hamilton," Wynne said. The words came without deliberation—spoken the way you'd name a place you'd already been heading toward.

His expression changed—not surprise, exactly. More like a man reaching for a protocol he'd never had to use. "Of course, sister. Hamilton is six steel chits. Next northbound runs day after tomorrow, 0600."

Wynne unfastened her belt pouch. Tipped the contents into her palm—small copper discs stamped with the Order's geometric seal. She held them through the bars.

He picked one up. Turned it between his fingers. Set it down carefully—not dropped. Placed.

"My apologies, sister. I'm not permitted to accept monastery marks for transit fare. They'd need to be exchanged for standard currency first." He glanced at the coins on the counter. "The trading houses on Front Street might take them, but I can't say at what rate."

"I understand. Thank you."

He held her gaze a moment longer than the transaction required. Young—not much older than her, ink-stained fingers, a pen tucked behind his ear that he'd forgotten was there. "The morning train boards at quarter to six. If you find a way to make fare, I'll hold a seat."

"I appreciate that," Wynne said.

She stepped away from the window. Poured the coins back into the pouch.

She chose a bench at the far end of the platform, away from the cluster near the ticket office. Staff leaning against her shoulder.

Her stomach twisted. The smell of frying meat from somewhere nearby turned the dull ache into sharp hunger. She watched a forklift shuttle a pallet from a warehouse bay to the nearest cargo car. Its rear wheels lifted slightly as the load tipped forward on the turn. A vendor hawked roasted nuts. A boy swept the platform for dropped coins. Six steel chits. How many hours of sweeping added up to six?

Voices carried from the cargo yard to her left.

"Bring it in another two feet. Two feet—there. Hold."

"That pallet's not seated. Back it out."

"I can see it's not seated, Pede. Fork's pulling left again."

Wynne turned. A cargo car stood open, its heavy sliding door racked back on rusted tracks. Inside, a man guided a pallet into position while another operated the forklift from the platform. A third waited inside with a strapping tool, ready to secure.

A fourth stood apart. Older. Grey beard, one arm bandaged and held tight against his ribs. His weight shifted with every movement of the cargo, reading it, tracking it.

"We'll never make Wednesday's departure at this pace."

"We're doing what we can, Pede. Short-handed as it is."

"I can see that." He glanced at his strapped arm.

Wynne rose. Walked toward them.

The forklift operator paused, engine idling. The men inside the cargo car looked up.

Pede turned as she approached. His gaze ran over her the way hers ran over a room.

"Help you?" he asked.

"You need hands," Wynne said. "I'll work. In exchange for a fair wage."

The young one on the forklift—Harlan, she'd learn—leaned out of the cab. "We're hiring from the monastery now?"

Pede lifted his good hand. The comment died. He studied Wynne for a beat longer. "You ever done cargo work? Strapping, load-securing, any of it?"

"No."

"Then why are you offering?"

"I'm a fast learner. And I'm stronger than I look."

"Everyone says that." But he was still looking. He'd been doing physical work his whole life. He knew what a trained body looked like even under monastery white.

"Here's what I've got. Interior car work. Once the freight's through the door, it needs positioning, bracing, strapping down. I'm down a pair of hands—" he gestured at his bound arm, "—and the kid on the lift can't be in two places at once."

He pointed into the open cargo car. "Al and Mickie will show you what goes where. You strap a load wrong, it shifts in transit. Shifts in transit, it damages. Damages, I eat the cost." He held her gaze. "Understood?"

"Understood."

"Work today. We'll see how it goes."

"That's enough."

He grunted. "You got a name?"

"Wynne Kaede."

"Ned Harren. Most people call me Pede." He gestured into the car. "Tall one's Alfred—"

A lean man with rolled sleeves looked up from a ratchet tensioner. "Al."

Pede's jaw tightened, but he moved on. "—and that's Mickie." The shorter one, broad-shouldered, already threading strapping through a floor anchor. "The kid on the lift is Harlan." A nod toward the young worker, who'd already turned back to his machine.

"You do what Al and Mickie tell you. Don't damage the cargo. Don't get in the way of the lift. And eat something if you find the time—you look like you missed more than one meal."

Wynne said nothing. He was right.

"Get to it."

She propped her staff against the platform wall and climbed into the car.

⊙

Steel walls rising on three sides. The floor—heavy planking, oil-darkened—ran thirty feet to the far wall. Anchor points studded the floor and walls at regular intervals. The air was closed, warm, heavy with diesel and old freight.

Al held up the tensioner—a mechanical ratchet with a heavy strap threaded through it. "This is your new best friend. Feeds through the anchors, over the load, ratchet it tight. You'll feel when the strap goes from slack to tension. That's your stop point."

He demonstrated. The ratchet clicked—steady, rhythmic, the strap drawing flat against the crate with each pull. When it caught, the sound changed. Shorter. Harder. The strap hummed.

"Hear that?"

Wynne listened. Nodded.

"That's snug. Go past it and you'll crack the crate or pop the anchor. Either one comes out of Pede's pocket." He released the tensioner. "Want to try?"

She took it. The weight was solid in her hands. Fed the strap the way he'd shown her—through the floor anchor, over the crate, down to the opposite anchor. Started ratcheting.

The mechanism had a rhythm. She found it on the third pull—the resistance building, her forearms reading the tension the way they read resistance in a staff bind. When the sound changed, she stopped.

Al checked the strap. Tugged it. Pressed his palm flat against the load and pushed. Nothing shifted.

"Not bad," he said.

"Next one's coming," Mickie called from near the door. "Heavy. Watch the floor."

The forklift's engine rose. A shadow filled the door. Then the load appeared—a wide pallet stacked with crated machine parts, the forks sliding it onto the car's threshold. The whole car shifted under the new weight, the floor flexing, the frame protesting in its couplings.

Wynne felt it through her feet. The car's balance changing—center of gravity pulling toward the door, the floor angling a degree she registered in her ankles before her eyes confirmed it.

"Push it home," Al said. "Mickie on the left, you on the right. Guide it—don't shove. Floor's not level anymore."

She set her hands on the crate. Felt the weight through her palms, her wrists, her shoulders. The pallet wanted to drift left—she could feel it, the same way she felt an opponent settling their weight before a strike. She adjusted. Pressed from the right, steady, using her legs and hips to drive it.

Mickie matched her on the other side. They moved it together—six feet, eight, ten. The pallet found its place against the wall.

"Hold it." Mickie braced the load while she fed the straps. Ratcheted. The sound changed. She stopped.

Mickie checked her work. Didn't fix anything. Moved to the next anchor point.

The hours built.

⊙

Heat pressed in—subtropical sun baking the cargo car's steel walls until the air inside felt solid. Sweat ran down her arms and made the tensioner grip slick. She wiped her hands on her tunic. Kept working.

Each load had its own problem. Some were balanced. Some were not—weight shifting inside crates, off-center stacks that wanted to lean, awkward shapes that fought the straps. Al read each one before it came through the door, calling adjustments.

"That one's top-heavy. Brace the base first, then strap high."

"Fragile. Don't let the ratchet over-tension. Feel for the change."

Wynne listened. Followed. Adjusted. Her body found a pattern. Read the weight. Find the center. Anticipate the shift. Respond before it arrives.

After the sixth load, Al watched her guide the next pallet into position—reading the drift, correcting before Mickie called it.

"You've never done this before," he said.

"No."

"You move like someone who knows what weight wants to do before it does it."

"Training. Not cargo."

"Different problem." The corner of his mouth tugged. "Same instinct."

After the eighth load, Mickie handed her a dented canteen. "Drink. You're wringing wet and I haven't seen you eat."

She took it. Cool, metallic water—shocking after hours of heat. She drank deeper than she meant to. "Thank you."

He took it back with a grunt. "You're fighting the straps. Don't muscle the ratchet—let the mechanism do the work. Slow pulls, steady. It's a tool, not an opponent."

She adjusted on the next one. Slower. Letting the ratchet's gearing carry the load instead of her arms. The strap drew tight with half the effort.

"Better," Mickie said. "You pick things up fast."

"Good instruction."

He snorted, but the lines around his eyes eased.

Three loads from the end, her body called the debt.

She braced against a pallet, pushing it the last two feet into position. Her arms shook—not from the weight, but from the accumulation. Eight hours of sustained work on one piece of bread. Her vision narrowed. The pallet drifted left.

Mickie's hand caught the far side. Steadied it. One hand on her shoulder. Brief pressure. "Almost done. You'll finish."

Wynne nodded once. Drew breath. Reached for the next strap.

The sun dipped low. Orange light poured through the cargo door, flooding the car's interior, turning the steel walls to copper. Wynne straightened between loads and caught it—the whole car burning in the last of the day. For a breath, the ache in her arms fell away, and there was just the light.

Two loads left. Harlan stood at the cargo door now, no longer disappearing into the forklift cab between runs. Watching her work.

One load left.

The last pallet was heavy and awkward—long crates, banded steel, the weight distributed unevenly. The forklift slid it through the door and the whole car groaned.

Al and Mickie took positions without a word. Harlan stepped in beside them.

Four people. One load. Pushed home.

Wynne fed the straps. Ratcheted each one until the sound told her to stop. Mickie checked. Al checked. Everything held.

Done.

Wynne stepped back. Leaned against the car's steel wall and let herself breathe.

Platform lamps buzzed to life outside, trading the fading sun for small circles of yellow light.

⚙

Pede came into the car. Moved down the line of secured freight with his good hand, testing each strap—pressing loads, nudging edges, reading the work by touch the way Wynne read a sparring partner's weight. Thorough. Unhurried.

Everything held.

He stopped in front of Wynne.

"You held up," he said. "Cargo's clean. Strapping's tight. Not a thing out of place." His fingers brushed his bound arm. "First barefoot monastery girl I've ever put on a crew."

He studied her. The same assessment from that morning, but informed now.

"I'm down a man for the next two weeks, minimum. Doctor says six before this arm's good for real work." He flexed the fingers of his bound hand. They moved, but poorly. "I need reliable help. Work every day, fair wage in steel chits. Same deal as today—you do what Al and Mickie tell you, you don't damage cargo, and you show up on time."

"I'll be here," she said.

"Six o'clock. Not a minute past."

"Understood."

He dipped his head and climbed down from the car.

Al passed her on his way out. Clapped her shoulder. "See you tomorrow, Order girl."

Mickie was the last to leave. He ran a final check on the straps she'd set, his broad hands moving with unconscious sureness. Satisfied, he stepped down to the platform and looked up at her.

"You got a place to sleep?"

"I'll find the bench—"

"No." He picked up his jacket from where he'd thrown it hours ago. "I've got a room out back of my place. Nothing special. Linens are clean. Shower works. Hot water's a coin toss."

He rubbed the back of his neck. "You're on the crew now. Can't have you showing up stiff because you slept on a platform."

"Thank you, Mickie."

"Don't thank me yet. You haven't seen it." He slung the jacket over his shoulder. "You eat anything today?"

"Bread. This morning. From a baker in the market."

He stared at her. "You just did eight hours on one piece of bread."

"The Order trains for endurance."

"The Order trains for stupid, apparently." He held out a small cloth bag. "Eat this on the walk. I'll put something real together when we get home."

She took the bag. Collected her staff from the platform wall and shouldered it.

He started walking—not toward the station or the main road, but through a side gate where the yard gave way to a narrow lane between warehouses. He didn't check whether she followed.

Wynne followed.

The lane opened into a residential street. Smaller than the market roads—working homes, close-set, lights coming on in windows as evening settled. Mickie moved through it without hurry, nodding to a woman taking down laundry, sidestepping a dog that appeared from an alley to inspect his boots.

His place sat at the end of a row. Narrow front, weathered clapboard, a porch that leaned at one corner but held. He led her around the side to a door she might have missed if he hadn't pointed.

"Was a workshop. Converted it when my daughter moved out." He pushed the door open. "Like I said. Nothing special."

A single room. Cot against one wall, made up with a wool blanket folded square. A shelf. A basin. A narrow door to what she guessed was the shower he'd warned her about. The air smelled like sawdust and soap. Someone had swept.

"Towel's on the shelf. Lock works from inside." He stepped back. "Kitchen door's around front. You're up before me, don't touch the coffeepot—it's temperamental and I'm the only one it trusts."

The corner of her mouth lifted. "Understood."

He turned to go. Stopped.

"You did good work today, Wynne Kaede." Quieter now. Without the crew to hear. "Rest up. Tomorrow's harder."

His footsteps retreated around the corner. A door opened, closed. The small sounds of a man settling into his evening—water running, a cabinet, the low murmur of a radio finding its station.

Wynne set her staff against the wall. Sat on the cot. The mattress was thin but gave in a way that meant someone had bothered.

She opened the cloth bag. Bread. A wedge of cheese. An apple.

She forced herself to eat slowly, no matter how loudly the hollow in her gut howled. The bread rough but solid—each bite expanding in her mouth. The cheese sharp enough to sting, salt and fat hitting her system like a shock. The apple so sweet it made her eyes prickle.

Or that might have been something else.

Through the wall, the radio found its station. A woman's voice reading news from somewhere far away. The words indistinct, but the cadence even.

Wynne drew breath. Four counts in. Held for four. Released for six.

Her breathing slowed.

Tomorrow. Six o'clock.

10 | Peri

2191.111 · 21:06
Gate 31

The truck rolled through Gate 31. The engine cut out—tick of cooling metal, the warehouse dark ahead of them.

Peri sat there a moment longer than she needed to. Hand on the door handle. The warehouse in front of her. Same corrugated walls, same loading dock, same concrete she'd crossed a thousand times.

She stepped down slowly, shoulders stiff, calves tight from the climb.

Connor moved around the truck with practiced ease, already unloading—toolboxes first, then the field radio with its antenna folded flat, testing gear last. Same order he'd packed them. Same silence.

She carried the pack just inside and set it down where no one would trip over it. The fastener tore apart as she opened the flap; three glass cells clinked softly when she pulled them free. Two were nearly dark, spent down to a faint glow. One still burned bright, stronger than the others.

She crossed to the charging rack. Twenty-three cells in their wooden frame. She slotted the three into open spaces and started to turn away.

Kitt was still asleep at her bench.

Peri looked back at the rack. Then at Kitt. Then at the rack again.

She blew a curl off her forehead.

Brightest in front. Left to right. Or was it right to left?

She pulled one cell and moved it two slots over. Paused. Shook her head. Shifted another. Paused again. The gradient had a logic—she'd watched Kitt arrange it that morning, watched her fingers skip past the bright ones and pull the steady ones, watched her do it like breathing. It had made sense when Kitt was doing it.

"How the hell does she keep this in her head?" she muttered.

Two more cells traded places under her hand as she squinted at the gradient like it might suddenly reveal its logic. Blue light played across her hands, each cell a slightly different shade she had no name for.

She stepped back. Studied the result. Tilted her head.

"Good enough," she muttered, entirely unsure whether she'd fixed it or made it worse. Kitt would know in three seconds. Kitt always knew.

Her gaze caught on Kitt's workbench.

Kitt was slumped over it, head pillowed on folded arms, dark hair sticking up in sleep-pressed angles, a few strands flat against her cheek. Soldering iron cold in its stand. Pages scrawled with diagrams scattered, components sorted into careful piles that had outlasted her consciousness. Her fingers still curled slightly, holding tools that weren't there anymore.

Peri walked closer, boots soft on the concrete.

Kitt's breathing was deep and even. A smear of flux streaked one cheek. She'd been at it for hours—the whole time since getting back from the dam, Kitt had been here. Working. Waiting for the radio checks. Making sure the repairs held from her end.

Behind her, Connor's footsteps moved in their usual rhythm, gear going back to its places.

Another set of steps sounded from the office corridor. Heavier. She knew them before they arrived.

Kataero filled the doorway. He looked at her.

She didn't bother with words. Just crossed the distance and stepped into him, arms wrapping around his solid weight.

His arms came around her instantly. She buried her face in his shoulder—machine oil, winter air, and underneath, the scent that was simply him.

One broad hand cradled the back of her head. His lips brushed her forehead.

His other hand moved in circles between her shoulders.

She breathed.

"I'm sorry," she murmured against him. "About yesterday."

"I know." His voice rumbled through his chest against her cheek. "I'm sorry too."

They stood like that. The warehouse settled into evening quiet around them—Connor's footsteps still moving, the creak of the building as the air cooled. She could feel his heartbeat, solid and unhurried, and she matched her breathing to it without deciding to.

Eventually Peri eased back and looked up at him.

"The repeaters are fixed," she said. "Network's up. Full coverage north to south."

Kataero nodded, his hand settling briefly on her head, gentle despite the calloused palm.

"Good work," he said.

He let her go and moved toward Kitt's bench.

Peri fell in beside him, her steps soft against his.

He stopped at Kitt's side and stood there for a moment, just looking down at her. His hand settled on her back and started rubbing in slow circles, the same pressure he'd used on Peri's shoulders. The same hands. The same care.

Peri watched him. The way his face changed when he looked at Kitt—the lines easing, the set of his jaw softening into something private.

She waited for the sting.

It didn't come.

"Kitt." His voice low. "Bedtime."

Kitt stirred, made a sound that wasn't quite a word.

"Come on. You'll wreck your back sleeping like that."

Kitt's head came up a fraction, eyes still squeezed shut. Her arms lifted instead, reaching blindly toward him.

"Carry me," she mumbled, thick and small—the same request she'd been making since she'd been small enough to carry.

Kataero's expression softened. His hand moved to her hair, smoothing it flat. "I'll never make it up those stairs."

"He's saying you weigh a ton," Peri put in.

Kitt's eyes snapped open. Locked on Peri.

Her hand closed on the nearest soft object—a crumpled, oil-stained rag—and she flung it with unfair accuracy for someone who'd been snoring thirty seconds ago.

Peri dodged, laughing. "Hey!"

Kitt launched herself off the stool. "Take it back!"

Peri bolted, boots hammering on concrete as she darted around the bench and wove between crates. Kitt came after her, faster than she had any right to be.

"I'm gonna kill you!"

"You've got to catch me first!" Peri shouted back, laughing so hard her ribs ached.

"Girls."

Kataero didn't raise his voice.

Peri froze mid-duck behind a crate, chest heaving. Kitt skidded to a stop a few strides behind her, equally breathless.

"It's late," he said. "Get your asses in bed."

Kitt glanced at Peri. Peri met her eyes.

"Fine," Kitt muttered, trying for dignity and completely ruining it with hair sticking up in chaotic angles.

"Fine," Peri echoed.

They headed for the stairs together. Peri reached them first, started up, then eased her pace on the third step until Kitt drew level.

Peri's arm slid around Kitt's shoulders.

Kitt's arm wrapped around Peri's waist without a pause.

They climbed in step.

"You know," Peri said lightly, "I basically did everything today. Connor just sat there watching snow melt off the tower."

"I'm sure he did," Kitt replied, voice dry as dust.

"I mean, I handed him every single tool. Multimeter, strippers, solder. He'd still be staring at frostbite if I hadn't pointed everything out."

They topped the stairs. The hallway stretched ahead, lined with familiar doors.

Bathroom door at the end. Hot water. Soap.

"I call first shower!" Peri announced, already angling for it.

Kitt was faster. Somehow. Unfairly.

She reached the door first, slipped through, and slammed the lock home with a decisive click.

"Don't use up all the hot water this time!"

"I can't hear you."

"Kitt!"

The water roared on. A small scream—the pipes hadn't warmed up yet.

Peri smiled at the closed door.

She leaned her forehead against the wood grain. The laughter was still in her chest, and she held it there for a moment before pushing off.

She wandered back to the railing overlooking the warehouse and folded her arms along the cool metal.

Below, the space was going dark by degrees. Kataero moved along the far wall, hitting switches—fluorescents dying in sections. Workbenches first. Then the storage rows. Then the loading dock.

Connor stood by the office door, waiting, arms folded. Kataero reached him and stopped, one hand landing on Connor's shoulder. He said something—too low to carry—and his free hand swept a broad arc through the air, something that had Connor's shoulders shaking. Connor answered with smaller, precise gestures, and whatever he said made Kataero's laugh boom up through the open space and find her where she stood.

The big exterior door rumbled closed, sealing them in. The sound rolled through the warehouse and settled.

The two men headed through the office doorway together, still talking. The doorway swallowed them. Their voices faded.

Peri rested her head on her folded arms.

Below her, the warehouse sat in near-darkness—just the charging rack's blue glow and the green power light on Kitt's radio. The building ticked and creaked as metal cooled. Somewhere in the walls, the pipes hummed, carrying hot water to her sister.

Her hand didn't reach for the stopwatch.

She noticed that.

She let her eyes close. Let the stillness hold.

11 | Wynne

2191.090 · 5:50

Pede-Meyers Madison Yard | UAD Port Madison

Day 2

The cargo car was already open when she arrived. Ten minutes early. Al was earlier.

He stood inside with a clipboard—actual paper, grease pencil tucked behind his ear—running down a manifest. Didn't look up when she climbed in.

"Grab the number-four tensioner off the wall rack. Not the three—the ratchet's stripped. And put these on." He tossed something without looking. Work gloves, leather, stiff with age but intact. "Mickie's are too big for you, but they'll keep your hands from tearing up before the week's out."

Wynne caught them. Pulled them on. The leather was thick, the fingers loose—Mickie's hands were half again the size of hers. But the grip held.

"Today's different from yesterday," Al said, finally looking up. "Yesterday was a tryout. Today you learn the job." He tapped the clipboard. "Every car gets a load manifest. Weight, dimensions, placement order, center-of-gravity notes for anything that's not standard. You don't read it, you don't load. Pede gets fined if the rail authority pulls a car and finds the weight distribution off."

He showed her the manifest for the first car. Columns of figures in neat handwriting—not Al's, she guessed. Pede's.

"This column is total weight per pallet. This one's the CG offset—how far off-center the heavy side sits. Anything over six inches gets braced before it gets strapped." He handed her the grease pencil. "Mark the floor where each pallet seats. I'll check your spacing."

Wynne crouched. Read the numbers. Began marking.

She got the first two right. The third was off by a foot—she'd misjudged the clearance needed for the strapping hardware.

"Closer together," Al said. "The tensioner arm needs eighteen inches of swing. Less than that and you can't get the ratchet over. More than that and you're wasting floor space, which means the last load doesn't fit, which means—"

"Pede eats the cost."

"She learns." He almost smiled. "Remark it."

By midmorning, Harlan was shuttling pallets to the door and Wynne was positioning them inside with Mickie. The rhythm was building—not the stop-and-teach of yesterday, but something closer to flow. Read the manifest. Mark the floor. Receive the load. Position. Brace. Strap.

Her hands were starting to understand the tensioner. Not just the mechanism—the feedback. Each strap talked through the ratchet handle. Tension that built evenly meant the load was seated right. Tension that spiked meant something was binding—a strap twisted, a brace out of line, the load canted on its skid. She could feel the difference in her forearms before she could see it.

Al noticed. Said nothing. But the corrections came less often.

Late afternoon. The last pallet of the day was in place, strapped and checked. Wynne's shoulders burned. Her hands, even inside the borrowed gloves, had found new places to ache.

Al pulled his grease pencil from behind his ear. Made a small mark on the clipboard—a check, next to a line she couldn't read from where she stood.

"Same time tomorrow," he said.

⊙

Day 5

Pede was in the yard when she arrived. Not watching from the sideline—standing at the manifest table, his good hand flat on the paperwork, arguing with a rail dispatcher about a scheduling change. His bound arm moved when he gestured. Not much. But more than it had on Day 1.

The shoulder was loosening. The fingers flexed more naturally. A man healing faster than he'd admit to his doctor and slower than he'd accept.

The dispatcher left. Pede caught her looking.

"Few more days," he said, flexing his bound hand. The fingers closed most of the way. "Few more days and I'll be back in the cars with the rest of you. Tired of standing around doing nothing." He glanced at the dispatcher's retreating back, then at the rail yard, then at his own useless arm. "I look like a bloody Assemblyman."

Mickie, passing with a tensioner over his shoulder, snorted without breaking stride.

The morning went smooth. Three cars to load—routine freight, well-manifested, nothing unusual. Wynne worked the interior with Mickie while Al coordinated from the platform, reading manifests and directing Harlan's forklift to each door in sequence.

She'd stopped thinking about the tensioner. It lived in her hands now the way the quarterstaff did—the feedback an extension of her own awareness, wrist and forearm knowing what the eyes hadn't seen yet. When a strap resisted wrong, she adjusted before the thought fully formed. When a load drifted during positioning, her body answered first—hips turning, weight shifting, hands guiding the pallet's momentum instead of fighting it.

Al had stopped correcting her two days ago.

The fourth car was different. Heavier freight—industrial parts, dense and awkward, some of the pallets stacked higher than Wynne's head. Harlan brought the first load to the door and the car groaned under the weight, its suspension compressing with a sound she felt in her knees.

Al was inside, checking the floor anchors near the back wall. Crouched, back to the door, tensioner in his hands.

Harlan's forklift brought the second pallet. Wider than the first. The forks slid it onto the car's threshold—and Wynne heard it. Not with her ears. With the floor.

A shift. Subtle. The pallet settling on the forks at an angle that wasn't right, the weight distribution off from how it should have sat. She'd felt correct loads come through this door for five days. This one was wrong.

The forklift raised the pallet to clear the threshold lip.

The high side tipped.

Not fast. Not yet. But the geometry was already decided—two thousand pounds of industrial parts on a pallet that wasn't fully seated on the forks, the center of gravity migrating past the tipping point with mechanical certainty. In two seconds, it would go. And Al was crouched directly under the fall line, back turned, ten feet from the door.

Wynne was moving before the thought finished.

Three strides. The floor jolting under her bare feet with each one. She hit Al at the shoulders—not a shove, a redirect, both hands driving him sideways and down, using his crouched position to roll him clear rather than blast him flat.

Al went sideways. Wynne went with him. Her hip struck the steel wall. Pain flared and she ignored it.

Behind them—a sound like the world breaking its knuckles. The pallet hit the car floor where Al had been kneeling. Steel parts burst free of their banding and scattered across the planking. The car rocked on its bogies. Something heavy rolled past her foot close enough to feel the air move.

Then silence.

Wynne was on the floor, one hand still on Al's shoulder. Her hip throbbed. Her breath was even.

Al lay against the wall where she'd put him. Eyes wide. Looking at the wreckage where he'd been crouching, then at Wynne, then back at the wreckage. The tensioner still in his hand, knuckles white.

Mickie stood at the cargo door. He hadn't moved—there hadn't been time. His face was gray.

Harlan sat frozen in the forklift cab, hands locked on the controls, staring at the toppled pallet.

The silence held for three heartbeats. Four. Five.

Al sat up. Looked at the scattered steel where his back had been. Looked at Wynne.

"How?" Quiet. Not *how did you save me. How did you know.*

"The floor," she said. "The weight was wrong when it came through the door."

He stared at her.

Mickie climbed into the car. Went to Al first—hand on his shoulder, checking. Then he looked at the pallet. At the debris field. At the dent in the floor planking.

Pede's voice came from the platform. Tight. Controlled.

"Everyone whole?"

"We're good," Mickie called back. Steadier than his face suggested.

Pede climbed into the car. Took in the scene—the toppled pallet, the scattered parts, Al sitting against the wall, Wynne beside him. His good hand went to his beard. Pulled once.

He looked at Harlan in the forklift. "That pallet seated when you picked it up?"

"I thought—" Harlan's voice cracked. "I checked it. I thought it was good."

"Clearly it wasn't." No anger in Pede's voice. Something worse—the flat calm of a man staring at the exact cost of what he'd almost lost. "We're done with that forklift until I inspect the forks myself. And you're going to tell me exactly what you checked and what you assumed."

Harlan nodded. Pale.

Pede turned to Wynne. Studied her the way he'd studied cargo—looking for what held and what didn't.

"You pulled him clear."

"Yes."

"Before it fell."

"Yes."

She watched him do the math. Five days of cargo work didn't explain what he'd just seen.

He didn't ask how. He looked at his bound arm. At the car. At Al, who was getting to his feet with Mickie's help, moving on legs that worked but didn't trust themselves yet.

"Alright," Pede said. Quiet. To himself as much as anyone. Then louder: "Take thirty. Everyone. Water, air, whatever you need. We clean this up after."

He climbed down from the car. Wynne heard him start in on Harlan. Not shouting. Worse—the steady, thorough dismantling of every assumption the kid had made, delivered in the tone of a man who'd just been reminded what shortcuts cost.

Al was on his feet. Brushing dust from his clothes. His hands were shaking. Delayed.

He stopped in front of Wynne.

"Thank you."

She nodded. That was enough.

He walked out of the car. Slowly. His hand trailed along the door frame as he stepped down.

Mickie stayed. He picked up the fallen tensioner. Turned it in his hands without looking at it.

"That was fast," he said.

"Training."

"That wasn't training." He met her eyes. "Training is what I saw the last five days—you learning the ratchet, learning the manifests, getting better at the job. That—" he gestured at the wreckage, "—that was something else."

Wynne said nothing.

Mickie seemed to understand that. He set the tensioner down.

"You're a strange kid, Wynne Kaede."

"So I've been told."

He almost smiled. "Come on. Thirty minutes. I know where Pede hides the good coffee."

⊙

Day 7

Morning found her before the sun did.

She dressed in the dark—not the white robes, which hung from a nail on the wall where she'd put them the first night. Shorts that ended above the knee. A fitted halter that left her arms and shoulders bare. Clothes for moving, not for modesty. The Order hadn't trained modesty into her. They'd trained function.

She took her staff and went outside.

Mickie's backyard was a narrow strip of beaten earth between the house and a low fence. A clothesline sagged between two posts. A garden that someone—his daughter, maybe—had once tended, now half-wild.

Enough room.

She began.

The first position arrived before she reached for it. Hands settling on the staff, weight dropping through her hips, and the morning air arriving on skin the robes usually covered—cool across her shoulders, strange against the flat of her stomach. She had never felt the forms in open air like this. Never felt a breeze track the motion of the staff.

First position flowing into second. Not remembered—inhabited. The wood whispering past her ear, the counterweight pulling through her shoulders, each strike rooted in her hips and driven upward through her core.

Slow at first. Centering. Her body had spent five days learning new patterns—the tensioner's rhythm, the cargo's weight language, the particular ache of muscles asked to push and hold instead of strike and recover. The forms asked for something older. Each sequence peeled the new work back in layers until what remained was the architecture underneath.

Then faster.

The staff blurred. Combinations she'd drilled since she was seven—strike patterns, defensive rotations, the flowing sequences that Master Mar had shaped into her until they were structure, not memory. Her bare feet turned on packed earth, finding grip. Cool where sweat gathered in the hollow of her back. Warm where the first light broke over the fence and found her shoulders.

She finished a sequence. Held the last position—staff extended, weight forward, breath cycling. The garden quiet around her. Her mind quiet inside her. Nothing to read, no weight to anticipate, no room to assess. Just the body in its oldest language, speaking to no one.

"Not sure what I expected under all that."

The voice pulled her back. Fence. Clothesline. Morning.

Mickie stood at the corner of the house, coffee mug stopped halfway to his mouth. His eyes had the same wideness they'd carried in the cargo car—something that didn't fit, rearranging itself behind his eyes.

She watched him try to figure out where to look. His gaze tracked her shoulders, moved to her arms, dropped to the staff, came back to her face. Landed nowhere. The robes had done more work than she'd realized.

"But it wasn't... this." He gestured vaguely. At all of her.

Wynne lowered the staff. Waited.

She saw the moment he heard his own words back. Color climbed his neck.

"That's not—I don't mean—" He set down the coffee mug on the porch rail. Picked it back up. "You're not—what I'm trying to say is—"

He was getting worse with every word.

"Mickie."

He stopped.

"Perhaps a long shirt would make you more comfortable."

He exhaled. "Yeah. That. Please."

She went inside and came back wearing one of his work shirts, long-sleeved, the hem past mid-thigh. Mickie's posture unlocked. He picked up his coffee with steadier hands.

"I'm sorry about—" He waved a hand at the general concept of the last two minutes.

"There's nothing to apologize for."

"There might be. I'm still not sure what I said."

Wynne smiled. "Neither am I."

He sipped his coffee. Studied the staff leaning against the fence. The wideness in his eyes had settled into something quieter—not the fumbling of a minute ago, but the same recalculation she'd seen after the pallet.

"So that's what pulled Al clear," he said.

"Part of it."

"How long have you been training like that?"

"Since I was seven."

He processed that. Sipped his coffee. Processed some more.

"Would you like to learn something?" she asked.

The pivot caught him off guard. "Learn what?"

"Something useful." She set the staff against the fence and turned to face him. "Give me your hand."

He hesitated. Then extended his right hand—broad, thick-fingered, callused from thirty years of ratchets and rigging.

Wynne took his wrist. Gently. Rotated it inward—not far. A few degrees. Her thumb settled on the joint, finding the space between the bones where leverage lived.

"Try to pull away."

He pulled. His hand didn't move.

His eyebrows went up. He pulled harder—and his knees buckled. Not because she'd forced them to, but because the joint lock gave his body exactly one option for relieving the pressure, and it was down.

"What the—" He was on one knee, arm extended, Wynne holding his wrist with two fingers and a thumb. "Okay. Okay. Point made."

She released him. He stood, flexing his hand, staring at it like it had betrayed him.

"Damn. You're strong."

"It isn't strength. It's leverage and position." She showed him the grip—where the thumb pressed, how the rotation created the lock. "The body protects itself. Bend the wrist past its natural line and everything below the elbow follows. You don't need to be strong. You need to be precise."

"The Order teach you that?"

"The Order doesn't separate body and mind. They're the same practice."

He flexed his wrist again. "Huh."

"Huh, indeed."

He laughed. Short, surprised—the kind that escaped before he could decide whether to allow it. "Alright. Show me again. Slower."

She did. Walked him through the grip, the rotation, the angle. His hands were too big and too strong and entirely wrong for the technique—he kept trying to muscle it, his forearm tensing against the rotation instead of allowing it.

She adjusted his thumb. Showed the angle again. The correction came out of her mouth in Mar's cadence—the same patient precision, the same way of naming what the body was doing wrong without making it a failure. She'd been on the receiving end of that voice for fifteen years. She hadn't known it lived in her own.

On the fourth try, he got it right. She felt the lock engage, felt her own wrist answer the way his had. Her knees started to go and she broke the hold with a twist he hadn't learned yet.

"Almost," she said.

"Almost." He was grinning now—the unselfconscious grin of a man who'd just discovered he could still learn something new. "My daughter would love this. She keeps telling me I need a hobby."

"Is disarming people a hobby?"

"In this neighborhood? It's practically a public service."

They went back and forth for another twenty minutes. The morning warming around them, light catching the overgrown garden—the wild things that had taken the beds since his daughter left. Mickie's coffee going cold on the porch rail. He never got it perfect. She didn't expect him to. But by the end, his hands understood the principle—that control wasn't about force, and that the body could be directed by anyone who understood its architecture.

When they finished, Mickie stood in the yard, rubbing his wrist.

"Laundry day," he said. "You know how to work a washboard?"

"Mickie. I grew up in a monastery."

"Right." He picked up his cold coffee. "Stupid question."

⊙

Day 12

The last morning came the way the first one had—before the sun, in the dark, with the sound of Mickie's radio through the wall.

Wynne dressed in her white robes. Folded the borrowed linens and left them squared on the cot. Set the work gloves Al had given her on the shelf. The room was exactly as she'd found it—clean, spare, ready for the next person who needed it.

She took her staff and went to the yard.

Everyone was there. Too early for the shift. They hadn't come to work.

Al leaned against the cargo car with his arms crossed, the clipboard nowhere in sight. Mickie stood with his hands in his pockets, looking at a point somewhere past the rails. Harlan sat on a pallet, quiet for once. Pede stood apart, his arm free of the sling for the first time—still stiff, still careful, but out.

Wynne stopped at the edge of the platform.

Pede spoke first. He came forward, reaching into his jacket with his good hand—the other moving at his side, testing its freedom.

"Twelve days' wages. Fair count." He held out an envelope. "I added a day for the one you spent learning before you were any use."

"That's not—"

"It is." He pressed the envelope into her hand. "And I put a note in there. Addressed to a man named Collin Meyers—my partner, runs our Hamilton depot. If you need work up north, show him that. He'll take you on."

She took the envelope. Felt the coin through the paper.

"Thank you. For the work. For the chance."

"You earned the work. The chance was free." He stepped back. His jaw worked once. Then:

"You be careful up there. Hamilton's not Port Madison. People move faster and care less." He glanced at his crew. "Down here, we look out for each other. Up there, you've got to find your own people."

"I think I've had good practice."

His mouth twitched. He extended his hand. The one that had been bound.

She took it. His grip was careful, the strength returning but not yet trusted. He held on a beat longer than a handshake required. Then released, turned, and walked toward the yard office.

Al came next. No ceremony—just walked over, pulled something from his back pocket, and held it out.

A grease pencil. His grease pencil, the one that lived behind his ear, that marked manifests and floor positions and had checked off each day of her progress on his clipboard.

"For the road," he said. "In case you need to mark where things go."

"Al—"

"You earned your marks." He said it the way he said everything—plainly, without performance. "I've been doing this twenty-two years. I've trained a lot of new hands. Most of them learn the job." He paused. "You understood it. That's different."

He clapped her shoulder. Held it a beat. Then let go and walked away, hands finding his pockets.

Harlan stood as she approached. Shifted his weight. Looked away, then back.

"I'm sorry about—the forklift. The pallet. I should've—"

"You learned from it," Wynne said. "That's what matters."

He nodded. Quick, grateful, still carrying it.

Mickie was last.

He stood at the edge of the platform, hands still in his pockets, watching the rails run north toward a point where they merged and disappeared. He didn't turn when she stopped beside him.

They stood there for a moment. The yard waking around them—engines warming, the first forklift coughing to life, the distant clang of couplings.

"You're going to want platform three," he said. "Northbound. Should be boarding in about forty minutes."

"Mickie."

He turned. His jaw was set, but his eyes weren't.

"Thank you," she said. "For everything."

"Don't." He pulled his hands from his pockets. One of them held a folded cloth bag. "My daughter sent this. Enough for the train and then some." He pushed it into her hands before she could argue. "She says anyone who can put her old man on his knees deserves a proper send-off."

"You told her about that?"

"She asked about the bruise on my wrist. I made the mistake of demonstrating." The corner of his mouth pulled up. "She put me down in two tries. Two. Took you four."

Wynne laughed. The sound surprised her—open, warm.

Mickie took her hand. Not a handshake. He held it, both of his wrapping around hers.

"You listen to me." Quiet. Just for her. "The world's going to look at you and see the robes and the staff and a girl who doesn't know anything. Don't let them. You know plenty. And what you don't know, you learn faster than anyone I've ever seen."

He released her hand. Stepped back.

"Safe travels, Wynne Kaede. Don't let Hamilton chew you up."

She bowed. He returned it with a nod.

She turned and walked toward the ticket office. Staff across her back. Envelope in her pack. The morning air cool on her face.

Behind her, Mickie's voice—calling to Al, to Harlan, to the day's work already waiting.

The squat building looked the same. The painted sign, the barred window. No queue this early—just the clerk behind his ledger, the same man from two weeks ago.

He glanced up. Paused. His pen stopped moving.

"I was hoping I'd see you again, sister." He set down his pen. "I'm not supposed to do this," he said, lowering his voice. "But there's an open seat in the business class coach. I'll charge you the standard fare." He was already writing the ticket. "Better seats. Quieter. You look like you could use the rest."

"That's very kind. You don't have to—"

"Six steel chits." He slid the ticket through the bars. "Platform three. Boarding in thirty minutes."

Wynne counted the chits from Pede's envelope and passed them through. The clerk took them with none of the careful hesitation he'd shown the monastery marks. Steel on wood. A clean transaction.

"Thank you," she said. "For holding the seat."

"I said I would." He picked up his pen. Then, without looking up: "Safe travels, sister. Hamilton's a long way from here."

She pocketed the ticket and walked to platform three.

The northbound train sat on the rails, engine idling, heat shimmer rising from its hood. She found the business class coach—cleaner than the standard cars, the seats wider, the windows larger. A woman in a pressed uniform checked her ticket without comment and gestured her aboard.

Wynne chose a seat by the window. Set her staff against the wall beside her. The seat gave under her weight. Cushion, not wood. Her body registered the difference immediately, every bruise and ache from twelve days settling into the give of it.

The train pulled away from Port Madison. The yard slid past—the cargo cars, the platform, the warehouse where she'd learned to read a manifest and strap a load and feel a shift before it happened. Then the buildings. Then the market. Then the hill, green and rising, where the monastery sat behind its oak-and-iron doors.

She didn't look away. She watched until the hill dissolved into the coastline and the coastline dissolved into distance and all that remained was the rail stretching north.

She drew breath. Four counts in. Held for four. Released for six.

Hamilton.

The train carried her toward it.

Part 2

"The reopening of the Hammison Corridor represents more than infrastructure—it represents promise. For too long, our citizens have endured rationing, scarcity, and the indignity of depending on those who operate outside proper channels. When Gate 20 opens, legitimate commerce flows. Quality of life will return to the plains of Calinoka, the shores of the North Sea, and the rural mountains of Kyjorh. Not through lawlessness—but through order."

— Chief Minister Shori Ashford
Address to the Continental Council, 2190

12 | Peri

2191.112 · 07:50
Gate 31

The service road climbed ahead, the same broken pavement she'd memorized, the same weeds forcing through split asphalt. But this morning, everything felt different—against her skin, in her lungs, in the pulse keeping time beneath her ribs.

Her legs settled into rhythm without thought. Each footfall landed true, the impact rolling clean through calves and thighs. The braid Kitt had woven that morning swung between her shoulder blades, tight and secure. The stopwatch sat warm against her hip.

She hadn't looked at it once.

Her breathing stayed easy despite the grade. Not fighting the hill like she used to—working with it, leaning into the slope, letting each step drive her forward. She could hear water trickling toward the canal below, thin and constant under the cadence of her breath.

She'd lost track of the miles somewhere around the third ridge, too absorbed in how it felt to bother counting. Sweat sheened along her hairline, gathered warm at her temples.

Emma Chen burst from one of the houses as Belfast Mills rose ahead—eight years old and made entirely of motion. Dark hair bouncing in an uneven ponytail, legs pumping.

"Peri!" Both hands windmilling overhead. Thrilled as always. Absolutely delighted by the simple fact of Peri existing in her morning.

Peri lifted a hand and waved back. The smile came without her building it first.

"You look fast today!"

"Feel fast today," Peri called—and meant it.

Emma dropped back quickly, but she kept waving with both hands until Peri crested the next rise.

Her pace picked up without her choosing it. Not strain. Just anticipation. Her legs felt clean and powerful.

She reached the warehouse approach, boots thudding onto packed gravel. Let herself drop to a jog, heart rate easing. Then a walk. Hands on hips, long even breaths. Steam rising off her shoulders.

Now.

Her hand found the stopwatch. She pulled it free.

Seventy-nine minutes, forty-three seconds.

She stared at the numbers. Read them again to be sure.

Her breath caught. Heart still pounding from the run—but for a different reason now.

Faster than she'd run that stretch in months. Not by seconds. By minutes.

A sound escaped before she could stop it—half laugh, half whoop. She glanced around quickly, almost guilty. Warehouse doors shut. Approach road empty. Her and the numbers.

Then she jumped. Both feet off the ground, fist punching the air. Pure reflex. Joy breaking through before discipline could catch it.

"Yes." Quiet, but fierce. "Yes!"

She slid the watch back into her pocket. The grin stayed welded in place, splitting her cheeks.

She needed to tell someone. Too big to hold alone.

Kitt would get it. Kitt always understood when numbers meant something.

Peri headed for the warehouse with quick, eager strides.

⊙

The cool hit her first—interior air finding sweat-damp skin, raising goosebumps along her arms. Machine oil and metal shavings. The warehouse's permanent weather.

Kitt's voice reached her before the rest of the room resolved. Technical. Tight. Already mid-sentence.

Kataero stood near the workbench, one hand resting on the bench edge, reading something over Kitt's shoulder. Connor leaned against a storage crate, eyes tracking whatever discussion had been happening before she walked in. Papers spread across the bench—diagrams, notes, facility layouts.

The endorphins were still humming. The number still on her tongue.

"How was the run?" Kataero looked up first.

"Good. Really good, actually." She looked for Kitt—wanted to catch her eye, share the number. "Kitt—seventy-nine—"

"—MERIDIAN's hardware-gated." Kitt's voice went tight, oil-darkened fingers tracing lines on the diagrams. "Closed system. Physical authorization. Every access leaves a trail."

The number died in Peri's mouth.

Kitt hadn't heard her. Hadn't looked up. Focus locked somewhere Peri couldn't follow.

Peri stood there for a beat with the grin still fading, the words still shaped in her mouth. Seventy-nine forty-three. The best run of her life, and the room had no place for it.

She swallowed the number. Let her face reset.

Later. Tell her later.

She moved closer, cooler air making her shirt stick to her back. "What's all this?"

Connor shifted against the crate. His gaze dropped to the layouts, then back to Kitt.

"I've used systems like that," he said. "Back when I had clearance."

"So you know how they work," Kitt said.

"I know they don't forget." His gaze stayed on the layouts. "Someone always notices."

"Cipher has cargo types and a rough window. But departure times, route changes, guard rotations—that's all locked in MERIDIAN. We're blind without it."

Connor straightened from his lean. "Getting into a Continental Authority security station isn't a supply run."

"No kidding." Peri stepped fully up to the workbench, close enough to see the layouts clearly. Walls, checkpoints, restricted zones—danger made neat and orderly on paper. Her weight shifted forward onto the balls of her feet. "This is what you've been working on?"

"Part of it." Kitt's tone carried that energy Peri recognized too well. "The northern station handles regional rail coordination. Twenty minutes on their terminal—"

"Twenty minutes inside a Union compound." Peri's voice went flat. "Do you hear yourself?"

"It's doable. Two people. One on the console. One watching the door."

Peri stared at the diagrams. Then she shoved the papers.

"Unknown security protocols. No backup plan. Continental Authority jurisdiction." Her eyes moved across the three of them. "If we get caught in there, we don't come home."

Connor nodded once. "Black site. No trial. No contact."

"Exactly." Peri pointed at him, eyes still on Kitt. "So no. We're not doing this."

"But the dam—"

"Will have to wait."

"How long?" Kitt's voice thinned. "We don't know if we have ten days or five. Every day we sit here is a day we might not have."

Peri hesitated. The layouts sat there, making the impossible look almost reasonable.

"If we had more time to plan—"

"There isn't another way." Kitt leaned forward. "This is the way. You know it is."

"No."

Kitt stood so abruptly her stool scraped concrete. The sound ripped through the warehouse quiet.

"You see Emma every morning. You know what's happening to this town." Her voice climbed. "And you're saying no because—"

"It's suicide!"

"Because you don't think I can handle it!"

The warehouse went quiet.

Peri stared at her sister. Kitt stared back—hands balled, chest heaving, daring her to say no again.

The same accusation. Different mouth.

Her hands were trembling. She shoved them in her pockets before anyone could see. Her fingers found the stopwatch, still warm.

Water dripped somewhere in the warehouse depths. Lock gates groaned distantly.

Connor cleared his throat. "And if we don't get the schedule information?"

Kitt flipped open her notebook, jabbed at a column of figures. "Without the terminal? Four departure windows, three cargo rotations, two possible routes. Twenty-six percent probability of successful intercept." Her voice tightened. "I don't build things at twenty-six percent."

Kataero studied the papers, one thumb tracing the edge of a layout. After a long moment, he looked up.

"Is there anyone who might have access to this kind of information? Layout, rotations, schedules?"

The question wasn't directed at anyone in particular. But Peri felt it land on her anyway.

She didn't answer right away.

Her gaze stayed on the diagrams. On the clean lines and boxed hazards and all the places things could go wrong. She dragged a hand down her face, thumb pressing hard at her temple.

"...I might know someone."

Kataero's hand stilled on the layout. "Who?"

Peri hesitated just long enough to make it clear she wished she hadn't opened her mouth.

"Rhowan."

The name landed flat. Wrong.

Kitt's face tightened. "Him?"

"Gods." Peri scrubbed at her forehead. "I know. But he runs with Union contractors. Maintenance crews. People who move through Authority buildings without setting off alarms."

“So he could help us?” Kitt asked.

“Maybe.” The word came out like it cost her. “But that's before we factor in trusting someone who burned us on Bethshelm.”

Confusion crossed Kitt's face. “He what?”

“Tipped off Continental Authority patrols to our route.” The memory still stung—patrol lights where there shouldn't have been any. The cold certainty that someone had talked. “We paid for it.”

She looked back down at the diagrams.

“I don't like this option,” she said quietly. “I don't trust it. And I don't want to owe him.”

Then, softer. Honest.

“But I don't see another door.”

Kataero was quiet for a long moment. Then: “We proceed. But properly. If we're infiltrating a Continental Authority station, we need real intelligence, proper timing, and contingencies. No shortcuts.”

He looked at Peri. “First step is the contact. Find out what he knows, what he can provide, and what it costs.” Then to Connor: “Where's the terminal?”

Connor was still for a moment. That stillness he carried when weighing whether to open a door he'd rather leave closed.

“Gate 20,” he said. “Hammison Lock.”

“You're sure?”

“Northern security station, second floor. Administrative section.” A pause. “I've been there.”

Kitt leaned forward. “What's the layout like?”

“Two years out of date.” He met her eyes. “They've been renovating. Guard posts, access points, protocols—could all be different now.”

“All the more reason we need current intelligence,” Kataero said. He looked directly at Peri. “Are you prepared to make contact?”

She opened her mouth to object one more time—to list all the reasons this was insane, to explain why trusting Rhowan was asking to get burned.

She closed it again.

Looked at Kitt's expression. The way her chin lifted. The way her hands rested flat on the papers. Waiting.

Rhowan. Not the betrayal. That practiced smile. The way his voice dropped when he leaned close, like they were sharing secrets no one else could hear. The way she couldn't quite hold his gaze whenever he looked at her like she was the only interesting thing in any room.

Her jaw tightened. *Don't.*

Part of her wanted to see him. That was the problem.

Part of her had been looking for an excuse.

"Shit," she breathed. The word tasted like surrender.

She nodded. "I'll talk to him."

Nobody said anything. The warehouse felt smaller.

Kitt started gathering her papers. Her hands steadier now.

Peri watched her work. Seventy-nine forty-three. She'd tell her later.

She already knew she wouldn't.

13 | Wynne

2191.101 · 16:08

Hamilton Rail Station | CAD Hamilton

The train groaned to a stop. Brakes hissing, metal shuddering through the floor and up through Wynne's bare feet.

She was already standing. Eleven days of rail, and the countryside outside her window had changed three times—coast to farmland to the dense gray sprawl that announced the capital hours before arriving.

Through the window, Hamilton's station rose around the platform—iron and glass, the vaulted ceiling climbing so high she had to tilt her head back to find its peak. Light poured through in geometric patterns that shifted as clouds moved overhead. More space enclosed under one roof than her body knew how to process. Her shoulders pulled inward before she caught herself.

The doors opened. She stepped down onto polished stone, cool and impossibly smooth against her soles.

Thousands of people moving around her—each one purposeful, destination already decided. No one wandered. No one hesitated.

No one recognized her.

In Port Madison, her platinum stubble and white robes had drawn nods, waves, the quiet vocabulary of a town that remembered monks. Here, eyes slid to her and slid away—the brief, assessing pause before they moved on. A woman changed course to avoid her path without breaking stride. Two men in merchant's clothes leaned together, voices dropping.

"—the hair. You see that?"

"Some kind of performer?"

"No. That's—I don't know what that is."

Wynne kept walking. Head high. Stride measured.

She stepped through the exit doors into full sun and Hamilton opened before her.

Her feet stopped.

Buildings climbed—not just higher than Port Madison, but impossibly high. Ten stories. Fifteen. Twenty. Stone and steel and glass rising until her neck ached from trying to find where they ended. Streets stretched in clean lines, paved and maintained in ways Port Madison's cobblestones had never been. People moved through it all like blood through veins—organized, purposeful, part of something vast and functioning.

She flexed her toes against pavement smoother than anything at the monastery—worn by so much traffic it had achieved a kind of perfection.

She drew breath. Four counts in. Held for four. Released for six.

Security was everywhere. Men and women in dark gray uniforms, body armor strapped tight, rifles held ready but not aimed. Standing at corners, watching intersections. Wynne read them without thinking—

weight distribution, hand placement, sight lines. Trained. Professional. Not soldiers expecting combat. Sentries maintaining order.

Every one of them clocked her. The robes, the staff, the bare feet. Eyes tracking, assessing, dismissing. She felt their attention pass over her and release, one checkpoint at a time, like moving through doors that opened but never quite welcomed.

One step, then the next.

She stopped at an intersection. Four streets running in four directions, all of them purposeful, none of them hers.

Something settled in her chest. Not a thought. Closer to gravity.

"The library's a good place to start, if you're new."

A voice beside her. Male. Unhurried, with the careful pronunciation of someone who chose words deliberately.

Wynne turned—and read him the way she read anyone. Body first.

He stood with his weight shifted left, a cane in his right hand taking the difference—brass-headed, worn smooth at the grip. Not leaning on it. Partnered with it, the way she carried her staff. Someone who'd walked this way long enough that it had become simply how he moved.

Young. Early twenties, though his bearing suggested more. Auburn curls catching copper in the sunlight. Green eyes that studied her with the same quiet attention she was giving him.

He gestured down the street. "They have city records, historical archives. Maps, guides for newcomers. I'm heading there now for research."

"I'm unfamiliar with that location," Wynne said. "Is it far?"

He leaned into his cane. The corner of his mouth lifted—not quite a smile. "Not far. If you can keep up."

Wynne looked at the cane. Back to his face. The almost-smile waiting.

The corner of her mouth twitched despite herself.

"I'll manage," she said.

"This way then."

⚙

He set off at an easy pace. Each step grounded by the soft tap of his cane against the pavement. Wynne walked beside him. Let her stride adjust to his without making a show of it.

The city unfolded around them. Towers rising on either side, stealing sunlight and casting the walkway into alternating bands of brightness and shade. The smell shifting with each block—fresh bread, then leather, then the sharp bite of something chemical and industrial.

The silence between them felt natural. She'd spent nineteen years in a monastery where silence was discipline, where every shared quiet had structure and purpose. This was different. Easier. Two people walking in the same direction who didn't need to fill the space between them.

"I'm Jaden," he said at last. Still facing forward. "Jaden Oram."

"Wynne Kaede."

"Welcome to Hamilton, Wynne Kaede." He glanced over. "First time in the capital?"

"First time anywhere outside Port Madison."

His eyebrows lifted a fraction. "That's a long distance for a first journey."

"I needed to leave."

He inclined his head once. Left it there. No follow-up question.

They passed a security checkpoint. Two officers standing watch. Both tracked Wynne immediately—white robes drawing their attention like a signal. Hands shifting on rifles.

Jaden raised his free hand slightly. A greeting. Practiced. Easy.

One officer nodded back. The tension thinned.

They turned a corner. A building rose ahead, larger than the others on this street. Stone facade, wide steps leading up to massive doors—wooden, dark, heavy. Words carved into the lintel:

HAMILTON PUBLIC LIBRARY

"Here we are," Jaden said. He started up the steps. Slower now. Cane finding each level carefully.

Wynne climbed beside him. Watching from the corner of her eye. Ready if needed. Not offering.

At the top, he stopped. Turned.

"The archives are extensive," he said. "What are you looking for?"

Wynne looked at the doors. At this stranger who'd offered direction without asking for anything in return.

"I don't know yet."

Jaden smiled. "Then this is exactly where we start."

14 | Peri

2191.112 · 08:52
T-37 N to Braelocke Hollow

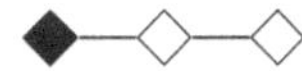

Peri moved through the warehouse, checking supplies. Water, food, rope. Usual gear for a multi-day run. Routine. Simple. The kind of task her hands knew without her mind needing to guide them.

She expected Connor to appear any moment with the truck keys.

Instead, footsteps crossed the concrete. Too heavy to be Connor's.

Kataero walked past carrying his travel bag, worn canvas over one shoulder.

Peri stopped. Her hand froze halfway to the next crate. "Where are you going?"

"Braelocke Hollow." He set the bag near the door with care. "I'll be coming on this one."

"You?" She stepped back without meaning to. "Who's going to keep the monsters at bay in the shadows?"

"Connor's helping Seth and Marcus flush the lock hydraulics." He pulled on his jacket, shoulders rolling into the weight of it. "Ice cracked a few seals over winter—needs handling before the spring barges start running. He can hold things down while we're gone." A pause. "Been a while since it was just the three of us together."

Kitt appeared from the back, her own bag already packed and slung over one shoulder. She stopped at the edge of the workspace. "Wait, you're coming?"

"I want to meet Rhowan myself."

Peri stopped. "Why?"

"You told us he burned you. Tipped patrols." Kataero picked up his bag. His tone stayed level. "What you didn't mention was that Rhowan asked for your help personally—and you said yes before you even knew what it was."

The words landed before she could brace for them.

"That's not—" She cut herself off. *How does he know that?*

Kataero didn't react to the edge building in her voice. "So I'm coming. I assess the contact myself."

He walked outside to load the truck.

The door swung behind him, settling half-closed. The echo rolled through the warehouse.

The second he was out of earshot, Peri rounded on Kitt.

"Did you ask him to come?"

"What?" Kitt's eyes widened. Her bag slipped on her shoulder and she caught it automatically. "No. I thought you asked him to come."

Peri stared at her. "Why would I do that? This is already awkward enough without—"

"You're lying."

The word hit harder because it was quiet.

Peri's jaw snapped shut. "I am not lying. You probably said something about Bethshelm and now he wants to—"

She heard how stupid it sounded even as the words left her mouth. She'd told the whole room about Bethshelm yesterday. Kitt had learned about it in the same conversation everyone else did.

"I didn't say anything about Bethshelm." Kitt's voice rose, heat flooding her cheeks. "Not a word."

Peri opened her mouth. Closed it.

"...Connor," she said flatly.

Of course it was Connor. Connor who saw everything. Connor who remembered details. Connor who still thought in debriefs and risk assessments. Connor who she'd trusted on a mountain with the worst parts of herself—and who'd handed it to Kataero like a field report.

"Well maybe Connor had a point—"

"Connor needs to keep his damn mouth shu—"

"I can hear you both."

Kataero's voice carried through the half-open door. Flat. Patient.

Peri and Kitt looked at each other. Kitt's face was flushed. Peri could feel the same heat burning in her own cheeks.

"Great," Peri muttered.

"This is going to be fun," Kitt muttered.

⊙

The first hour passed without words.

Peri drove. Kataero had taken the back seat without discussion. Kitt rode shotgun, notebook open across her lap, marking signal locations with careful pencil strokes. The scratch of graphite filled the quiet between them. Kataero sat in the back, watching the country through the window.

Just the engine's low rumble vibrating through the steering wheel. Tires on cracked pavement. The occasional rattle over rough patches.

Peri's hands gripped the wheel. Too tight. White-knuckled. Her shoulders rode up near her ears, neck muscles knotted. Every few minutes she'd force herself to loosen her grip, settle back into the seat, drop her shoulders. It never lasted.

Road stretched ahead. Empty. Pavement and fields and the occasional abandoned structure with dark, hollow windows. Four hours to Braelocke Hollow. Maybe five depending on conditions.

Five hours of this.

In her peripheral vision, Kitt had drifted. Leaning against the passenger door, pencil tapping absently against her temple, eyes unfocused on the notebook in her lap.

Kitt's head came up. Eyes adjusting to the road ahead.

"Oh—Peri. You need to stop."

Peri's hands jerked the wheel left before her brain caught up—truck lurching toward the shoulder, tires biting gravel. She overcorrected right, the vehicle swaying before she wrestled it straight.

"What? What's wrong?"

Kitt was already pointing through the windshield. "Carrington Station. There's a bakery next to the fuel depot." She looked back at Kataero, eyes bright. "They make these lemon muffins. You'd hate them."

Peri's hands hadn't stopped shaking. "You almost gave me a heart attack. For muffins?"

"They're really good muffins."

From the back seat, Kataero's low chuckle filled the cab, and the silence that had held for sixty miles cracked open.

Peri pulled off at the junction. Hands still unsteady.

Kataero climbed out first, joints popping as he stretched. He started filling the tank, the pump clicking off gallons. Kitt disappeared inside, already on her muffin mission.

Peri leaned against the truck. Metal warm from the sun, heat seeping through her jacket. The station was half-shuttered—one working pump, weeds cracking through the lot. Another place holding on. She watched the pump's counter turn. Gasoline sharp in the air.

"You're angry," Kataero said.

"I'm fine."

"You're angry I'm coming."

Peri didn't answer. Her fingers found the edge of her jacket pocket, worrying at the seam.

"I'm not here to supervise you." His voice stayed calm. "I'm here because if something goes wrong with this contact, I want to know who we're dealing with."

"Nothing's going to go wrong."

"Probably not." He finished filling the tank, replaced the nozzle. Stood there for a moment, hand still on the pump. "But probably's never been good enough. Not with you two."

He walked inside to pay.

Peri stood there. Hands in her pockets. Empty road stretching both directions, heat shimmering off pavement.

She pulled her hands free and slapped both thighs, hard, the way she did before a run. Shook out her arms. Rolled her neck until it cracked. The reset traveling through her body the only way it knew how — through motion.

⚙

Two hours later, Kitt finished her third muffin.

She licked lemon glaze off her thumb, entirely satisfied with herself, and wadded the paper wrapper into the cupholder with the other two.

The radio crackled. Static first, then a DJ reading weather reports in a monotone that suggested deep boredom. Then music—one of those old songs that played on every frequency, recycled until everyone knew the words without trying.

From the back seat, Kataero started humming along. Quiet at first, just a low sound in his throat. Then louder. Then words—singing now, his voice rough around the edges but sure.

Peri caught his reflection in the rearview mirror. Head back against the seat, eyes half-closed, fingers drumming against his knee in time with the beat.

Kitt glanced at Peri, eyebrow raised. Then she started humming too, adding her voice to Dad's off-key contribution.

Peri felt the corner of her mouth twitch. She tried to stop it. The smile won anyway.

She joined in. Just humming—she didn't remember most of the words. But the melody was there, buried in memory from hearing it a thousand times.

All three of them making noise together. Off-key in places. Too loud when the chorus hit.

Her grip on the wheel went easy.

The song ended. Another started, less familiar. None of them could find the harmony. It didn't matter.

Kataero settled back, breathing evening out. Not sleep—rest.

Kitt returned to her notebook, pencil scratching soft patterns. The faint smile still at the corner of her mouth.

Peri kept driving. Grip loose. Road rolling under them, warm afternoon light filling the cab.

The outskirts of Braelocke Hollow rose against the horizon. Old rail yard in the distance—rusted tracks catching light, abandoned cars standing like monuments to commerce that used to flow through here. The Fractured Bazaar somewhere beyond, hidden in the maze of repurposed buildings that bloomed wherever people gathered to trade.

"We're staying at the inn tonight." Kataero's voice came easy from the back seat. "Tomorrow morning we find your contact."

"Sounds good," Peri said. And meant it.

Kitt closed her notebook and watched the town grow closer.

15 | Wynne

2191.101 · 19:34

Hamilton Public Library | CAD Hamilton

Hours of stillness, and Wynne's body was starting to argue.

But everything else in her was content. More than content—absorbed in a way she hadn't expected. The monastery's library had been a single room. Three walls of shelves, maybe two hundred volumes, every spine memorized by the time she was twelve. She'd assumed all libraries were like that.

Hamilton's library had an entire floor dedicated to geography alone.

She'd started there. Maps of the Union spread across tables larger than the monastery's dining hall—trade routes inked in red, rail lines in black, cities marked with population counts that made Port Madison look like a footnote. She'd found Hamilton and traced the distance from the coast with her finger. Touched the dot that was Port Madison. Measured the space between who she'd been when she arrived and who she was now.

Then Jaden had pulled a chair to her table, set down a stack of trade records, and started talking. And somehow that had been four hours ago.

Evening light had long since faded from the high windows. The reading room had settled into after-hours quiet, lamps clicking off one by one in the empty rows behind them.

Her quarterstaff leaned against the table edge. Jaden had set his cane beside it without thinking, and now the two supports rested against each other—wood on wood.

"This is fascinating." He looked up, eyes bright. "The trade corridor through Valcross Junction was established in 2167, but the regulatory framework wasn't implemented until 2171. Four years of completely unregulated commerce through a strategic chokepoint."

The way he said it—not lecturing, just alive with the discovery—reminded her of Master Rev reading aloud from the oldest texts. The same quality of attention. As if the information itself deserved excitement.

She found herself leaning forward despite the hours of sitting.

"Do you know what that means?" he asked.

"Someone profited significantly."

A smile broke across his face.

"Exactly! And look—" He pulled another book from the stack, pages snapping as he flipped through. "Import taxes during that period increased by three hundred percent. But the treasury records—" He grabbed another volume. "—show only half that increase in actual revenue."

He paused, looking at her over the stacks.

"Someone was getting very, very rich."

A laugh escaped her. She didn't press her lips together. She didn't look away. She just laughed—open, unreserved—and let it be.

His eyes narrowed with amusement. "You find economic fraud amusing?"

"No. I find it interesting that you find it exciting."

"It is exciting. This is—" He caught himself, rubbed the back of his neck. "My mentor would say I'm reading the infrastructure as power structure rather than engineering. Follow the gaps in regulation and you find who benefits from the absence." He tapped the page. "She taught me that. Changed how I see everything."

He reached into his satchel and pulled out two cloth-wrapped parcels. Unwrapped the first—bread, cheese, dried fruit—and paused. Looked at the food. Looked at Wynne.

"You haven't eaten."

Not a question.

"I'm fine."

He was already dividing the portion. Half the bread. Half the cheese. Most of the fruit pushed toward her side. "Eat."

The second parcel he left wrapped, set at the empty chair to his left.

Wynne looked at what remained in front of him. The math didn't balance in his favor. She ate anyway. The bread was good—not the baker's bread from Port Madison, but solid, and her body received it with quiet gratitude.

⊙

Footsteps approached from the stacks. Working boots on stone, unhurried.

Her weight shifted automatically, finding balance over her center.

The man who emerged wore a security uniform with the library patch on his shoulder. Forties. Sandy blond hair grayed at the temples. He carried his weight slightly left, favoring his right side. Knuckles that had been broken and healed poorly.

He stopped at a comfortable distance. Clear sightlines to both exits.

"Evening, Mr. Oram." His eyes moved to Wynne, then to the divided food, then back to Jaden. "Don't often see you with company."

"Paul, this is Wynne Kaede. She arrived in Hamilton today. Wynne—Paul Finney. Night security here for six years."

"Five this November. Was hired six years ago, settled into this." Paul extended his hand.

Wynne stood and took it. His grip firm, straightforward, despite what her training read in the rest of his posture.

"Ms. Kaede."

"Mr. Finney."

"Just Paul." He released her hand and picked up his parcel from the table. Unwrapped it. Broke the bread in scarred hands. "You're a lifesaver, Mr. Oram."

"You say that every time."

"True every time." Paul's attention returned to Wynne. "First day in Hamilton and you've already found the best research partner in the city. That's either very good luck or very good instincts."

"I haven't decided which," Wynne said.

Paul's laugh was low and genuine. His eyes stayed on her a beat longer than the moment warranted.

"Fair enough."

He took a bite. "Now, Mr. Oram—making any progress on your grandfather's records?"

The ease dropped from Jaden's posture. "Another dead end. These council minutes reference an amendment vote, but the amendment itself isn't in the file."

Paul's brow furrowed. "Amendment texts from that period... they're not filed with council minutes. Different system back then." His hand traced a path across the library floor. "Lower Archives. Sub-level two, east wing. Cross-referenced by session date rather than subject."

"Paul, you're invaluable."

"Always happy to help, Mr. Oram." Paul finished his bread. "I should finish my rounds before my daughter accuses me of skipping dinner again." He shook his head. "Pretty sure I'm supposed to be the adult, not her."

His attention moved to Wynne. "I hope to see you again, Ms. Kaede."

"And I you, Paul."

He moved toward the next reading room. Wynne tracked his footsteps until they disappeared.

"He seems helpful," she said. Night security who knew exactly where amendment texts were filed and which cross-reference system applied to which decade.

"He is." Jaden was already pulling books, energized. "That man found me asleep on this table once, put a blanket over me, and locked me in for the night." He laughed. "The morning clerk found me still here, blanket-wrapped and confused. Gave the poor girl a proper fright."

Jaden stood, gathering volumes in his arms. "Lower Archives. Sublevel two. This might finally give me what I need." He looked at her.

She reached for her quarterstaff.

"Lead the way."

⊙

They crossed the main floor, past empty reading rooms where chairs sat pushed in and lamps stayed dark. Through a door marked ARCHIVES—RESTRICTED ACCESS.

Cold rose through the stone beneath Wynne's bare feet as they descended. The air dry, sharp with chemical preservation.

The hallway stretched narrow, doors on both sides labeled with decades and subjects. Fluorescent lights hummed overhead—flat, harsh, nothing like the amber warmth they'd left behind.

Jaden stopped at one of the doors. "2170–2175. Council Records."

He pulled a key from his pocket. Metal scraped as he turned it.

Nothing happened.

The key ground against tumblers that wouldn't catch. Wynne watched his hand—pressure increasing, angle adjusting. He tried again.

Still nothing.

His hand gripped the doorknob. His whole body had gone still. The key turned over in his fingers. Once. Twice.

"They changed the locks."

The words came out flat. Final.

Her hand settled on his arm.

"It waited this long," she said quietly. "It can wait one more day."

He stared at the door. She watched the grief cross his face—brief, naked, too large for a locked door.

Then he straightened. Turned. The smile that found his face was real—reaching his eyes.

"One more day."

He pocketed the key and started toward the stairs.

⊙

They climbed back to the main floor. Jaden organized books with renewed purpose, marking pages for tomorrow.

Wynne shouldered her pack and gripped her staff.

Outside, the city had transformed. Cool air hit her face—different from Port Madison's salt-heavy nights. Cleaner. Thinner. The mineral smell of stone, and beneath it the faint electrical hum of lights that didn't flicker. The pavement under her feet was releasing the day's heat in slow waves, each block slightly cooler than the last.

Street lamps cast steady circles of light—electric, unwavering. Between them, shadow pooled in doorways and alleys. The security patrols moved differently after dark. Weight forward instead of settled. Hands closer to weapons. Eyes scanning rather than monitoring.

They passed a checkpoint. Eyes tracking. Jaden's cane tapped its rhythm on pavement. One officer's gaze followed Wynne's staff for three steps before releasing.

"I just realized," Jaden said after several blocks. "You arrived today. Do you have lodging?"

"No."

"I've kept you in the library all day and didn't even think—" He shook his head. "There's an inn near the university district. Clean. Reasonable rates." He paused. "I can show you."

"Thank you."

They turned down a side street. Older buildings. Windows glowing from within.

"You know," Jaden said, "the trade gaps we found today—the unregulated corridor, the missing revenue—that pattern isn't unique. It keeps appearing in the records, the same shape repeated across decades." He was thinking aloud, the way he did when something connected. "The Pendleton Act of 2155 was supposed to close exactly those kinds of loopholes. Understanding why it failed is half of what I'm trying to prove."

"I'm glad you came to the library today, Wynne Kaede."

"So am I," she said.

They walked on. His voice filling the quiet between streetlamps, and the tap of his cane keeping time beside her.

16 | Peri

2191.113 · 09:15 | Z3

Braelocke Hollow | Bexley Transfer Station

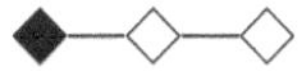

Peri spotted Rhowan at the far end of the bazaar.

Bodies pressed close—too close, shoulder to shoulder, breath to breath. The smell hit first: rust, rotting canvas, the sour stink of too many people crammed into too little space. Overhead, patchwork tarps and corrugated metal filtered the morning light into shifting patterns across the mud-packed ground.

She hated being here. Hated asking him for anything. Not after Bethshelm.

But they needed papers. And Rhowan was the only one who could get them fast enough.

Kitt walked beside her, tension coiled tight in her shoulders. Every few steps her eyes swept the crowd—assessing threats, marking exits, cataloguing faces. Kataero moved somewhere behind. Peri didn't need to look. She always knew where he was, the way she knew where her own hands were.

Rhowan stood at his stall, dark hair swept back from his face, coat too fine for this place. Dark wool that said money without shouting it, cut close at the shoulders, falling just past his hips. He was talking to an older woman, her hands shaking as she counted coins from a worn leather purse. The line behind her had grown to three people, but Rhowan waited. Patient. Not rushing her, not glancing at the customers he was losing.

The woman came up short. Peri could see it in the way her shoulders dropped, the tremor that ran through her fingers as she counted again.

Rhowan shook his head. Pressed the coins back into her palm. Slid a small package across the counter toward her.

"On the house, Mrs. Tierney. Give my regards to your grandson."

The woman's face crumpled with gratitude. Her mouth worked, trying to find words that wouldn't come. She clutched the package to her chest and shuffled away, disappearing into the crowd.

Rhowan watched her go.

Then he looked up.

His gaze cut through the crowd and found Peri. Dark. Sharp.

That grin spread across his face—the one that started slow and never quite finished.

"Red." His voice carried across the noise. Low. Pleased. "And here I thought my day would be tragically predictable."

Two years. Two years since Hammison, since he'd called her that while she was still flustered from the beautiful eyes comment, and he was still doing it. She'd told him to stop. Multiple times. Told him it wasn't her name. Told him she'd break his fingers if he kept it up.

He kept it up.

She looked away before he could read her face. The way she was standing. Where her hands were. Whether her face was giving anything away.

She moved toward his stall, and people shifted out of her way without being asked.

"Still running your mouth, I see."

"Only because your entrance demands commentary." He dismissed the next customer with a wave—some nervous man clutching a corroded device—and gave her his full attention. Leaned forward on his elbows, that smile still playing at the corners of his mouth. "You move through this place like you own it. One day, perhaps you will."

She forced her expression into a scowl.

She reached the counter. Crossed her arms. Canvas pulled tight across her shoulders with the motion. "Save the lines for someone who's buying."

"You look well, though." His gaze tracked her face. Something quieter than his usual performance. "Rested."

Liar. She hadn't slept properly in weeks. But the observation landed anyway.

Her eyes cut sideways. Kitt had drifted toward a nearby stall, examining something mechanical. Not watching.

Peri tucked stray hairs behind her ear without thinking. She leaned in—quick, quiet.

"You look well too."

She pulled back immediately. Too fast. The words already out, already his, already something she couldn't take back. She fixed her gaze on the goods behind him—salvaged electronics, coiled wire, things she couldn't name—as if they'd suddenly become fascinating.

"So..." His eyes swept the crowd behind her. "No shadow today? Don't tell me Connor's lurking somewhere calculating how long my body would take to sink."

"Connor's back home. Warehouse business."

"Shame." Rhowan leaned against the stall frame, arms crossing over his chest. "I rather enjoy his quiet disapproval. Like being judged by a very disappointed monument."

Despite herself, a smirk tugged at her mouth.

Rhowan caught it. His grin widened—

Then his gaze snagged on something over her shoulder. The easy confidence drained from his face.

"Oh gods," he muttered.

Peri didn't need to turn to know what had caused that reaction.

The crowd parted.

Kitt materialized beside her, carrying twice Peri's menace in half the space. Hair cropped to a dark pixie cut, sharp lines framing sharper eyes. That look she got when someone was about to have a very bad day—the one she'd inherited straight from Kataero.

Rhowan straightened. Recovered his composure with visible effort.

"Miss Ota." He inclined his head. "Always a pleasure."

Kitt's gaze settled on him with uncomfortable weight. "Surprised you're not lying about something already."

"I'm offended." Hand over heart, though the gesture lacked his usual conviction. "I haven't started yet."

"Play nice," Peri said. But her attention had already moved past them.

Kataero stood three stalls away, examining a display of salvaged tools. Not looking at them directly.

"Does the Black Marshal always tag along now," Rhowan asked, pitched just low enough to stay private, "or are we about to invade something?"

"We need something," Peri said.

His smile returned, curling at the edges. "So you came to me."

"Don't make me regret it."

The charm slid away. "What do you need?"

Kitt leaned closer, voice dropping below the market noise. "Papers. Administrative clearance. Maintenance pass for a restricted facility."

Rhowan's eyebrows rose. "That's ambitious. And dangerous." He glanced toward where Kataero stood, then back to them. "Planning a social call somewhere you shouldn't be?"

"Can you do it or not?" Peri pressed.

He studied her face. The tension around her eyes. The way she held herself too rigid.

"Depends on specifics." He pulled a leather-bound notebook from beneath the counter, flipped through pages covered in notations only he could read. "Different facilities, different security features. The wrong detail gets you shot, not just turned away."

"Hammison Lock," Kitt interrupted, precise as clockwork. "Gate 20. Something that gets two people inside for routine maintenance work."

Low whistle. "Gate 20. That's not just serious—that's Continental Authority serious." His finger traced down a column of text. "Maintenance credentials for a restricted facility. The forging isn't the issue. It's the verification codes—they change weekly, and they have to match current registry books at the gates."

He looked up from the notebook. Met Peri's eyes. "Wrong materials, wrong codes—you might as well announce yourselves wearing signs that say ARREST ME."

"So that's a no?" Peri challenged.

"I didn't say that." He straightened. "I have contacts. People who left the right facilities with the right souvenirs. People in the Code Office who owe me favors."

"Timeline?" Kitt asked.

His fingers drummed against the counter. Thinking. "Normally? A week. Maybe five days if I push hard and call in markers."

"We need them faster," Peri said. "Two days. Maybe less."

The drumming stopped.

"That's not pushing timelines." His voice flattened. "That's setting them on fire and hoping nobody notices the smoke."

"Can you do it or not?"

He closed the notebook with deliberate finality. Studied her with renewed intensity.

"I can try. But the price just tripled."

"Name it."

Rhowan leaned forward. Elbows on the counter. Eyes locked on hers.

"Dinner. The Crook and Chase in North York. Just you and me. One evening."

The bazaar noise pressed in around the silence between them. Just his face. His eyes.

Dinner. With Rhowan. Alone.

Kitt made a disgusted noise beside her. "You can't be serious."

"I'm always serious about dinner."

The nerve of him. "You've got some balls asking that after Bethshelm."

"Huge," Kitt added flatly.

Rhowan's expression flickered. "That is a misunder—"

"What's to misunderstand?" Peri's voice went cold. Precise. "How Connor and I spent twenty-four hours in a cell while someone else finished our job? The job that you asked us specifically to do. And somehow... you still ended up with the goods that we were supposed to get paid to lift."

"Hold up." Kitt turned to face her fully. "You spent the night in jail? That's not what you told—"

Peri's gaze cut to her sister. Sharp. Final. "We aren't discussing that."

Kitt's mouth closed. But her look promised they absolutely were discussing that later.

Rhowan's hands came up, defensive. "No, that's not—"

"Not what?" Peri exhaled hard through her nose. Then leaned forward across the counter. "Not what it looked like? I sat between two sweaty drunks all night because you sold us out. Do you have any idea how long it takes to get that kind of odor out of this hair?" She gestured at her copper braid. "Weeks."

"It was pretty awful, actually," Kitt confirmed. "I could smell her from across the warehouse. We had to air out her room."

Peri turned back to Rhowan. "And you want me to trust you again."

"That's not—that's not how it happened."

"Then explain it." Arms crossed, blue eyes waiting.

"I can't. Not here. Not now." He glanced around the crowded bazaar. Bodies moving past. Vendors within earshot. "Please."

Peri held his gaze. The word had landed different from anything else he'd said.

"Convenient."

His hands gripped the counter edge, knuckles whitening against the wood.

"That's it?" Her words came out level. Cold. "One dinner and you'll risk your contacts, your reputation, your neck getting these papers on an impossible timeline?"

"Yes."

"Why?"

He didn't waver. Didn't slip into charm or deflection.

"Because I want to know you when you're not looking at me like I'm about to stab you in the back."

The bazaar pressed in. All that heat and noise. But the space between them had gone quiet.

He placed his hands flat on the counter. "One dinner. We talk. You get the papers. Take it or find another forger who can deliver on your timeline."

Peri stared at him.

Kitt shifted beside her. Voice low, reluctant. "The northern tower signal's been degrading. We need to hit the closest repeater anyway." A pause. Weight in it. "It's near North York."

Giving her an out. A practical reason that had nothing to do with dangerous smiles.

"Fine." The word scraped her throat like broken glass. "But I leave when I want." She leaned forward, matching his posture. Close enough to see the flecks of copper in his eyes. "And if you try anything—any trickery at all—so help me gods, you won't have to worry about Connor sinking your body somewhere."

The corner of his mouth lifted, slow and genuine.

"Tomorrow evening then. The Crook and Chase." He paused. "I'll make reservations."

He held up a finger. "Oh, wait—how many passes do you need? Just you and Miss Ota, or...?" He glanced toward where Kataero stood, then back to them with exaggerated innocence. "I could make one for the Black Marshal, but the man's face is on half the Continental Authority recruiting materials. Bit conspicuous for maintenance work."

Kitt's mouth twitched despite herself.

"Two passes," Peri said, fighting down her own smile. "Just us."

"Sensible." Rhowan nodded gravely. "Much easier to forge documents for people who aren't wanted walking legends."

A shadow fell across the counter.

Peri went still. She hadn't heard him approach—nobody ever heard Kataero approach—but he was there now. Standing close enough that Rhowan had to look up.

Rhowan straightened immediately. Spine going rigid, all trace of humor vanishing. The color left his face. "Marshal. Always an honor."

Kataero didn't acknowledge the greeting. His eyes settled on Rhowan. Held there.

Peri caught his arm. Gave him a look. "Dad."

The word quiet but pointed. Meaning: *stand down.*

Kataero's expression didn't soften, but it shifted—adjusting. He glanced at Peri, then back to Rhowan.

"She's vouching for you." Voice quiet. Final. "Don't waste it."

Rhowan held his gaze. "I won't." Quiet. Certain.

Kataero studied him another moment. Then nodded once. Sharp.

He turned and walked away. The crowd parted without him asking.

Rhowan let out a breath. His hands unclenched on the counter. The color crept back into his face in stages.

"Your father," he said, "is terrifying."

"I know," Peri said. Almost gentle.

Kitt caught Peri's arm. Pulled her back a step. Voice low. "Something is off about the papers."

"What about them?"

"The timeline. His timeline." Kitt's words came fast, precise. "He already has them. He knew we'd need them before we asked."

"Or maybe he has incentive to make the impossible, possible."

"I just hope I don't end up in a cell for twenty-four hours," Kitt muttered.

The thought landed cold in Peri's gut.

"We'll find out tomorrow," she said.

Kitt looked toward where Kataero had disappeared. Then back to Peri. Her expression softened.

Go.

Kitt's hand landed on Peri's shoulder. Gentle push.

"Coming, Dad," she called, already moving into the crowd. Answering a summons that never came.

Peri stayed.

She looked at him sidelong—at hands still pressed flat against the counter.

Words rose in her throat. Real ones. Dangerous ones.

She swallowed them.

"This better not be a waste of time."

"It won't be." A pause. "I promise."

She turned to leave.

"Peri."

She froze. Surprised he didn't call her Red. A little hurt that he didn't. She couldn't look back. Couldn't breathe. Hearing her own name in his voice—intimate, careful, real.

"Tomorrow. I'll have everything you need."

She stopped. Pulled her hair back behind her right ear. Looked over her shoulder, found his eyes one last time, and let the smile come.

Then she walked into the crowd, following the path Kitt had carved through the press of bodies.

⊙

Kitt was talking about timelines. The repeater. How they'd need to leave before dawn to make the window work.

Tomorrow.

She should be focused on the mission. The risk. All the reasons trusting Rhowan was a terrible idea.

Instead she was cataloguing what she owned. The jacket that fit well but smelled like diesel. The shirt that didn't have visible repairs. Whether her hair would cooperate or fight her.

"Peri?" Kitt's voice cut through. "You listening?"

"Yeah." She forced her attention back. "The repeater. Before dawn."

Kitt's eyes narrowed. Held.

Then the corner of her mouth twitched—barely.

She didn't say anything.

She didn't have to.

17 | Kitt

2191.114 · 08:26 | Z2

East toward Northern Coast Tower | North York

Kitt climbed back into the truck, the cold metal of the door handle biting through her glove. "Peri's not even up yet. Probably pacing a hole in the floor about tonight. Best we aren't around to see it."

Kataero smiled from the driver's seat. Already had the engine running—rumble traveling through the seat, deep and warm. "Where to?"

"East toward Reed's Harbor." She pointed through the windshield. "About an hour out. Tower's on the coastal ridge."

The truck pulled away from the inn, gravel crunching under the tires. North York fell behind them—orderly streets giving way to rutted roads, farmland thinning to scrub brush, hills rising ahead. The cab smelled like engine heat and old leather and the coffee they'd finished before leaving.

They drove without talking. Shoulders brushing when the road pitched them sideways. His hands sure on the wheel, reading the ruts.

"How's the network holding?" he asked.

"Better. Southern repeaters are stable. Western chain's solid." She pulled out her notebook, the leather cover worn soft from constant handling. "This one's been degrading for two weeks. Signal strength dropping five percent every three days." She tapped the page. "If we don't fix it today, we lose the northern coverage entirely."

"And you think it's at the tower?"

"Has to be. Base station's fine. Power's consistent. It's either the antenna array or the waveguide connection." She closed the notebook. "Hoping it's the array."

"Ground work?"

"Desperately." She glanced at him. "Much rather troubleshoot at eye level than two hundred feet up in this wind."

⊙

The tower came into view forty minutes later. Lattice structure climbing from a cleared ridge—metal framework against gray sky, red and white paint faded to primer where weather had stripped it. Guy-wires taut and humming with tension she could hear through the closed windows. Platform at the top, barely visible.

Kataero parked at the base. The engine cut and the wind filled in immediately—constant, pushing against the truck hard enough to rock it on its springs.

Kitt moved to the equipment shelter. Five minutes inside told her everything and nothing—every indicator green, every reading nominal, the base station humming along like the problem existed somewhere else entirely.

She emerged. Looked up at the tower. Followed the lattice framework as it climbed until her neck ached from the angle.

"Well?" Kataero asked. His tone said he already knew.

"Everything down here is perfect. Which means it's at the top."

She grabbed her tool bag from the truck bed. Started strapping on the climbing harness—nylon webbing stiff from the cold, buckles clicking as she threaded them through. Each connection checked twice. Hips. Thighs. Chest. Seated properly, tension even, nothing binding.

"The waveguide's probably corroded. Or something's nesting in the feed assembly." She cinched the last strap. "Won't know until we're up there."

Kataero pulled his own harness from the back. His fingers tested each clip and carabiner gate, the same methodical check she'd learned from watching him do it a hundred times. "Been a while since I climbed."

"Two months. The western repeater." She remembered the halfway point. How he'd paused, one hand on the rung, breathing harder than the altitude justified. She'd stopped too. Pretended to check a clip. Waited until he was ready without making it a conversation.

"Feels longer," he said.

She handed him the secondary tool bag. Their gloved fingers brushed in the handoff. "Try to keep up, old man."

⚙

The climb took twenty minutes.

Hand over hand. Metal rungs cold through her gloves. The wind trying to find the gaps between her harness and her jacket, between her collar and her neck.

Clip in. The carabiner gate snapping open and clicking shut—that sound meant the system was working. Meant the line would hold.

Climb. Hands finding the next rung by feel. Her fingers were already losing dexterity in the cold. She'd have maybe forty minutes of fine motor work at the top before her hands became a liability.

Clip in again.

The lattice vibrated under her grip—each gust traveling through the steel like a signal through wire. She could feel the tower's resonant frequency in her palms, the whole structure flexing and recovering, flexing and recovering. Sound engineering. Built to move, not to resist.

Kataero climbed below her. His breathing audible—heavier than it used to be. But even. Controlled.

No rush. Safety over speed. His rule.

At the platform, she pulled herself over the edge. The grating was solid under her knees. She stayed there a moment, hands flat against metal, letting her grip recover. Her forearms had tightened up on the last thirty feet.

Then she looked up.

The coastline stretched north. Gray water, gray sky, the line between them lost somewhere in the distance. Reed's Harbor a cluster of shapes to the northeast.

She'd never been this high on this tower before. The network map in her notebook showed Tower Six as a red dot on a ridge. This was what the red dot actually looked like from the inside.

Kataero came up beside her. Breathing hard but steady. He moved to the equipment housing, hands sure on the latches despite the wind.

Kitt was already there. Her fingers found the waveguide coupling, tracing the metal joint, feeling for the roughness of corrosion. There—scaling under her fingertips. And something else. A smell underneath the sharp bite of oxidized metal. Organic. Damp.

"Oh, you've got to be kidding me."

"What?"

"Bird's nest. Right in the feed horn." She pulled her flashlight, the beam cutting into the housing. Twigs and grass and down feathers packed tight. "Solid. Weeks of work in here—they built it up gradually." She shook her head. "Patient little bastards."

She set down her bag. Started pulling tools out and laying them on the platform in order—needle-nose pliers, wire brush, contact cleaner, the small inspection mirror. Each one placed where her hand could find it without looking.

"What do you need?"

"Hold the light. Hand me things when I ask." It came out softer than she'd meant.

They worked.

"Needle-nose pliers."

He rummaged. Held up a pair.

"No, the other ones. Yellow handle."

He held up another pair. Also yellow.

"The bent ones, Dad. The tip is angled."

"They're all yellow. Why do you have four pliers with yellow handles?"

"They're not the same. Different jaw widths. Different grips. Different purposes."

"Tell that to my eyes."

She bit back a smile. Kept working.

The nest came apart piece by piece—packed tight by time and weather, each twig resisting before it gave. Her fingertips going numb from the cold and the repetitive pulling. She could feel her dexterity window closing. Twenty minutes of fine work left. Maybe fifteen.

"Wire brush."

He found it on the first try. Small victory.

"Contact cleaner."

He handed her the multimeter.

"That's not—" She glanced back. Frustration and amusement fighting for his face. She took it. Set it aside. Found the contact cleaner herself.

"I'm better at other things," he said.

"I know, Dad."

She scraped corrosion from the waveguide. The sound harsh against the wind. Tested connections—the multimeter needle swinging, settling, holding. Good readings. Clean signal path. The nest had been the primary obstruction, the corrosion secondary. Both cleared.

He held the flashlight without wavering the entire time. That much he could do.

She reconnected the waveguide, fingers working the coupling despite their numbness. Feeling for the click that meant it had seated. Tightened the seal—one turn, two, three. Correct torque by feel, the way she'd learned to do it when her hands were too cold for a torque wrench.

She pulled out the field radio. Keyed the mic. "Station Thirty-One, this is Tabby. Signal check."

Static—

Then Connor's voice, clear and strong: "Tabby, Thirty-One. Reading you five-by-five. Signal strength back to normal."

She grinned. Couldn't help it.

"Confirmed. Tower Six operational. Tabby out."

She clipped the radio to her belt. Started packing tools, her movements quick.

Kataero was quiet beside her. She caught him watching her hands instead of the equipment.

"What?" she asked, pausing.

"Nothing. Just..." He set down the flashlight. Metal on metal, soft against the grating. He paused. The way he did when words weren't coming easy. "You've gotten good at this."

"I've been doing it for three years."

"I know. But there's a difference between doing something and being good at it."

She lined the pliers back in the bag. Didn't look up.

"I'm proud of you."

Her hands stopped on the tool bag. She stayed like that—kneeling on the platform, fingers on canvas, wind pulling at her jacket.

"I couldn't have done it without—" she started, but the sentence came out wrong. She tried again. "You taught me everything."

"I held the flashlight." A pause. "And handed you the wrong pliers."

She looked at him then. The wind had put color in his face. The gray in his beard. The lines around his eyes that hadn't been there three years ago.

She looked away. Packed the last tool.

"Come on," she said. "Before we freeze up here."

She should have stood. Should have started the climb down.

Instead she moved to the edge of the platform. Sat. Let her legs hang over the grating, boots over nothing.

Kataero settled beside her. Close enough that his shoulder pressed against hers. She could feel his breathing through the contact—deep, even.

She leaned into it. Into him. The way she had in the garage when she was fifteen, grease on her hands and an engine running behind them.

His arm came around her. Pulled her in.

The wind cut across the platform. Below them, the coastline stretched gray and silver. The tower hummed beneath them—functional, transmitting, carrying signal because she'd made it so.

She closed her eyes. Let his shoulder take the weight.

They'd climb down soon. Drive back. Walk into whatever tonight would bring. But for now the tower was fixed and her father was warm beside her and the radio was reading five-by-five.

Systems nominal.

⊙

The climb down was quieter. Easier. Gravity doing most of the work, her arms loose, the wind at her back instead of in her face.

At the bottom, she unclipped her harness. Stowed the gear. Started toward the truck—then stopped.

She turned and looked up.

The tower rose against the gray sky, lattice and guy-wire, paint stripped and steel holding. Humming. Carrying signal north along the coast because she'd climbed it and cleaned it and put it right. Her hands still smelled like corrosion and contact cleaner.

The warmth from the platform hadn't left her shoulders.

"We good?" Kataero called from the truck. He was checking the tie-downs on the bed. "We didn't leave anything up there, I hope."

Kitt smiled.

"No." She turned back and pulled open the passenger door. "I got what I needed."

She swung herself in. Buckled up. Knocked her knuckles twice against the dash.

"Let's find you some food before I start seeing the hangry Black Marshal."

Kataero started the engine. His laugh carried them out of the clearing.

18 | Wynne

Mid Spring | 2191.112 · 19:08
Hamilton Public Library | CAD Hamilton

Nearly two weeks, and Wynne still couldn't name why she was here.

The pull had gone quiet somewhere in the second week. Not gone—she could still feel it underneath, the way a river's current pressed through the hull of a boat even when the surface was glass. But it wasn't speaking. Wasn't pulling. Just present. Waiting.

Which left her with routine. And routine, it turned out, suited her better than she'd expected.

Mornings she trained in the courtyard behind her inn—quarterstaff forms in the gray light before the city woke. The forms were the same ones she'd practiced since she was seven, but the courtyard changed them. Stone walls threw back sound differently than the monastery's open yard. The staff's arc had to account for a low-hanging eave on the eastern side.

After training, the city.

She'd mapped Hamilton on foot, one district per day. The harbor district smelled of tar and fish and the metallic bite of welding. The university quarter was quieter, its streets lined with trees that had been allowed to grow old—a luxury Port Madison couldn't afford. The government blocks were clean and watched, security at every corner.

But the working neighborhoods between them were where she kept returning. Narrow streets where laundry hung between buildings and children played in doorways and the vendors knew each other by name. Less polish. More life.

⊙

She was cutting through the market district when the sound reached her. Worse than shouting. The crowd pulling back like water from a hot pan.

A security officer had a man by the collar. Pressed against a wall. The man's hands were up—not fighting, not resisting. Just up. His face turned sideways against the stone.

"I said where did you get it." The officer's voice was controlled. Professional. But his weight was forward, his grip bunching fabric, and the angle of his arm said he was ready to escalate.

"I told you. The salvage market. I have a receipt—"

"You have a piece of paper." The officer shifted his grip. The man's breath caught.

A dozen people watched. None moved.

Wynne's feet had stopped before she'd decided to stop.

She read the officer. Trained. Tense but not panicked. The grip was for show as much as control. She read the man. Afraid but not guilty. His hands weren't trying to escape—they were trying to become smaller.

She didn't step between them. She didn't raise her voice. She walked to a spot three paces to the officer's left—visible, unhurried—and stood. Hands at her sides. Staff across her back. Weight settled.

The officer's eyes found her. Tracked the robes, the hair, the staff. His grip loosened by a fraction. An audience of one who wasn't looking away, wasn't pretending. Just standing. Watching.

The man looked at her too. His face opened—recognition that someone was there.

The officer released the collar. Smoothed the man's shirt with a gesture that was meant to look reasonable. "Get your documentation in order," he said. "Next time I won't ask twice."

The man gathered himself and walked away. Didn't run. Kept his dignity.

The officer looked at Wynne one more time. She held his gaze. He turned and moved on.

The crowd reformed. Market noise resumed.

Her heart was beating faster than it should have been.

She didn't know what to do with that.

⚙

Evenings, she returned to the library.

To Jaden and his research. To Paul, who appeared from the stacks each night with coffee or conversation or both, lingering longer than his rounds required.

Tonight she arrived to find him already deep in the 2160s trade records, three books open simultaneously, notes scattered across the table in handwriting she'd learned to decode.

"You're early," she said, setting her staff beside his cane. The two supports found their lean, settled now, practiced.

"I found something." He looked up. Eyes bright. "The revenue discrepancy from the Valcross corridor—it doesn't just appear in the 2170s. I found the same pattern in 2162. And again in 2158. Same shape. Same gap between collected taxes and reported treasury intake."

"Someone's been doing this for decades."

"At least. Which means it's not opportunism—it's infrastructure. Built into the system." He tapped the page. "My mentor always said, follow the absence. What's missing tells you more than what's present."

"Your grandfather saw this," she said.

Jaden nodded slowly. "I think he did. I think that's exactly what he saw."

The weight of it settled over the table.

"We'll find it," she said.

He looked at her. That smile—the one that arrived before he could decide whether to allow it. "You sound very certain for someone who didn't know what a television was three weeks ago."

"Certainty is one of the few things I brought with me."

"I've noticed."

☼

Paul appeared from the stacks carrying two cups of coffee and an expression of mild conspiracy.

"Don't tell the evening clerk," he said, setting the cups on the table between stacks of trade records. "She's decided I'm enabling your unhealthy research habits."

"You are," Jaden said, accepting the cup without looking up.

"I prefer the term facilitating." Paul leaned against the shelf beside their table, arms crossed loosely. His usual spot.

He turned to Wynne. "You were in the market district this morning."

"You heard about that?"

"Word travels. A barefoot woman in white robes staring down a security officer without saying a word." He sipped his coffee. "That took courage."

"It took standing still."

"Same thing, sometimes." He moved on, the way he always did—touching something real, then stepping back before it became a conversation. "Sophie would've approved. She's got a thing about fairness. Stubborn about it. Gets into arguments with other kids about sharing equipment at the workshop." He shook his head. "Last week she spent an hour explaining to a boy twice her size why cutting in line was a structural injustice."

Wynne laughed. "Structural injustice?"

"Her words. She reads too much." The pride was right there in his voice. "Wants to be an engineer, but I think she'd make a terrifying lawyer."

"She sounds wonderful," Wynne said.

"She is." Something brightened in his eyes. Stayed there. "Clock gears in the kitchen drawer. Broken radios on the dining table. I haven't had a clear surface in my house since she learned to use a screwdriver."

"Bring her by sometime," Jaden said. "I'd like to meet the girl who's teaching structural injustice to Hamilton's youth."

"Maybe." Paul's smile didn't waver. "She's not great with new people. Takes after her old man that way."

He pushed off the shelf. "I should do my actual rounds before they realize I'm spending all my time socializing." He paused. Looked at Jaden's notes. "How far did you get in the 2160s records?"

"Just started. The filing in that section is a disaster."

"Try the Regional Development Committee minutes. They cross-referenced differently back then—subject rather than date. Might get you closer to the revenue trail."

"Paul, what would I do without you?"

"Read the wrong files for another five years, probably." He grinned. "Back in an hour."

He moved into the stacks. Wynne tracked his footsteps until they faded.

"He knows this library better than the librarians," Jaden said, already reaching for the section Paul had suggested.

"He does," Wynne agreed. And went back to her reading.

⊙

Later. Coffee cold. The library's deepest quiet—only Paul's rounds breaking the silence.

He reappeared carrying a small cloth-wrapped bundle. "Sophie made cookies." He set the package on their table. "Too many. She'd want them shared."

Wynne took one. Bit into it. Simple. Good. Made with care by hands that knew the recipe from memory.

"Thank you."

"Thank Sophie." He settled into his lean against the shelf. "Did I ever tell you about the first time Mr. Oram here requested archive materials?"

Wynne looked up, interested.

"Paul..." Jaden didn't look up from his book.

"He comes in. Must've been nineteen, twenty. Still had that university-student intensity." Paul turned to Wynne. "Walks up to the desk with a list. And I mean a list. Seventeen documents. Specific volume numbers. Archive references. The works."

He paused for effect.

"The archivist looks at this list and says, 'Sir, are you writing an encyclopedia?' And Mr. Oram here, dead serious, says 'No, just checking a footnote.'"

Wynne's lips pressed together, fighting the smile.

"A footnote!" Paul's laugh was genuine. Full. "Seventeen documents for one footnote. She told me later she'd never seen anything like it."

"It was an important footnote," Jaden said, but the corner of his mouth had betrayed him.

"And that time you reorganized the entire 2160s trade ledger section because the filing system was 'structurally inefficient'?"

Jaden finally looked up. "That was a public service. It was chaos."

"It was alphabetical."

"Alphabetical is insufficient for chronological data sets."

Paul looked at Wynne with solemn gravity. "He spent three days refiling everything by date and category. The head librarian wanted to thank him. Couldn't find him. He'd moved on to another section."

Wynne stopped fighting the smile.

"You're making me sound obsessive," Jaden said.

"You are obsessive." But Paul said it with affection. "This library's better for having you haunt it."

The evening settled around them. Three people in a library after hours. Cold coffee. Scattered books.

Eventually Paul straightened. "Closing time. For real this time."

They gathered their things. Wynne shouldered her pack. Staff in hand.

Outside, night had fallen. Cool air. The faint electrical hum of street lamps. Pavement releasing the day's last heat under her bare feet.

Paul locked the doors behind them. Tested them twice.

"Tomorrow?" Jaden asked.

"Tomorrow," Paul confirmed.

"Goodnight, Paulie," Wynne said.

Paul's face brightened. Surprised.

"Goodnight, Ms. Kaede. Mr. Oram."

He headed toward the staff entrance. His footsteps faded around the building.

Wynne and Jaden turned down the main street. His cane finding rhythm on the pavement. Her bare feet on cooling stone.

"Paulie?" Jaden said after a block.

"It suits him."

"I never considered it. Known him for years. Always just 'Paul.'"

"Because you're formal even when you're friendly."

"Fair point." A beat. "Though I think he appreciated it."

"He did."

"He's a good man," Jaden said quietly.

"He is."

⊙

They walked in comfortable silence. His voice had gone quiet—thinking, not talking, the particular stillness he settled into after good evenings. Two weeks of walking together had made the rhythm automatic—cane tap, footfall, her steps adjusting without thought.

The pull was still there. Quiet and patient behind her ribs. It hadn't led her anywhere new in days.

She wasn't sure whether staying was patience or comfort. Whether the routine she'd built here was discipline or just a nineteen-year-old who'd found good coffee and interesting company and a city that had started to feel like it could be hers.

Either way, she'd be back at the library tomorrow. And the day after that.

"Goodnight, Wynne Kaede," Jaden said at the corner where their paths diverged.

"Goodnight, Jaden Oram."

She watched him go. Cane tapping. Lamplight catching the copper in his hair.

She turned toward the inn. The night air cool against her arms, the staff settling into its familiar weight across her back.

Tomorrow.

19 | Peri

2191.114 · 13:00

North Longshore Inn | North York

The inn room was small. Four steps to cross. Three to the window. Not enough space to pace out the restless energy building under her skin.

Six hours until dinner.

Six hours, and every time she tried to picture sitting across from Rhowan without a job between them, without angles to work or negotiation to hide behind, the thought slid sideways and wouldn't finish.

Her hands wouldn't stay still. Kept finding things to touch—the doorframe, the window latch, the fabric of her jacket. Aimless motion that went nowhere, solved nothing.

Peri changed into running clothes. Thermal layers, jacket, boots laced tight. Found the stopwatch in her pocket, turned it over once. Metal cool against her palm.

She headed downstairs, boots loud on wooden steps. Needed to move more than she needed to measure.

⊙

North York smelled like fish and diesel and salt water. Docks stretched along the waterfront—trawlers, workers, machinery. Voices calling over the noise. Seagulls screaming over all of it.

She ran west along the waterfront, pushing her pace faster than she needed to, the burn building in her calves, in her lungs. Past the fishing operations into the industrial section where warehouses gave way to salvage yards. Mountains rose in the distance, gray peaks touched by clouds.

The rhythm wouldn't come. Not fully. Her legs worked but her mind kept slipping—the restaurant, the table, his face across it.

Boots striking pavement. Breath in, breath out. Heart rate climbing but the zone staying just out of reach.

One yard caught her eye as she passed.

Marine surplus. Hand-painted sign weathered by salt air. Open gate. Inside, bins overflowed with components—copper piping, valve assemblies, coils of wire. In the front bin, clearly visible from the street: copper strips, zinc plates, graphite brushes. Battery terminals green with corrosion.

I need those.

Peri slowed. Jogged on. Made a mental note of the location—gate width, sight lines, the owner bent over something in the back. Older man, silver in his beard, absorbed in his work.

The run carried her another mile west before she turned back, but the salvage yard stayed in her head the whole way.

⊙

Inside her room, she washed her face in the basin. Cold water shocking against flushed skin. She straightened up, breathing hard. Still flushed. Still restless. The run hadn't burned off what it was supposed to.

The salvage yard kept turning over in her head.

She could buy the parts. Walk in with money. Pay by weight like an honest customer. Simple. Easy. Safe.

Or.

Heart kicking. Not from the run.

Better than sitting here thinking about dinner for another five hours.

Peri changed clothes. Dark pants. Plain shirt. Jacket left open—casual, unremarkable.

She headed west, hands in her pockets.

⚙

The salvage yard looked the same. Gate still open. Owner working near the back—older man up close, silver in his beard. Work-worn hands. Sure. Fast. Not thinking about it.

Her thumb found the stopwatch through the fabric. The button gave under the pressure. *Click.*

Peri walked through the gate with her hands loose at her sides and that crooked half-smile already forming.

"Help you?" The man didn't look up from his inventory.

"Just browsing. Heard you had marine electrical components."

"Got a bit of everything." He gestured vaguely at the bins. "Front's mixed salvage. Priced by weight if you find something useful."

She moved to the bins, footsteps unhurried. Pushed aside valve assemblies, copper piping, examined a length of wire and set it down. Working toward the battery components underneath. No rush.

"You do boat repairs?" The man stood, wiping his hands on a stained rag.

"My sister does radio work. Always needs parts." She picked up a corroded relay and turned it over, eyebrows lifting like she'd found something interesting. Set it down again. "Field communications. She's always tinkering with something. Drives my father insane."

The man chuckled. "I know the type. My son was the same—took apart every radio in the house before he was twelve."

"That's Kitt." Peri grinned. "She took apart Kataero's field radio when she was nine. He didn't speak to her for two days."

"Did she fix it?"

"Better than it was before." She leaned against the bin, settling in. "He still won't admit that."

The man laughed outright. Wiped his eyes with the back of his hand. "Fathers and daughters. Same story everywhere."

She asked about the ships. Where the salvage came from. Whether the old trawlers still had decent copper in them. He lit up—told her about the decommissioned fleet, the ones they'd stripped before the Continental Authority impounded the rest. His hands moving as he talked, shaping hulls and engine rooms in the air.

Peri listened. Asked the right questions at the right moments. Let him talk. Let him enjoy having someone who cared about the answer.

"I might have some vacuum tubes in the back," he said, already turning. "Old stock but sealed. Your sister might want them."

"Maybe. Show me?"

He led the way toward his workshop. Peri followed two steps behind.

Her hand dropped into the front bin as she passed. Zinc plate—cold, solid, satisfying weight. Into her pocket without breaking stride.

She kept walking.

Graphite brushes from the second bin. Fingers finding them by texture—smooth cylinders, slightly waxy. Gone.

Copper terminals last. Rough with corrosion against her fingertips. Two of them, slipped into the opposite pocket to balance the weight.

Her breathing never changed. Her stride never hitched.

The man pulled vacuum tubes from a drawer lined with yellowed newspaper, handling them gently. He explained about the old ships, the careful work of preservation, seals that had held for decades. His hands gentle with the glass.

"These are beautiful," Peri said. And meant it.

She bought two. Handed over coins while the stolen components sat warm against her hips. The man counted the money, wrapped the tubes in newspaper with care.

"Your sister's lucky to have someone sourcing parts for her," he said.

"She's the talented one. I just fetch things."

The man smiled. "Well, you fetch with purpose. That counts for something."

She took the package. Nodded. Opened her mouth to say something—thank you, maybe, or goodbye—and found nothing there she trusted.

"Good luck with your sister's work," he said.

Peri walked out through the gate. Her thumb found the button without her telling it to. *Click.*

The smile held until she reached the street.

⚙

Back in her room, Peri emptied her pockets onto the bed. Zinc plates—two of them. Graphite brushes in a row. Copper terminals still green with corrosion. Vacuum tubes she'd actually paid for, wrapped in paper that crinkled too loud in the quiet room.

She arranged them on the worn bedspread. Stared at them.

Components Kitt needed. And a kind man's trust, cracked open and emptied out for thirty seconds of feeling like she was good at something.

He'd told her about his son. He'd laughed at her story about Kitt. He'd wrapped the tubes in newspaper with careful hands.

She wrapped the stolen pieces in a shirt from her bag. Tucked them into the bottom of her pack where no one would see them.

Evidence. Shame. Gift.

Peri washed her hands in the basin. Cold water. She scrubbed longer than she needed to.

The water ran clear but her hands still felt like someone else's.

She looked at the clock on the wall.

Two-fifteen.

Four hours.

She still had no idea what to wear.

The stopwatch sat in her jacket pocket. She knew the number without looking—her body always knew the number.

She didn't pull it out.

This sucks.

20 | Peri

2191.114 · 19:00

Crook & Chase | North York

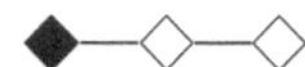

Three outfits spread across the bed.

Peri held up the first—dark pants, long-sleeve shirt. Fabric stiff under her fingers, worn smooth at the elbows. She rolled her shoulders. Too tight across the back. She'd spend the whole night adjusting. Tossed it aside.

The second—cargo pants, fitted shirt. Every other day of her life. Like someone who hadn't even tried.

The third—

She held the sleeveless shirt against herself and looked in the cracked mirror above the washbasin.

Her arms reflected back. The curve of her shoulders from years of pull-ups on scaffolding. Forearms corded from hanging off ledges. Muscle shifting under skin when she moved. Calloused palms rough enough to catch on the soft fabric. Fingernails cut short because anything longer got caught in locks.

This was what she had.

She pulled on the sleeveless shirt. Dark pants that actually fit. Let her hair down from its braid, fingers working through copper strands that fell past her shoulders in waves still kinked from being bound. One strand refused to fall with the rest—the same copper curl that escaped every braid she'd ever tied. She tucked it back. It fell forward again.

Scarier.

No makeup. She didn't own any. Wouldn't know what to do with it if she did.

In the mirror, a young woman looked back. All angles and evidence. Freckles that wouldn't hide under anything. Hands that picked locks. Arms that scaled walls.

She grabbed her jacket and headed downstairs.

⊙

The spring rain had passed through North York an hour ago, leaving the streets clean and the air sharp. Puddles reflected lamplight in scattered pools of gold. Salt air from the harbor mixing with wet stone and new growth.

Her boots splashed through shallow water. The sound oddly pleasant in the evening quiet.

Rhowan waited outside the Crook and Chase, leaning against the stone wall. He'd dressed well—not overdressed, but intentional. Dark coat, well-fitted pants, shirt open at the collar. His dark hair was combed but still looked like he'd run his hands through it once or twice. Nerves.

And yes, that was definitely cologne. Cedar and something sharper underneath.

He turned when he heard her boots in the puddles.

His face changed. He straightened from the wall without seeming to realize it.

"Red," he said softly. Then caught himself. "Peri. You look..."

"Like someone who owns three outfits and picked the least terrible one?"

"Beautiful," he finished. Simple.

The word landed in her chest. Stayed there.

She looked away.

"We should go in."

⊙

The Crook and Chase was intimate. Tables spaced far enough apart that conversations stayed private. Wood worn smooth by years, soft lighting, the smell of roasted meat and herbs and warm bread. Rich enough to remind her she'd barely eaten all day.

The hostess seated them in a corner. Away from windows, away from other patrons. Rhowan's doing—she watched his eyes track the room even as he held her chair.

They ordered wine. Studied menus. Made the kind of conversation that fills space without touching anything real—the food, the weather, how the rain had cleared.

Peri watched his hands as he talked. The way he gestured when he explained something about the wine—fingers moving with easy grace. The way he held the glass, stem between thumb and forefinger.

But underneath. The slight tension in his shoulders. His free hand tapping against his thigh before he caught himself.

"You're nervous," she said.

Rhowan stopped mid-sentence. "I'm sorry?"

"Your hand." She nodded at it, now deliberately flat on the table. "And your shoulders are up."

He set the glass down. The charm flickered—the smooth surface cracking just enough to show something real underneath. "You're very observant."

"I read people for a living."

"And what are you reading?"

"Someone trying very hard to impress me."

His laugh came out thin. More exhale than sound. "Is it working?"

"No."

The word hung between them.

She watched the performance ease—not gone, but loosening at the joints.

"Fair enough," he said quietly. "Fair enough."

Silence.

She could feel it building. The test she'd been designing since she'd said yes to this dinner. Show him what's underneath. Watch his face. See if he flinches.

Because if Rhowan was going to leave, she needed him to leave now. Before this became something she couldn't walk away from. Before she woke up one morning and found the space beside her empty with no explanation on the table.

"Can I tell you something?" Her voice came out rougher than she'd expected.

"Anything."

"I'm not good at this." She gestured between them. The table. The wine. Whatever this was. "I don't mean the conversation. I mean—the sitting still part. The part where you let someone see you and hope they don't leave."

She watched his face. Watched for the flinch. The polite retreat. The careful words that meant *I'm going to finish this wine and find a reason to leave.*

Rhowan didn't move. Didn't look away.

"I'm a mess, Rhowan. The real kind. And I don't always know why, but I know what it looks like from the outside." Her fingers found the stem of her wine glass. Turned it slowly. "You already know about Pepper. You know what she did. So you know what happens when I let someone in."

The last part came out quieter than the rest.

"So if you're going to decide this isn't what you signed up for, do it now. While it's still just dinner."

The restaurant hummed around them. Other conversations. Silverware on plates. The soft sounds of people who weren't taking themselves apart over wine.

Rhowan was quiet for a long time.

"I coerced you into this dinner," he said. Voice low. Stripped of the usual smoothness. "I knew you'd never say yes if I just asked. Not after Bethshelm. Not after you stopped showing up."

He met her eyes. "You just showed me something real. So here's mine." Hands flat on the table. "I'm terrified right now. Because I wanted this—you, across a table, talking to me like I'm a person—and now that it's happening I have no idea what to do with it."

A sound that wasn't quite a laugh. Self-conscious.

"That's not a line," he added. "I don't have any left."

Peri looked at him. Past the dark eyes and the cologne and the coat that cost more than her wardrobe.

"Okay," she said.

"Okay?"

"Okay." She picked up her glass. Drained half of it. "So we're both disasters. At least the food smells good."

He laughed—surprised out of him, cracking his face open into something unguarded. His eyes crinkling at the edges, younger than she'd ever seen him look.

⊙

He told her about growing up near here. His mother's house, the garden she'd kept even when nothing else grew. The harbor in summer—fish and salt and hot metal from the shipyard. He told her about leaving. Not why, not yet, but the way his mother had stood in the doorway and not asked him to stay.

Peri told him about Kitt taking apart Kataero's field radio at nine. About Connor's quiet disapproval that could make you feel three inches tall from across a room. About the way the warehouse smelled in winter—machine oil and cold concrete and the warmth of Kitt's workbench lamp.

She didn't plan what she shared. It came pulled out of her by wine and his attention and the unfamiliar relief of being listened to by someone who wasn't family, wasn't obligated, was just there.

Food grew cold on plates they barely touched. The wine bottle emptied without either of them tracking who'd poured last.

"Bethshelm," she said eventually.

The ease left his face. "Yes."

"Tell me what happened."

Fingers tracing the rim of his glass.

"Someone else knew you were coming," he said. Voice low. "Someone who'd set up worse than jail." He lifted his eyes. "The patrols kept you safe while I dealt with the real problem."

"What kind of problem?"

"The kind where people don't come back."

She stared at him. The story she'd been carrying since Bethshelm—*Rhowan sold us out, Rhowan took the goods, Rhowan can't be trusted*—shifting under her feet like bad footing on a hillside.

"You let me hate you for months."

"Better you hate me than end up dead." He met her eyes. "I'd make that trade every time."

Months of anger. Months of Bethshelm being proof that she couldn't trust anyone outside the family. And now the ground underneath all of it was giving way and she didn't know what was down there.

She picked up her glass. Empty. Set it down again.

"I don't know where to put that."

"You don't have to do anything with it tonight."

⊙

He walked her out. The restaurant's warmth giving way to cool spring air that raised goosebumps on her bare arms. The rain had left everything scrubbed clean—wet stone bright under the lamps, sounds carrying farther than they should.

He stopped walking. Turned to face her.

Cedar. Wine. The heat coming off his skin in the cool air.

"I should say goodnight," he said. "And walk away."

"Is that what you want?"

"No."

He leaned forward. Pressed a soft kiss to her cheek. Brief. Gentle. His breath against her skin.

He started to pull back.

She turned her head.

His lips hovered there—so close to the corner of her mouth she could feel the heat of him. One movement. One breath.

Her hands caught his shoulders. Fingers curling into the wool of his coat. Solid. She could feel the muscle underneath, the tension of him holding still, letting her choose.

Her pulse kicked everywhere at once—throat, wrists, stomach. Her whole body pulling toward him like gravity had shifted, and the want hit her so hard she couldn't breathe. Not the clean adrenaline of a job. Something she had no name for, no training for, no defense against.

Gods.

She stepped back.

It took everything she had.

Night air rushing into the space between them.

She shoved her hands in her jacket pockets before he could see them shaking.

"Goodnight, Rhowan."

"Goodnight, Red."

She didn't correct him.

She turned and walked. Boots on wet stone. Not looking back.

⊙

Somewhere between the restaurant and the inn, he'd slipped the envelope into her jacket pocket. She found it on the stairs—paper smooth against the stopwatch's familiar chrome where her fingers had expected metal first.

She opened it in her room. Layout of Gate 20. Camera positions. Guard rotation patterns. Service entrance on the east side.

A note in his handwriting: *Passes fell through. Found another way. This is what I have. The rest is on you.*

She studied the layout until the lines blurred. Then she set it on the table and sat on the edge of the bed.

She could still feel the wool of his coat under her fingers. The heat of him. That moment where the whole world had narrowed to the space between his mouth and hers.

She pressed her palms flat against the mattress. Breathed.

She lay back. Street lamp shadows shifting with the wind.

She didn't sleep for a long time.

21 | Wynne

2191.115 · 12:17

The Vance Memorial | CAD Hamilton

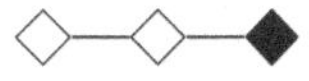

Midday sun had pulled half the district outside.

The Vance Memorial sat at the center of Hamilton's government quarter—a circular stone path ringing a small lake, the water so still it doubled the sky. Aldric Vance, Chief Minister before Jaden's grandfather took the post. The path honored him and the Continental Authority's founding in equal measure: bronze plaques set into the stone at measured intervals, each one marking a moment the Authority considered worth remembering. The founding charter. The first infrastructure compact. The integration of the eastern territories. Names of ministers, engineers, military commanders—the Authority's chosen heroes, pressed into metal and mortared into the walk.

Wynne had read every plaque her first week. Some of the names appeared more than once.

Pence Garda's was near the eastern curve, where the path bent closest to the Hamilton Public Library. A modest plaque compared to Vance's—smaller lettering, fewer dates. But the stone around it was worn smoother than its neighbors, polished by years of feet that paused there longer than the walk required.

Jaden never paused at it. Wynne had noticed that.

The memorial grounds spread wide around the lake—old hardwoods throwing shade across stone benches and low walls, the grass kept short and even. Office buildings rose on three sides, glass and steel climbing fifteen stories, their lobbies emptying onto the paths as the lunch hour took hold. The fourth side opened toward the library's west entrance, stone steps descending from the reading rooms to the memorial grounds.

It was where Wynne had started doing her morning forms. The flat stone near the lake's edge, where the sun hit earliest and the space was wide enough for staff work without crowding the joggers and the government workers cutting through on their way to the Authority complex. Two weeks of it. Every morning.

Now she sat cross-legged on the low wall bordering the path, staff balanced across her knees, eating an apple. Bare feet on sun-warmed stone.

Two weeks in Hamilton. The security checkpoints had stopped being checkpoints. She passed through them the way she passed through doorways—acknowledged, assessed, released. The detail assigned to the memorial grounds knew her face if not her name. The tall one at the library entrance had started nodding. The woman who covered the south approach during morning shift had stopped tracking her staff like it was a weapon.

Small things. But Wynne noticed every one.

The grounds were full. Office workers eating lunch on benches. A group of children chasing each other along the path, their mothers watching from the shade. Two members of the security detail leaning against the wall near the library steps, body armor loosened in the heat, rifles slung. Off duty or close to it—she read the difference in their posture. Weight back. Hands away from their weapons. Eyes moving but not hunting.

Sanchez was watching her.

Not the way security usually watched her. He'd been stealing glances for a week, always when she did her morning forms by the lake. Staff work—the combinations Mar had drilled into her until the patterns lived in her joints rather than her memory. She'd caught him twice mimicking a wrist rotation when he thought no one was looking.

Mid-thirties. Compact, broad through the chest, a scar nicking his left eyebrow from something he definitely had a good story about. The kind of man who drew greetings the way a bonfire drew people—three strangers had said hello to him in the ten minutes Wynne had been sitting here. He'd returned every one by name.

His partner nudged him. Said something low. Sanchez shook his head. Then pushed off the wall.

He didn't cross the path the way most people approached her—careful, measuring. He walked over like he was heading to lunch and she happened to be in the way. Already talking before he stopped, the way a man does when the decision to speak happened three sentences ago in his head and his mouth was just catching up.

"Hey—so I gotta ask, because it's been bugging me." No introduction. No excuse me. He was already in it. Stopped six feet out. Stance easy. Hands at his sides. "Every morning, same spot, same routine. The staff work." He mimed a rotation—rough, wrong, but recognizable. "That's combat training, right? Real combat. Not the fitness stuff they sell at the gyms downtown."

"It is."

"I knew it." He turned halfway back to the wall where his partner leaned. "Walsh said it was exercise. I said that's a woman who knows how to hit someone."

Walsh—taller, longer reach, a runner's build where Sanchez was a wrestler's—lifted a hand from across the path. "I said it could be exercise."

"You were wrong." Back to Wynne. "So the monks—you still train with those? The staffs? For actual fighting?"

"That is one of the techniques we master, yes."

"You master." He let the word sit. Rocked back on his heels. "So hand to hand too."

Wynne said nothing.

"I'll take that as a yes." The energy was building in him now—not aggressive, just a man who'd been sitting on a question for a week and finally had the conversation he wanted. "See, I boxed. Fifteen years. Golden Gloves regional, couple amateur titles, before I went into security work. I know what trained looks like. And what you do out there every morning—" He pointed at the flat stone by the lake. "—that's not just trained. That's something else."

Her eyebrow lifted.

"I'll take that as a yes too." He grinned. "Look—I'm not asking for a fight. I know better than to throw hands with a monk in front of a memorial." He glanced at the crowd, the kids, the mothers on benches. "But I am curious. You ever test yourself against someone outside the monastery?"

"The Order trains against many styles."

"Trained-against and tested-against aren't the same thing." He said it without challenge. Just a man who knew the difference from experience. "So here's what I'm thinking. Nothing rough. No strikes, no blocks. All I gotta do is reach you—hand to shoulder, hand to arm. Two taps. I win."

A few of the lunch crowd had noticed now. Heads turning. Conversations pausing.

"Simple enough, right?" He tilted his head. Sizing her up the way you'd size up a locked door—not with doubt, but with professional interest.

"You would think."

Walsh had pushed off the wall, arms crossed, already grinning.

Wynne set the apple core on the wall beside her. Read Sanchez properly now. Weight distribution even, which meant his training was recent enough to hold at rest. Right hand dominant—he'd reach with it first. Knees slightly bent. He had speed. She could see it in the way his weight sat forward, coiled in his calves. Fifteen years in a ring lived in that stance whether he knew it or not.

She stood. Laid the staff on the wall behind her.

"Whenever you're ready."

He moved.

Fast. Credit to his training—he didn't telegraph with his shoulders the way most people did. Straight line, right hand reaching for her upper arm.

Wynne stepped left. Not far. Six inches. His hand passed through the space she'd been in, fingers closing on air. His momentum carried him a half-step past her.

He reset. Faster this time—feinted right, shifted left, hand sweeping for her shoulder.

She read it in his hips. The left one dropped a quarter-inch before his weight committed—the body deciding before the mind confirmed. She pivoted on her back foot. Let his arm cross in front of her. She was already behind his reach before he completed the motion.

A low sound from the growing crowd. Not quite a cheer. Interest.

Sanchez's eyes narrowed. The grin had shifted—still there, but something grudging underneath it now. Respect arriving through the side door.

"How is it you move so fast?"

"I'm not fast." Wynne settled her weight. "Perhaps you should be faster."

His eyes caught fire. The look of a man who'd just been told the mountain was taller than he thought and had decided to climb it anyway.

Without the gear, he was faster. Close enough to matter. Not close enough to win.

"Nope." He planted his feet. Hands on his knees. "Alright." He straightened and jerked his chin at Walsh. "Get over here."

Walsh dumped the pile and stepped into the space the crowd had naturally cleared along the path—joggers rerouting, a few stopping to watch.

Two of them now. Flanking positions. Sanchez front, Walsh circling right.

Wynne read both at once. Mar's training—when facing multiple opponents, don't track hands. Track hips. The hips commit before the hands decide.

They came together. Coordinated—one high, one low. Better than she expected. They'd trained for this, the kind of paired approach used for crowd control.

Wynne dropped her center of gravity two inches. Sanchez's left hip loaded—high reach, right side. She let it pass over her shoulder. Stepped through the gap between them—the space they'd left because two bodies can't occupy the same line—and came out behind Walsh, who was still reaching for where she'd been.

She tapped his shoulder blade with two fingers.

Laughter from the crowd. A few people clapping. One of the children broke free from his mother and ran a lap around the lake path, arms spread like wings.

Walsh spun. Stared at Sanchez. "She touched ME."

Sanchez stood there, hands on his hips, shaking his head slowly. Not angry. Something better. "Yeah she did."

"That's not—" Walsh turned back to Wynne. "That's not the game."

Wynne let the corner of her mouth lift. "It could be."

⊙

Sanchez was demonstrating something to a cluster of detail—hands moving, weight shifting, Walsh standing behind him helpfully reenacting the moment he'd been tagged—when Jaden appeared at the top of the library steps.

He stopped. Took in the scene—the gathered crowd, the security detail out of position, Walsh miming Wynne's pivot for an audience, Sanchez talking with his whole body. A paper bag in one hand. Two glass bottles tucked against his side with the other, condensation running down their necks.

He made his way down the steps. The cane finding each level, unhurried. He crossed the path to where Wynne had resettled on the low wall, staff across her knees, watching the crowd with the quiet attention of someone who'd just done something physical and was letting her body cool.

"Stopped by Mel's on the way back." He held out the bag and one of the bottles. "Two sandwiches. What's happening here?"

Wynne took the bottle. Glass, cool and wet in her hand. She uncapped it and drank—lemonade, tart and sweet, the cold cutting through the heat she'd built. "Sanchez wanted to play a game."

"I can see that." Jaden eased himself down onto the wall beside her, settling the cane between his knees. He watched Sanchez's demonstration with the expression of a man reading a text in a language he found amusing but didn't speak. "And how did the game go?"

"He lost."

"Naturally." He opened the bag between them. Two sandwiches wrapped in waxed paper. He handed her the larger one without comment. "Walsh too?"

"Walsh too."

"Both of them. At the same time?"

"They volunteered."

Jaden unwrapped his sandwich. Took a bite. Chewed. Watched the crowd—the way it hadn't fully dispersed, the way people were lingering at benches and on the path, glancing toward Wynne between bites of their own lunches.

"You know they'll be back tomorrow," he said.

"I know."

"And they'll bring friends."

Wynne bit into her sandwich. Roast turkey, sharp mustard, something pickled. Good. "I'm counting on it."

He glanced at her. She caught it from the edge of her vision—the quick, studying look he gave when something she said landed in a place he hadn't expected. He didn't follow up. Just turned back to his sandwich and the sun and the crowd.

They ate. The grounds settling around them. Children back at the lake. The security detail drifting toward their posts, Sanchez's voice carrying across the path as he said goodbye to someone by name. Cut grass and warm stone. The lemonade still cold in her hand.

Movement from the path.

Sanchez, walking back toward them. But not alone. Two detail trailed him—one she recognized from the library entrance, one she didn't. And behind them, others. A young woman with a government lanyard and grass stains on her knees from sitting on the grounds. Two mothers with children balanced on their hips. A girl, maybe fourteen, with a runner's build and her hair pulled back tight. Three women from the office buildings, blazers off, sleeves pushed up. A boy in school uniform who'd clearly decided lunch hour was no longer about eating.

Sanchez stopped at the edge of the path. He'd put the vest and belt back on, gear squared away, looking like a man on duty again instead of a man who'd just been made a fool of in front of forty people. The others gathered behind him—not in formation, not organized. Just present. Waiting.

"So," he said. Arms crossed. The grin back, but different now—less swagger, more honest. "We were thinking. If you'd be willing—some of us would like to learn."

Wynne looked past him. Counted. Fifteen. Eighteen. More drifting over from the edges of the grounds, drawn by whatever the crowd had left behind. Mothers and office workers and detail who'd watched her morning forms for two weeks and never quite found the moment to ask.

Beside her, Jaden set his sandwich down. She felt him shift—the stillness that came over him when something clicked. He didn't say anything. Just looked at her the way he looked at a document when the last piece fell into place.

She met his eyes. He tilted his head toward them—barely a movement. *They're asking you something.*

She set her sandwich down on the waxed paper. Stood.

"Give me five minutes."

She picked up her staff and walked down to the path.

She found the spot she used every morning—the flat stone near the lake's edge where the sun hit longest, where the path widened enough for a group. The water still and bright beside them. Aldric Vance's name cut into the stone twenty paces to her left. Pence Garda's somewhere behind her, near the eastern curve.

She set her staff down. Faced them.

"We start with breathing." Her voice carried across the grounds without effort. Nineteen years of training halls and open courtyards. "Four counts in through the nose. Hold for four. Release for six through the mouth. This is how we center ourselves."

She drew the breath. Showed them. Watched eighteen chests try to follow—some too fast, some holding too long, Sanchez exhaling like he was trying to blow out a candle across the room. The fourteen-year-old got it right on the first try. One of the mothers swayed gently, her toddler asleep against her shoulder, breathing in perfect unconscious rhythm.

"Slower," Wynne said. "The breath is not a race."

She took her position. Feet apart. Weight centered. Hands open at her sides.

"Watch first. Then follow."

She began the first form. The opening sequence—the one Mar had taught her before anything else. Before strikes, before blocks, before the staff. Just the body learning where it lived in space. Weight shifting. Arms rising. The slow, deliberate architecture of someone discovering what their hands could do when they stopped reaching and started listening.

In the memorial grounds, eighteen people breathed together for the first time.

Wynne moved through the form. Sun on stone. Spring air off the lake, clean and still.

She was smiling.

And when she turned at the form's apex—arms wide, weight settling, the movement carrying her gaze back toward the wall—Jaden was there. Not watching the way a spectator watches. Leaning forward, cane forgotten between his knees, her sandwich beside him carefully rewrapped. The expression on his face open in a way she hadn't seen before. Like he was solving something that didn't have numbers.

She held the turn a breath longer than the form required.

Then she faced her students, and kept teaching.

22 | Kitt

2191.115 · 04:45

North Longshore Inn | North York

Kitt woke to the smell of coffee.

She lay still. Eyes closed. Darkness under the door—not even gray yet. The radiator ticking as it cooled. Her brain ran startup diagnostics: location confirmed, threat level minimal, hair situation critical.

The coffee smell hit again. Stronger.

Her arm reached toward the door before the rest of her decided to move.

Coffee. Now.

She sat up. Grabbed the oversized t-shirt from the floor—*PROBLEM SOLVED*, crossed wrench and screwdriver, faded to near-illegibility. Sweatpants that had given up on dignity sometime around year three. She shuffled toward the door, already making grabbing motions at nothing.

The door creaked. Kataero stood at the small stove, pouring from the percolator. He glanced over his shoulder at her zombie approach.

"You really do love me," she muttered, both hands reaching for the cup before he'd finished pouring.

Something tugged at the corner of his expression. "Good morning to you too."

She wrapped her fingers around the ceramic. Warmth bleeding into her palms. First sip. Eyes closing.

"Mmm." Second sip. "Okay. Human now."

She shuffled toward her radio housing, then caught the cold creeping up her hip where the sweatpants had slipped. Tugged them up one-handed without thinking. "Gonna shower. Just need to check the cells and—"

"Hold up."

She paused. Turned. Leaned against the doorframe, coffee cup held close to her chest like a shield.

"What?"

"What do you know about him?"

"Who?"

"Rhowan Cade."

Ah. There it was.

She took another sip. Watched him over the rim. He'd settled into the chair by the window—not moving, not pacing. Just waiting. The way he did when he'd already made up his mind to worry and was looking for permission.

"You mean the guy you let Peri go to dinner with last night?" The smile came slow. "Little late."

"Better late than never."

"True." She pushed off the doorframe, moved to her radio housing. Peeled back the velcro patch with one hand, coffee in the other. Three glass batteries glowed phosphor-blue inside—steady, even, no dimming at the seams.

She logged that automatically. The way she logged everything.

"On the surface? Nothing alarming." Eyes on the cells. "Dockworker. Warehouse clerk at North Docks Shipping—that's his official file. Unofficially, he's an information broker out of the Lower Loops. Forged documents, trade intelligence, supply chain facilitation. We already knew that part." She resealed the velcro. Flicked the toggle. Vacuum tubes humming to life.

"That doesn't seem so bad."

"You'd think." She moved back toward the doorframe, reclaimed her leaning spot. "But I dug deeper. And that's where it gets interesting." Another sip. "Someone scrubbed his history. Not recently—a couple years back, maybe more. Employment records before North Docks are clean. Too clean. No gaps, no irregularities, no former employers with bad things to say. That kind of background doesn't happen by accident for a twenty-four-year-old running a black market stall."

She watched Kataero process that. The stillness sharpening.

"There's more. About two years ago, he started asking questions about Canton Cusk waste acquisition patterns. Ferrosalt shipments moving through channels they shouldn't have been in. The kind of questions that get people noticed by the kind of people who don't like being noticed."

"And?"

"And he's still alive." She let that sit. "Which means either he stopped asking—or someone decided he was more useful asking than silent. Either way, whoever cleaned his trail had resources. Real resources. Not street-level."

Kataero's jaw tightened. Not anger—calculation.

"You've been tracking him."

"Peri's mentioned him. Their paths cross." She settled against the frame. "First time was about two years ago. Supply run in Hammison. She came back mentioning someone 'aggressively charming' who was 'probably running a con.' Annoyed he'd called her eyes beautiful. Thought he was working an angle."

"That's right." Kataero's voice shifted—recognition settling in. "I forgot about Hammison. He seemed... smaller."

Kitt's grin widened. "Next to you, everyone is smaller."

His mouth almost gave in.

"And every time they cross paths," Kitt continued, "he gets this look when he sees me. Like he's trying to remember if he's said his prayers."

Despite himself, Kataero's expression softened.

"You've been intimidating him."

"I've been assessing him." Another sip. "The intimidation is a bonus."

"And your assessment?"

"No outstanding warrants. No gambling debts, no broken hearts or wives with angry husbands, no bodies I can find." She shrugged, one shoulder lifting. "He's clean on the surface. But someone with real weight is behind him, and I can't see who. That's the part I don't like."

Kataero was quiet. Still in that chair. Waiting.

Kitt sighed. Shifted her weight against the frame. "Dad, she's fine. She was home early. Nothing happened. Peri is a lot of things, but she's far from stupid. Impulsive, yes. Stupid, no."

"That doesn't answer my question."

She looked at him then. Really looked. The gray in his beard. The stillness that wasn't peace—just patience worn into bone.

"You want to know if he's good for her."

"Yes."

She was quiet for a moment. The radio hummed behind her. Steam curled from her cup.

"He's terrified of me. Which I appreciate."

He actually laughed at that. "Why?"

"Because the first time we met, I asked him exactly three questions." She ticked them off on her fingers, coffee cup dangling. "What he wanted. Why he wanted it. What he'd trade for it." Her grin returned. "That's when the charm stopped working."

"Good."

"I thought you'd approve." She straightened from the frame, heading for the bathroom. Paused at the door. "And Dad—she was humming when she came home. The kind she does when she thinks no one's listening."

She glanced back at him. The stove's glow caught the lines around his eyes. Made him look older than she liked to think about.

"You know she likes him, right?"

She watched amusement settle across her father's face. "The tower really wasn't failing, was it?"

Kitt's eyes widened.

"Technically... yes. Would it have failed tomorrow? No. Probably not next week or next month."

"Mmhmm..." He smirked into his coffee.

"She was going to say no. And I know that is not what she wanted. So... I... gave her an option to say yes."

Kataero held his cup, studying her face. Something flickered across his—tender, almost soft. Then it shifted. Something pulling inward, retreating behind his eyes.

She knew that look.

She turned away before the memory could settle.

"Now, if we're done with the protective father routine—"

"Honey."

Kitt stopped. Not her name—the word he used when something was about to hurt.

Kataero hadn't moved. Still facing the window. When he spoke, his voice was careful. Measured.

"I just don't want to see her give herself to someone who could leave."

Her smile vanished. The coffee cup suddenly heavy in her hands.

His worry about Peri routing straight to his own loss—the wound finding a path through his daughter's happiness like current through a short circuit. She could see the whole diagram.

The radiator ticked in the silence.

"Gate 20 tonight," he said, voice returning to normal. "I want Connor there. Just in case."

Kitt forced her voice steady. "You calling or should I?"

"I'll handle it."

She crossed to him. Kissed his cheek—stubble rough against her lips—and headed for the bathroom before her face could betray her.

Behind her, the click of the field radio's toggle. His voice, steady: "Wolfhound, this is Panther."

Static.

Then Connor, clear despite the hour: "Panther, Wolfhound. Go ahead."

She closed the bathroom door. Locked it.

Turned on the shower. Hot. Full blast. The sound filling the small space like white noise.

She made it to the sink before her hands started shaking.

Someone who could leave.

She gripped the porcelain. Knuckles white.

"Don't do it." Barely a whisper. Her own voice, thin against the tile. "Don't."

She'd been nine. Leaning against the table in their old kitchen, watching Mom's hands work through Peri's hair. Over, under, pull. Over, under, pull. The rhythm of it. The way the copper strands caught the morning light.

Kitt had memorized every movement. The angle of her mother's wrists. The tension she kept in each section. The little tug at the end to test the hold.

She hadn't known it was the last time. Hadn't known her hands were learning something her mind would need to keep—that years later she'd repeat those same movements every morning, her fingers finding the pattern in Peri's hair like muscle memory of a woman who wasn't there anymore.

"Don't—"

The sob broke through anyway. She clamped her hand over her mouth, pressed hard, but it came out muffled and ugly against her palm.

She couldn't talk to Peri about this. Peri didn't want Pepper in her head—flinched at the name, went cold at the mention, carried the leaving like a blade she kept sharp on purpose. And Kataero—she'd just watched his wound open in real time, watched him route his own abandonment through his daughter's happiness. She couldn't hand him hers too.

So this stayed here. Behind locked doors. Under running water.

The only place she was allowed to miss her mother.

Sometimes it slipped through anyway and Pepper's face was right there—the smell of her hair, the warmth of her lap, the sound of her humming while her fingers worked through the copper strands. The kitchen full of morning light. Kitt on the other side of the table, watching. Learning without knowing she was learning.

And Kitt just wanted to see her. Once. Just once. Wanted to ask her if it ever stopped hurting. Wanted to ask why she left. Wanted to sit in that kitchen again and memorize something new because the old memories were wearing thin from use.

She stayed there until her breathing steadied. Until she could swallow the rest back down where it lived.

Then she wiped her face. Stepped into the shower. And let the water take whatever was left.

23 | Peri

2191.115 · 05:37
T-29 S to Hammison Lock (Gate 20)

Peri drifted somewhere between sleep and waking, the truck's rumble a distant thing beneath her. Her fingers had found her cheek without her telling them to—tracing the spot where his lips had pressed.

Cedar. She could still smell it on her skin, faint beneath motor oil and cracked leather.

"So," Kitt said.

Peri's hand dropped to her lap. Fast. Guilty. She straightened in her seat, blinking the last of sleep away.

Here it comes.

She kept her gaze fixed on the window, watching a fencerow march past. Gray wood, weathered and splintering.

"How was dinner?"

The question landed soft but loaded. Peri was grateful for the dim light.

"Fine," she said, keeping her tone flat.

"Fine." Kitt's voice sharpened. "You had dinner with Rhowan Cade at one of the nicest restaurants in the territory and it was 'fine'?"

"Yes."

"Did he give you the intel?"

"Yes."

"Is it good?"

"Haven't gone through it all yet."

Silence filled the cab again—heavier this time. Tires humming against asphalt.

Then: "What did you wear?"

Peri's hands curled into fists in her lap. "Clothes."

"Peri."

"What?"

"You know what." Kitt's knuckles went white on the steering wheel. "I want details. What did you wear? What did you eat? What did you talk about? Did he—"

"We talked. We ate. I got the papers. That's it." Each word clipped. Defensive.

"That's it." Disbelief. "You're telling me you spent three hours with Rhowan Cade and nothing happened?"

Nothing. The wool of his coat under her fingers. The burn of stepping back.

"Nothing happened."

"Did he try anything?"

"No."

"Did you want him to?"

Gods yes.

Peri's head snapped toward her sister. "What kind of question is that?"

Kitt's eyes stayed locked on the road, but her smirk was unmistakable—even in profile, even in the dark.

From the back seat came a quiet sound. Not quite a cough. Not quite a laugh. Kataero's version of amusement.

Peri twisted around, leather creaking. "You have something to say?"

Kataero continued looking out his own window, expression neutral as carved stone. "Not at all."

"Then why—"

"Your sister asked a reasonable question." The calm in his voice landed harder than any accusation.

"It wasn't reasonable."

"It was extremely reasonable," Kitt interjected, grin widening. "You came back to the inn at ten-thirty. I heard you come in. I was still awake working on the radio housing, and I heard your footsteps in the hall. You were humming."

"I was not."

"You absolutely were. Some tune I've never heard you hum before." Kitt's delight was audible now. "So it was more than 'fine.'"

Peri crossed her arms. Turned back to the window, watching hills begin to rise in the distance. "Can we please focus on the job?"

"We have thirteen hours until we reach Gate 20," Kitt said, bright with sisterly torture. "Plenty of time to focus on the job. Right now, I want to know what you wore."

Her teeth ground together. "The sleeveless shirt. Dark pants. The usual."

"The sleeveless shirt." Kitt climbed higher, delighted. "The one that actually shows your arms?"

"Yes."

"The one you never wear because you think it's too—what was the word—revealing?"

"I didn't say that." But her words wavered, unconvincing even to herself.

"You absolutely said that. Last summer when I suggested you wear it to the Belfast Mills festival, you called it too revealing. Said you'd rather wear your jacket. Didn't want people staring."

"I don't remember that."

"I do. Vividly." Kitt's grin was a living thing now. "So you wore the revealing shirt. For Rhowan. At a nice restaurant."

"For myself."

"Sure. Did you wear your hair down?"

Peri said nothing.

"Oh my gods, you wore your hair down." Kitt's satisfaction radiated across the cab. "He noticed, didn't he?"

Peri's silence was answer enough.

Kitt's laugh burst out, filling the truck with genuine delight. "What did he say?"

"Nothing." But even Peri heard how weak that sounded.

"Peri."

The words burst out before she could stop them—defensive and raw. "He said I looked beautiful, okay?" Her voice cracked on the admission. "He said I looked beautiful and we had dinner and talked and it was nice. That's it. Can we drop it now?"

The cab went quiet, different now—softer, less teasing. Just engine rumble and tires on asphalt.

Then Kitt, gentler: "It was nice?"

Peri forced herself to answer. "Yeah. It was nice."

"Nice" wasn't enough. Wasn't anywhere close. But it would have to do.

"Good." Kitt's voice had lost its teasing edge. "You deserve someone who looks at you like you're not just Dad's errand girl."

Peri turned back to the window. Said nothing. Couldn't say anything.

I just fetch things.

Her jaw tightened enough to ache. She kept her gaze fixed on the gray landscape rolling past.

Kitt must have felt the shift. "Hey. I didn't mean—"

"It's fine." Flat. Clipped.

"Peri—"

"I said it's fine."

The quiet came back heavier. The truck's engine filled the void.

Kataero's voice cut in from the back seat: "Did he explain Bethshelm?"

Peri turned, grateful for the redirect. Kataero was still gazing out his window, not looking at her. But his attention—that particular focus he brought to everything.

"He said someone else knew we were coming. Someone who'd set up worse than jail." She went quiet. "Said the patrols kept us safe while he cleaned up the real problem."

"Do you believe him?"

Did she?

"I don't know," she said finally. "But I think he believes it."

Kataero nodded once. Said nothing else.

"And the job?" Kitt asked after a while. "Did he come through?"

The envelope sat against her ribs, tucked inside her jacket. She could feel its edges through the fabric.

"Yeah." She kept her voice even. "He came through."

Kitt's eyes flicked toward her. "Details?"

"Intel. Access points. Enough to work with." She shifted in her seat. "I'll lay it out when we stop."

Kitt pressed her lips together. Wanting more. Reading something in the answer—or in what wasn't there.

"You trust it?"

"I trust that he wanted to impress me more than he wanted to play an angle."

Silence. Then Kitt, quieter: "That might be worse."

Peri didn't argue.

Miles passed. Fence posts thinning out, replaced by low stone walls half-reclaimed by moss, the land going wilder as they moved south.

At some point, Kitt had gone quiet. She drove one-handed now, construction schedules propped against the steering wheel. Pages she'd been collecting for weeks—contractor manifests, build timelines, equipment requisitions. Peri watched her flip to a floor plan, lips moving as she traced corridors with her finger. Administrative wing. Second floor. The kind of details that lived in procurement paperwork if you knew where to look.

"You've memorized that thing," Peri said.

"Getting there." Kitt didn't look up. "I want to know the layout before we're standing in it."

⚙

Peri glanced back over her shoulder. Kataero was watching her—but something had shifted in his face. Not his usual stillness. Softer. The corner of his mouth almost curved.

Something she didn't know how to answer. Her hand twitched toward the gap between the seats—toward him—before she caught herself.

Then it changed.

Between one breath and the next, his face closed. Eyes going distant—fixed on the gray fields but not seeing them. Seeing something else entirely.

He turned back to the window. Just her father watching the landscape.

Peri faced forward. Let her temple rest against cool glass.

Goodnight, Red.

She let herself hold that. The way he'd said it—soft, like a secret.

The truck rolled on toward Gate 20.

24 | Wynne

2191.117 · 07:20

Garda Square Farmer's Market | CAD Hamilton

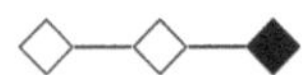

The market woke early in Hamilton.

Wynne moved through it as the sun climbed, bare feet finding the rhythm of cobblestones she'd walked for two weeks now. Same platinum stubble. Same white robes. Same quarterstaff across her back.

Different city. Different response.

"Morning, Miss Kaede!" A fruit vendor lifted a hand as she passed—the same man who'd watched her with wary silence that first day. Now he tossed her an apple without waiting to see if she'd catch it. She did. Bowed her thanks. He was already turning to his next customer.

She bit into the apple as she walked. Sweet. Crisp. Given freely.

Two children darted from an alley—the baker's daughters, she'd learned. They skidded to a stop in front of her, blocking her path with exaggerated formality.

"Lady Monk." The older one, maybe eight, performed a bow so deep her nose nearly touched her knees.

Wynne returned it. Just as deep. Just as serious. Holding the posture until the girl straightened.

The younger one dissolved into giggles. They ran off, bare feet slapping stone, laughter trailing behind them.

Even the security detail at the corner gave her room. One nodded as she approached. She nodded back. They let her pass without the tracking eyes she'd felt those first days.

The crowd parted around her now. She moved with them. Part of the rhythm.

⊙

Movement caught her attention. A coffee shop on the corner, windows open to the morning air.

Paul sat inside. Back to the wall—he always chose seats that way. Arms crossed, but his left hand resting near his ribs. That unconscious touch she'd seen before, the one that came when he was thinking hard or when the cold got into old injuries.

Newspaper on the table, forgotten. Coffee cup beside it, steam long since faded. He'd been here a while.

He was watching the market. Not her specifically—the whole square, the way he watched any room he sat in. But when their eyes met, the usual warmth didn't settle in right away. A beat too long. Something underneath—tired, maybe. Troubled.

Wynne raised her hand. Small wave.

Paul lifted his cup in response. The smile came, but it had to travel a distance to reach his face.

She moved on, letting the market carry her forward. Everyone had bad mornings. Even Paulie.

⊙

She finished the apple near the fountain at Market Square and tossed the core into a waste bin.

A bookstall caught her eye.

Jaden.

She caught herself mid-step. Noticed the catch. Kept walking. Normal pace. Measured. Controlled.

Jaden stood examining a leather-bound volume with exaggerated interest. Turning it over in his hands. Reading the spine. Flipping to a random page. Reading nothing at all.

His cane leaned against the stall's edge. His weight shifting left to right, right to left. The bookseller watched him with the patient expression of someone who'd realized ten minutes ago this customer wasn't actually buying anything.

He was waiting. Trying very hard to look like he wasn't waiting. Failing completely.

She approached from his blind side. Let her footsteps announce her.

Jaden's head came up. The book snapped shut. Relief broke through before he could catch it. Eagerness underneath.

"Ms. Kaede." Too formal. Compensating. "I was just—" He gestured vaguely at the bookstall. "Browsing."

"You've been browsing that same book for a while." The bookseller's voice was dry. "Erta's Guide to Freshwater Fishing. Third edition."

Jaden looked down at the cover. His ears went slightly pink.

"Research," he said. "For a project."

"Mm-hmm." The bookseller looked to Wynne before turning to help another customer, smile barely hidden.

Wynne took the book from his hands. Set it back on the display. "The new credentials came through?"

The mask cracked. Genuine excitement bleeding through. "Full access. Clara sent word this morning. We can finally—" He stopped himself. Glanced around at the crowded market. Lowered his voice. "We should go."

"We should."

But she didn't move yet. Just watched him—fingers drumming against his cane, body tilted forward, energy coiled beneath his careful composure. Six years of searching. Two weeks of dead ends. And now, finally, real access.

She touched his arm. Brief. Grounding. "Ready?"

Jaden met her eyes, looked down to her hand, then back up.

"No." Small smile. "Let's go anyway."

They walked toward the library together. The market parting around them the way it did now—two people moving with shared purpose through a city that had learned to recognize them.

⊙

Hamilton Public Library in morning light was nothing like the evening quiet Wynne had grown accustomed to.

She pushed through the heavy entrance behind Jaden and stopped just inside the threshold.

Dozens of young voices echoing off high ceilings, the acoustic chaos of stone and wood amplifying everything into a wall of noise. Three school groups at once, children between shelves like dropped marbles, teachers calling for attention that dissolved before it could land.

"Bloody zoo today."

Paul stood near the entrance, uniform rumpled. But he smiled when he saw them—and this time the warmth arrived without delay. Whatever had been troubling him in the coffee shop didn't survive contact with people he was glad to see.

"Morning, Paulie."

"Ms. Kaede. Mr. Oram." He nodded toward the chaos. "Field trip season. Three schools decided today was library day. At once." He shook his head. "I've been directing traffic since dawn."

"You look it," Jaden said.

"Flatterer." Paul's smile stayed. He touched Wynne's arm briefly—light, familiar. The easy contact of someone who'd become part of her daily life without either of them marking the moment it happened. "Careful in there. The little ones have discovered the rolling ladders."

They wove through the crowd carefully. Jaden moving with the deliberate care his body demanded, choosing paths that avoided sudden movements. Wynne stayed close, her body positioned to shield his weaker side.

At the circulation counter, a blonde woman in her forties looked up from a stack of return cards. "Jaden. Thank god."

"Morning, Clara. I need access to the restricted archives. 2170 to 2175 council records."

"We just got the authorization this morning." She found a brass key in an envelope tucked beneath the counter. Handed it to him, metal catching the overhead lights. "Full access."

A crash from the children's section. Something toppled—wood hitting wood.

Clara's jaw tightened. Behind her, one of the other staff members was already moving toward the sound, but the disorder was building.

Jaden pocketed the key. "I'll head down—"

"Go," Wynne said, cutting him off gently. "I'll be down shortly."

He looked at her. At the chaos spreading through the library. Understanding crossed his face—the slight widening of his eyes, the small nod.

He moved toward the archive door, weaving between clusters of children with practiced care.

⊙

Wynne stepped into an open section of floor between the reference desk and the children's area. Set her pack down.

Her muscles ached for proper movement. The courtyard behind the inn was too cramped for full forms, and even the memorial grounds required restraint—public space, joggers to account for, sequences trimmed to fit the audience she'd started drawing. She hadn't performed for pure discipline in days. Just connection. Just teaching.

She drew her quarterstaff from its carry position. The weight settling into her hands. Smooth wood warm against her palms despite the morning cold.

A few children noticed. Stopped talking. Turned to watch.

Wynne didn't explain. Didn't announce. Just centered herself the way Master Rev had taught her. Found the connection between breath and balance and purpose.

Then moved.

First form came clean. Simple. Her body remembering what days of teaching and abbreviated public forms had softened—the way movement felt when mind and body aligned completely without consideration for who was watching.

Staff spun. Her body followed. Not leading, not chasing. Just being the motion itself.

More children stopped. A cluster formed, the chaos drawing inward.

The running footsteps slowed. The voices dropped—not from being hushed but from finding something more interesting than their own noise. Even the children on the ladders paused, hands gripping the rails, bodies still.

Wynne flowed through the sequence. Staff spinning in controlled arcs. Each motion bleeding into the next. Not performance. The pure discipline of it. Connection she'd been reaching for during these weeks of public practice.

She reached the final position. Planted the staff with a sharp crack against the floor.

Perfect stillness.

Then the children erupted. Applause. Delight. Questions bubbling up like something uncorked.

A small girl approached from the cluster—seven, maybe. Long dark hair in braids. Brown eyes serious despite the smile trying to break through.

She stopped exactly three feet away. Hands at her sides. Still in a way the other children weren't.

"Could I learn?" the girl asked quietly.

"Yes," Wynne said. "Anyone can learn. As long as they're patient and willing to make the effort."

The girl's face transformed. Seriousness breaking into genuine joy—small, private, full of possibility.

She ran back to her class, already talking excitedly to the children beside her.

Wynne stood. The room had settled. Teachers managing their groups with renewed purpose, the chaos organized into something more intentional. Clara caught her eye from the circulation desk and mouthed *thank you.*

She turned back toward the archive door.

Jaden stood there. Just inside the frame. Watching her.

His cane hung loose in his hand, forgotten. His weight fully on his injured leg without seeming to notice. The analytical mask—gone. Just him, unguarded, looking at her the way he looked at a pattern that had finally resolved.

She crossed to join him, floorboards solid beneath her bare feet.

He blinked. Surfaced. The analytical mind reassembling itself—but slower than usual. Pieces not quite fitting back together.

"I've read about it," he said. "Monks and their forms. I always thought it was—" He stopped. Shook his head. "I have no frame of reference for what I just watched."

"Then we should go," Wynne said. "Before you find the frame and lecture me for an hour."

The corner of his mouth twitched. Not quite a laugh—but the shape of one.

He cleared his throat. Looked down at the brass key in his hand as if rediscovering it. "Right. The archives."

He turned toward the door. Inserted the brass key. Tumblers clicked—solid, precise, old engineering refined over generations. The lock that had refused them weeks ago, that had held Jaden's grief—opening now. Easily.

Cool air rose from below, carrying the scent of old paper and preservation chemicals and the particular mustiness of spaces rarely disturbed.

Jaden glanced back at her.

Then he started down the narrow stairs, his cane tapping against each step.

Wynne followed.

Into the archives.

25 | Peri

2191.115 · 19:14

Gate 20 | Hammison Locks

Night had fallen over Hammison Lock. Shadow and dim lamplight. Air sharp with rain and concrete dust. Water dripped from scaffolding somewhere in the darkness, steady and rhythmic.

She crouched behind a stack of steel girders, cold and slick beneath her gloved fingers. Scaffolding ahead. Steel skeleton against dark cloud. The gate structure half-built, half-exposed. Cold air pulling through the gaps.

Beside her, Kitt adjusted her pack. Leather straps creaked softly, buckles clinking.

Then again.

"Stop fidgeting," Peri whispered. "You look nervous."

"I'm not nervous." Kitt's hands stilled on the straps, but her shoulders remained tight, drawn up toward her ears. "I'm checking my equipment."

"You've checked it four times."

"I like being thorough." But Kitt's fingers found the buckle again anyway.

Peri understood. Her own hand found the stopwatch in her pocket, thumb tracing the worn chrome.

Kataero stood several yards back, arms crossed, gaze fixed on the access road. Seven o'clock had come and gone. Now it was seven-fifteen.

Peri's eyes moved without her telling them to. Open ground north, equipment yard. Hard road east, fast. The truck to the south. Three ways out. All of them wet.

Headlights appeared on the access road. A truck. Moving slowly, engine growling low.

It parked with a hiss of brakes. Connor climbed out, tool bag slung over his shoulder, walking like he had all the time in the world. Like fifteen minutes late was exactly on schedule.

"Thought we said seven," Kataero called out, carrying across the site without shouting.

Connor set down his bag with a heavy thump against wet gravel. "Fuel line cracked on the drive over." He pulled out a rag, began wiping his hands with slow, methodical movements. Even from here, Peri could smell diesel on him. "Had to patch it roadside."

"Could've radioed."

"Could've." Connor folded the rag, tucked it away. "Figured you'd survive fifteen minutes without me." He glanced up. "Miss me that much?"

Kitt snorted—caught between amusement and exasperation. Peri grinned. Couldn't help it.

Kataero's expression didn't change. But the corner of his mouth twitched. "Let's move."

⊙

"Records terminal is in the administrative section," Kitt said, pulling out her notebook. Her shoulders dropped slightly—that shift when she could focus on facts.

"Guard rotation?" Peri asked.

"Every forty minutes according to the construction schedules I copied." Kitt flipped a page, showing neat diagrams. "Two guards per shift. Gate entrance and interior patrols."

Peri nodded. Her gaze traced the scaffolding running up the north side—skeleton's ribs against the sky. Service entrance at the base. Darker shadow against concrete.

"North side entry," she said. "Scaffolding to service entrance."

"How do you know about the cameras?"

"Camera mount's empty." She pointed toward the gap—that dark space where light should be. "They don't wire those until the build's done."

Kitt's eyes lingered on her for a moment. Then back to the facility. "Makes sense."

Kataero looked at Connor. Connor's chin dipped a fraction. Whatever it meant, they'd already agreed. Then Kataero's attention shifted to Peri and Kitt. "You two get closer. Confirm the entry point and guard patterns. Eyes only. Don't engage. Report back when you have a read on the security."

"Got it," Peri said. Movement. Action. Finally.

"And Peri?"

She stopped. Turned back.

"Watch the wet ground." His dark stare held hers. "Tracks show easy after rain."

She nodded. Started moving forward, Kitt falling into step behind her.

⊙

They stayed low, using construction equipment and material stacks for cover. Ground slick in places where rain had pooled, muddy in others where it had churned beneath boots and machinery. She tested each step before committing her weight, choosing dry patches without thinking about it.

Behind her, Kitt's boots squelched once—sudden and loud.

Peri stopped. Looked back.

Kitt froze mid-step, face twisted in a grimace, one boot sunk ankle-deep in mud that gleamed in the lamplight.

"Lighter steps," Peri whispered. "Watch where I walk. Step exactly where I step."

Kitt nodded, pulling her boot free with a soft sucking sound that made them both tense. The night stayed still.

They kept moving. Slower now. Peri's awareness sharpened until she could feel every texture beneath her boots—gravel, concrete, mud, grass. The difference between disturbed earth and settled ground registering through her soles.

"Breathe deeper," she murmured without turning. "You're making too much noise."

Kitt's next breath came slower. More even.

At the facility perimeter, she stopped behind a concrete barrier that still smelled of wet cement—recently poured and curing. The main entrance visible from here: pools of light from security lamps, shadows where guards stood or patrolled. Two of them. One near the gate, leaning against the guardhouse wall like he'd rather be anywhere else. One patrolling the exterior—methodical, unhurried, the pace of someone who'd done this same circuit a hundred times.

She watched. The exterior guard moved north wall. Pause. East corner. Pause. South wall. Back to the entrance.

She watched him do it again.

"Twelve minutes," she said. "Full circuit. Same corners every time."

Kitt pulled out her notebook, scribbled a mark. Looked up. "You counted that fast?"

Peri kept her eyes on the guard. "He's a creature of habit."

She pointed as the guard turned toward the south wall. "When he's on the south side—two minutes to reach the scaffolding unseen."

"Peri, wait—"

But Peri was already moving, tapping Kitt's wrist as she broke from cover. They sprinted low across the open gap and onto the scaffolding, metal rattling faintly under their boots as they climbed.

They reached the second level. The service entrance sat ten feet away—a plain metal door with a heavy industrial lock.

Kitt caught her breath, shot Peri a look that needed no translation. She flipped open her notebook, pencil tapping as she reviewed her timing marks. "Guard loop confirmed. Entry point viable." She looked up. "We should head back. Report to Dad befo—"

"Or we go in now."

Kitt blinked. "Now?"

"Window's open. Ninety seconds before the guard loops back."

"Peri, we don't know—"

"I know." She was already turning toward her sister's pack, fingers quick and sure as she dug through the side pocket where Kitt kept her precision tools. "Trust me."

"That's not the mission." Kitt's hands twisted around the notebook. "Dad said eyes only. Scout and report."

Eyes only.

Scout and report.

Fetch.

"Kataero says a lot of things." She selected the tension wrench and a short rake—their weight settling into her hands. "I say we move."

She crossed to the door and knelt, already sliding the wrench into the lower half of the keyway. Metal kissed metal. The world narrowed.

Kitt's voice climbed somewhere behind her. "Peri! We can't just decide to break in!"

"We're not deciding. We're doing."

Her fingers found the first pin. Pressure. Resistance.

Good girl. Fetch.

Click.

The first pin set. The voice stumbled, lost a step.

She tilted the wrench, feeling for the second. The tool an extension of her fingers, her awareness narrowing to the microscopic landscape inside the lock. Pins and springs and the beautiful simplicity of a problem with a solution.

"Doing is deciding!" Kitt caught herself, dropped to a hiss. "We can't just—"

"Watch me."

Second pin. The rake found it, tested it. *Dad's errand girl—*

Click.

Cut off mid-word. The doubt thinner now, further away.

Just her and the lock and the perfect clarity of doing something she was good at.

"What if we get caught?" Kitt's breathing had gone quick, shallow.

"We won't."

"You don't know that. Not here. Not in a—"

Third pin. She didn't have to search for it. Her fingers knew. Metal sang against metal—that particular frequency that meant everything was aligning.

I just fetch things—

Click.

Gone. All of it.

The world went quiet.

"Relax, Kitten." She smiled without meaning to.

"Don't call me—"

Fourth pin.

Click.

The cylinder turned. Perfect. Clean.

The lock opened like a gift.

She stayed there for a moment. Kneeling. Tools warm in her palm. The open lock hanging loose and defeated in front of her.

This. This she was good at.

Peri rose. Tools sliding back into her palm. Reached into her jacket. Pulled out two cards—Rhowan's addition, tucked behind the layouts in the envelope. They'd been in her jacket since she'd opened the envelope. Just in case.

She clipped one to her collar, held the other out to Kitt.

Kitt stared at it. "What's this?"

"Put it on. Just don't let anyone look too close."

"Peri." Kitt's voice dropped. "What is this?"

"It's an ID card. Close enough to pass from a distance. Just a precaution."

Kitt turned the card over in her hands. Generic photo. Generic name. The kind of thing that might survive a glance from ten feet away but would fall apart under any real scrutiny.

"Where did you—"

"Put it on."

Kitt's mouth thinned. She clipped the card to her jacket. Her eyes stayed on Peri a beat too long—something working behind them that wasn't nerves. Something colder. The look of someone realizing they'd been managed.

Peri reached up. Blew the copper curl out of her face—the one that fought every tie-back. Then she pulled the handle.

The door swung inward, fresh paint and concrete dust spilling into the night air.

She held it open. Looked back—not at Kitt, but past her. Past the scaffolding and the construction site. To the distant edge where the truck sat. Two shapes barely visible against the dark.

Kataero. Connor. Waiting for a report that wasn't coming.

She turned back to Kitt. Saw her sister frozen at the threshold—jaw tight, hands pressed flat at her sides. The war playing out across her face. The part of Kitt that knew this was wrong, that they were breaking protocol, ignoring direct orders, risking everything on Peri's impulse.

And underneath—the part that needed to know if she was right.

"Coming?"

Kitt's expression flickered. Something that would keep.

"Always following," she muttered.

Peri grinned—sharp, bright, trouble.

Sorry, Dad.

She stepped through the doorway. Her hand found the pocket. The chrome. Cool and certain beneath her thumb.

"Let's do this."

Click.

26 | Kataero

2191.115 · 19:18
Gate 20

◇—◇—◇

Kataero watched them disappear into the darkness. Two shadows moving low across the construction site, using cover the way he'd taught them. Peri leading, Kitt following. The way it always was.

Connor settled against the truck's tailgate, pulling out a radio component and his soldering kit. Sharp smell of flux drifted on the night breeze. "They'll be fine."

"I know." But Kataero's attention stayed fixed on the point where they'd vanished.

He forced himself to turn away. Their gear was stacked near the truck—tool bags, supply packs, the equipment they'd need for the train job in three days. He started checking it methodically. Inventory, condition, readiness. The kind of task that kept his hands busy.

Peri's pack sat on top. He lifted it, testing the weight.

Heavier than it should be.

He opened it.

Standard gear on top. Lock picks, flashlight, rope, the usual tools.

Then, wrapped carefully in newspaper and tied with string—two vacuum tubes. Pre-Authority manufacture. The kind Kitt had been asking about for months. Newspaper showed a price mark in faded ink. Twelve marks each.

Underneath those, bundled hastily in one of Peri's own shirts—more components. Zinc plates. Graphite brushes. Copper terminals green with corrosion. No packaging. No markings. Still carrying traces of dirt and grime like they'd been pulled straight from a salvage bin.

Kataero went still.

He lifted one of the vacuum tubes in its newspaper wrapping. Set it aside. Then lifted the shirt bundle. Unwrapped it slowly.

Everything in the newspaper: purchased.

Everything in the shirt: stolen.

She'd had money. Had made a legitimate purchase. And stolen anyway.

His teeth set.

He started rewrapping the components. Purchased items back in their newspaper. Stolen goods back in her shirt. Careful. Exact. The way he'd been taught to handle evidence in another life.

His hand brushed paper. Thicker than newspaper. Folded.

He pulled it free.

An envelope. Unsealed. Inside: a hand-drawn layout—not architectural blueprints, but detailed enough. Someone had sketched the facility's footprint with care. Camera positions marked with small circles, several annotated *unwired* or *mount only*. Guard rotation patterns noted in columns along the margin—shift times, circuit duration, coverage gaps.

A service entrance on the east side circled twice, with a note: *maintenance traffic after hours, badge check but no name log.*

Access points. Patrol windows. Blind spots. Everything someone would need to get inside.

Kataero stopped.

He didn't recognize the handwriting. Not Peri's—hers was quick and angular. Not Kitt's precise print. Not Connor's.

Rhowan's. Had to be. The dinner that was supposed to be about forged passes had produced something else entirely. Someone with contacts inside a Continental Authority facility had mapped it for his daughter, and his daughter had kept it from him.

She'd walked into this job tonight already knowing the layout. Already knowing the camera gaps and guard circuits and which entrance to use. And she hadn't said a word.

The envelope marked the east side service entrance. She'd pointed north—the scaffolding. She hadn't even used Rhowan's route. She'd studied the intel enough to find a better one.

He folded the papers. Slid them back into the envelope. Placed it carefully on top of the pack.

Evidence. For a conversation that would happen later.

He zipped the pack closed. The metallic rasp of the zipper sounded too loud in the quiet night.

"What've you got there?"

Kataero glanced up. Connor had stopped soldering, iron still in hand.

He held up the newspaper-wrapped tubes in one hand, the shirt-bundled components in the other.

Connor stared at the two separate piles. "She bought something to cover the theft."

"Or she bought what she needed. Then saw the rest and couldn't help herself." Kataero's voice stayed flat. "Either way, she walked into a vendor's stall, made a legitimate purchase, and walked out with goods she didn't pay for."

The words hung between them.

"There's also an envelope." He kept his voice level. "Hand-drawn layout of this facility. Guard rotations. Camera blind spots. Access points. Handwriting I don't recognize."

Connor's expression hardened. The humor that usually lived somewhere behind his eyes went dark. "Rhowan."

"Has to be."

"She didn't mention it."

"No. She didn't."

Wind carried the distant sound of machinery from the construction site.

Connor set down the soldering iron. "She's in there right now with intel we've never seen."

"With her sister beside her."

Kataero looked at Connor. "Did you know about this?"

"How could I?"

"Because she trusts you." The words came out harder than he intended. "More than anyone. I find it hard to believe the one person she actually talks to didn't know any of this was going on."

Connor was quiet for a long time. When he spoke, his voice was careful. Controlled. The way it got when he was choosing between honesty and kindness and landing on honesty.

"Maybe as her father, you could have seen it better."

Kataero's mouth opened. Closed.

Connor held his gaze. No apology in it. No retreat. Just the unflinching look of a man who'd said something true and wasn't going to take it back.

Kataero looked at the pack. Zipped shut. Ordinary. Carrying everything he'd missed.

The theft wasn't new. He'd suspected—small things going missing from jobs, components appearing without receipts. He'd told himself it was resourcefulness. Told himself she was being practical in a world where practical meant survival.

He hadn't wanted to see the pattern. A father's blindness, dressed up as trust.

The silence between them had changed. Heavier. The kind that could calcify if someone didn't break it.

"That was out of line," Kataero said. "What I said."

"Yeah." Connor picked up the soldering iron. Turned it over in his hands. "Mine too."

"No. Yours was fair."

Connor looked at him. Held it for a beat. Then nodded once and went back to his work.

Done. The way it always was with them. The hurt would sit where it sat. But the focus was back where it belonged.

On the copper-headed girl doing god knows what inside that facility.

⚙

Fifteen minutes.

Kataero laid out the infiltration gear across the truck bed. Lock picks in graduated sizes. Voltage tester. Wire cutters. Slim pry bar they'd need for the terminal cabinet. Everything organized, checked, ready.

Connor leaned against the hood beside him, binoculars raised. Somewhere in that illuminated grid, two shadows that didn't belong.

Temperature had dropped. Spring cold settling in, the kind that found its way through jacket seams and made metal sting to touch.

He set down the lock pick case. Picked up his radio. Keyed it. "Falcon. Tabby. Report."

Static.

Twenty minutes.

Connor lowered the binoculars. "Still just construction crews and perimeter guards. Standard rotation."

"And?"

"No sign of them."

Which meant they were either very good or very gone.

Kataero grabbed the binoculars. Scanned the facility himself.

Guard towers at the corners with mounted searchlights that swept the perimeter in lazy arcs. Two-man patrols along the fence line, evenly spaced, rifles slung but present.

Nowhere to hide. Nowhere to move unseen for long.

Connor's voice was low. "They're being thorough. Taking their time to map the patterns."

"Kitt doesn't know the patterns." Binoculars stayed fixed. "She doesn't have the field sense to read guard rotations on the fly. To feel when to move and when to freeze."

"Peri does."

"Peri does." He lowered the binoculars. "And Kitt will follow wherever Peri leads."

Connor shifted his weight. "Kitt's smart—"

"Smart doesn't help when a searchlight finds you." He could see it—white light sweeping across concrete, catching a shadow that moved half a second too late. Kitt's face illuminated. The freeze. "She'll be watching her sister instead of the threat."

Wind cut across the open ground.

"You taught them both," Connor said quietly. "Trust that."

Kataero turned. Met his partner's gaze.

"She may be my daughter," Kataero said, "but you're her guardian. Sometimes I wonder if you just watch her walk into trouble so you can pull her out."

Silence. Connor held his stare with the patience that had carried them through two decades together.

"That's not fair," Kataero said. "I know that."

Connor didn't release him from the look. "No. It's not." He paused. "But I'm not the one who missed the envelope."

Kataero took that. Let it sit where it sat.

The memory rose before he could stop it.

Margos. Six years ago. Peri fifteen and convinced she was ready for real work. Not training. Not controlled exercises. The real thing.

He'd said no. Told her to wait another year. But she'd gone anyway—recruited two kids from Belfast Mills, planned it herself, executed it without telling him until it was done.

Almost done.

He'd found her in an alley three blocks from the target. Slumped against brick, one hand pressed to her left shoulder, blood seeping through her fingers and soaking into her jacket. Dark. Too much of it. The two kids she'd recruited were gone—scattered when things went wrong, leaving her alone and bleeding.

The man who'd stabbed her lay five feet away. Dead. Peri's knife still in his ribs where she'd put it after he'd put his blade in her shoulder.

She'd looked up when Kataero dropped beside her. Fifteen years old. Copper hair matted with sweat and rain. Face pale with blood loss. But her eyes—

See? I can do this. I'm good enough.

Even bleeding out in an alley with a dead man at her feet, she'd been trying to prove something.

He'd carried her six blocks to where Connor was waiting with the truck. Had held pressure on the wound while Connor drove, Peri's blood warm and slick against his hands. She'd stayed conscious the whole way—watching him, waiting for him to say something.

He hadn't trusted himself to speak.

The scar was still there. Puckered tissue on her left shoulder, visible whenever she wore anything sleeveless.

Six years ago.

And here they were again. Different facility. Different risk. Same pattern. The same girl running past every guardrail he'd built, and him standing on the wrong side of it wondering when he'd stopped being able to reach her.

And he'd sent Kitt with her.

His hands needed something to hold. He grabbed the voltage tester. Turned it over without seeing it. Set it down. Picked up the wire cutters. Set those down too.

"She learned from it," Connor said.

"Did she?" Quiet. Dangerous. "Or did she just get better at hiding how close to the edge she runs?"

Connor was quiet. His hand moved to the back of his neck—held there. The first crack in his composure all night.

Twenty-five minutes.

⊙

Thirty minutes.

Cold had worked its way deep. Into Kataero's bones. His joints.

He grabbed his radio. Keyed it. "Falcon. Tabby. Report."

Static.

He tried again. "Falcon. Tabby. Report."

Nothing.

Connor pushed off the hood. The humor had drained from his expression entirely. "Maybe they had to wait for a patrol."

"Or they went inside." The pieces assembled with terrible clarity. One after another. "They went inside and they're not coming back to report because they're already committed."

"You don't know that."

But he did. The same way he knew when a job had gone wrong before anyone said a word.

"I know Peri." He stared at the construction site. "Window opens, she takes it. Doesn't wait for clearance. Doesn't wait for backup. Just moves."

"Kitt wouldn't let her—"

"Kitt follows her sister. Always has." The truth of it settled. "And Peri knows it. Counts on it."

Searchlights swept the perimeter. Same lazy arcs. Guards walked their routes. Everything normal.

Except somewhere in that grid, his daughters were doing something they'd been explicitly told not to do. With intel he'd never vetted. From a source he'd never cleared. Because his daughter had decided she knew better, and he hadn't seen it coming.

Should have seen it coming. The theft. The hidden intel. The way she'd known exactly which entrance to suggest without hesitation. He'd been standing right there when she'd pointed to the north side scaffolding, and he hadn't asked how she knew. The envelope said east. She'd chosen north. She'd already improved on the plan before they'd arrived.

A father's blindness.

His body moved before his mind caught up. Two steps toward the facility. Into the lights and the guards. No intel. No plan.

Connor's hand caught him. "And do what?"

He stopped. Didn't turn.

"We don't know where they are." Level. Patient. Same tone Connor used when someone was about to make a mistake they couldn't take back. "You go in blind, you make it worse."

His muscles corded with the effort of staying still. Of not moving. Of being patient when patience felt like cowardice.

"How long?"

"Shift change is in forty minutes." Connor's grip stayed firm. "If they're not back by then..."

He didn't finish.

Kataero nodded. Barely.

"Forty minutes."

Connor released him. Stepped back.

"Trust her," Connor said quietly.

Kataero turned toward the facility one last time. The lights and the shadows and the complete absence of his daughters.

Trust her.

Girl who stole to cover stealing.

Trust her.

Girl who'd kept intel from her father and led her sister into a facility on a stranger's word.

Trust her.

Girl who never failed when people depended on her.

He turned away. Settled back against the truck. Metal cold against his spine.

Forty minutes.

He'd wait.

27 | Peri

2191.115 · 19:23
Gate 20

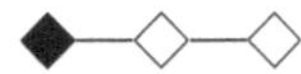

Emergency lighting cast everything in sickly green. Hallway stretching ahead—institutional tile, concrete walls, nothing that told her where anything was.

They were inside.

Peri's eyes adjusted quickly. Space opened around her—the way air moved, where sounds would echo, which shadows offered cover.

Somewhere deeper in the building, machinery hummed. Water moving through pipes in the walls.

Kitt pulled out her notebook, hands shaking enough that the pages rustled. She oriented herself against the mental blueprint, comparing what she'd memorized to the reality of concrete and tile. "Terminal should be...

second floor. Administrative wing." Her whisper barely stirred the air. "East side of the building."

"Then let's move." Peri's voice stayed low. Confident in a way that usually pulled Kitt out of her spirals.

Not this time. Kitt's breathing was too fast, too shallow.

Peri reached out. Found Kitt's wrist in the darkness. Squeezed once.

Kitt's pulse hammered beneath her fingers.

"Hey." Softer now. Just for her. "Breathe."

Kitt's eyes found hers in the green dark. Wide. Too much white showing.

"Stairs?" Peri asked.

"End of this hall. Turn left." Kitt's voice steadied a fraction. Finding focus in the navigation. "Second floor, east wing, third door past the—"

Footsteps.

They both froze.

Sound came from around the corner ahead. Heavy boots on tile. Measured pace. Someone walking a patrol route, not rushing. Just making rounds.

Peri saw the alcove before she thought the word—maintenance recess, three feet deep, barely visible in the emergency lighting.

She pulled Kitt into it. Pressed them both against the back wall, her body between her sister and the corridor. The way she always did.

Footsteps grew louder. Each boot strike amplified by proximity and fear until it was the only thing in the world.

Behind her, Kitt had started shaking—tremors running through her shoulders, vibrating against Peri's back. Breathing coming faster, harder.

Peri turned in the narrow space. Faced her sister. Found her shoulders in the dark.

"Kitt." Barely a breath. "Shh. Easy."

Kitt's eyes were squeezed shut. Fingers twisted in the straps of her pack like she was trying to hold herself together by gripping something.

Peri pressed her palm flat against Kitt's sternum. Firm. Steady. An anchor.

"Breathe. Feel your heartbeat."

Kitt's breath caught. Hiccuped.

"Slow and easy." Peri kept her hand there, kept the pressure constant. Felt the wild hammering underneath and didn't flinch from it. "I have you. Nothing bad is going to happen. Trust me."

Kitt nodded. Small, jerky movements. Her breathing still ragged but reaching for the rhythm Peri was offering.

"That's it." Peri matched her own breathing—slow in, slow out—and felt Kitt's chest begin to follow beneath her palm. "We got this."

Another nod. Steadier.

The footsteps reached their hallway.

Peri turned back toward the opening. Pressed Kitt against the wall behind her. Went still.

A guard appeared. Older. Thick around the middle. Flashlight in one hand, coffee in the other. Night shift—bills to pay, no glory in it. He swept the flashlight down the corridor, beam passing over their alcove—

Peri stopped breathing. Made herself nothing. Just shadow and concrete and empty space.

The beam moved past. Kept going. The guard's attention already elsewhere—his coffee, his remaining hours, anywhere but this empty corridor.

He turned the corner. Disappeared.

The sound of his boots faded.

Kitt's breath released in a shudder against Peri's shoulder blade.

Peri counted to twenty. Listening. Making sure he wasn't coming back. Making sure Kitt had time.

"Okay," she whispered. "We're okay."

Kitt nodded against her shoulder. Didn't speak yet.

She turned back to face her sister. Found Kitt's eyes in the dim light. Still scared. But present.

"Can you do this?"

"Yes." Stronger than Peri expected. Kitt's jaw setting the way Kataero's did when he'd made a decision. "I can do this."

"Good." Peri pulled them out of the alcove. "Because we're almost there."

Kitt followed. Her breathing still controlled—the rhythm Peri had given her, held and carried like something borrowed.

⊙

They found the stairs. Darker than the hallways. No emergency lighting here, just whatever filtered down from the floors above. Peri led with one hand on the railing, boots finding each step on the edges where concrete met wall, where the structure was solid and silent.

Second floor. Door opened onto another hallway—darker. Admin offices lined both sides, doors closed, windows black. Just ambient glow from exit signs at either end.

"Which way?" Peri asked.

"East." Kitt's whisper came with more certainty now. She was in her element too—mapping space, tracking blueprints, finding patterns. "Third door on the right."

They moved down the hallway. Peri led, her footsteps silent on tile. Moving the way she moved through the warehouse at dawn—her body knowing exactly how much sound a boot made and exactly how to prevent it.

Third door appeared. Plain metal. No window. A card reader mounted on the wall beside it, indicator light blinking red.

Locked.

Kitt tried the handle. Door didn't move.

"Badge access," she whispered. "Print only—no electronic strip. We need—"

"Wait here." Peri was already moving back down the hallway.

"Where are you going?"

"To get us in."

"Peri—"

But she was already through the stairwell door, letting it close soft behind her.

⊙

Guard was on the first floor. His footsteps echoed up the stairwell—still making his rounds, that same rhythm of routine.

Peri descended. Silent.

She reached the first-floor landing. Cracked the door.

There he was. Twenty feet down the corridor. Back to her. Flashlight sweeping corners out of habit, not attention. Keys on his belt. Badge on a retractable reel clipped to his waistband.

She watched him. Three sweeps with the flashlight. Pause to check something on his clipboard. Forward ten paces. Repeat.

Three sweeps. Pause. Forward. Repeat.

Guard completed another cycle. Getting closer to the cross-corridor where the break room sat—she smelled old coffee, saw the faint glow of a vending machine around the corner.

He'd go there. He'd refill.

Peri moved into the hallway, staying to shadows. Matched his pace from thirty feet back.

Guard reached the break room and turned the corner.

She closed the distance. Quick. Silent. Twenty feet. Ten.

Stopped just before the corner. Listened.

Coffee machine hissed. Liquid pouring into a cup. Guard muttered something about institutional coffee that couldn't keep anyone awake.

Peri pulled the copper curl from her face. Drew a breath. Let her body settle into it—just another employee, working late, tired, looking for caffeine.

She walked around the corner.

Guard looked up, startled. Hand going to his belt—

"Sorry!" Peri stumbled slightly, like she'd been half-asleep and surprised to find someone. "Didn't mean to scare you. Just need coffee before I finish the filing upstairs." She gestured vaguely toward the ceiling. "Deadline stuff. Always is before the monthly reports."

Guard's hand dropped. Took in her appearance—young, tired, harmless. "Didn't know anyone else was still here."

"Just me and spreadsheets." She moved to the coffee machine. Grabbed a cup from the stack. Let herself sway slightly on her feet. "This coffee any good?"

"It's terrible." But his voice carried humor now. Just two tired people stuck working nights. "But it's hot."

"I'll take it." She poured. Coffee smelled burned. Looked like mud. She took a sip, made a face. "You weren't kidding."

He chuckled. Set his clipboard down. Pulled out his own cup for a refill.

One step closer. "How late are you—" She stumbled—accidentally—and her shoulder caught his arm, coffee sloshing, her hand grabbing his jacket for balance. "Sorry, sorry! These late nights—"

"It's fine." He steadied her, his free hand catching her elbow.

Her other hand found the reel. Thumb on the clip. She pressed—

It caught. The spring-loaded clip bit into his belt loop instead of releasing clean. Her thumb pressed harder. His weight shifted—half-turning toward the snag, brow creasing.

"Really am sorry about the coffee—" She tugged his sleeve with her other hand, pulling his attention left while her thumb found the angle.

Pressed again. The clip released with a faint click, masked by her continued fussing with the coffee stain on his sleeve.

The badge pressed cool against her palm.

"Thanks," she said, stepping back. "I should get back to it."

"Good luck with those spreadsheets."

She smiled. Tired. Genuine.

"Thanks. Have a good rest of your shift."

She walked away. Not too fast. Not too slow. Just another employee heading back to their desk.

Reached the hallway. Turned the corner. Kept walking until she couldn't hear the break room anymore.

Then she ran. Up the stairwell, two steps at a time, silent even at speed. The badge warm in her hand.

Kitt nearly jumped out of her skin when the stairwell door opened.

"Relax." Peri materialized from the darkness, barely breathing hard. "It's just me."

"You've been gone—" Kitt's voice pitched too high. "I thought—"

"Got it." Peri held up the badge. Retractable reel dangling from her fingers. RAMON TORRES, NIGHT SECURITY.

Kitt stared. "You stole a security badge."

"Borrowed." Peri moved to the terminal room door. Swiped the badge.

Reader blinked. Green.

Lock disengaged with a mechanical click that sounded impossibly loud in the quiet hallway.

"That's not borrowing," Kitt hissed. "That's theft. From a guard. Who's going to notice in about—"

"Then we better be quick." Peri pulled the door open. "You coming or not?"

Kitt's mouth pressed shut.

Then she stepped through the door.

⊙

The room was small. File cabinets against one wall, metal gray and institutional. Desk with papers stacked neatly. And against the far wall—

Kitt stopped. Stared.

The terminal filled the far wall. Massive. Six feet wide, four feet tall, metal housing in institutional beige. Tubes glowed orange and blue through ventilation grates, heat pouring off the machine in waves. The hum went through the floor and into her boots—deep, mechanical, alive. A screen in the center cast eerie brown-green light across the room, cursor blinking.

Everything that had threatened to unravel Kitt since they'd entered—gone.

"Williams-Haworth Series VII," she breathed. Wonder and something that felt like coming home. "They actually have one."

She pulled tools from her bag, hands steady now. Eyes locked on the terminal like nothing else existed.

Peri moved to the door. Cracked it open just enough to see the hallway. Empty. Fluorescent lights humming. Distant sound of voices—guards somewhere else in the building.

Fifteen minutes. Maybe twenty if Torres takes his time with that coffee.

"How long?" she asked without turning.

"Twenty minutes. Maybe more."

Cutting it close.

"I'll keep the monsters away."

Kitt didn't respond. Already lost in the machine. Already seeing past the housing to the circuits and logic gates underneath.

Peri settled against the doorframe. Where she could watch the hallway and her sister both. Hand near her knife. Breathing steady. Footsteps, voices, the rhythm of guards on patrol—all of it registering through the building's bones, through the floor under her boots.

Behind her, the quiet rasp of a screwdriver against metal. Kitt's shoulders relaxed as her hands found their work.

Peri watched the empty hallway. Counted seconds.

Fourteen minutes and forty-three seconds.

Fourteen minutes and forty-two.

28 | Kitt

2191.115 · 19:33

Gate 20

Her fingers found the nameplate first. Brass, slightly raised, warm from the heat pouring off the housing. She traced the letters without thinking—*Williams-Haworth Series VII*—the way someone else might touch a photograph. A thing she'd only ever read about. Real now. Under her hands.

She pressed a key.

CLUNK.

Tactile feedback solid, certain through her fingers. Each keypress a physical commitment. She pressed another just to feel it again.

CLUNK. Perfect.

Behind her, Peri's hand appeared over her shoulder. Torres's badge, retractable reel still attached. Kitt took it without turning and pressed it to the reader mounted on the terminal's side.

The machine hummed. Processing. Vacuum tubes flared brighter through the grates. Thirty seconds of waiting while circuits closed and opened, while analog systems verified authorization through hardware she'd never seen outside of a textbook.

The display changed:

CLEARANCE VERIFIED

SUPERVISOR RAMON TORRES - LEVEL 4

FACILITY: GATE 20 SECURITY

PASSWORD:_

Kitt stared at the prompt. Cursor blinking. Waiting.

How am I supposed to know the password?

She looked at the badge. As if it would suddenly reveal Torres's password.

Nothing.

The shit you get me into, Peri.

She typed guesses. Obvious sequences. Factory defaults if they even had them.

ACCESS DENIED

ACCESS DENIED

ACCESS DENIED

Three strikes. The screen flickered a warning:

WARNING: FAILED AUTHENTICATION

ADDITIONAL ATTEMPTS WILL TRIGGER SECURITY ALERT

Kitt's hands hovered over the keys. One more wrong password and alarms would sound. Guards would come. Done.

Her eyes tracked over the terminal. Housing. Ventilation grates. Access panels.

Access panels.

This wasn't some modern sealed system. This was MERIDIAN. Analog computing. Mechanical switches and vacuum tubes and physical circuits. Everything accessible. Everything serviceable.

Everything bypassable if you understood the hardware.

⊙

Password verification. Authentication protocol. Has to check the credential against stored data. Stored data means memory storage—magnetic core, ferrite matrix. The comparison circuit queries memory, compares values, returns true or false.

Which means the comparison logic would be deeper. Behind the main housing. Where the core systems lived.

Behind.

Kitt circled the terminal. There—rear access panel. Larger than the side panels. Four screws. Positioned low, near the floor where cooling vents exhausted hot air.

She knelt. Pulled out her screwdriver.

First screw. Second. Third. Fourth.

The panel came free. She set it aside carefully.

And stared into a maintenance nightmare. Authentication circuits sat deep—maybe eighteen inches back, surrounded by vacuum tubes glowing orange and blue, bundles of wiring running in every direction, circuit boards stacked at angles that made no engineering sense whatsoever. Heat poured from the opening. And the only way to reach those circuits was to climb up, squeeze between the terminal's bulk and the wall, and lie on her back with her head lower than her feet while reaching down into the guts.

Who designed this?

Kitt stripped off her jacket. Tossed it aside. Tank top and overalls would have to do. Already sweating and she hadn't even started yet.

She tested the route first. Because getting IN was one thing. Getting OUT was survival.

Hand hold here—the corner of the terminal's frame, solid metal that wouldn't break. Another there—edge of the desk, bolted to the floor. She could pull herself up if needed. If she didn't get stuck. If nothing went wrong.

She climbed. Wedging herself into the gap between terminal and wall. Her boots finding purchase against the baseboard. Her shoulders scraping paint off the wall. The space narrower than it looked. Much narrower.

The top edge of the terminal's housing caught her overalls. Right in the worst possible spot.

Wedgie. Immediate and uncomfortable.

"Oh..." She grabbed the fabric. Yanked it free with more force than necessary. *She is going to pay for this.*

Kitt adjusted. Settled in. Let herself slide down slightly until her back rested against the wall at an angle. Head lower than her feet. Looking up into the terminal's guts from below. Dust drifted down. Coating her face. Getting in her short hair. The fans blowing hot air directly at her.

She pulled out her testing probe. Flashlight clenched between her teeth. Reached up—no, down? Direction got confusing upside down—into the maze of components.

Wiring. So much wiring. Color-coded at least. Blue for power. Red for signal. Yellow for ground. Following the paths with her eyes. Tracing circuits through the tangle.

There. Input circuit routing to... comparison logic. The authentication gate. Physical switches built from tubes and resistors. Everything exposed. Everything accessible if you were willing to be uncomfortable enough to reach it.

Fans blew dust into her face. She blinked it away. Kept working.

Compact design. That's what they'd called it. Efficiency. Packing everything tight. Never mind the poor bastard who'd have to maintain it someday.

Engineers. Probably never had to fix anything they designed in their lives.

Her fingers found the circuit board. Warm.

So if I bypass the comparison... interrupt the signal. Make it think the passwords match even when they don't...

Comparison circuit. Two inputs—one from the keyboard, one from memory storage. Output going to an authorization gate.

If I bridge the output... force it high regardless of input...

She pulled out a thin wire from her tool bag. Had to reach back awkwardly—arm bent at wrong angle, shoulder protesting. Got it. Brought it up into position.

One end to the authorization gate's output. Other end to the power rail. Forcing the circuit to read as TRUE no matter what the actual comparison said.

Her hands shook slightly. Not panic. Just awkward angle. Heat. Dust in her eyes. Being upside down while trying to do precision electronics work.

If she fried the authentication circuit Torres wouldn't be able to log in later and they'd know something was wrong. But if she didn't do this they got nothing.

She made the connection. Careful. Precise despite everything.

The terminal hummed louder. Heat increased. Fans spinning faster.

Now she needed to get back to the keyboard. The bypass was set—but the system was still waiting for input. A comparison circuit needed something to compare, even if the answer was rigged.

Carefully. Very carefully. She started pulling herself up. Hand hold on the terminal frame. Other hand on the desk edge. Boots scraping against wall. The overalls catching again—she yanked them free—and then she was out. Sliding down to the floor. Dusty. Sweaty. Tank top sticking to her back.

She scrambled around to the front of the terminal.

Cursor still blinking. Still waiting. The lockout warning still glowing above it like a threat.

One shot. If her bypass didn't hold—if the wire had slipped, if she'd bridged the wrong rail—the next keystroke would trigger every alarm in the building.

Her fingers hovered over the keys.

What's the password, Kitt?

She typed the first thing that came to mind.

P. CLUNK.

E. CLUNK.

R. CLUNK.

I. CLUNK.

Eyes shut. Breath held. Fingers still on the keys because she couldn't make herself let go.

Her finger found ENTER. Pressed it.

CLUNK.

The machine worked. She could hear it—relays clicking behind the housing, tubes cycling, the comparison circuit running her four stupid letters against Torres's actual credentials and finding, thanks to one thin wire on one small rail, that they matched perfectly.

Three seconds. Four.

She opened her eyes.

Phosphor glowed:

AUTHENTICATION SUCCESSFUL
WELCOME TO MERIDIAN-4 NETWORK

"Ha!" The sound escaped before she could stop it.

Behind her, Peri's voice cut through. "Kitt. Shut up."

You have no idea.

Right. Stealth. She bit down on the victory, swallowing the rest of her excitement.

Time went elastic. The way it always did when the work took over.

She looked at the wire still attached inside—her bypass visible through the open rear panel. Temporary, but evidence. She'd disconnect it after. Carefully. Everything back to normal. Torres would never know someone had bypassed his password by literally jumping past the verification logic with a piece of wire and some uncomfortable climbing.

Then she turned back to the keyboard.

Okay. Okay. Now let's see what you've got.

Her fingers found the keys. Started typing. Each CLUNK victorious now.

Behind her, Peri shifted position by the door. Still watching. Still guarding.

⚙

The interface was text only. Typed commands in, text out. No graphical elements. Just amber text against brown-green phosphor, the glow painting her hands gold.

She positioned her notebook at the screen's edge. Pencil ready. Everything she pulled up would be captured—line by line, in her neat block printing. The way she'd done it a hundred times transcribing signal data. Only faster. Much faster.

Kitt navigated through menus. Each command typed carefully. Each keypress echoing too loud in the small room.

NETWORK_MAP

DISPLAY: AVAILABLE_NODES

The screen filled with text. Facility names. Communication hubs. Sprawling web of MERIDIAN terminals connecting Continental Authority installations across the region.

GATE 20 ADMINISTRATION

GATE 20 SECURITY [CURRENT]

GATE 20 OPERATIONS

HAMMISON DEPOT - RAIL

VALCROSS JUNCTION - RAIL

KYJORH TRANSFER STATION COORDINATION

CONTINENTAL GENETIC WELLNESS FACILITY - GRAPHTON

She found it immediately—the last entry. Continental Genetic Wellness Facility. *Why is a medical center on a Continental Authority network?*

Her fingers hovered over the keys. Curiosity pulling at her. Same instinct that made her take apart perfectly good radios just to see how they worked. Just to understand.

Her finger trembled over the ENTER key. *Don't do it.*

She typed anyway.

CONNECT: CGWF_GRAPHTON

The terminal hummed. Processing. Establishing connection across the network. Twenty seconds of waiting while she committed to a detour that had nothing to do with train schedules.

The screen changed:

CONNECTION ESTABLISHED

CONTINENTAL GENETIC WELLNESS FACILITY

GRAPHTON REGIONAL CENTER

AUTHORIZED ACCESS: LEVEL 4

DISPLAY: AVAILABLE_RECORDS

Text scrolled. File directories. Patient intake logs. Treatment schedules. Equipment inventories. Pharmaceutical records.

Kitt leaned forward. Scanning the data. Medical files. Patient records. Prescription databases. Everything you'd expect from a healthcare facility.

Just medical files. Not what we need.

But something nagged at her. A pattern her engineer's brain kept circling back to. Why would patient records need Continental Authority network access? Why would a wellness facility be listed alongside military coordination and rail transport? The architecture was wrong. The security level was wrong.

She started typing deeper. Navigating through directories.

PATIENT_RECORDS

ACCESS: INTAKE_LOG

ACCESS DENIED

INSUFFICIENT CLEARANCE

LEVEL 6 AUTHORIZATION REQUIRED

Level 6? For patient intake logs?

She tried another directory.

TREATMENT_SCHEDULES

ACCESS DENIED

INSUFFICIENT CLEARANCE

LEVEL 6 AUTHORIZATION REQUIRED

What kind of medical facility needs Level 6 clearance for basic—

She backed out. Returning to the network map. But the wrongness lingered. Like a circuit that didn't quite close.

She shook her head. Pushed it aside.

DISCONNECT

CONNECT: HAMMISON_DEPOT

The terminal processed. Tubes glowing brighter as it worked.

CONNECTION ESTABLISHED

HAMMISON DEPOT - RAIL OPERATIONS

AUTHORIZED ACCESS: LEVEL 4

Better. Much better.

RECORDS

TRANSPORT

RAIL_MANIFEST

SEARCH: NORTHERN_ROUTE

The screen went blank for a moment. Processing. The machine working through databases. Thirty seconds that felt like hours while she waited, muscles tense, ready to abort if—

Data appeared. Line by line. Filling the screen.

RAIL MANIFEST SCHEDULE – NORTHERN ROUTE

TRAIN 47 – SERVICE DATE 2191.116

ORIGIN: CGWF GRAPHTON (Z1)

DEPART: 0400

STOP 1: UAD BELTMOIRE DEPOT (Z1)

ARRIVE: 1442 / DEPART: 1530

STOP 2: KYJORH TRANSFER STATION (Z2)

ARRIVE: 0224 / DEPART: 0300

STOP 3: VALCROSS JUNCTION (Z2)

ARRIVE: 0627 / DEPART: 0902

STOP 4: NORTH SHORE TRANSFER STATION (Z2)

ARRIVE: 1134 / DEPART: 1142

DESTINATION: NORTH YORK PORT (Z2)

ARRIVE: 2100

Her pencil slid out of her fingers and clattered softly against the terminal casing.

2191.116.

Kitt settled onto the stool and tugged the back of her overalls free from where they'd ridden up. Hanging upside down for ten minutes had consequences.

Her pencil hovered over the page. Tapped once. Twice.

2191.116.

She squinted at the number. Frowning at it the way she frowned at components that didn't match their spec sheets.

"Who in their right mind counts days of the year," she murmured, tapping the pencil against her temple now. As if that might jog something loose.

Okay. Fine. Math.

"Thirty-one... thirty... twenty-eight—" She paused, scowling. "Wait, is it twenty-nine this year?" She was pretty sure it was twenty-nine. Maybe twenty-eight. "—thirty-one... thirty..."

She trailed off, losing count. She could calculate signal propagation delay across a three-hundred-mile relay chain in her head, but ask her what month day one-sixteen fell in and the whole system crashed.

Her gaze drifted to the terminal screen. Lower right corner, where system status lived on every MERIDIAN unit she'd ever worked with.

2191.115 · 19:47 Z2

Her pencil slid out of her fingers and clattered softly against the terminal casing.

Day 115.

The train departed on day 116. Tomorrow. Not next week. Not ten days from now. Tomorrow.

Her hand found the edge of the terminal. Gripped hard.

Departure from Graphton at 04:00. It was 19:47 now. That was—she counted—roughly eight hours. Eight hours until the train was moving. Eight hours to get out of this building, back to Gate 31, wake the crew, brief them, load equipment, and—

Her gaze tracked back to the manifest. **CGWF GRAPHTON (Z1).**

Z1.

She looked at the terminal clock. Z2.

"No."

Graphton was eastern zone. She was central. 0400 in Z1 was 0300 in Z2. She hadn't gained an hour. She'd lost one.

"Oh, that's—" She pressed her knuckles into the desk. "That is worse. That is objectively worse."

Seven hours. Seven hours and thirteen minutes, if she was being precise, and she was always precise when precision made her miserable.

What is the point of time zones. Not a question. A grievance. "This is a strong case for everyone to just run off one clock and adjust their own damn wake-up times."

The numbers refused to rearrange themselves.

Seven hours until the train left Graphton. But the train didn't need to be in Graphton to be a problem. Once it was rolling it was rolling—eating track at whatever speed a loaded freight managed, heading north through Beltmoire, through Kyjorh, through every stop on that schedule whether her crew was ready or not.

She looked at the stops. Dwell times. Beltmoire: forty-eight minutes. Kyjorh: thirty-six minutes. Valcross: two hours thirty-five minutes—crew change, guard rotation. North Shore: eight minutes. Fuel and water.

Valcross was the window. Had to be. Longest stop, most personnel movement, most chaos. If they were going to intercept, that was where.

Kyjorh was closer—home ground, middle of the night, thirty-six minutes of dwell time. Tempting. But thirty-six minutes wasn't enough to offload two boxcars of generator equipment, not without a crane they didn't have and a staging area they couldn't hide. And hitting a Continental Authority train within spitting distance of Belfast Mills was the fastest way to bring the Authority straight to their door.

No. Valcross. Distance was safety.

0627 arrival at Valcross. Z2—her time, at least. That much she didn't have to convert.

From now to then. She counted backward. Roughly eleven hours. Minus the drive back to Gate 31. Minus briefing. Minus loading. Minus the drive to the intercept position. Minus setup.

"This whole calendar and clock shit is stupid," she muttered. But her pencil was already moving again. Copying the stop times. The dwell windows. Every number on that screen transferred to paper in her neat block printing because paper didn't crash, paper didn't need a password, and paper didn't care what time zone you were in.

Not the week they'd expected. Not the ten days Cipher's window had suggested. Hours.

Who. Is. Planning. This. Job?

I am.

The responsibility found her. Not panic. Closer to gravity.

We can do this. We have to do this.

She forced her hand to move. Pencil finding paper. Muscle memory taking over while her mind raced through contingencies.

Come on, show me what you're carrying.

More data scrolled:

CARGO INVENTORY:

CAR 1: GENERAL FREIGHT

-CONSTRUCTION MATERIALS (BULK)

-INDUSTRIAL SUPPLIES (MANIFESTED)

CAR 2: MEDICAL TRANSPORT

-EQUIPMENT (VARIOUS)

-PHARMACEUTICALS (CONTROLLED)

-[RESTRICTED] MT-7719 CLEARANCE REQUIRED

CAR 3: GENERATOR COMPONENTS

-TURBINE HOUSING (QTY 2)

-ROTOR ASSEMBLY (QTY 4)

-CONTROL SYSTEMS (QTY 1)

-WIRING HARNESS (QTY 6)

-VOLTAGE REGULATORS (QTY 8)

CAR 4: ELECTRICAL EQUIPMENT

-TRANSFORMER UNITS (QTY 3)

-SWITCH ASSEMBLIES (QTY 12)

-INSULATION MATERIALS (BULK)

Her hand went still. Pencil hovering over the page.

Turbine housing. Rotor assemblies. Control systems.

Everything we need for the dam.

The whole power generation system sitting in two boxcars. If they could get Car 3 and Car 4, Belfast Mills wouldn't just survive—it would thrive. Real power. Consistent power. Emma's question answered in steel and copper: *If you had the right parts, could you fix it?*

Four turbine rotor assemblies—if they were six-pole synchronous with those voltage regulator ratings... if the turbine housing fit the existing mounting points at Kyjorh... if the control systems could integrate with the dam's forty-year-old infrastructure...

They could actually do this.

Hours. Not even a full day.

Focus. Keep recording. Get everything. Panic later.

Car 2 nagged at her. MT-7719. Same Level 6 clearance as the Graphton patient logs.

She tried anyway.

DISPLAY: CAR_2_MANIFEST_DETAIL

The screen flickered:

CARGO CAR 2: MEDICAL TRANSPORT

EQUIPMENT (VARIOUS) - STANDARD MANIFEST

PHARMACEUTICALS (CONTROLLED) - STANDARD MANIFEST

[RESTRICTED CARGO]

HANDLING CODE: MT-7719

CLEARANCE: LEVEL 6 REQUIRED

OVERRIDE: CONTINENTAL COUNCIL AUTHORIZATION ONLY

There it was again. Same clearance level. Same wall. A medical facility with military-grade network access, and a medical cargo with Continental Council override. Two data points on the same circuit—and circuits went somewhere.

Not her problem. Not tonight.

She typed rapidly now. Each CLUNK urgent. Purposeful. Drilling into Valcross—the one stop that mattered.

ROUTE DETAIL: VALCROSS JUNCTION (Z2)
ARRIVE: 0627 / DEPART: 0902
CREW CHANGE (15 MINUTES)
GUARD ROTATION: STANDARD
CARGO ACCESS: AUTHORIZED PERSONNEL ONLY
SECURITY DETAIL: 6 ASSIGNED / 3 SHIFTS / 2 ACTIVE
COMMS: ENCRYPTED – CHANNEL 7
COMMANDER: K. PRAEMEN

Two active guards during a crew change. Fifteen minutes of handoff where attention split between incoming and outgoing personnel. Security focused on the cargo, not the perimeter. Encrypted comms meant coordination would be tight—but tight coordination also meant predictable patterns.

She logged it all. Times, durations, personnel data. Pencil moving in tight efficient lines. Then weather forecasts for 117. Sunrise times. Visibility conditions.

The complete picture building line by line on twelve pages of notebook paper. Thorough intelligence. The difference between clean and disaster.

Enough. Time to clean up.

She moved back to the rear of the terminal. Her bypass wire still visible inside the open panel.

Back up. Into the gap. Wedging herself between terminal and wall again. The route known now at least. Still uncomfortable. Still hot. But faster.

She reached in. Found the wire. Disconnected it carefully from the power rail first, then from the authorization gate. The circuit returned to its normal state. Torres could log in tomorrow and never know someone had been here.

Wire back in her tool bag. Panel lifted into place. One screw. Two. Three. Four. Everything buttoned up.

She slid back down. Grabbed her jacket. Still sweaty, still dusty, but the physical evidence was gone.

Kitt allowed herself one breath. Badge in her pocket, notebook in her bag, bypass removed. Nothing left behind but heat dissipating from the housing.

Now the session traces. Analog systems kept their own kind of memory—relay positions holding the last command path, session counters ticking up with each login, magnetic impressions on the core showing which network nodes had been accessed. Not logs you could delete with a keystroke. Physical states you had to manually reset.

She reached for the keys. First the session counter—every MERIDIAN unit had one, a mechanical odometer behind the front panel that tracked authentications. She'd need to roll it back one. Then cycle the relay bank to clear the command path, degauss the routing matrix so the core wouldn't hold a magnetic ghost of every node she'd touched. Fifteen minutes of careful work. Maybe twenty.

Then—

Voices in the hallway. Close.

Too close.

"—check the records room, maybe the badge fell somewhere—"

Kitt's hands froze. Session counter still showing one extra login. Relay bank still holding the path from Hammison Gate 20, to Graphton, to Valcross. Every node she'd accessed tonight mapped in magnetic residue across the core like footprints in snow.

"Kitt." Peri's whisper sharp. Urgent. "Now."

No time. No time for any of it.

She killed the active session. That much she could do—one command, one CLUNK, screen returning to the login prompt. The counter, the relays, the magnetic traces—those would stay. Evidence she couldn't erase. Torres might not notice. Maintenance might not check. But the footprints were there for anyone who knew where to look.

Her hand found Torres's badge in her pocket. She started toward the door—

Footsteps were right outside. Boots on tile. Crackle of a radio.

Peri's hand shot out. Grabbed Kitt's arm. Pulled her toward the far corner. Behind the file cabinets. Barely enough space for both of them. Metal cold against Kitt's back. Smell of old paper and dust.

They pressed flat. Notebook crushed against her chest. Twelve pages of handwritten notes. Everything they'd come for.

Everything except the tool bag sitting next to the chair.

Her breathing. Her heartbeat. Both too loud.

The handle rattled.

The door opened.

29 | Peri

2191.115 · 19:48
Gate 20

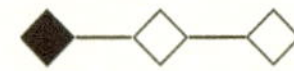

Guard was three feet away. Two.

Peri pressed flat against the wall behind the file cabinets, Kitt crushed against her, both of them breathing through their mouths. The guard's flashlight swept the room—beam sliding across the desk, the terminal's glow, the chair where Kitt's tool bag sat in plain view.

Beam stopped. Tracked back toward the chair.

Held.

His radio crackled. "Henderson, anything?"

He keyed his radio. Eyes still on the chair. "Negative. Records room is clear."

"Copy. Check the sublevel maintenance areas."

"En route."

He turned. Walked back to the door. Stepped into the hallway.

Door closed.

Kitt exhaled slowly. Silently. Her whole body shaking with adrenaline she couldn't release. When she swallowed, her face twisted—jaw tight, eyes squeezed shut.

Peri waited. Ten seconds. Twenty. Listening for footsteps, for voices, for any sign the guard was coming back.

Nothing.

She shoved Kitt out from behind the cabinets. Not hard. Just enough to unstick her. Kitt stumbled forward a step, caught herself.

"Gods, you sweat when you're nervous." Peri wiped Kitt's dampness off her palm and onto her jacket. "I'm surprised we didn't get nicked by your smell."

Kitt lifted an arm. Sniffed. "I don't stink."

"Reminds me of rotten cabbage."

"Really?"

"Kitt. Focus." Peri nodded toward the chair. "Don't forget the bag."

Kitt grabbed the tool bag. Slung it over her shoulder, hands still shaking. Her mouth opened—words already forming, the terminal, the data, the whole night trying to spill out.

"The session counter," she whispered. "The relay bank. I didn't have time to reset them."

"Will it matter tonight?"

"No. But if anyone checks the routing matrix—"

"Later. Exit first." Peri moved to the door. Cracked it open.

Empty hallway. Emergency lighting casting everything in sickly green. Distant voices fading toward the sublevel.

She gestured. *Let's go.*

Kitt stepped close behind her.

Peri held up a hand. "Don't stand too close."

The shaking hadn't stopped. Twelve pages of intelligence in Kitt's bag and all of it useless if they didn't make it out of the building.

Peri looked at her. Really looked. The joke falling away.

"Hey." Quieter now. "We're almost done. You did the impossible—I'll take care of the possible. I'll get us out."

She caught Kitt's forearm. Felt the tremors under her grip. Squeezed once.

Kitt held her gaze. Nodded. Peri felt her start to relax.

Peri turned back to the door. Cracked it open. Checked the hall.

"Now."

And they were through.

⊙

They moved quickly. Not running—just employees finishing a job, eager to clock out. Nothing suspicious.

Peri felt the building around her. Where the air moved cooler—exits. Where the corridor widened—junctions. Where the light changed—stairwells. The route back unspooling under her feet the way a trail did on the return leg of a run.

Behind her, Kitt's footsteps hit concrete with too much force.

"Lighter," Peri whispered.

"I'm trying." Kitt's voice tight.

She was trying. Peri could hear the hesitation, the way Kitt was second-guessing every step. Thinking instead of moving.

But the stairwell was ahead and there wasn't time for a lesson.

They reached the door. Peri pressed one ear against cold metal. Listened.

Nothing. Just the distant hum of ventilation.

She cracked it open. Slipped inside. Started descending.

Kitt followed, her breathing harsh in the enclosed space. Gripping the railing so tight Peri heard the squeak of skin against painted metal.

Ground floor. Peri cracked the door.

Main corridor. Busy. Evening shift change. Workers moving between offices with coffee cups and tired conversations. Too many faces that might remember faces that didn't belong.

"Not this way."

She led them further down. Another level. Concrete walls unpainted, rough. Sublevel—mechanical systems, maintenance spaces, the building's working guts.

Warmer down here. The air tasted like machine grease and concrete dust. Something overhead groaned—pipes settling, ductwork vibrating against its mounts. Harsh light every twenty feet, shadow between.

And at the far end: a loading dock access door, partially open, letting in the smell of night air.

"There." Peri pointed. "That's our exit."

Her shoulders loosened. Thirty feet of empty concrete between them and out. Clean operation. They were going to walk out without a—

Metal on metal. Stairwell door opening with a sharp clang. Footsteps descending fast. Voices echoing through concrete:

"—Ramon's badge pinged the records terminal twenty minutes ago. That's not coincidence—"

"—check all maintenance corridors, they might still be in the building—"

Her fingers found Kitt's arm. "Run."

They sprinted.

Loading dock door ahead, the rectangle of dark growing larger—

Halfway across the sublevel, she saw it: a drainage channel cutting across the floor. Wide. Deep enough that the bottom disappeared into shadow. Access grate gone.

Behind them, voices spilling into the sublevel.

Peri didn't slow. Three running steps—one-two-three—feeling the rhythm in her legs. She launched.

Airborne. Channel dropped away beneath her. Boots hit concrete. She landed in a rolling crouch on the far side, momentum absorbed through her legs. Came up turning back—

Kitt was still running toward the edge.

Tool bag bouncing against her side. Eyes wide.

"Jump!" Peri called.

Kitt jumped—wrong angle, not enough height, all panic and no technique. She hit the far edge chest-first. Air driven from her lungs in one brutal exhalation. Hands scrabbling at concrete, fingers finding nothing, boots kicking against the channel wall.

Her fingers started slipping.

Kitt.

She lunged. Grabbed Kitt's wrists. Locked her grip.

Kitt's full weight hit her arms like a sledgehammer. Peri's boots scrabbled for purchase on the concrete edge. Shoulders screaming. The angle wrong—all of Kitt's weight pulling down while Peri fought gravity and momentum trying to take them both over.

"Stop kicking!" Peri braced her feet. "You're making it worse!"

Kitt's legs thrashed—panic overriding sense, the tool bag swinging heavy with stolen data, its weight working against them.

Peri hauled. Arms burning. Kitt scrambled—got one elbow over the edge, concrete scraping skin, then the other.

Peri slid her grip to the collar of Kitt's overalls and heaved with everything she had left.

Kitt tumbled over the lip. Collapsed on the concrete. Both of them gasping. Harsh, ragged pulls of air that hurt. Blood on Kitt's elbows where concrete had scraped through fabric.

Her eyes caught it immediately—Torres's badge, corner poking out of Kitt's overalls pocket. White plastic against dark fabric. Might as well be a flashing sign.

She snatched it.

"Hey—"

Peri flicked her wrist. Badge spun through the air, caught the work light for a moment, then disappeared into the drainage channel. Distant splash.

"Bye bye, Torres." Peri wiped her hand on her pants. "Thanks for the assist."

"Wait—" Kitt pushed up on her elbows, staring at the channel. "You can't just leave that there. It's evidence."

"Evidence that Torres dropped his badge in a construction trench. Careless guy. Happens all the time."

"But—"

"You want to climb back down there and fish it out?"

Kitt's mouth opened. Closed.

"Didn't think so. Up. Let's go."

"I hate you," Kitt gasped.

"You love me. Come on." Peri grabbed her arm, pulling her up.

⚙

Voices behind them—closer now. Flashlight beams cutting through the shadows.

"There! Movement near the loading dock!"

Peri pulled Kitt to her feet. Supply crates ahead, thirty feet from the loading dock door.

She dove. Pulled Kitt with her. They pressed flat against the concrete floor, dust and cardboard filling her nose, cheek against grit.

Two guards burst into the sublevel. Radios crackling. Flashlights sweeping arcs through the shadows, close enough that Peri saw dust motes dancing in the beams.

"Negative contact. Must've gone up the access ramp."

"Copy. Exterior team, check the loading dock area."

Guards moved toward the ramp on the far side—away from them.

Peri counted to ten.

Then lifted her chin toward the door. *Move.*

They slipped out from behind the crates. Through the loading dock door—hinges blessedly silent—and up the exterior ramp. Every second expecting a shout behind them, a hand on her shoulder, the command to stop.

They crested the ramp. Night air hit. Cold and sharp. Chain-link fence twenty feet ahead, gate hanging open on broken hinges. Beyond it, the maze of industrial buildings and narrow alleys that made up the Yards.

Home territory.

Peri grabbed Kitt's hand and pulled her toward the fence, toward the shadows, toward out.

They disappeared into the Yards.

Truck was a quarter mile east. Dad was waiting.

She pulled the stopwatch free. Clicked it. *Forty-nine minutes.*

Perfect.

She could already see it—Dad's face when she told him.

⊙

Fifty yards ahead, leaning against the chain-link fence: Kataero and Connor. Waiting. Arms crossed, weight balanced—but something in the set of her father's shoulders. The tightness in his jaw even from this distance.

The triumph that had been building in her chest began to curdle.

They reached the fence. Kataero's eyes went immediately to Kitt, scanning her for injuries. Saw the scraped elbows. The dust covering her. The way she was still breathing too hard.

Then his gaze shifted to Peri.

Something colder than anger. The wall coming down between them.

"You alright?" His voice level. Calm. The tone that meant whatever he was actually feeling was locked down tight.

"I'm fine," Kitt said.

Kataero nodded, his attention lingering on Kitt a moment longer. Then back to both of them. "Any problems?"

"Nothing we couldn't handle," Peri said. She watched his face. Waiting for something.

His expression didn't change.

"Did you get the data?"

Kitt pulled the notebook from her bag. "Everything. Train schedule, cargo manifest, guard rotations, security protocols."

He took the notebook. Turned it over once before pressing his thumb into the cover. "Good work."

He looked at Kitt when he said it. Not at Peri.

"Let's go."

He started walking, his hand briefly touching Kitt's shoulder before he moved ahead. Connor fell into step beside Kitt, asking her something quiet about the terminal access.

Peri followed a few steps behind.

Kataero stayed close on Kitt's right. Connor on her left. The two men bracketing her, the angle of their bodies closing around her.

A triangle. A shield.

With Peri on the outside.

Kitt almost fell. Of course he's checking on her.

She kept walking. Rain started to spit—light, barely more than mist.

Peri caught up, inserting herself back into the group. Refusing to stay outside.

"So that drainage channel," she said. Light. Conversational. "I cleared it pretty smoothly. Good form. Real athletic."

Nothing from Kataero. Not even a glance.

Kitt's head snapped toward her. "Are you seriously—"

"Just saying. Some of us are natural athletes."

"Some of us didn't pickpocket a supervisor and force us to run through maintenance tunnels!" Kitt's voice rising, color flooding her cheeks.

"Some of us think fast under pressure."

"Some of us don't create the pressure in the first place!"

Connor coughed—suspiciously like a poorly disguised laugh.

Kataero glanced back. Just there, at the corner of his mouth, the tiniest twitch. "You both did good. Now stop bickering before you draw attention."

They walked in silence for half a block. Rain on their shoulders.

Then Kitt, her voice quiet: "You did pull me up pretty fast."

"You're welcome."

"I didn't say thank you."

"You should."

"I'm not going to."

Kitt's hand found Peri's. Squeezed once—quick, there and gone.

Peri squeezed back. Kitt's fingers cold against hers, trembling slightly.

They kept walking.

30 | Peri

2191.115 · 20:27

T-38 E to Gate 31 | Hammison Locks

Hands on the wheel, eyes fixed on the road, the engine's rumble a low drone under everything else. Six hours back to Gate 31. The job was over and her body knew it—the sharpness bleeding out of her, the high draining the way heat left metal after the forge went dark.

Behind them, Connor's wagon followed at a fixed distance. Insurance. Backup. An escape route they hadn't needed.

They'd gotten out clean.

Kitt sat twisted sideways in the passenger seat, unable to face forward. The adrenaline came late for her—no crash, just ignition—and now it hummed through her, restless. Her hands moved as she talked, cutting the air, replaying every second like it might change if she said it enough times.

"—and I couldn't believe it worked!" she was saying, her voice pitched high with excitement. "I mean, Dad, I *knew* the theory was sound—magnetic core memory has to store authentication credentials somewhere accessible—but actually finding the credential circuit? In that wiring mess? While upside down?"

She laughed—high, unrestrained, pure victory.

In the back seat, Kataero made a low sound of acknowledgment. Not quite agreement. Just listening. That tone he used when Kitt was explaining something technical and he wanted every detail.

"Upside down?" he asked. Calm. Interested.

"Behind the terminal!" Kitt twisted further in her seat, practically kneeling now to face him fully. "Eighteen inches deep, Dad. Heat everywhere. Dust coating everything. Fans blowing straight in my face. And the terminal housing—" She gestured at her hip. "—gave me the worst wedgie of my life getting in there. Knickers nearly cut me in two. Gods, I still hurt from that."

Behind Peri, fabric shifted. Kataero leaning forward slightly.

"Sounds uncomfortable," he said.

"It was *awful*. But worth it. Because once I got the wire positioned—just this tiny bypass, forcing the authentication gate high—the whole system opened up. Terminal thought Torres had logged in legitimately when really I'd just jumped past the verification logic entirely."

Kitt laughed again, bright and breathless. "And Peri—Dad, you should have seen her. She was AMAZING."

Peri's hands tightened on the wheel.

The word landed wrong. *Amazing.* Kitt was telling Kataero she'd been amazing while he sat in the back seat and his silence pressed against Peri's shoulders like a hand.

"She just walked right up to this Torres guy," Kitt continued, "like she belonged there. Full confidence. Asked about the coffee. Did the bump—you know the bump?—and his badge was *gone*. He didn't even notice. Just kept talking about how terrible the coffee was."

"Oh, she did, did she?" Kataero said. Mild as anything. No edge. No anger. Just observation.

Kitt missed it entirely.

In the rearview mirror, Peri caught a glimpse of Kataero's face. Eyes steady. Taking it in.

The road pulled her eyes forward again.

"It was *smooth*, Dad. Like, I've watched Peri work before, but this was different. This was her being completely in her element. No hesitation. No doubt. Just reading him, adjusting on the fly, making it look natural."

"And then you went with her," Kataero said. Quiet. Following the thread.

"Well, yeah." Kitt pulled out her notebook, already flipping to her terminal notes. "She needed someone who could actually use the terminal once we got access. And I'm glad I did, because the data we pulled—Dad, wait till you see it."

"I'm waiting," he said. Patient. The way he always sounded when he wanted someone to keep talking.

Peri's teeth set. Her hand moved to her pocket. Found the stopwatch. Chrome warm against her palm.

It didn't help.

"Tell me about getting out," he said.

Kitt's energy surged again. "Oh gods, that was *terrifying*. I copied down everything—train manifests, cargo lists, security schedules—all by hand while guards were searching the building. And then we heard them coming and we had to run."

She gestured animatedly. "Made it almost to the loading dock and there was this drainage channel. Eight feet wide. Peri cleared it clean—just launched herself across like it was nothing."

She went quieter. "I didn't make it. Hit the far edge chest-first. Started slipping. Tool bag pulling me down."

In the rearview, Kataero's posture shifted. Tension coiling underneath the calm.

"Peri grabbed me," Kitt said. "Just shot her hand out and hauled me up. Arms burning, shoulders screaming, but she got me over."

She laughed, already moving past it.

Peri kept her eyes on the road. Her grip on the wheel white-knuckled. Her hands still remembered what her sister had already let go of.

She made her fingers loosen. Made her eyes fix on the center line.

"And then we hid behind these supply crates," Kitt was saying, "and the guards came right past us—close enough I could see the dust in their flashlight beams—but they moved away, and we just slipped out. Through the loading dock, up the ramp, through the fence."

She grinned, turning that grin toward Peri. "We made it out clean. Didn't we?"

"Yeah," Peri said. Rougher than intended. "Clean."

⊙

"Dad." Kitt's voice changed. "The schedule."

"What about it?"

"The train." Kitt's pencil stopped moving. "It's not next week. It's not even days out."

Silence from the back seat.

"The train leaves Graphton at 0400," Kitt said. "That's Z1 time. Which is 0300 our time." She paused. The math she'd already done at the terminal, done again now in the hope it had changed. "That's in about seven hours."

Peri sat up straighter. Her hands adjusted on the wheel.

"Seven hours," Kataero repeated. Flat. Processing.

"By the time we get back to Gate 31 it'll already be rolling." Kitt's voice had gone thin. "But it doesn't reach Valcross Junction until 0627. That's where the longest stop is—crew change, guard rotation, two hours and thirty-five minutes on the ground."

Seven hours. The number sat in Peri's chest the way eighty-six minutes used to.

She kept driving.

Kitt talked through the rest. Four cargo cars. Car 1 general freight. Car 2 medical transport with a restricted cargo designation—MT-7719, Level 6 clearance. Car 3: turbine housing, rotor assemblies, control systems, wiring harnesses, voltage regulators. Car 4: transformers, switch assemblies, insulation.

"Cars 3 and 4," Kataero said. "Everything for the dam."

"Everything for the dam," Kitt confirmed. "If those rotor assemblies are six-pole synchronous and the housing fits the Kyjorh mounting points—Dad, we could have real power. Consistent power."

Kataero was quiet for a long moment. Just the engine and the road and the dark.

⊙

The fuel stop came at the halfway mark. A depot on the edge of a dark crossroads—pumps standing like sentinels, a single light buzzing above them.

Peri killed the engine. Her hands stayed on the wheel for a moment before she made herself let go.

Connor pulled alongside. Topped off his wagon without a word.

Kataero crossed to Connor's window. Spoke low—the train, the timeline, the stops, the cargo. Connor listened. Asked nothing. Nodded once.

Kataero walked back to the driver's side.

"You're tired," he said. "I got it from here."

Peri moved to the back seat without argument. Shoulder against the door, legs stretched out. Watching from the dark.

Kitt hadn't moved. Still passenger side, still sideways, notebook still open. She barely registered the swap.

Kataero adjusted the seat. Adjusted the mirrors. Hands at ten and two. Engine rumbling back to life.

He drove the way he did everything—steady, unhurried, like the truck was something worth respecting.

⊙

"Give me the notebook."

Kitt looked at him. "You're driving."

"Give me the notebook, Kitt."

She handed it over. Kataero reached up and clicked the dome light on. Propped the notebook against the steering wheel, one hand holding it open, eyes dropping to Kitt's neat block printing.

The truck drifted. Not much. Just enough.

Kitt's hand caught the wheel. Held it steady.

Kataero didn't look up. Just kept reading. His other hand turned a page.

Kitt adjusted her grip. Both hands now, leaning across from the passenger seat, keeping the truck centered while her father studied her work. She glanced at the road. Glanced at him. Back to the road.

"Dad. You're not even looking."

"I'm looking." He turned another page. "You've got the wheel."

Kitt huffed. But she held it. Steady. Her arms stretched across the cab, her body twisted at an angle that couldn't have been comfortable, steering from the wrong seat while Kataero absorbed twelve pages of intelligence at highway speed.

From the back seat, Peri watched them. Father and daughter. One reading, one steering. Neither willing to stop what they were doing to let the other finish.

"Six guards," he murmured. "Three shifts, two active."

"At any time," Kitt said, eyes on the road. "Hourly patrols. Encrypted comms, Channel 7. Commander named Praemen."

Kataero turned a page. Read. Turned another.

The truck drifted again. Kitt corrected. Again.

"The Valcross stop," he said. "Two hours thirty-five minutes. Crew change. Guard rotation."

"That's the window. Has to be. Longest stop, most movement, most—"

"Can't do it."

Kitt blinked. Her grip on the wheel loosened for a half-second before she caught it.

"What?"

"Can't hit a stopped train at Valcross." Kataero's voice had shifted. Not the calm father listening to his daughter. The Black Marshal working a problem. "Too many guards concentrated in one place. Crew change means more personnel on the platform, not fewer. Extra eyes. Station lighting. And the stop time doesn't help us—we can't offload two boxcars worth of generator equipment with six guards and a station crew watching."

Kitt's mouth opened. Closed. Her hands stayed on the wheel.

"What about Beltmoire? Forty-eight minute stop—"

"Same problem. Shorter window, same exposure. Any scheduled stop means the train is expected. Personnel are alert. Infrastructure is lit."

"Kyjorh?"

"Thirty-six minutes. Middle of the night, better cover, but it's a transfer station. Coordination hub. Too much traffic."

Kitt stared through the windshield. Steering. Watching her father close doors on every number she'd pulled from that terminal.

"North Shore is eight minutes," she said. Quieter now. "That's nothing."

"That's nothing," Kataero agreed.

He closed the notebook. Set it on the dash. Both hands returned to the wheel—his fingers settling over Kitt's. She let go. Pulled her hands back to her lap.

Silence. Engine droning. Connor's headlights steady in the mirrors.

"So what do we do?" Kitt asked. Small. Not defeated—searching.

He clicked off the dome light and the dark rushed back in.

"We don't hit the train when it's stopped," he said. "We slow it down enough to board it while it's moving."

The conversation had tilted. From intelligence report to operational planning. From what Kitt had found to what Kataero would do with it.

"Is that even possible?" Kitt asked.

"With the right terrain. The right approach." Kataero's eyes stayed on the road. "A loaded freight climbing a grade—heavy consist, full cars—she's not making speed. Maybe eight, nine miles an hour on a steep enough pull. Walking pace."

"Walking pace," Kitt repeated. Testing the idea.

"It's been done. Rail workers used to board moving trains to set brakes on grades before they had air systems. You just need to know where the train slows down and have a way to reach it."

Kitt was quiet. Processing. Peri could see her sister's engineer brain turning it over—not the tactical question of how to board, but the physics. Mass, momentum, friction, grade percentage. The math of a heavy train fighting gravity.

"The route goes through mountains north of Valcross," Kitt said slowly. "I saw elevation changes in the track layout. If there's a grade steep enough..."

"Get some rest." Kataero's voice gentled. Back to the father. "We've got a long day ahead."

"But—"

"You did the hard part. Let me work the rest for a while."

Kitt looked at him. At the notebook on the dash. At the road unwinding ahead.

"We came this far," she said. Not a question. Needing to hear it confirmed.

"We did." Kataero reached over. His hand settled on the top of her head for a moment. Brief. Warm. "We'll make this happen."

Kitt exhaled. Something in her loosening—the last of the adrenaline, the last of the panic, the weight of seven hours she'd been carrying since the terminal clock stole her breath.

She turned forward in her seat. Pulled her jacket tighter. Her head tipped against the window the way it always did when sleep was winning.

Then she was out. Breath fogging the glass in slow, even clouds. Notebook still on the dash. Pencil still tucked behind her ear.

Peri watched her sister sleep. The dome light off now, just dashboard glow and the shapes of the road.

⊙

Kataero waited. Five minutes. Ten. Until Kitt's breathing had gone deep and steady and her hand had fallen open in her lap.

Then he reached for the radio mounted on the dash. Keyed it. Low volume—just enough to carry.

"Wolfhound, Panther."

Pause. Static. Then Connor's voice, clear and unhurried.

"Go ahead, Panther."

"What's the name of that train loop outside Valcross Junction? The one that climbs into the mountains."

Shorter pause this time. Connor already thinking.

"Chapi Grade. Why—what are you thinking?"

"Looking for a spot to jump on that train."

The radio was quiet for a long moment. Just the hiss of the carrier signal. Connor processing.

Then: "I have an idea." Silence. "Peri's going to love it."

Kataero looked at the rearview mirror. Found Peri's eyes in the dark.

She held his gaze. Didn't blink.

The radio clicked off. The truck rolled on through the dark. Connor's headlights steady behind them.

⊙

Gate 31 came into view just before 0300.

The warehouse sat dark against the canal, a solid shape blocking out stars. No lights in the windows. Loading dock doors closed.

Kataero slowed the truck. Pulled around to the side entrance. Killed the engine.

Silence rushed in. The tick of cooling metal. The distant sound of water moving through the canal locks. Kitt's breathing, soft and even against the passenger window.

Behind them, Connor's wagon rolled to a stop. His headlights clicked off.

Kataero opened his door quietly. Boots on gravel, barely a sound.

"Full brief at 0800," he said through the open door. "Get what sleep you can."

Then he was moving toward the warehouse, a shadow among shadows.

Movement beside her. Kitt stirring, blinking against the dark.

"We're home?" Her voice thick with sleep.

"Yeah." Peri climbed out. Her legs stiff from the back seat, hands empty without the wheel. "We're home."

They grabbed their bags. Moved through the side door into the warehouse's cold quiet.

Connor was already inside, his gear bag over one shoulder. He caught Peri's eye as he passed. One nod. Brief.

Kitt shuffled toward the stairs, still half-asleep, her notebook clutched against her chest like a child holding a stuffed animal. She paused at the bottom step.

"Peri?"

"Yeah?"

"We make a good team."

Then she was climbing, her footsteps fading into the upper dark.

Peri stood alone in the warehouse. Everything waiting for tomorrow. For the brief. For whatever Kataero was already building in his head.

She climbed the stairs. Found her room. Closed the door.

Jacket on the chair. Boots by the door. Stopwatch on the nightstand—chrome catching the faint light from the window.

She lay on the bed. Staring at the ceiling.

Kitt's voice, somewhere in the hours behind them: *We make a good team.*

The words lodged somewhere warm despite everything—despite the silence and the rearview mirror and the white-knuckle memory that still lived in her hands.

We do.

She closed her eyes.

31 | Wynne

2191.117 · 10:10
Hamilton Public Library

The archive room stretched deeper than Wynne had expected—rows of massive metal shelving units mounted on floor tracks, each labeled with decades and subjects in faded paint. The air down here older than the main library above. Preservation chemicals and aging paper. Cool enough that her throat tightened when she breathed.

Cool concrete pressed through her soles. Archive cold—the kind that settled into the bones of a room and didn't leave.

Jaden moved to the first shelving unit, his cane tapping softly against concrete. He read the label, lips moving slightly. Moved to the next. Then the next.

"2165 to 2168. Municipal Planning." He kept walking. "2168 to 2171. Trade Regulations." Another step. "2171 to 2173. Economic Development."

His cane stopped tapping. He looked up at the next unit's label.

"2173 to 2174. Council Proceedings."

He grabbed the three-pronged wheel handle mounted on the unit's side. Started cranking. Metal ground against metal—deep and grating, the entire shelving unit rolling on its floor track with surprising smoothness despite the noise. The gap widened between units.

CLUNK.

Unit locked into position.

"Remarkable engineering," Jaden said, slightly breathless from the effort. He traced the wheel's spokes with his fingertips. The weight of however long he'd been searching fell away from his face. Just a man delighted by clever design.

"You're enjoying this," she said.

"The archives? Absolutely." He flashed her a small smile. "The quiet down here is its own kind of charm."

He stepped into the confined passage. She followed.

Shelves rising floor to ceiling like canyon walls bound in dark cloth. Volumes packed tight. Decades of council proceedings.

"2173," Jaden murmured, tracing along spines. "January through March. April through June." He kept moving. "July through September. October through December. 2174. There."

He pulled down a volume—heavy enough that his breathing shifted as he took its weight.

"You're always keeping track of the room," he said conversationally, opening the book with careful hands. "Even now, eyes flicking to the entrance."

"Habit."

"Useful one." He turned a page. "Do you ever let that go?"

"No."

He turned another page, softer now. Smiled gently—not pressing. Just observing.

⊙

Something fell.

A small card, cream-colored, fluttering between them.

Wynne bent, picked it up. Cardstock thick and expensive, embossed lettering catching the light.

Victoria Colwell

Executive Aide to Chief Minister Pence Garda

Continental Authority — Hamilton District

She handed it to Jaden.

He stared at the card, spinning it slowly between his fingers. "Victoria Colwell." Recognition colored his words. "She was my grandfather's aide. I remember her from when I was young. She used to bring me sweets when she visited the house." He turned the card over. Blank. "Why would her card be here? In council records from three years after his removal?"

He opened the volume fully, pages crackling softly.

Wynne watched his face. Saw the exact moment something shifted—breath catching, hand moving to cover his mouth. When he looked up, his eyes were wet.

"He voted against it." Thick. Roughened. "Environmental Protection Adjustment Act. My grandfather argued it was unconscionable. Called it corporate exploitation masquerading as environmental protection." His finger traced along the text. "He fought this. Voted no. Every single session. Tried to build opposition. Even after—"

He looked up, tears bright and unashamed. "This is it. Proof. Evidence the official record was altered. The public documents all say he supported this act. Used it as justification for his removal—claimed he'd lost perspective, become too industry-friendly. But here—" His voice cracked. "Here's the truth."

"Jaden." She kept her voice quiet. "You found it."

"I found it." Wonder and grief tangled together. "They destroyed him for this. Everything he stood for. Rewrote the record to make him the villain, and he—"

⚙

She felt it before she heard it.

Not sound—the absence of sound. A shift in the quality of the silence behind them, the archive's dead air disturbed by someone who knew how to move quietly but couldn't prevent the space from registering the displacement. The training caught it the way training always did—not thought, not decision. The body knowing before the mind could name what it knew.

Her spine straightened. Breathing dropped into combat rhythm. Staff sliding through her grip to fighting position.

She moved between the darkness and Jaden in one fluid step.

Jaden looked up from the book. "Wynne, what—"

"Quiet."

Movement in the shadows beyond their aisle. Someone approaching.

Paul stepped into the fluorescent light.

And Wynne's stomach dropped.

Same uniform. Same face. Same sandy hair. But the man standing at the mouth of their aisle was not the man who'd touched her arm in the library this morning. Not the man who'd told stories about Sophie's clock gears, who'd laughed at Jaden's footnotes, whose face had brightened when she called him Paulie.

That man was gone. And what stood in his place was someone she'd never met—someone who'd been standing behind Paul's eyes this entire time, watching through them, waiting.

Everything she'd filed away and forgiven—the broken knuckles, the exit awareness, the body that held itself ready—all of it reassembled in a single instant. Not old habits. Not a former life.

Current. Active.

He stopped twenty feet away. Close enough to matter in this confined space. Far enough to create uncertainty about what came next.

"Easy, child." His voice came flat. The warmth gone from it like heat from stone after sunset.

"Paulie?"

The word came out before she could stop it. The name she'd given him.

Something crossed his face—fast, uncontrolled. Pain. Real pain. The kind that lived in the same place the warmth had lived, which meant the warmth had been real too, which made everything worse.

Then it was gone. Sealed behind whatever he needed to be to finish this.

⊙

"You really aren't supposed to be here, Mr. Oram." He said it without looking at Jaden. His eyes hadn't left Wynne.

"Paul, what are you doing here? Clara said you were—"

Paul's hand moved. Deliberate. Slow enough not to be immediately threatening. Fast enough to make his point.

His palm settled on the gun at his belt.

Wynne's awareness crystallized. Distance. Angles. The shelving units boxing them in. Twenty feet of straight line between her and that hand. No room to maneuver laterally.

She could do it. Probably.

But probably meant Jaden died if she was wrong.

"Don't." Quiet. Not to Paul. To Jaden.

"Your brains would be all over these books if I hadn't announced myself first." Paul's voice stayed flat. "Keep that in mind before you decide to pull my limbs from their sockets."

Why announce himself? A man with a gun in a confined space—if he'd wanted them dead, they'd be dead. He'd walked in loud enough for her training to catch. Stopped at twenty feet instead of five. Put his hand on the weapon instead of drawing it.

He was giving her time. Giving himself time. Which meant this wasn't decided yet.

"What is this, Paul?" Her voice came out steadier than it should have. Staff angled—ready to strike, ready to defend. But she was talking to him. Not threatening. Asking.

His mouth pulled tight.

"You were supposed to stay upstairs, Mr. Oram." He still wouldn't look at Jaden. "Keep chasing your grandfather through documents that would never quite give you answers."

Behind her, Jaden's breathing stopped.

"A lead here. A cross-reference there. Just enough to keep you looking." Each word dragged out of him. Not a briefing. A confession. "But you got new credentials. Full access. Which means someone above me decided it was time to let you find something—or make sure you stopped looking."

"You've been—" Jaden's voice cracked. "All this time—"

"Keeping you alive." Paul said it like it cost him something. "By keeping you from finding what you're looking for. Yes."

The silence that followed was worse than the gun.

Wynne felt Jaden behind her—the way his breathing changed, the shift in his weight as something foundational gave way. Six years of Paul's helpful suggestions, Paul's friendly guidance, Paul's coffee and stories. All of it recalculated in an instant.

"Then she showed up." Paul's focus returned to Wynne. His eyes tracked her stance—the way she held the staff, her balance, the discipline in her positioning. "And things got complicated."

⚙

"So here's what happens." He straightened. Hand still on the gun. "You put that book back. Forget that card. We go upstairs and continue like none of this happened. You keep researching. I keep you alive. Everyone walks out of here."

"No." Jaden's voice came from behind her—quiet but absolute.

"Mr. Oram—"

"He was my grandfather." The words strengthened as he spoke. "Someone destroyed everything he stood for. Falsified the record to justify removing a man who refused to be bought. I can't walk away from that. I won't."

Paul looked at Jaden for the first time. Really looked. And Wynne saw it—the thing she hadn't wanted to see. Underneath the mask, Paul cared. Had always cared. The manipulation and the affection had lived in the same body for six years, and neither one had been a lie.

"I trusted you." Jaden's voice cracked with anger. "All these years, Paul. I trusted you."

Paul's expression flickered—shame, fast and real, before the mask reassembled.

"Aye." His voice went harder. "And you're an easy target, Mr. Oram. If we live through all of this, you might thank me for this lesson."

"I won't."

"Probably not."

Wynne held her position. Staff ready. But something underneath the training was fracturing—not her resolve. Something quieter. The place where *Paulie is a good man* had lived for two weeks. It was empty now, and she didn't know what to put there. The overlay said *read him, assess him.* Her training said twenty feet, straight line, one chance. But underneath all of it, in the place where the monastery's teachings lived: *he announced himself. He hasn't drawn. He's still talking.*

People who want to kill you don't tell you stories first.

"What's it going to be, Ms. Kaede?" Paul's eyes found hers. "You going to fight me? Close that gap before I draw?"

"Yes." No hesitation.

His mouth quirked. "Probably right. You're fast. Properly trained." He tapped the gun. "But I don't need to outrun you. Just need one clear shot. And in this space—straight line. No room. You'd have to come right at me."

"I know."

"And you'd do it anyway." Something close to respect in his voice. "Because that's what your kind does. Commits. Even when it's stupid."

He shook his head. Something surfacing despite his efforts—rawer than the mask, older than the operation.

"You remind me of someone. Made the same calculation once." His left hand found his ribs. Pressed. "She won. Put me down hard enough that I never fully got back up."

His right shoulder rolled forward—the protective instinct she'd noticed from the first day. The injury she'd attributed to old life, old work. Not old at all.

"She was right about everything." His voice went quiet. "And it destroyed her anyway."

Wynne held her ground. Staff steady. Heart hammering. But listening.

"And you're just standing there," he said, almost to himself. "Not negotiating. Not pleading. Not trying to talk your way out. Just standing between me and him like it's the most natural thing in the world."

His jaw ground. His hands opened and closed at his sides.

"Do you have any idea how hard you are to point a gun at?"

⊙

Paul stared at them. Wynne in front with her staff ready. Jaden behind with his book and his truth and his stubborn refusal to walk away.

He sighed. Ran his free hand through his hair.

"Not long ago, Sophie started on me." His voice went quieter. The man underneath surfacing because he couldn't hold him down anymore. "You know how kids are. She wanted to know what I'd done that mattered. What I'd accomplished that she could point to when she talks about her old man."

He touched the gun at his belt. Let his hand fall.

"I told her about the library. Preserving knowledge. Important work." His mouth twisted. "She said, 'But what have you done, Dad? What choice did you make that meant something?'"

He looked at Jaden. Really looked.

"You are many things, Mr. Oram. Daft, obtuse... hell, a bloody bore with your constant research." His voice roughened. "But I'll give it to ya—you kept at it. And here I am with a pistol at my belt and you still won't stop."

"And you—" He looked at Wynne. Something broke behind his eyes. "You're not broken. Not like me. Not like her."

The gun came up. Pointed at them properly for the first time.

Wynne's body went electric. Twenty feet. Straight line. Her weight shifted to the balls of her feet, staff angling for the strike—one chance, full commitment, close the distance before his finger finished the pull.

Jaden's breathing stopped behind her.

Paul's arm was steady. Eyes flat.

She didn't speak. Didn't move. Just stood there being exactly what she was—the thing between him and the person behind her.

Paul's arm held.

His throat moved.

His eyes didn't match the rest of him.

Paul laughed—short, rough, exhausted. The sound of surrender.

He tossed the weapon.

The gun spun through the air—dark metal catching fluorescent light—then clattered into the shadows between shelving units. The sound echoed through the archives. Sharp. Final.

He stood with his hands empty. Staring at nothing.

"Six years." His voice came out raw. Scraped clean of everything—the warmth, the mask, the sardonic armor. "Six years of living, tossed aside for a monk and a bookworm." His mouth twisted. "That's me dead, then. Can't unfuck that."

Wynne held her position. Staff ready. But the air between them had changed.

Paul stood with empty hands, staring at the space where the gun had disappeared.

"Come with us."

Paul blinked. Stared at her like she'd spoken a language he'd forgotten.

"You're kidding."

"Paulie." She held his gaze. The name tasted different now—like something being tested. Something she was choosing to offer again, deliberately, knowing what it cost. "Come with us."

Behind her, Jaden's voice cut through—sharp with disbelief.

"You're joking."

Paul's mouth quirked.

"I just said that."

"You point a gun at us, tell us you've been lying for six years, and now she's inviting you along?" Jaden's anger hadn't faded—the absurdity sharpened it. "After everything you just—"

"Mr. Oram." Paul's voice went flat. Tired. "I just burned every bridge I had. Every contact, every employer, every favor I've collected in twenty years of doing work most people won't touch." He gestured toward the shadows where the gun had disappeared. "The moment I don't report in, people start asking questions. The moment they realize what happened here, I become a liability. And liabilities in my line of work don't retire. They disappear."

He looked at Wynne. Fighter to fighter.

"I've spent six years watching this one chase truth." He jerked his chin toward Jaden. "Two weeks watching you be something I forgot existed." He swallowed hard. "Someone needs to make sure that survives what's coming."

"So you're protecting us now?" Jaden's voice still carried disbelief.

"Don't get romantic about it." The sardonic edge returned—armor rebuilding because armor was all he had left. "I'm choosing the side that doesn't make me hate myself when I look in the mirror." He touched his ribs. "Already broken enough as it is."

Wynne lowered her staff. Not all the way. Enough.

Paul looked at the staff. At the angle. At what it meant.

"Well then," he said. "Where are we going?"

32 | Peri

2191.116 · 05:48

Gate 31 | Kiron Hills Locks

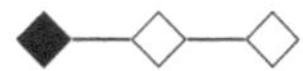

Peri stepped out of her room, jacket on, boots laced. The stopwatch sat heavy in her palm—chrome worn smooth, surface curved. Her thumb found the button without thinking.

Finally. Back to what she knew. Back to the run.

Below, the warehouse sat dark except for Kitt's workbench—scattered parts catching light under a single work lamp. But Kitt wasn't there.

Kataero stood at the bench instead. Waiting.

The stillness of him made her pause at the top of the stairs. Her fingers tightened around the stopwatch.

"Where's Kitt?"

"Still sleeping." He turned, and even across the dim warehouse she read his posture. Decision made. No negotiation coming. "Not today."

"What?"

"The run." He moved toward the door, each step measured. "Come with me."

Peri descended. The button pressed into her palm. "I need to—"

"You need to come with me." He opened the door. Cold air rushed in—canal water with its mineral tang, morning frost. "Bring your blade."

Her hand tightened around the stopwatch.

"You won't need that," Kataero said, not looking back.

She stared at the chrome surface. Her reflection distorted in the curve.

She set it on Kitt's workbench. Her hand felt too light without it. She grabbed her training sword from the rack instead and followed him out.

They walked in silence through the industrial sprawl. Past equipment sheds with rusted roofs dripping condensation. Past cranes standing sentinel against the lightening sky. Down toward the locks, where mist hung low over the water.

The Kiron Hills canal stretched dark ahead, water still as black glass. The massive lock gates rose like silent monuments—metal and stone built to move water, control flow. The air smelled of wet iron and algae and the particular cold of deep water.

He led her to the spillway platform. Flat concrete, fifty feet square. Chains and gears stacked along one edge, tools scattered where workers had left them. Otherwise, empty.

Their breath misted in the predawn chill.

Kataero turned to face her.

His hand found the wrapped grip at his back.

Finally.

Steel in her hands. An opponent across from her. Something she could answer. Not words. Not explanations. Not the silence in a truck.

Just proof.

He drew the weapon in one fluid motion—blade clearing the shoulder harness with a whisper of steel against leather. The Sabaki. Long-hafted, curved blade at one end, weighted counterbalance at the other. A weapon built for patience. For distance. For fights measured in breaths rather than heartbeats.

She drew her training sword before he'd finished settling into stance.

He stood with the Sabaki balanced across both hands. Still as the lock gates behind him. Reading her the way he read everyone—patient as stone.

She rolled her shoulders. Bounced on the balls of her feet.

She grinned. Couldn't help it.

Come on, old man.

"Let's do this!"

She launched forward, blade leading, her whole body committed to the strike. Fast. Aggressive. Close the distance before reach could—

The Sabaki's shaft swept horizontal.

Not the blade. The back end. Catching her sword mid-strike with a sharp crack of wood on steel, redirecting her momentum sideways. She stumbled past him, balance compromised, boots scraping concrete.

He hadn't moved his feet.

She reset. Circled. Cold air burning in her lungs. She watched him track her with that patient stillness—the blade end drifting to follow her movement, the shaft balanced easy across his palms.

She attacked again. Faster. Feinting low toward his knee, then snapping high. The combination that worked on sparring partners, that created openings through speed and misdirection.

The Sabaki's blade descended.

One movement. Unhurried. Like he'd known what she would do before she'd done it. Her high strike met curved steel and slid sideways. Dismissed. The shaft was already rotating, back end sweeping toward her ribs in a motion that had started before her attack finished.

She threw herself backward. Felt the wind of it passing.

Both ends. One motion flowing into the next, no gap between defense and counter. Hakari. The form she'd abandoned years ago.

"Again." His voice came easy. He wasn't even breathing hard.

Sweat stung her eyes. The grin was gone.

She drove forward. The combination she'd built herself—the one that had never failed. High feint drawing the guard up, then drop to a crouch, blade sweeping low, and the moment the opponent shifted weight, explode upward. Rising strike under the guard. Fastest thing she had.

He gave ground. Step by step, retreating.

Yes—

The retreat was a lie.

His back foot planted. The shaft caught her extended sword arm at the wrist—the moment she was most committed. Most exposed. Most certain she'd won. Her grip broke and her blade spun away, clattering across concrete.

The blade end stopped at her throat.

She hadn't even seen him reverse it.

Breath ragged. Pulse hammering against cold steel. His eyes held hers—patient, assessing. Waiting.

"You keep trying to close distance," he said. Not winded. "Fighting like reach is a problem to solve." The blade stayed steady. "It isn't. It's the fight itself."

The blade withdrew. He stepped back. Settled into ready position.

"Again."

She retrieved her sword. Her wrist ached where the shaft had struck—not hard enough to injure. Just enough to teach. Her fingers trembled on the grip.

This time she waited. Let him come. Defensive. Reading his movements the way he'd taught her years ago—before she'd decided speed was the only thing that mattered.

He advanced. The Sabaki moving in measured arcs—every angle controlled. She blocked the first strike. Impact jarred through her arms into her shoulders. Blocked the second. Muscles screaming.

The third strike didn't come.

The shaft hooked behind her ankle. Swept.

She hit concrete. Hard. Air punched from her lungs. The braid slapped against stone beside her head. The cold of the platform seeped through her jacket into her spine. Sky wheeling above—gray bleeding into pale blue, the first stain of orange where the sun was reaching for the horizon.

The blade touched her chest. Light. Almost gentle.

"You're faster than me." Calm. Patient. "Younger. Your reflexes are better." The blade didn't move. "But you fight like speed is the answer. Like closing distance is victory."

Three exchanges. Three defeats. Each one easier for him than the last.

"What if the fight never lets you close?" He withdrew the blade. Offered his hand. "What if reach isn't the problem—what if it's the lesson?"

She took his hand. Let him pull her up. Legs trembling. Arms aching.

The sky was lighter now. Gray giving way to blue, clouds catching fire at the edges. Kataero stepped back, and something changed in his posture. The Sabaki's tip touched concrete. Both hands on the wrapped handle, weight easing through the shaft. Shoulders lowering.

Ready position. But not for fighting.

"You're fighting the wrong fight," he said.

Her legs trembled. "What does that mean?"

"You're fighting yourself. Trying to prove you're still good enough. Still fast enough." He paused. "But the bar keeps moving. It's never enough."

Heat built in her gut.

"You run every morning. Perfect times. Always chasing a faster number." His gaze tracked toward the warehouse. "But there's no test, Peri. There's no finish line. Just you, measuring yourself against something that will never tell you you're enough."

Her throat closed.

"They do mean something." Defensive. Thin. "The times mean—"

"What crown are you competing for?"

She opened her mouth. Found nothing.

"Seventy-nine minutes." His voice quiet now. "I gave you that watch to measure your growth. Not to build a cage."

The sun broke the horizon. Orange light touched the water, reflected off the lock gates. The wind shifted—bringing the smell of coming weather. Red sky in morning.

"The salvage vendor," he said. "North York."

The platform tilted. Cold crawled up her neck.

"Kitt needed them."

Too quick. Too desperate. She heard the hollow ring even as the words came out.

"You had money to buy them." Each word measured. "You risked yourself for no reason. Not for Kitt. Not for the network." He paused. "For the feeling."

Shame burned under her skin.

"And Gate 20." Harder now. "I told you to scout. Eyes only."

Her teeth set.

"The layout. The rotations. Torres's coffee break. You knew things you shouldn't have known." His eyes held hers. "I found the envelope in your pack. Hand-drawn layout. Rotation schedules. Handwriting I didn't recognize."

She couldn't breathe.

"Where did it come from?"

"Rhowan." Small. Caught.

"You took his intel at face value. Kept it from me. Then you led your sister into a Continental Authority facility based on information I never saw and never had a chance to verify."

"It was good intel—"

"You didn't know that." His voice didn't rise. Didn't need to. "You hoped. You gambled. And you bet Kitt's life on it."

"If any of that information had been wrong—" He stopped. Let the silence fill with everything he wasn't saying.

"But it wasn't," she said.

"This time." He stepped closer. His voice dropped. "Who pays when your luck runs out?"

She saw it then. Not anger. Fear. A father watching his daughter walk toward edges she couldn't see.

"You put her at risk." Not loud. Worse than loud. "You made a choice that could have gotten her killed. And for what?"

She opened her mouth. Closed it.

"The bar keeps moving, Peri. You'll never catch it. And the crowns you're chasing wilt the moment you touch them."

"That's not fair—"

"People are depending on you. Not just for food or medicine. For hope. They look to you and see—"

"No." The anger came up hot and fast. "They look to you. You're the Black Marshal. You're the one they follow." Her voice rose. "I'm just running errands. Fetching things."

"You're more than—"

"I'm Kataero Ota's charity case." The words came out sharp. Meant to wound. "The Blackwood brat you got stuck with when my father died."

She saw it hit. The flicker—quick, controlled. His breath catching. Just slightly. Just enough.

Pain.

She should have stopped.

"Isn't it?" Her voice cracked. Something breaking loose. "They all look to Kitt to follow in your shoes. She's your legacy. Your blood. Your real daughter." The word came out venomous. "Don't worry—I kept your lineage safe at Gate 20."

Silence. The kind that follows a blade going in.

"Go talk to her about this and leave me—"

"Peregrine."

Not Peri. Her full name—slow, deliberate. The one he only used when he wanted her to stop spiraling and let him reach her.

Her body reacted before her mind could. Breath hitching, shoulders dropping. The old instinct to pause and listen.

She hated that it still worked.

Fuck this.

"Am I wrong?" Hands up, shaking. "Tell me I'm wrong. Tell me I'm not the one who always gets left behind—"

"You're not wrong that your mother left. You're not wrong that Lin died." His voice steady. "But you're wrong about what they mean."

"My mother walked away from me when I was thirteen." Raw. Scraped from someplace deep. "Just gone. No note. No goodbye."

She wasn't explaining anymore. She was throwing it at him.

"I was thirteen and I didn't even get to ask why. Didn't get to ask what was so broken about me that she couldn't—"

The sob came without permission. She tried to swallow it. Couldn't.

"And Lin—at least he died for something. At least he chose to protect someone instead of just walking away like I was nothing."

Her breath hitched. The words kept coming.

"There are two people responsible for me being here. One died. One left. And I keep trying to sand myself down—file off whatever reminds you of her and build up whatever people swear came from him." Her voice broke. "Like if I get it right, you won't decide I'm too much trouble to keep."

Kataero didn't move. Didn't interrupt. Just watched her, still as stone.

"All I have is the job. The run. And that fucking stopwatch." She laughed—harsh, broken. "Measuring nothing. Because none of it matters. I could run a four-minute mile and it wouldn't change the fact that everyone I've ever loved has either died or decided I wasn't worth staying for."

"And now you're standing here telling me to be something I never asked for. Some hero from stories I never knew." Her voice cracked. "Everyone talks about Lin like I should remember him. Like I should be him. Like his ghost is a template I'm failing to match every day."

"I don't see Lin when I look at you."

Quiet. Certain. Cutting through.

She kept going like she hadn't heard. "I don't have memories of him. Just stories. Just people finding me wanting."

"I don't see Lin when I look at you." Slower this time. Making sure.

She heard it. Felt it reach for something in her chest.

She couldn't let it.

"I see you, Peri. I always have."

Too much. Too close to something she couldn't afford to believe.

"I'm trying," she said. Small now. Worn to the bone. "I'm doing the jobs. I'm keeping things running. What more do you want?"

"I want you to stop running from yourself."

Silence.

"And I can't make you see it. I can't force you to understand." He paused. "You have to choose to see it yourself."

He drove the Sabaki into the concrete.

Steel screamed. The blade sank. The hilt stood upright between them.

He turned. Walked toward the edge of the platform.

Stopped.

"You have me." So quiet she almost missed it. "You've always had me. That hasn't changed."

Then he was gone. Boots echoing. Fading.

⊙

Peri stood alone.

The sun climbed. The sky bled red—streaks like warnings smeared across the clouds. Canal water caught the light and threw it back, fractured.

Her training sword hung at her side. Too heavy.

Sweat cooled on her skin. Her face tight where tears had dried to salt.

The lock gates groaned somewhere behind her. Metal settling. The world moving on.

She'd wounded him. Had aimed for it.

Charity case. The Blackwood brat you got stuck with.

His face. The flicker—quick, controlled. The pain he'd tried to hide. She'd seen it open and she'd kept cutting.

And he'd taken it. Every word. Didn't defend himself. Didn't strike back.

Just let her bleed him.

And then—

You have me. You've always had me. That hasn't changed.

The wind shifted. Cold through her sweat-damp shirt. The smell of coming weather.

Seventy-nine minutes. Pride that lasted half a morning. Gate 20—forty-nine perfect minutes, the high already fading before they'd reached the truck. The zinc plates. The vendor's smile, his trust. Always fading. Always needing to be replaced.

She stared at the Sabaki. Steel buried in concrete. Handle rising against the burning sky.

What crown are you competing for?

She didn't know.

I don't see Lin when I look at you.

Kataero had never compared her to her father. Not once. Not in any conversation she could remember.

That had been everyone else. The neighbors who remembered Lin's laugh. The old contacts who saw his eyes in her face. The strangers who heard Blackwood and expected something she didn't know how to give.

But not him. Never him.

So who—

She was the one. Measuring herself against a dead man's shadow. Holding every accomplishment against a ghost and finding it wanting. Building the impossible standard and blaming everyone else when she couldn't reach it.

Running from a ghost she'd conjured herself.

If she'd been holding the knife to her own throat this whole time—if there was no one to outrun—

Then what was left?

Your real daughter.

She hadn't meant—she'd been angry, she'd been—

You have me.

The thing that was true and she wished it wasn't.

Like if I get it right, you won't decide I'm too much trouble to keep.

But everyone else did. Everyone else looked at her and saw a dead man's eyes and a gone woman's face and expected her to be the best of both and none of the worst and she was so tired—

Pepper in the doorway. Except she didn't have that memory. She'd built it from nothing—from the empty space where a goodbye should have been—and she'd been carrying a fabricated image for eight years like it was evidence.

Her father's face. She didn't have that either. Just Connor's stories. Just the knife on Connor's belt and the gap where a person should have been.

Two ghosts. One she'd invented. One she'd inherited.

And she'd been measuring herself against both of them her entire life and calling it trying.

Her chest locked. Air wouldn't come. Her hands pressed against her temples—everything flooding in at once, filling every space she'd kept empty, every room she'd kept locked—seventy-nine forty-three with nobody to tell and the click of the stopwatch at the salvage yard gate and Pepper's empty hallway and Lin's empty grave—

"FUCK!"

She hurled her sword.

It spun end over end, steel catching the red-streaked light. Flashing. Falling.

Splash.

Gone.

Thirteen years. Every lesson. Every bruise. Every morning drill before the sun came up. The blade he'd put in her hands when she was eight and said *this is yours now.*

Gone.

Her hands shook. Empty.

The lock gates stood unchanged. Patient. Indifferent.

Kataero's Sabaki still stood where he'd left it. Blade buried in concrete. Handle rising against the red sky.

Not his judgment.

His question.

Still waiting.

She turned and ran.

South, into the hills. Away from the warehouse. Away from his words.

Her boots pounded concrete. Then dirt. Then grass. Each impact sharp, the shock traveling through her bones. Her breath tore in and out, ragged, burning. Cold air slicing her lungs.

She pushed harder. Waiting for the shift—the moment her mind went quiet and her body took over. The moment the thoughts stopped and there was nothing but rhythm and ground and air.

It didn't come.

You've always had me.

She ran faster. Heel striking wrong, shoulders climbing, arms locked tight against her ribs. Pushing past the form, past the training, past everything her body knew about how to do this right.

You've always had me.

The Sabaki standing in the concrete behind her. His question still waiting.

She couldn't outrun it. She'd known that before she started.

She ran anyway.

PART 3

"INFRASTRUCTURE IS CIVILIZATION'S SKELETON. WITHOUT IT, COMMUNITIES WITHER INTO DEPENDENCY—ON SMUGGLERS, ON THIEVES, ON THOSE WHO PROFIT FROM SCARCITY. THE HAMMISON CORRIDOR WILL END THAT DEPENDENCY. THOSE WHO HAVE BUILT THEIR LIVES STEALING FROM THE MARGINS WILL FIND THOSE MARGINS CLOSING. THIS IS NOT A THREAT. IT IS SIMPLY PROGRESS."

— CHIEF MINISTER SHORI ASHFORD
CONTINENTAL INFRASTRUCTURE ADDRESS, 2191

33 | Kitt

2191.116 · 06:31 | Z2
Gate 31

Kitt descended the metal stairs, one hand trailing the rail, the other covering a yawn that made her jaw crack. Her slippers—one blue with white dots, one gray striped—shuffled down each step. Mismatched socks showed where her pajama bottoms rode up. She'd grabbed whatever was clean in the dark.

Cold bit through the thin cotton of her tank top. The warehouse held onto night temperature like a grudge—concrete and metal drinking in the chill, refusing to let go even as dawn pushed gray light through the tall windows. She pulled her bathrobe tighter. The worn terry cloth did almost nothing.

Should've put on real clothes.

But the radio schedule didn't care about warm layers, and she was already awake, so down she went.

Her breath misted in the dim warehouse. She reached the bottom and moved toward the main breaker panel, toes curling in her slippers against the cold concrete.

Her fingers found switches by memory. Click. Click. Click.

Overhead bulbs flickered to life in sequence, struggling against insufficient power, fighting their way to maybe seventy percent brightness. Each one hummed as it warmed—transformers waking reluctantly, coils heating, the whole system protesting the demand.

She stopped at the charging rack first. Habit. Twenty-three glass cells seated vertically in their wooden frame—some glowing strong phosphor-blue, some dim, three completely dark. The rectifier hummed in the corner, steady and low, doing its work while she slept.

One cell sat wrong. Third row, second position—bright phosphor glow where there should be dim. Fresh cell rotated forward, out of sequence.

Kitt's eyes narrowed.

Dammit, Peri.

She pulled the misplaced cell, held it up to the gray light. Too fresh. Might not hold under field conditions. She rotated it back where it belonged, moved the stable ones forward. Brightest to dimmest, left to right. The order Peri never remembered no matter how many times Kitt explained it.

Her fingers worked stiff, but the ritual steadied her. Small thing. Fixable thing.

She crossed to her workbench, still yawning. Reached for the power strip—

Her hand stopped.

The stopwatch sat on her workbench. Chrome catching the struggling light. Forty-nine minutes frozen on the dial.

Kitt stared at it. Her hand hovering six inches away. Not touching. Not moving.

Peri's stopwatch. The one she carried everywhere. The one she checked compulsively before every run, every job, every moment she needed to prove something to herself.

What's this doing here?

Her eyes tracked up to the second floor. To Peri's window. Dark. Empty.

She'd left for her run then. Before dawn. But she never—

The radio crackled to life behind her.

Static first. White noise filling the warehouse. Then a tone cutting through. Three short pulses. Two long. One short.

Pattern she'd been waiting for.

Kitt turned from the stopwatch. Her slippers scuffed against concrete as she moved to the communications station. She grabbed the microphone, hands still stiff from the chill.

"Tabby. Reading you. Go ahead."

"Good morning, Tabitha." Cipher's voice filtered through clear despite the distance. The same measured cadence as always—each word placed like a component on a board. "I trust yesterday's operation concluded successfully?"

"Affirmative." She kept her voice level. But her eyes kept pulling back to the stopwatch on the bench. "Gate 20 terminal access achieved. Full manifest data retrieved. Generator components confirmed on Train 47."

A pause. Longer than usual.

"The timeline," Cipher said. Something careful in his tone now. "I understand it was... not what we anticipated."

Not what we anticipated. Kitt's hand tightened on the mic. A week. He'd said a week, maybe two. They'd built their entire planning window around that estimate. And now—

"Thirty-four hours," she said. Flat. "We had thirty-four hours from the moment I read that terminal. We have less than twenty-four now."

Static hissed. When he spoke again, his voice carried something that wanted to be regret.

"Schedules shift. The intelligence was sound at time of acquisition." A beat. "Access to the MERIDIAN terminal at Gate 20 verified the cargo's existence. Confirmed you haven't missed the window."

Confirmed you haven't missed the window. As if that were the same as having adequate time to plan. A week compressed into a day because his intelligence was stale and they were the ones absorbing the cost.

"We could postpone," Kitt said. The words came out before she'd fully decided to say them. "Wait for the next shipment. Plan properly."

"And when would that be?" His cadence didn't change. But an urgency she hadn't heard before pressed against the patience—three years of measured calm, and now this. "These components move irregularly. Months between shipments, sometimes longer. Belfast Mills has been waiting three years, Tabitha."

She thought of the dam. Four hundred kilowatts where six megawatts should be. Unit One grinding itself apart. The brownouts getting longer. Emma crouching by a dead turbine asking if she could fix it.

"The window exists," Cipher continued. "Narrow, yes. But your team is capable. Your planning is sound. The only variable is whether you trust yourself to execute."

Her gaze drifted to the stopwatch again. Chrome face. Frozen numbers. Peri's absence sitting on her bench like a physical object.

Where is she?

"You sound distracted, Tabitha."

Kitt straightened. Hand tightening on the mic. "Negative. Local conditions nominal."

"Of course." A pause. Static hissed softly between them. "There was restricted cargo noted in the manifest as well, yes? Medical transport?"

"Car 2." She pulled her notebook closer. Something to focus on. "Level 6 clearance. Handling code MT-7719. Couldn't access details."

"Likely pharmaceutical security theater."

"Level 6 is military grade." The words came out before she could stop them. "Same clearance as the Graphton wellness facility on that network. That's not theater. That's—"

"That's not your objective." His tone stayed even. Patient. But something underneath had closed—the way a relay clicks shut and locks. "Generator components. Cars 3 and 4. That's what Belfast Mills needs. That's what you're there for."

She waited for more. An explanation. A reason why military-grade clearance on a medical shipment didn't matter.

Nothing came.

"Right," she said finally. "Generator components."

"Excellent. Trust your preparation, Tabitha. Trust your team." A pause. Then, firmer: "Trust it."

Three times. The same word, three times in close succession. Cipher didn't repeat himself. His speech patterns were precise—state once, move on. She'd listened to him for three years. He didn't do this.

She filed it. Couldn't process it now.

The main warehouse door opened.

Cold air rushed in. She turned.

Connor.

He stepped inside and closed the door quickly behind him, his breath misting. Heavy jacket, work gloves, boots suited for the cold. He took one look at Kitt—pajama bottoms, mismatched slippers, bathrobe—and something shifted in his expression.

Not quite a smile. More like recognition.

He moved toward the equipment storage, pulling canvas bags from shelves. His movements economical. Purposeful. Storm-gray eyes taking in the scene—Kitt at the radio, the tension in her shoulders, the stopwatch on the bench.

His gaze lingered on that last one. Just for a heartbeat.

Then he kept moving. Started checking gear.

"It sounds like you have capable people around you," Cipher said through the radio.

"Yeah." Kitt watched Connor work. Steady. Unshakeable. "We'll make it work."

"Then I'll leave you to your preparations. Maintain radio silence unless absolutely necessary. Contact me when the operation is complete."

"Understood."

"Good luck, Tabitha."

Signal faded. Static rising. Then nothing.

Meter needle dropped to zero.

Kitt set down the microphone. Warehouse quiet now. Just Connor moving equipment. Hum of struggling electrical systems. Occasional drip of condensation from the high ceiling.

She turned back to her workbench. To the stopwatch sitting there.

Peri never left it behind. Never.

"Kid."

Connor's voice. She turned. He'd set down a bag, was watching her with those gray eyes.

"You ready for this?"

Kitt looked at the stopwatch. At the notes spread across her bench. At three years of preparation compressed into tomorrow's fifteen-minute window.

"I don't know." Honest. Quieter than she'd intended.

"We control what we control." He crossed his arms. Same tone he used when teaching her to shoot, to drive, to not panic when things went sideways. "Preparation. Execution. Response when things go sideways." He moved toward the vehicles. "Coffee's in the thermos."

Then back to work. Loading. Checking. Methodical. Like tomorrow was just another job.

Behind her, footsteps on gravel. Heavier than Connor's. The particular measured cadence she'd know anywhere.

The door opened. Quieter than before—held, controlled, eased shut.

Kataero.

He moved across the floor with that economical precision she recognized. But something was wrong. His face too carefully controlled. His jaw set harder than usual.

His jacket was damp. His hair disturbed by wind. He'd been outside—by the canal, maybe. Somewhere that had broken something inside him.

He crossed toward his office without looking at anyone. His hand came up—just for a moment—and touched his cheek. Wiped something away.

Kitt went still.

The stopwatch on her bench. Peri gone before dawn. Kataero coming in from outside with his face wet. Something had happened between them—or something had happened to one of them that the other couldn't reach. She could trace the sequence but couldn't read the values. The data points were there. The meaning wasn't.

But he'd already disappeared into his office. Door closing with a soft click.

Connor had stopped loading gear. Was looking at the closed door. Then at the stopwatch on Kitt's bench. Then at the warehouse door—the one that led outside.

"Keep the world running, kid." He was already pulling his gloves back on. Already moving.

"Connor—"

"Get some real clothes on."

The door opened. Cold air. Then it closed, and he was gone.

Kitt stood alone in the warehouse. The stopwatch on her bench. Her father behind a closed door. Her sister somewhere in the hills. And Connor going after the one who ran, because someone had to.

She didn't move for a long moment.

Then she pulled the oscillator closer. Touched the probe to the test point. The multimeter's needle settled.

Point-zero-zero-three.

She watched it. Held her breath the way she had morning after morning at this bench, waiting for the drift, waiting for the reading to creep back to where it shouldn't be.

The needle held. Steady. The thermal compensation stable, the network repairs feeding clean signal back through the system. The fault she'd been chasing since that first morning—gone. Not because she'd solved it at the bench. Because she'd climbed repeater stations and cleaned junction boxes and rebuilt the infrastructure the oscillator depended on.

The reading held because the network held. Because the work she'd done out there had fixed what was wrong in here.

She set the probe down.

One day left.

She'd make sure they were ready.

34 | Wynne

2191.117 · 10:30
Hamilton Public Library

Paul moved first. Shoulders loose, walking as if nothing had happened. Wynne followed, staff angled down, eyes tracking the aisles between the shelving units. Jaden came last, cane tapping softly against concrete, the book with his grandfather's truth clutched against his chest.

Paul bent, retrieved the gun from where he'd thrown it. Checked it. Started to holster it.

Wynne watched him. Eyebrow raised.

"What?" He slid it into place. "You expect me to live a new life naked?"

"I expect you to understand something." She kept her voice level. "If your methods contradict my principles, we will correct your methods."

Paul's eyes narrowed. "You threatening me, Ms. Kaede?"

"I'm establishing boundaries. I won't compromise what I am to achieve what I want."

Silence stretched between them.

Then Paul laughed—short, genuine. "You really are like her, aren't you?" He shook his head, almost fond. "Fine. You want rules? Here's mine. I've got your back. Not his." He pointed at Jaden. "Yours. If it comes down to choosing between keeping you alive and helping him find his truth? I'm choosing you. Every time."

"Why?"

"Because he's chasing truth. Noble. The kind of thing that gets a man killed." He glanced back at Jaden. "His choice. His road."

"I'm still here," Jaden said. His voice carried the careful control of a man whose composure had cost him something to maintain. "Still quite present. Still, I might add, baffled as to why a man who betrayed me, held a gun in my direction, and threatened my life is now traveling with us as if none of that ever happened."

Paul didn't turn around. "Because I'm useful."

"Useful." Jaden's cane struck the floor harder than necessary. "The man who was sent to mislead me. To keep me distracted. To ensure I never found what I just found. That man is now useful?"

"More useful than you know." Paul's voice stayed flat. "You have no idea what finding that book just set in motion."

"Enlighten me."

"Later. When we're not standing in the place where I failed my assignment." He started toward the stairs. "Move."

Wynne caught Jaden's eye. Confusion there. Anger. But underneath—fear. The dawning recognition that he'd stepped into something larger than his grandfather's letters.

She gave him a small nod. *Later.*

They started up the stairs toward the main library, footsteps echoing in the narrow stairwell.

Paul stopped at the top. Hand on the door. Not opening it yet.

He looked back at Wynne.

"Watching you move this morning. The way you commit. The way you know exactly what you stand for." He paused. "I used to know what that felt like. Before I got good at compromising."

He held her gaze.

"Everything out there is going to try grinding you down into someone like me." His voice caught. "I'd rather it didn't."

"It won't." She held his gaze a beat longer. "For now, that has to be enough."

"Good enough."

Paul pressed his ear against the wood. Listening.

"Sounds normal. Move fast but look calm. Don't run—running draws attention." He glanced back. "And Ms. Kaede? Keep that staff down. Last thing we need is you looking ready to fight."

"I am ready to fight."

"I know. That's the problem." Almost approval in how he said it.

He pushed the door open.

⊙

The library looked exactly as they'd left it.

Children's voices carried from the reading corner—a teacher explaining something about the pictures in a book, small voices asking questions that had nothing to do with the answers. Morning light fell through tall windows, catching dust motes that drifted without urgency.

Normal. Unchanged. A world that had no idea what had just happened below.

Wynne took it in. The exits. The sight lines. The security officer near the front door, attention on his newspaper. Clara at the circulation desk, head bent over paperwork.

Paul set the pace—unhurried but purposeful. A man with somewhere to be but no particular rush to get there. Wynne matched it. Jaden's cane tapped a measured rhythm beside her, his breathing carefully controlled.

They passed the history section. The reference desk. The reading table where they'd spent two weeks of evenings—books and coffee and the cane and staff leaning against each other. She didn't look at it.

Clara looked up as they approached the circulation desk. Professional smile forming—the automatic greeting of someone who'd spent years welcoming strangers.

The smile faltered.

Her eyes moved from Paul to Wynne to Jaden. Took in the tension in their shoulders. The way Wynne's hand stayed close to her staff. The way Jaden held the volume like a lifeline.

They were past her before she could speak.

The main entrance. Glass doors. Morning light beyond.

Paul pushed through first. Wynne followed. Jaden last, his cane crossing the threshold with a sound like punctuation.

Outside.

The air hit her—cold, clean, carrying the smell of the harbor and something cooking from a cart down the street. Hamilton in its morning routine. Security on corners. Workers heading to factories and offices. Vendors calling prices for bread and fish and yesterday's newspapers.

No one looked at them twice.

Paul led them left. Away from main streets. Into narrower paths where the buildings pressed closer and the shadows lasted longer.

"Stay close. Look normal. Just three people taking a morning walk."

"We're fugitives," Jaden said quietly.

"Not yet." Dark humor threading through Paul's voice. "Give it an hour. Then you're fugitives. Right now you're just persons of interest."

"How comforting."

"Wasn't meant to be." Paul's pace quickened slightly. "Someone's going to check the archive. Find it disturbed. Find me missing. Find that—" he gestured at the book Jaden carried "—gone. When that happens, the clock speeds up considerably."

"How considerably?"

Paul didn't answer. Which was answer enough.

⊙

Paul shrugged off the wool jacket three steps past the library's side entrance. Didn't fold it. Just let it drop onto a steam grate where condensation was already darkening the fabric. He rolled his shoulders—working out the stiffness, or shedding the last of whoever he'd been in the library. Hard to tell.

He moved differently now. Wynne tracked the change the way she'd track any shift in a fighter's stance. The library Paul had ambled—weight settled, pace unhurried, a man comfortable in his territory. This Paul cut through the alleys with an economy that stripped every unnecessary movement. Turns taken without hesitation. Eyes scanning intersections before his body arrived at them. The gait of someone who'd mapped every shortcut, every hiding spot, every place the patrols didn't bother checking.

Not a security guard anymore. Whatever he'd been before the library.

They moved deeper into the service alleys. Narrow corridors between buildings that official city maps probably labeled "maintenance access" but felt more like veins—dark, damp, carrying the city's waste and secrets.

Jaden looked up at the buildings pressing close on either side. Brick and stone blackened by decades of coal smoke. Laundry lines strung overhead, dripping water that pooled in the uneven cobblestones.

"I've read the city planning documents," he said quietly. "They describe these as 'service corridors.'" He stepped around a puddle of something dark. "They didn't mention the smell."

"Brewery runoff," Paul said over his shoulder. "Mixes with the sewage near the junction points. You get used to it."

"Do you?"

Paul didn't answer. Just kept moving. Left, then right, then through a narrow gap between two buildings that barely fit them single file.

They emerged into a wider alley. Loading docks on one side, residential back entrances on the other. Paul picked up his pace, angling for a cross street ahead where Wynne could see morning light cutting between the buildings.

She stopped.

Something—

Not sound. Not quite. Something underneath the brewery smell and sewage—garlic. Strong. Sharp. The kind of smell that came from a body, not a kitchen.

"Paul."

Quiet. But he heard it. Turned back.

She pointed down the passage to their right. Forty feet, then a corner.

Paul went still. His eyes tracked from the corner to Wynne's face, checking her read against his own knowledge of these streets.

"Bloody Remy," he said quietly. "Breath could strip paint off a warship. Good nose."

Not quite a compliment. More an acknowledgment.

He checked the alley behind them. Clear. Looked at the cross street ahead—too exposed. Then back to Wynne and Jaden.

"Wait here."

"Paul—" Jaden started.

But Paul was already moving. Not toward the corner where Remy waited. The other way—through a service door Wynne hadn't noticed, moving with the ease of someone who'd used that entrance a hundred times.

Gone.

Silence settled. Just the drip of water from overhead lines. The distant rumble of cart wheels on cobblestones.

Wynne's gaze tracked the alley. The far end where Paul had indicated. The service door. The cross street beyond. Her body doing what it always did—reading the space, mapping the geometry, finding the lines of approach and retreat.

Jaden stood beside her, watching the door Paul had disappeared through. That analytical mind working through probabilities and outcomes. Holding that book against his chest like it could protect him from what it contained.

She looked at him. At the way his hand gripped the cane—knuckles white, the only part of him that admitted what the rest was trying to hide. At the man who'd just had six years of trust demolished in a basement and was still standing. Still thinking. Still holding the evidence.

Something settled in her chest. Quiet. Sure. The pull—not leading her anywhere new. Just confirming where she already was.

Jaden turned, catching her looking. "What?"

"Nothing." Her gaze returned to the alley corner.

Jaden looked at the door Paul had disappeared through. Back to Wynne.

"I'm still trying to get my head around this," he said. His voice carried that same dry edge—academic precision applied to an absurd situation. "All these years working together. And now we're just following him through the underbelly of the capital as if his sudden and rather spectacular betrayal of trust didn't just happen."

His hand shifted on the book. The grip that had been steady since the archive—white-knuckled, absolute—loosened for just a moment.

Then it tightened again. He noticed her noticing.

"Yes," she said. "We are."

A beat. Then Jaden smiled. Small. Genuine. The kind she hadn't seen from him since before the archive.

"There are perhaps worse ways to die."

Wynne felt her feet on the cobblestones. The staff across her back. The buildings pressing close on either side—a city that had become hers and was now becoming something she'd have to leave.

"There are. But not today."

Jaden's chin lifted slightly. The analytical tension in his face eased—not into softness, but into something steadier.

Movement. The service door opening again. Paul emerged, flexing his right hand. Breathing normal. No blood visible. No urgency in his movements.

"Handled." He gestured back the way they'd come. "Best move before he wakes or his friends find him."

He walked past them, angling for a different route now. Away from the cross street. Deeper into the maze.

Wynne followed. After a moment, so did Jaden.

Behind them, around the corner where Remy had been standing, nothing moved.

Paul led them deeper. Toward the rail yard.

35 | Peri

2191.116 · 08:57
Gate 31

Peri's legs burned wrong as she approached Gate 31. Not the clean ache that came after a good run. Something uglier. Something she'd earned by running until her body begged her to stop and then not stopping.

What crown are you competing for?

Her stride faltered. She forced it steady again.

How long? An hour? Two? Sun was higher now, hot on her shoulders. Her throat raw from breathing hard in cold air. Sweat had soaked through her shirt and dried, leaving it stiff against her skin. Her right ankle throbbed where she'd turned it on a hillside root without slowing. Her lips were cracked. She could taste blood when she licked them.

Her hand went to her pocket out of habit, fingers searching for chrome.

Empty.

Both loading dock doors stood open. Voices inside. Metal on concrete. The sounds of people working toward something.

She walked in.

Sunlight to shadow. The warehouse swallowed her whole—dark after the brightness outside, everything reduced to shapes and sound. She blinked. Waited for her eyes to catch up. The voices sharpened before the room did.

"I'm telling you," Marcus was saying somewhere to her left, "if you pack the winch cable under the come-alongs one more time, I will end your bloodline."

"My bloodline's doing fine." Thomas. Wheezing, which meant Marcus had him in a headlock again. "Your mother said so last night."

"Oh, that's it—"

"Children." Seth's voice, patient and dry. Tap of metal on metal—the tire iron he used as a pointer. "Can we maybe load the truck before we commit fratricide?"

The shapes resolved. Flatbed half-loaded with gear. Crates stacked along the wall. Carter at the rear axle with his tire gauge, writing in his notebook, checking it twice. The crew doing what crews did. Bickering and shorthand and hands that didn't need to think.

The job. The train. Valcross.

It hit her standing there in the dark with salt on her skin and blood on her lips—she'd forgotten. Two hours of running and she'd forgotten the thing they'd spent weeks building toward. The thing Kitt had found and mapped and bled for. The thing that was happening tomorrow.

And they were all here. Packing. Loading. Ready.

Marcus let go of Thomas. The laughter shifted register—that half-second adjustment a room makes when someone walks in and nobody wants to be the first to ask.

She felt them see her. The swollen ankle. The dried sweat. The wild look she couldn't control because she didn't know it was there. And no stopwatch. Everyone in this warehouse knew what that watch meant.

Carter stood. Crossed to the water station without a word. Filled a tin cup. Brought it back and held it out.

Peri took it. Drank the whole thing standing there, water running down her chin, her hand shaking just enough that the cup rattled against her teeth. Cold spreading down her throat, into her chest. She breathed.

"Thanks, Carter."

She held the cup out. He took it, nodded, and went back to his tire gauge.

She moved. One foot, then the next. Across the warehouse floor toward the stairs. Shower. Gear. Get out the door. That was all she needed. Three things. She could do three things.

Marcus and Thomas had their backs to her. Working. Giving her the mercy of not watching, even though she could feel the effort it cost them.

Stop reading the room. Just walk.

Kataero was at Kitt's workbench. She saw him in her peripheral—his shape, his stillness. He'd gone motionless when she entered. That particular stillness that meant he was aware of everything while appearing to study the notebook open in front of him.

You have me. You've always had me.

She adjusted her line. Three degrees left. Enough to pass wide of the workbench without it looking deliberate. Without it looking like she was avoiding him.

It looked deliberate. She knew it looked deliberate. She did it anyway.

He didn't look up. Didn't come to her. Just turned a page like it required his full attention.

Giving her room. Or something she couldn't tell apart from room.

Kitt intercepted her halfway to the stairs.

Her sister's face did the thing it always did—the quick read, the assessment, the worry she couldn't quite keep out of her eyes. She was holding something.

Stopwatch. Chrome catching the warehouse light.

"You left this at my workbench."

Not *forgot.*

Left.

Peri looked at the stopwatch in her sister's hand.

She should leave it. That was the point, wasn't it? The cage. The crown. The bar that kept moving.

Her fingers closed around the chrome.

Not yet.

She pocketed it. "Thanks."

Kitt's mouth opened. The question forming.

Peri was already moving. "Twenty minutes."

The stairs were fifteen feet away. She could see the bottom step. She could count the distance in strides—eight, maybe nine with the ankle.

Connor materialized at her flank. Not blocking. Just there. His hand coming up—that gesture she'd seen a thousand times, reaching to steady, to check, to pull her back to center the way he'd been doing since she was small.

Her hand came up between them. Not a push. A boundary.

Not now.

He read it. His hand dropped. He stepped back.

Seven strides. Six. Five.

She reached the stairwell. Took the first three steps at a normal pace because they could still see her.

Then she was around the corner and she took them two at a time. Up and away. From the crew and the truck and the job she'd forgotten. From

Kataero's patience and Connor's worry and Kitt's careful word choices. From every pair of eyes that had looked at her and seen someone who needed help and not one of them knowing that the thing she needed help with was herself.

Hot water. Closed door. Twenty minutes.

She could fall apart for twenty minutes.

36 | Kitt

2191.116 · 09:01
Gate 31

Above, a door closed. The sound carried through the warehouse—solid, final.

Twenty minutes, she'd said.

Kitt turned back to her workbench. Three field radios waited in pieces. Battery housings exposed, contacts cleaned, ready for cells. Nine cells total. Standard loadout for a job this size.

Her job. Her planning. Her intel that found the train, her network that carried the communications, her twelve pages of handwritten notes. Tomorrow morning, all of it would either work or it wouldn't, and every variable she could control was accounted for.

She had twenty minutes to fill and her hands were already moving.

First radio. First cell seated—glass sliding into brass housing with a soft click. Blue glow disappearing behind the velcro patch. Light blocked. Charge preserved.

Then the pipes groaned. Water moving through old metal. Peri's shower starting.

Thought I'd try going without.

The words sat wrong. Peri's voice when she'd said them—rough, defensive. The way she'd pocketed the stopwatch like it burned her. The way she'd slipped past Connor without letting him touch her.

Second cell. Click. Velcro sealed.

Whatever was happening with Peri, it would have to happen around the job. Not instead of it.

Third cell. Housing closed. Connections verified. One radio operational. Two to go.

Seth's boots announced him across the concrete. He stopped at the charging rack. His hands hovered over the rows of phosphor-blue, not touching. Waiting.

"Front row?"

"Middle of the rack." Kitt didn't look up. "The ones on the ends are bleeding charge too quickly. They'll need to be torn down and rebuilt."

Seth nodded. Started collecting cells with careful hands—three, six, nine. Each one examined briefly against the light before he set it on the bench beside her. No questions about which shade of blue meant what. No skepticism about her system.

Just trust.

She started on the second radio. Fingers finding their rhythm now—the quick, sure movements that came when her hands knew the work better than her thoughts could follow. This was the part she was good at. The preparation. Making sure every piece of equipment would perform when it mattered.

Tomorrow it would matter.

"Daddy, who lives up there?"

Emma's voice echoed through the warehouse, bright and curious. Kitt's hands paused.

"Kitt, dear."

"Can I go up there?"

"You might have to ask her, honey."

Kitt glanced toward the loading bay doors. Marcus stood just inside, Emma's hand in his. Sarah beside them—dark hair pulled back, watching her daughter with the quiet patience of someone who'd long since accepted that Emma would touch everything in any room she entered.

Emma was already pointing. The charging rack. The tool wall. The stairs leading up.

"What's that? What does it do? Can I touch it?"

Marcus answered each question with the same gentle patience. Sarah's hand found his arm.

Then Marcus turned to Sarah.

Their foreheads touched. Her hand came up to his chest, fingers spreading over his heart. He pulled her close—the kind of embrace that knew exactly how they fit together. Practiced. Certain.

Emma squeezed between them. Forced her way into the hold until both parents adjusted to include her. Three becoming one for a moment.

Sarah pulled back first. Hand still on his chest. Small pat—once, twice.

Kitt's hands went still on the radio.

Hand on chest. Fingers spread. Pat—once, twice.

Copper hair catching morning light. Green eyes.

Kataero stood at the same loading bay doors. Younger. No gray in his beard. No lines around his eyes. The weight that would come later not yet settled into his shoulders.

Pepper beside him. Her hand on his chest. Fingers spreading over his heart.

Peri squeezed between them. Nine years old and already tall for her age, already restless, bouncing on her toes even while trapped in the embrace. Already asking when Daddy would be home. Already looking toward the door.

Kitt sat on the stairs. Five years old. Hair long then, falling past her shoulders in dark tangles that Pepper kept threatening to brush properly. Overalls with grease stains on the knees—she'd found a broken radio in the warehouse that morning and spent an hour taking it apart, not understanding yet what any of the pieces did, just wanting to see how they fit together.

She didn't see Pepper's fingers tighten on his shirt. Didn't notice the brightness in her mother's green eyes. Didn't know yet what that brightness meant.

She was five. The world was small and certain and her father always came home.

Pepper pulled back. Hand still on his chest. Small pat—once, twice.

"Bye Daddy!"

Kitt blinked.

Emma. Now.

Sarah was leading her toward the road, their hands linked. Marcus watching them go with that look she'd learned to name in all the years since that staircase.

Emma turned back, waving with her whole arm. "Bye Peri!"

Her voice carried up toward the second floor. Toward the closed door. Toward the sound of water still running through old pipes.

No answer.

Emma's wave faltered. She looked to her mother, confused.

"She's getting ready, sweetheart. Come on."

They disappeared through the loading bay doors. Yellow coat swallowed by morning light.

Kitt looked up at Peri's room. Door still closed. Shower still running.

Marcus stood alone now, watching the empty doorway where his family had been. His hand came up to his chest—unconscious, touching the place where Sarah's palm had rested.

Then he turned back to the flatbed. Back to work.

Kitt turned back to the radios.

Third unit. First cell seated. Click. Second. Click. Third. Click. Velcro straps secured. All three housings closed. Connections verified—she keyed each one, listened for the carrier tone, checked the meter response. Clean signal on all three.

Three radios. Nine cells. Operational.

She ran through the rest of the checklist. Radios—done. Charging cells—loaded. Route maps—in her bag, annotated, every approach and fallback marked. Signal codes—confirmed with everyone last night. Tools for the cargo cars—Seth had those on the flatbed.

The planning was solid. Tomorrow, Chapi Grade. A loaded freight climbing into the mountains at walking pace. Kataero's window—not hers. She'd found the train. He'd found the way onto it. And somewhere between the grade and the summit, they'd have minutes to do what should take hours.

She allowed herself that. The small, private satisfaction of a plan that held together on paper and would hold in practice because she'd accounted for everything she could account for.

Above, the water cut off.

The pipes shuddered once and went silent.

Kitt waited. Counting seconds without meaning to. Fifteen. Thirty. A minute.

Movement upstairs. Footsteps crossing the floor. The creak of old boards.

But the door didn't open.

She looked around the warehouse. Everyone in motion. Seth and Thomas finishing the flatbed straps. Carter wiping his hands on a rag, tire pressure confirmed. Connor standing near Kataero's truck, arms crossed, watching the stairs with that patient stillness he did better than anyone.

Kataero at the hood, map spread flat. He'd folded and unfolded it three times in the last ten minutes.

They were all waiting. The whole operation—vehicles loaded, equipment checked, people ready—suspended on one person who wasn't coming down.

Marcus caught Kitt's eye. Raised an eyebrow. *How long?*

Kitt shook her head slightly. *Don't know.*

More minutes. The warehouse humming with engines.

Kataero folded the map again. His eyes went to the stairs, then away. Then back.

He didn't go up. Didn't call out. Just waited.

Enough.

"Peri!" Her voice carried up the stairs, sharper than she intended. "We're ready!"

Silence.

One heartbeat. Two.

Then footsteps. Quick. Determined.

The door opened, and Peri came down the stairs. Hair still damp. Tied back, not braided. Eyes tracking the room without settling on anyone. The version of her sister that people who didn't know her would mistake for fine.

Kitt knew. Her sister was not fine.

37 | Peri

2191.116 · 09:01
Gate 31

Door to her room closed behind her with a deep metallic sound. She leaned against it, breathing hard, shoulders pressed to cool metal.

Twenty minutes. She had twenty minutes to pull herself together.

The stopwatch was in her hand. She'd pulled it out without thinking. Chrome warming against her palm. Forty-nine minutes frozen on the dial.

She looked at it.

Not at the time. At the thing itself. The weight of it. The scratch across the crystal from a job two years ago. The engraving on the back she didn't need to read because her thumb had memorized every letter.

For Peri. —K.

This. This small bright machine. This thing she reached for before her mind caught up every morning, carried in her pocket like a heartbeat, held up against the sky after every run. Measuring. Always measuring. Eighty-six minutes. Eighty-three. Eighty-six again. Numbers that told her she was slipping and never told her why.

What crown are you competing for?

The stopwatch hit the desk. Not placed. Thrown. Chrome skidding across wood, leaving a crescent gouge before it came to rest against the wall. Forty-nine minutes still frozen on the dial. Staring up at the ceiling.

She turned away from the desk.

Boots first. Pulled off hard, dropped where they fell. Jacket thrown on the bed. Shirt—stiff with dried sweat, the fabric peeling off her skin in one long unstick. Pants. Everything. All of it on the floor or the bed or wherever it landed.

The weapons rack stood beside the door.

Her kukri hung in its spine harness, the leather worn to her shape. Below it—the empty pegs. Two of them, bare, the wood darker where the training sword had rested for ten years. The wrapped grip, the nicked edge, the weight of it in her hand since she was nine. Kataero's hands correcting her grip, adjusting her stance, running the same drill until her muscles didn't need her brain anymore.

In the canal now. Sinking in black water with everything else she'd thrown away this morning.

She crossed the room. Nothing on her. Nothing between her and anything.

The bathroom door was open. She pushed through.

Kitt's side of the vanity: organized, labeled, everything in its place. Small mirror above it, clean.

Peri's side. The mirror. And on the lower corner, the strip of tape she'd put there—she couldn't remember when. A month ago. Three months. Her own handwriting, cramped and decisive.

What's the point?

She'd written it about the dam. About Belfast Mills and the flickering lights and Emma Chen's brother nearly dying because medicine cost more than people had. About the grid that failed a little more every week and the roads that kept crumbling and the relay stations that corroded faster than Kitt could fix them. About getting up every morning and running ten miles and stealing supplies and patching things over and watching it all slide back toward the same slow collapse.

She'd written it about the world.

She looked at it now and the words had changed shape. Same ink. Same tape. Different question.

What's the point?

Get up every morning. Run every morning. Train. Steal. Fight. Come home bloody or sore or both. Push the body harder, leaner, faster—for what?

She looked at herself in the mirror.

Muscle and sinew and angles. Shoulders cut sharp. Arms defined in ways that had nothing to do with vanity and everything to do with years of asking her body to be a tool. Ribs visible when she breathed. The scar on her left shoulder, the ridge of it pale against her skin.

An athlete. A weapon. Anything but a woman.

She reached up and peeled the tape off the mirror. Slow. The adhesive pulling, leaving a faint residue on the glass. She held the strip in her fingers for a moment—her own handwriting, curling slightly now that it had nothing to stick to.

She let it fall.

The mirror was clean. Full. Just her.

She looked.

Not bracing this time. Not checking. Looking. The way you look when you're trying to find someone in a crowd.

Copper hair, dark with sweat, hanging loose around her shoulders. Sharp cheekbones. The line of her jaw.

Blue eyes.

She held them. Held her own gaze and looked deeper—past the blue, past the face she knew. The green that lived underneath. The woman behind the glass.

"I need you."

Her voice in the small bathroom. Quiet. Stripped.

The mirror gave her back blue.

"Mom." She leaned closer. Hands on the edge of the sink, weight forward, her face inches from the glass. "I need you. Please."

Nothing moved. Nothing shifted. The blue stayed blue. The face stayed hers.

She waited. The way you wait for a signal on a dead channel.

"Where are you?"

The bathroom tiles. The drip from the shower head. Her own breathing.

Her hands tightened on the sink.

"What? Got nothing to say now?"

Louder. The acoustics catching it, throwing it back at her.

"Where the fuck are you?"

The mirror didn't answer. The mirror never answered. The mirror had been giving her back her own face for eight years and her mother hadn't been behind it once—not really, not when it mattered, not when Peri was standing here with nothing on and nothing left and asking.

"Stay gone."

She said it to the glass. To the woman who wasn't in it.

Then quieter. Almost nothing.

"I don't need you."

She turned from the mirror. The shower. The knob. Her hand on it.

"You obviously don't need me."

The water came on. She stepped in before it warmed.

The cold shocked her scalp, her shoulders, ran straight down her spine. She stood into it. Waited.

When the heat arrived it came hard, water hammering the back of her skull, her neck, the tight muscles across her shoulders.

Get your shit together.

She reached for the soap and scrubbed. Hands moving through the motions because the motions were older than whatever was happening inside her. Arms. Shoulders. The scar she didn't linger on. Everywhere. Mechanical. Thorough.

She turned the water off. Stood in the steam. Water dripping off her hair, her elbows, pooling at her feet.

She dried off with rough efficiency. Hands finding the towel, the motions, the next thing and the next thing.

Fresh shirt, soft cotton. Reinforced pants. Layers for the trip, nothing restricting movement. Hair pulled back and tied. No braid. Not today.

The weapons rack.

Her kukri—she lifted it off the pegs and shrugged into the harness. Buckles finding their places, straps tightening where they always tightened. The weight settling between her shoulder blades, the blade riding the groove along her back where it disappeared under a jacket. Familiar. Right.

Her hand slowed on the last buckle.

The empty pegs below. The darker wood. Ten years of afternoons—his patience, her stubbornness, the sound of wooden blades meeting in the warehouse echo. All of it in the canal now. Gone because she'd needed something to throw and the sword was in her hand.

She finished the buckle. Pulled it tight.

Knife secured at her hip. Gear bag packed.

She moved toward the door.

The stopwatch sat on the desk where it had landed. Chrome dull in the gray light. Crescent gouge in the wood beside it. Forty-nine minutes frozen on the dial.

She stopped.

The empty pegs were behind her. Proof she could let go of something he'd given her. She'd done it once today already. She could do it again. Walk out. Leave the chrome on the desk. Let both relics go—the wooden blade in the water, the stopwatch in the empty room.

Her hand went to her jacket pocket.

Nothing there.

She stood in the doorway. The stopwatch on the desk. The door open. The stairs beyond it, and voices below, and a seven-hour drive, and a train at the end of it.

Leave it.

Her vision blurred. She blinked and felt the heat slide down her cheek. One. Just the one. She wiped it with the back of her hand before it reached her jaw.

"Fuck it."

She crossed back. Grabbed the stopwatch. Shoved it into her jacket pocket where it landed heavy and warm against her thigh.

Pulled the door open and went through it.

⊙

The stairs felt longer going down.

Each step bringing the warehouse back into focus. The sounds sharpening—engines idling, voices calling final checks, metal settling against metal.

Everyone was at the vehicles.

Thomas sat in the flatbed cab, adjusting mirrors. Carter loaded last-minute items into the bed, working around him without speaking.

Marcus stood near Seth's truck, hands in his pockets, watching the loading bay.

Kataero's crew cab sat ready. Doors open. Connor loading a bag into the back. Kitt at the passenger door, field radio case already secured, her hands checking straps that didn't need checking.

Kitt looked up when Peri reached the bottom of the stairs. Their eyes met.

"You okay?" Kitt asked.

Too soft. Too careful.

"Fine." Peri kept moving. "Let's go."

Kataero stood near the driver's door, map spread across the hood. Head down. Shoulders set.

Peri's feet carried her past his truck.

Past Connor, who straightened to watch her go. His hand dropped from the bag he was loading—reaching slightly toward her, then pulling back.

Past Kitt, whose hands stilled on the straps. Whose head turned to track her.

"Peri—"

She didn't stop.

Past the crew cab entirely.

Seth was at his vehicle, the older truck, rust bleeding through paint at the wheel wells.

He looked up as Peri approached. "You're riding with us?"

"That okay?" Casual. Like this was normal.

Seth glanced past her. Toward the crew cab. Quick. Reading the situation.

His eyes found Kataero—still bent over the map. Then Connor—watching. Then Kitt—frozen at the passenger door.

"Yeah." Careful. Neutral. "Sure."

Peri pulled open the front passenger door and climbed in. Old coffee and motor oil. Familiar in a different way than Kataero's truck. Less complicated.

She settled against the seat and let her gear bag drop to the floor.

Through the windshield, she could see them.

Connor near the crew cab. His eyes on her.

Kitt climbing slowly into the passenger seat of her dad's truck. Looking back at her through the glass.

And Kataero.

He folded the map with precise movements. Climbed into his truck. Pulled the door shut with controlled motion.

Marcus climbed into the back seat behind Peri without a word.

Seth started the engine. It caught on the second try, diesel rumble filling the cab.

Engines started in sequence. Kataero's crew cab smooth and immediate. Seth's truck settling into rough idle.

Convoy rolled out. Gate 31 falling behind them—the warehouse, the canal, the locks. Home.

Peri watched through the window as the loading bay doors shrank in the distance.

Her hand found the stopwatch in her pocket. Fingers wrapping around the chrome.

Warm now. Body heat seeping into metal.

Seth's radio crackled. Kataero's voice: "Convoy check. Everyone ready for a long day?"

Seth grabbed the mic. Quick glance at Peri as he keyed it. "We're good."

Road stretched ahead. Seven more hours to Valcross Junction.

38 | Kitt

2191.116 · 09:58

T-23 to Valcross Junction | Kyjorh Mountains

The back seat was empty.

Road surface had gone to hell two miles back—asphalt baked and rutted, grooves worn deep where years of heavy loads had ground the same tracks into softened tar. The truck wallowed through them, suspension catching every ridge. Kitt felt each one through the seat, through her hands, through the notebook balanced on her thigh.

She looked over her shoulder.

The spot behind Kataero. Where Peri always sat—knees up, boots on the edge of the bench, complaining about the music or the route or the temperature or whatever her restless mind had landed on that hour. Her gear bag sat there now. Nylon and buckles where noise and motion belonged.

Connor sat beside the bag. Silent. Greatcoat creaking when the truck caught another rut. If the empty seat bothered him, it didn't show.

She turned back to the windshield. Kataero's hands at ten and two. The road unspooling ahead through cracked pavement. Nobody had spoken in twenty minutes. The cab filled with the things that filled it when Peri wasn't here—engine noise, suspension groan, and the stillness Kataero carried like weather.

Her notebook sat open in her lap. Fuel consumption, elevation profiles, timing calculations—she'd built this route from the intelligence she'd pulled off the MERIDIAN terminal. Every gradient, every turn radius factored in. And now they were driving it, and the road was matching her numbers.

She allowed herself that. Quietly. The way she always did.

Her dad checked the rearview mirror.

She caught the motion in her peripheral. His eyes lifting, holding, returning to the road. Not checking the convoy spacing. Not scanning for threats.

Finding Peri. In Seth's passenger seat, two hundred meters back, copper hair catching sunlight through the window.

Again. Thirty seconds later.

Again.

She'd been six the first time she understood. Trail run behind the warehouse—Peri already disappearing around the bend with that effortless stride, not even winded. Kitt's lungs burning. Her legs too short. Falling further behind with every step until she stopped in the middle of the path, fists clenched, and hated her own body for the first time.

You're not built for that, little one. Come. I'll show you something better.

And he had. The workbench. The radios. The quiet satisfaction of making something that worked.

She'd stopped trying to keep up after that. Found her own thing. Made peace with it.

Most days.

Kataero checked the mirror again. Seven times now. She'd stopped actively counting after six, telling herself it was normal. But her brain kept the tally. The interval calculated itself—once every minute and twenty seconds, consistent as a carrier signal.

"Terrain's going to get worse about thirty miles ahead." She kept her voice even. Operational. Her finger found the elevation profile on the page. "Road narrows to single lane in places. We should maintain spacing through the switchbacks, but if visibility drops—"

"I know." Not sharp. Not dismissive. Just distant. "We discussed that earlier."

Right. They had.

Eyes back to the mirror.

She tried once more. Past operational. Into the space between them.

"That terminal at Gate 20—I've been thinking about the network architecture. The way they routed the CGWF node through the same backbone as military coordination. That's not standard. If we could access a MERIDIAN unit after the job, I could map the full topology. Find out what else they're running through that infrastructure."

She was offering him something real. Not route data he'd already approved. The next step. The bigger picture. The thing only she could see.

Kataero's eyes went to the mirror. Came back.

"Let's get through tomorrow first."

Gentle. The way you'd talk to someone whose contribution you appreciated but whose timing you couldn't accommodate.

I'm right here, Dad.

She looked down at the notebook. The fuel estimates tracking within three percent of her projections. The elevation profiles confirmed by every rut and grade change since they'd left. Good numbers. Her numbers.

She smoothed the page she'd creased earlier. The scar still visible.

⚙

Kataero reached for the radio. Lifted the mic from the dash mount.

"Convoy check. Call in."

His voice shifted—flat, professional. For the first time in an hour, his eyes left the mirror.

Kitt glanced back at Connor.

He was already leaning forward. Like he'd been waiting for the opening. His voice low, close to her ear.

"They had a fight this morning. By the canal."

Kitt's hands stilled on the notebook. She kept her eyes on the page.

Carter's voice came through the radio. "Lead vehicle, good." Clean signal. No drift.

"About what?" she whispered.

Connor's pause had weight to it. The kind of silence that knew more than it was offering.

"That's for your dad to tell you."

But he won't, will he? He'll check the mirror and say "got it" and let me sit here solving an equation with missing variables because the one person who has the answer is too busy watching the person who caused the problem.

Static on the radio. The channel open, waiting.

Peri's voice came through the speaker. Quiet but clear. "All good back here."

Kataero's shoulders dropped.

Just a fraction—half an inch, barely visible—but Kitt saw it. The tension leaving his frame like current draining from a circuit. His grip on the mic loosening. His eyes closing for just a half-second.

Click-click. Acknowledged. Mic back on the dash.

Peri's voice had come through clean. Strong carrier, minimal noise floor. Kitt had soldered those connections. Had seated those cells this morning—glass sliding into brass with soft clicks, blue glow disappearing behind velcro.

Her equipment carried her sister's voice across two hundred meters of mountain road and eased something in her father's chest.

That should have been enough.

His eyes went back to the mirror.

⊙

The relay tripped.

Not loud. Not dramatic. Just a switch thrown by a current she'd been accumulating all morning without measuring—every mirror check, every dismissed briefing, every "got it" and "I know" while he watched the road behind him instead of the daughter beside him.

He's my dad.

The thought surfaced clean and hard and certain.

Her father. Her blood. The man who'd put her on his workbench at three years old and let her hold a soldering iron—unlit, just the weight of it—because she'd reached for it and he'd seen something in the reaching. Who'd taught her to read schematics before she could read chapter books. Who'd held the flashlight steady every time she'd needed one, even when he handed her the wrong pliers.

Mine. And I'm right here. And I have been right here. Every convoy, every job, every morning at the workbench. I didn't run. I didn't fight. I showed up with my numbers correct and my equipment working and I have been right here this entire time.

And Peri fought with him. Ran from him. Chose Seth's truck over his.

And he was still watching the mirror.

And then—because her brain was a filing system and filing systems didn't care about timing—another drawer opened.

Last night. The drainage channel at Gate 20. Eight feet wide, twelve feet deep, access grate removed. Her chest hitting the far edge. Fingers finding nothing. The tool bag full of stolen intelligence swinging against her side, pulling her down.

Peri's hands locking around her wrists.

Stop kicking. You're making it worse.

The weight transfer. Concrete scraping her elbows through fabric. Being hauled over the lip by someone who'd already cleared the jump clean and come back for her. Lying on the concrete gasping while Peri snatched Torres's badge from her pocket and flicked it into the dark.

I hate you, Kitt had said.

Peri pulled her up. *You love me. Come on.*

Fourteen hours ago. The data in her notebook—every gradient, every fuel estimate, every turn radius they were driving right now—existed because her sister had caught her over a twelve-foot drop and hadn't let go.

The shame arrived.

Quiet. A slow warmth behind her sternum. The particular ache of catching yourself being unfair to someone who, fourteen hours ago, had your full weight in her hands and held on.

He's our dad.

She let the correction settle. Held it alongside the other thought—the hard one, the possessive one—because filing one away wouldn't make it untrue. Both things lived in her now. The claim and the correction. The jealousy and the memory of her sister's grip on her wrists, pulling her up.

She closed her notebook.

⊙

Miles rolled past. Convoy holding formation. Two hundred meters. Everything on schedule.

Through the side mirror, Seth's truck held the interval precisely. Steady. Unwavering.

Connor shifted behind her. She could feel his gaze on the back of her head. That quiet attention he gave when he was deciding whether to speak.

He didn't.

Kataero drove. Eyes forward, then mirror, then forward.

Kitt sat beside him. Notebook closed. Numbers correct. Equipment performing. Every system she'd designed working exactly as intended.

Close enough to touch him.

She felt the distance anyway.

39 | Peri

2191.116 · 12:12

Alba's Market at Ben's Corners | T-23 N

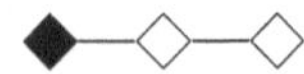

Seth's truck slowed, tires crunching over gravel. Gas station ahead—two ancient pumps, a small store with dirty windows, picnic tables weathered to old bone. Rural. Forgotten.

Convoy pulled in with practiced precision. Flatbed taking the first pump. Seth guiding his truck to the second. Kataero's crew cab parking near the store entrance where he could see everything.

Engines cut off. The tick of cooling metal. The distant hum of struggling refrigeration.

Seth stretched, vertebrae popping. "You coming in? Bathroom break?"

"I'm good."

He studied her for a moment. "You sure? We won't stop again for another hour."

"Yeah. Thanks."

He nodded. Climbed out. Left the door ajar. Fresh air pushed in—gasoline and sunbaked asphalt.

Peri stayed in the truck. Watched through the window as everyone else became part of the world again.

Carter at the pump. Thomas heading into the store. Marcus stretching beside the flatbed. Seth crossing toward the store with that easy walk of his, lifting a hand to Carter as he passed.

All of them out there. Moving through sunlight and air and each other's company like it was the simplest thing in the world.

She sat in the cab and watched them do it. The seat warm under her. Old coffee smell baked into the upholstery. Sun through the windshield heating her face, her hands, the tops of her thighs. The warmth stopped at the surface.

Her reflection in the side window—faint, transparent. The parking lot visible through her face. Through her eyes. Like she was already half-gone.

What crown are you competing for?

She let her head fall back against the seat. Hand over her eyes.

"Fuck."

Through the side mirror, she could see Kataero's crew cab parked behind them. Him standing beside his truck. Arms crossed. Not going into the store. Not stretching. Not doing any normal human thing.

Just watching Seth's vehicle.

Connor stood beside him. Said something. His mouth moved. Kataero shook his head once. Sharp. Final. Didn't look away.

Tap tap.

She flinched hard—elbow cracking against the door, heart slamming into her ribs. Knuckles on glass.

Kitt stood outside, hand raised to tap again.

Their eyes met.

She reached for the window crank. Glass descended with a squeal.

"Hey." Kitt's voice careful. Neutral.

"Hey." Hoarse.

"You okay?"

"I'm fine."

Kitt's dark eyes—Kataero's eyes—studied her face. Not believing it. "Dad's worried."

Of course he was. She could see him in the side mirror, still standing there. Still watching.

"I didn't ask him to worry," Peri said. Sharper than she'd meant.

Kitt's mouth pressed thin.

"No." Her voice went hard. Cold. "You never do."

Then: "You just do whatever you need to and the rest of us adjust around you."

Peri's chest seized. The air in the cab went thin.

Kitt had never talked to her like that. Not once.

"What's that supposed to mean?"

Kitt's mouth opened. Closed. Her breath came harder.

Then she stepped back. Shutting it down. "Nothing. Forget it."

"Kitt—"

"Everything's fine." Voice colder. Distant. The tone she used for strangers. "Stay in the damn truck. Better for all of us."

She turned. Walked away. Stiff. Boots striking pavement too hard.

Peri tracked her through the window. Kitt reached the others near the flatbed. Thomas said something—questioning tilt of his head.

Kitt's response was sharp enough that Thomas raised both hands, backing off immediately.

Peri let her head fall back against the seat. Glass warm from the sun against her skull.

Better for all of us.

Kitt braided her hair every morning. Handed her the stopwatch when she'd left it behind. Said *we make a good team* at the bottom of the stairs last night. Kitt was the one who stayed. The one who was always, always there.

And Peri had just watched those hands walk away. Just like their mother.

I'm the reason why.

The thought came before she could stop it. Ugly. True enough to bruise.

The kitchen. Morning light. Kataero behind her chair with a comb he didn't know how to use, trying to section hair he'd never learned to braid.

"No." Thirteen and furious, pulling away from his hands. "You don't do it like she does. Where is she? She knows how to do it so it's not too loose and it doesn't fall out."

"I'm sure she'll be home soon, honey. Why not just put it in a ponytail for now?"

"That's not—I—fine."

Then Kitt. Small voice from the doorway.

"I can do it for you."

Peri's head had snapped toward her. Sharp. The way it did when something caught her off guard and her whole body reacted before her brain caught up.

"What?"

Kitt hadn't flinched. Nine years old, still in her pajamas, hair tangled from sleep. Standing in the doorway like she'd been watching the whole time. Learning.

"I can do it. I know how."

Peri had stared at her. This small, serious kid with their mother's cheekbones and their father's steady eyes, offering something nobody had asked her for.

"You do?"

"Yes."

Peri looked at Kataero. Kataero looked at Kitt for a long moment. Then he stepped back from the chair.

"Okay."

Kitt had climbed onto the chair behind her. Stood on her knees to reach. Her fingers finding the part with too much pressure, pulling the sections too tight, getting the crossover wrong twice before muscle memory she didn't know she had took over.

It wasn't right. It wasn't Pepper's hands.

But it was close enough to breathe through.

And the next morning, Kitt was there again. And the next. And the next. Until Peri stopped flinching at the wrong fingers and they became the right ones.

Eight years of mornings. Eight years of small hands becoming sure hands becoming the only hands that knew the pattern.

And Peri had just watched those hands walk away.

She reached back without thinking. Found the ponytail. The weight of it against her back—tied, not braided. Wrong.

She didn't move.

Engines rumbled back to life. Convoy rolled out.

Peri turned and looked through the rear window.

Connor sat in the back of Kataero's truck, visible through two layers of glass. His eyes found hers across the distance.

Held.

Not accusatory. Not pitying. Just knowing.

Peri looked away first.

She was doing it again.

⊙

They made camp in the hills overlooking Valcross Junction as the sun dropped toward the horizon. Clearing sheltered by trees on three sides, open view of the junction below. Everything Kataero always looked for—sight lines, cover, escape routes. A place to control.

Fire built. Tents up. Canned stew heating in a pot that Carter had scrubbed clean before anyone else thought to ask. The crew settling into the evening the way crews did—Thomas and Carter talking quietly about tomorrow's rigging, Seth making nervous jokes that fell flat, Marcus cleaning his kit with the meticulous care of someone who needed his hands busy.

Peri sat near the fire. Close enough that the heat reached her face. Ate stew that tasted like nothing. Watched the flames and felt the warmth press against her skin the way the sun had pressed through the truck window.

Connor sat across from her, face half-lit by flames. Watching everyone without seeming to look at anything.

Kataero sat to her left. Close enough to be part of the group. Far enough that conversation wasn't expected. Five feet of firelit air between them carrying more weight than the seven hours of road behind them.

Their eyes met once across the fire.

He held her gaze.

Peri looked away first.

Kataero stood. The firelight caught the angles of his face, and for a moment he wasn't her father or her problem or the man she'd screamed at by a canal. He was the Black Marshal. The shift was physical—shoulders squaring, jaw setting, voice dropping into the register that had commanded battalions.

"Listen up."

Conversations died. Even Seth's nervous energy went still.

Peri straightened. Couldn't help it. That voice bypassed everything—the fog, the guilt, the hollow space in her chest. Twenty-one years of responding to that tone and her spine still answered before her brain did.

Kataero pulled Kitt's map from his coat and unfolded it across his knees. The map Peri had watched Kitt build from twelve pages of stolen intelligence—every detail pulled off a terminal that Kitt had bypassed, in a facility they'd barely escaped the night before.

"Train 47 is already moving. Left Beltmoire this afternoon—right now it's somewhere between there and the Kyjorh Transfer Station. Hits Kyjorh around oh-two-hundred, clears it by oh-three-hundred. Arrives Valcross Junction at oh-six-twenty-seven."

He let that settle. The fire crackled. Somewhere out there in the dark, the train was grinding north. Getting closer while they sat here eating stew.

"Fifteen-minute crew change at Valcross. Guard rotation—six total, two active at any time." He traced the route with one finger. "I don't want to hit it at the station. Too many eyes, too many variables."

His finger moved south of the junction. Traced the switchbacks of the Chapi Grade—the long climb where the track looped back on itself up the mountain.

"Train slows through the Chapi Loop. Nine miles per hour up the switchbacks."

Jogging speed. She could keep pace with the train on foot.

His finger stopped on the map. The flat spot at the top of the grade, where the track leveled out roughly a mile before Valcross.

"We stop the train here."

He looked around the fire. Making sure he had every pair of eyes.

"Car 3 is the primary target. Turbine housing, rotor assemblies, control systems, wiring harnesses. Everything Belfast Mills needs to bring the dam back. Car 4 has transformers and switch assemblies—secondary target if time allows."

"Six crates minimum from Car 3. More from Car 4 if we get the time. Twenty minutes from stop to departure. That's the math."

"Seth, you take Thomas and Carter. Position the flatbed at the flat spot before the train arrives. A-frame rigged, slings ready. Carter on the hoist. Thomas on the ground. Take my truck with you—Carter, you drive it over. I want all vehicles in one spot. No backtracking."

Seth nodded. Serious now.

"Marcus, you drive the drop team to the bridge. Once we're on, you take the truck to extraction and wait for the signal. Fill in the gaps."

"Connor, Peri, Kitt, and I will board the train on the loop."

"Me?" Kitt's voice sharp with surprise. "I'm not—"

"Her?" Peri. Same beat. Different fear.

Kataero looked at them both. Something flickered in his eyes—the briefest acknowledgment that his two daughters had just spoken in unison for the first time all day.

"You're with me on this one."

The words cut clean. Not harsh. Just closed. No room for debate because it wasn't a debate.

Kitt's mouth stayed open for a half-second. Then shut.

"How are we stopping the train?" Seth asked.

Kataero glanced at Connor.

"Connor and I will handle that. You worry about being ready when it stops."

"I got an idea," Connor said, poking the fire.

His elbow found Peri's ribs. Light. The kind of nudge you'd give a kid sister before a game. When she looked at him, he winked. One eye, quick, gone before anyone else caught it.

I've got you.

She almost smiled. Almost.

Kataero folded the map.

"No improvisation. No heroics. We get the generator components and we leave."

"What about the mysterious cargo?" Seth asked. "Car 2. MT-7719. We just ignoring that?"

"We focus on the mission." Steel beneath the calm. "Generator components only. Anything else is a distraction we can't afford."

His eyes swept the circle one more time. Landing on each face. Holding.

"Questions?"

She had one. She didn't ask it.

"Good. Get some rest. We move at oh-five-hundred."

⊙

Group dispersed. Connor banking the fire. Kitt heading for the tent she and Peri were sharing. Didn't wait. Didn't look back.

Peri sat by the dying fire. Not ready to sleep. Not ready for the tent and Kitt's silence and the canvas walls holding them both in a space too small for what was between them.

Kataero stood. Started toward his tent. Stopped. Looked back at her, his face all angles and shadow in the firelight.

Words gathering behind his teeth.

"You should get some rest," he said finally.

"I will."

He nodded. Turned. Walked away.

She watched him go until the darkness swallowed him.

Connor stayed on the log. Poking the embers the same way he'd been poking them all night. Patient. Unhurried. Like he'd been waiting for the clearing to empty.

"You planning to sleep at all?" he asked finally.

"Eventually."

"Might want to make it soon. Long day tomorrow."

"Says the guy still awake."

"That's fair."

Silence. Fire dying between them.

"He's not angry," Connor said quietly. Not looking at her. Looking at the embers. "He's worried. There's a difference."

"I don't want to talk about it."

"I know." He shifted on the log. Stared at the fire a long time. "You're both hurting. Both too proud to cross first."

"He left his Sabaki in the concrete and walked away."

"You threw yours in the canal and ran."

Peri's hands curled into fists.

"I went looking for you," Connor said. Still poking the fire. "All I found was the Sabaki. Nearly got a hernia pulling it out."

She could see it. Connor at the spillway in the early morning. Alone. Wrapping his hands around the hilt and hauling against concrete that didn't want to let go.

"He just walked away, Connor."

"What did you expect?" Not unkind. Just honest. "He's always been there for you. Taken every punch you throw. At some point, even he breaks." He let that sit. "And for a man like him, that's something."

The fire popped. Sparks drifted upward and died.

"I can't face him."

"This is one of them. He's your father. He loves you. Talk to him."

"Before tomorrow."

Pause. Heavy.

"Why?"

Connor held her gaze in the firelight. Serious in a way she hadn't seen since the mountain.

"Because tomorrow's dangerous. And if something goes wrong—"

Lin was a great man who found his purpose. What made him who he was... it's in you.

Fire crackled. A log collapsed inward, sending up sparks.

He stood. Looked down at her.

"Before tomorrow, Peri."

He walked away toward his tent.

She sat there for a long time. Cold seeping into her bones. Watching embers fade to ash.

Eventually the cold drove her to the tent. Kitt was already in her sleeping bag. Curled on her side facing the tent wall. Breathing slow and even.

Too even.

Peri knew her sister's sleep-breathing, and this wasn't it.

She climbed into her sleeping bag without zipping it. Pulled it over herself like a blanket. Lay there in the dark. Staring up at canvas she couldn't see.

She should say something. Bridge the gap Connor had told her to cross. But the words wouldn't come. They never came. She could plan a heist, read a room, talk her way past armed guards—but she couldn't find six words for her little sister in the dark.

Minutes passed. The canvas moved slightly in the wind. Cold air finding the seams.

Then Kitt shifted.

Not turning over. Not speaking. Just moving backward, closing the distance between them, until her back pressed against Peri's chest. Small and warm and deliberate.

Kitt's hand found Peri's arm. Pulled it across herself. Held it there—Peri's palm flat against her sternum, Kitt's fingers laced through hers.

The way they'd slept when they were small. When the dark was too big and Peri's arm was the thing that made it smaller.

Peri curled around her. Chin settling against Kitt's hair. Pulling her close. Kitt's body molded with hers.

Her sister's heartbeat against her palm. Steady.

Kitt's breathing changed. The too-even rhythm softening, loosening, becoming the thing Peri actually recognized—the real sound. The one that meant safe. The one that meant sleep.

Peri held on.

She was still holding on when she fell asleep.

40 | Wynne

2191.117 · 11:47

Hamilton Rail Station | CAD Hamilton

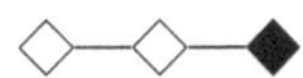

Rail yard spread before them—cargo containers stacked three high, creating narrow corridors that smelled of old grease and diesel exhaust. Wynne's bare feet found purchase on grit-covered concrete. Noon sun turned metal surfaces too hot to touch.

Security everywhere. More than usual. Guards moving with purpose rather than the lazy patrol of men counting hours. These were hunters looking for something specific.

Looking for them.

Paul's voice came low. "I'd say folks are going to take my skipping check-in as a sign that things didn't go as they'd have liked." His hand moved to his ribs—unconscious gesture, old injury remembered. "Best to get out of a city that has armed security on every corner."

"Agreed." Jaden scanned the yard, cane tapping softly. "Northern line runs through Barrowfield. Less populated, fewer checkpoints."

Paul snorted. "When was the last time that nose of yours left a book and traveled outside Hamilton?"

"You think I only know my way around a library."

"Not even. Too busy poring over your grandfather's work—you barely noticed I kept moving the books around."

Jaden's stride faltered. "You deceitful—"

Wynne stopped listening.

A voice carried from somewhere ahead. Familiar cadence—weathered authority giving orders to men who knew how to take them. She turned, scanning the maze of containers and cargo.

There. Sixty yards ahead. Broad frame, arm braced but working—a leather support strapped from wrist to elbow, the kind that let a man use his hands while reminding him not to trust them completely. He was lifting a manifest clipboard, checking cargo, directing his crew the way he always had. Back in the work.

Pede.

"I found us a way out of here."

Paul followed her gaze, irritation replaced by calculation. "Friend of yours?"

"I worked his crew for two weeks." She started moving. "Whether that extends to this, we'll find out."

They moved between containers, staying in shadows. Paul led, reading patrol patterns with the same economy he'd brought to Hamilton's alleys. Jaden followed, cane clicking against concrete. Twenty yards from Pede's position.

"You three! Stop!"

Two guards emerged from behind a container to their right. Weapons drawn but not raised—professional stance, doing their job. Wynne counted more converging on the shout. Four, six.

Paul's hand went to his belt.

"Run or fight?" His voice tight.

"Hands where we can see them!"

Wynne's staff came off her back. No ceremony. Six guards in a narrow space between containers, concrete and metal boxing them in. No room to maneuver, but the same constraint worked both ways.

Manageable. Maybe.

⊙

The first guard reached for her arm—shoulder dropping before the grab, weight committing forward. She read the intention a half-second before it arrived. Stepped inside his reach, caught his wrist, and redirected his momentum past her. Her staff swept his leading leg at the ankle and he went down hard, concrete unforgiving beneath him.

His partner was already moving. Baton up. The impact shuddered through her wrists when she blocked—the kind of force that came from a man who outweighed her by sixty pounds and knew how to use it. He pressed the advantage. She gave ground, felt the container edge cold against her back.

Trapped.

She dropped. His baton cracked against metal where her head had been—the sound enormous in the narrow space—and her staff drove up between his legs, lift and twist. He folded backward. Landed badly.

A body hitting metal to her left. Paul's work—she didn't need to look.

The sharp crack of wood on bone somewhere behind her—Jaden's cane, and a grunt that wasn't his.

Radio chatter cut through: "Section 7, multiple suspects engaged, requesting backup—"

More would come. Had to move faster.

Two more guards flanked her—coordinated, one going low, one high. She read the pattern, blocked the low guard's grab with the staff's base, but the high guard's baton caught her across the shoulder blade. Pain hit sharp and immediate. Her grip loosened for a fraction of a second.

Can't lose the staff.

She let the hit's force carry her into a spin—the momentum already there, fighting it would waste it. Staff came around in the rotation and caught the high guard across the ribs. She heard him grunt. The low guard grabbed for her ankle. She drove the staff's butt end down—not hard enough to break, just enough to make him let go.

More guards poured in from adjacent sections. Too many now to track individually.

One rushed Paul from behind. "Paul! Left!"

He turned too slow. Baton caught him across the forearm and his pistol fell, skittering under a container.

Wynne was already there. Staff came up, blocked the follow-up swing meant for Paul's head. Her shoulder screamed but she pushed through it, swept the guard's legs. Down.

Another charged. She stepped back—foot hit grease-slicked concrete. Balance shifted wrong. Her weight going where she didn't want it. The guard's hand closed on her staff before she could reset. Yanked hard.

Her grip tore free.

Wood clattered across concrete. Fifteen feet away.

For one breath, her hands were empty. And something in her chest seized—not fear. Something older than fear. Wood worn smooth by her hands alone, lying on oil-stained ground. Not her capability. Her history.

New rules. New distances.

The guard coming at her didn't know the difference. He saw an unarmed girl and committed—full speed, full weight, exactly the kind of mistake people made when they confused a weapon with the person holding it.

Wynne stepped into him. Not back. Into. Caught his wrist, rotated it past the joint's natural limit, used his own forward momentum to fold him over her hip. He hit the ground before he understood what had happened. She was already turning—elbow strike to the next guard's solar plexus, precise enough to empty his lungs without cracking his sternum. He doubled over. She drove her knee into his thigh, dead-legging him, and he dropped.

Faster now. Without the staff there was no distance, no time—just contact, read, respond, the fight happening at the speed of touch rather than reach. Master Kell's work. The close-quarters drills she'd resented at thirteen because she'd wanted the elegance of staff forms, not knowing exactly how much force a human knee could take before it stopped being a knee.

Another guard. Faster than the others—trained, not just equipped. He came in low, arms wide, trying to tackle. She read his weight, sidestepped at the last instant, caught his head as he passed and redirected him face-first into a container. The sound was ugly. He stayed down.

The remaining guards hesitated. Half a second of nothing. That was enough.

Movement in her peripheral. Paul—he'd spotted her staff on the ground, grabbed it, spun, threw it end over end. His shoulder caught halfway, the staff wobbling instead of spinning clean—

Wynne's hand shot up. Caught it mid-rotation, weight settling back into her grip like coming home.

But more kept coming, and radio chatter suggested reinforcements en route. The guards were learning now—staying back, waiting for openings rather than rushing in. Getting smarter. Which meant this was getting worse.

Paul moved beside her, breathing hard. He'd retrieved his pistol from under the container—raised it now at an approaching guard, arm steady despite the chaos, and Wynne saw the decision in his shoulders before his finger found the trigger.

Her staff cracked across his aim.

The shot punched into the sky. The sound ricocheted between metal walls—every guard in the yard knew exactly where they were now.

Paul rounded on her. Not just anger in his face. Disbelief. The particular fury of a man who'd just had survival taken out of his hands.

"What the hell?!"

A baton swung past them both—close enough to feel the air move. Neither flinched. For one held breath the fight continued around them and they stood in the center of it, locked on each other.

"Doing their job shouldn't cost them their lives."

She said it quietly. Just the line she would not cross, spoken aloud so it existed in the world between them. Her shoulder was screaming. Her wrists swelling inside her grip. She was losing this fight by degrees, and she had just made it harder.

And she would do it again.

Paul's expression went flat. She could see it building behind his teeth—all the practical reasons she was wrong. Every one of them valid. Every one of them true.

He blocked a baton with his forearm, grunted with the impact. Turned back to the fight because the fight didn't wait for moral philosophy. "Will make for excellent last words."

Wynne blocked another strike. Her shoulder had gone past pain into something duller—a deep, structural protest that meant she was borrowing from tomorrow.

"Maybe," she said. "But they'll be mine."

⚙

Jaden's hand on her arm. Hard. "They're herding us—east fence." Breathing between every other word. But his eyes were already somewhere else, reading what his body couldn't answer.

She saw it now. Four guards pushing from the left, three from the right. Herding them against the containers with tactical patience. Every choice not to break bones was a choice to fight the same man twice.

This isn't sustainable.

Pede stood thirty feet away. He'd stopped working. His crew frozen behind him—and she saw them now. Al, tensioner still in his hand. Mickie, broad shoulders squared, watching the fight with an expression she recognized. The same one he'd worn in the cargo car after the pallet save. Reading what he was seeing. Knowing what it meant.

Pede's eyes found hers.

No calculation. No weighing. He'd watched her work twelve days. Watched her save Al's life. Watched her leave on a train with his envelope in her pack and his partner's name in her pocket. He knew who she was.

Behind him, the cargo train's engine rumbled. Steam already building.

His mouth pressed thin. Decision made.

"First time I laid eyes on you, I knew you were trouble." He turned to his crew. "Asses on that train! NOW!"

Move.

Wynne spun, staff clearing a path. Not fighting anymore—just creating space, buying seconds. Paul was already running, hauling Jaden by the arm, half-carrying him toward the cargo car. Jaden's cane caught on a rail tie and he stumbled—Paul didn't slow, just gripped harder, kept them both moving.

Twenty feet.

A guard grabbed Wynne's arm with a grip that meant it. She twisted—not graceful, just desperate—brought her elbow up. Connected with his jaw. He let go.

Ten feet.

Paul reached the cargo car, hauled himself up, turned, grabbed Jaden's hand. Jaden's bad leg buckled on the step—for one terrible second he hung between the platform and the moving train, body weight pulling him down, Paul's grip the only thing between him and the wheels. Then Paul heaved and Jaden was aboard, landing hard on the cargo car floor with a sound that was half impact and half the breath driven out of him.

Wynne came last. Guards closing fast. One more swing cleared the closest two, her shoulder failing, her wrists throbbing, the staff feeling heavier than it had ever felt in her life.

Can't hold them.

Mickie's hand shot out from the cargo door. Caught her forearm. Pulled hard—the same grip that had steadied the pallet she couldn't hold, that had taken her hand on the platform the morning she'd left. Callus against skin.

She left her feet as the train lurched and landed in the cargo car. Stumbled. Mickie's other hand caught her shoulder, kept her upright.

"Easy," he said. The same word. The same voice.

Behind them, a guard scrambled to follow. Tried to jump aboard. Missed. Hit the platform hard.

Train picked up speed.

Pede appeared at the cargo door. Looked at her—bruised, winded, staff still in her hand.

"You good?"

She nodded.

He rolled the door halfway closed, leaving it cracked for air. She heard him shouting outside: "Clear! Keep moving!"

⚙

Wynne moved to the gap in the door.

Her shoulder was on fire. Her wrists swelling, bruises forming across her forearms in the shapes of every baton she'd blocked. Her body tallying the cost now that survival no longer demanded she ignore it.

She watched.

Guards picking themselves up throughout the yard. Helping each other stand—one reaching down for another the way men do when the fighting stops and they remember they're just men. One limping. Another holding his ribs, breathing carefully.

But standing. All of them standing.

That was hers. That was what her principles had bought—not victory, not escape. Just the knowledge that every person she'd fought today would go home tonight. Would eat dinner. Would sleep in a bed. Would wake up bruised and sore and alive because she'd chosen to make her own fight harder rather than make their lives shorter.

The math didn't balance. Paul would tell her so. The practical calculus said she'd nearly gotten them killed for a principle that the world didn't reward and the enemy didn't share.

She knew.

Through the narrowing gap, vehicles arrived. Fast. Blackcoats—Continental Authority enforcement—moving through the yard with a coordination that made the guards she'd fought look like a neighborhood watch. They spread through the yard. Weapons drawn. Converging on where the train had been, questioning workers, establishing a perimeter around nothing.

Sanchez was with them. Not Blackcoat—local detail, folded into the response the way security always folded into larger operations. She caught him by the way he moved before she found his face. Weight forward on his feet, directing two officers toward the warehouse line, hand signals clean and economical. Professional. Focused. The same energy he'd brought to the lake path, pointed somewhere else now.

He didn't look toward the train. He had a job to do.

The dockworkers still milling through the yard were just dockworkers. The guards were bruised and upright and had nothing to offer but a description. Buildings thickened, steel and brick cutting the view into narrower slices.

Gone.

Behind her, deeper in the cargo car, Al was already checking straps on crates that had shifted during the rushed departure—hands moving with the same quiet precision she remembered, the clipboard nowhere in sight for once. Mickie worked the far end, retensioning a line that had slipped its anchor, the ratchet clicking in steady rhythm.

They didn't look at her. Didn't need to. The work was the work, and the train was moving, and freight didn't secure itself.

Pede had made his choice. His crew had followed. The way crew followed.

Wynne stood at the door. Arms folded across her chest, staff cradled against her body. Her shoulder protested the position. She kept it anyway.

Jaden moved to her left. Paul to her right. Three of them watching Hamilton disappear.

"Blackcoats," Jaden said quietly. "That's Continental Authority."

Paul snorted. "Yeah."

Wynne said nothing. Just watched the city thin into farmland, the skyline she'd mapped over two weeks of walking reduced to a smudge on the horizon.

⊙

The hours passed in the rhythm of steel on steel, wheels singing against rails as morning stretched toward afternoon. The cargo car swayed with the motion, finding its pace as the train built speed through farmland and scattered forest.

Master Rev's voice surfaced from memory—arriving, as it always did, when she'd done something he would have argued against and couldn't have argued with:

The world is not what we told you it would be. You'll encounter the situations that made us withdraw—the impossible choices, the failures that break people. When you do, remember that we didn't fail. We chose differently than you're choosing now.

She'd understood the words then. Standing in the trial chamber, nineteen years old, bare feet on sand, certain she knew what the world was. Standing here with bruised wrists and a shoulder that would ache for days, watching farmland scroll past while Blackcoats searched an empty yard behind her—she understood something else.

He'd been afraid for her. That was what lived beneath the lesson. Not disappointment. Not warning. Fear that his student would walk into the world he'd retreated from and find out why he'd retreated.

She was finding out. And she was still standing.

Not the monastery's choice. Hers.

Paul sat against a crate, cleaning his gun with methodical attention. After a while, he spoke without looking up.

"Just making sure you know what you're choosing, Ms. Kaede." He glanced at her shoulder, at the bruises climbing her forearms. "Because it only gets harder from here."

Wynne leaned her head back against the cargo crate. Felt the vibration through wood and steel, through her whole body.

She closed her eyes.

41 | Peri

2191.117 · 04:50 | Z1
Outside Chapi Loop | Valcross Junction

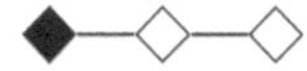

Peri woke to cold against her chest.

The space where Kitt had been. Gone now—sleeping bag zipped neat and rolled, the corner tucked under itself the way Kitt did everything. Precise. Considered. Even in the dark, even after.

She could still feel the shape of her sister against her ribs. The warmth that had been there all night, the heartbeat she'd tracked through her palm until sleep pulled her under. How long ago had Kitt slipped free? Minutes? An hour? She'd moved carefully enough that Peri hadn't stirred.

Outside—boots on frozen ground, voices low and professional, the clank of equipment being loaded. Team already preparing.

She'd barely slept. Maybe two hours total, fragmented and full of shadows—the sword falling through dark water, over and over, never reaching the bottom. Her body felt heavy. The kind of tired that lived in her bones. But the sounds outside were insistent. A machine already in motion, with or without her.

Peri sat up slowly. Canvas dark above her. Her breath misted in air she couldn't see. Temperature had dropped overnight—she felt it in the stiffness of her fingers as she reached for her clothes.

She dressed by feel. Layers in the order her body knew—the chill making her movements clumsy at first, then sharper as she woke up. The knife at her hip. She felt its weight settle where it always sat. Kukri along her spine beneath her shirt, handle where her hand expected it. Both where they should be.

The stopwatch sat on her pack where she'd set it before climbing into the sleeping bag. She found it by touch. Chrome cold under her fingers.

Peri held it.

Forty-nine minutes still frozen on the dial—not that she could read it in the dark. She didn't need to. She knew the number the way she knew her own pulse. She hadn't wound it. Hadn't started it. Just set it there like she could set aside everything it represented.

She turned it over. Worn reset button under her thumb. How many times had she pressed that? Thousands. Starting the timer. Stopping it. Checking her worth in minutes and seconds.

What crown are you competing for?

She set the stopwatch back on her pack.

Leave it.

She grabbed her gear bag instead. First aid, water, the small things she'd need. Stood and moved toward the tent flap.

Didn't look back.

Pushed through canvas into cold morning air—

And stopped.

Three steps from the fire pit. Frost crunching under her boots. Wind cutting through her jacket. The camp spread around her in the dark—

headlamps bobbing between vehicles, the shapes of tents coming down, the others moving with purpose between them. All of it registering at a distance, like watching through the truck window again.

Her hand went to her pocket.

Empty.

Weight missing from her ribs. Balance wrong. The world tilting slightly without that anchor, everything a half-step off center. Like running with one boot unlaced—she could do it, but every stride would feel like a mistake about to happen.

Her shoulders dropped. Head tilting back, eyes closing. Cold air against her face.

C'mon. C'mon, c'mon, c'mon.

She took a step. Stopped. Took another. Stopped.

Fuck.

She turned. Went back into the tent. Not thinking. Just moving. Compulsive. Inevitable.

Grabbed the stopwatch from her pack. Shoved it into her jacket pocket. Felt its weight settle against her ribs.

And stood there. Breathing hard. Staring at the dark where the canvas wall should be.

The whole thing took maybe fifteen seconds.

Fifteen seconds to undo the only thing she'd tried to change.

She pushed out of the tent before she could think about it anymore.

⊙

Camp was breaking down around her. Tents coming down, gear being stowed. The crew moving with the tight efficiency of people who knew the clock was running. Seth's team was already gone—flatbed and the crew cab, pulled out while she slept. Headed for the flat spot to rig the hoist.

Peri found a place at the edge of things—close enough to be part of it, far enough that nobody tried to talk to her. She ate something from a tin. Couldn't have said what. Washed it down with water so cold it hurt her teeth.

The sky was still black. Faintest glow on the eastern ridge—not light yet, just the promise of it. No wind at ground level, but the treetops moved—weather up high, coming down eventually.

Kitt was at the remains of the fire pit, packing the radio into its case by headlamp. Hands moving with that careful precision—velcro, clasps, the cells checked one more time. She didn't look up when Peri passed. But she didn't turn away either.

Kataero called the drop team together. Four of them in the dark. Final check.

"Train cleared Kyjorh two hours ago. It's on the grade now. Seth's team is in position at the flat spot." His eyes moved across them—Connor, Peri, Kitt. Landing on each face. "We're on the bridge in forty minutes. Twenty-minute window once it stops. We execute the plan, Belfast Mills has power by end of week."

No questions. Everyone knew their parts.

"Mount up."

Peri moved toward Marcus's truck—the remaining vehicle, the one Marcus would drive to the extraction point once the drop team was on the bridge.

She wasn't ready for this. Wasn't ready for the small space and the quiet that would press into every place she didn't fill. But the job didn't care what she was ready for.

Kataero was at the passenger door, checking gear by headlamp. Always checking.

She stopped beside him. Close enough to touch.

Her mouth opened. Her hand moved—almost reached for his arm before she caught herself, shoved it in her pocket. Found the stopwatch there.

"You ready?" he asked.

"Yeah."

His teeth set. That muscle in his jaw. The silence between them full of everything "yeah" couldn't carry.

"Good." He shouldered his bag. "Let's go."

He climbed in.

Peri stood there another heartbeat. The morning cold on her face. The taste of whatever she'd eaten sitting metallic in her mouth.

Then she climbed into the back. Kitt was already there—staring out the window at nothing, chin resting on her fist. Not the professional distance from the gas station. Something else. Quieter. The distance of someone who'd closed the gap in the dark and didn't know what that meant in daylight.

Connor took the front passenger seat. Marcus behind the wheel.

Doors shut. Engine rumbled to life.

Kitt glanced over. Her eyes dropped to Peri's hair—loose, tangled, shoved behind her ears. The mess of someone who'd slept hard and woken fast.

"Peri. Your hair."

Peri reached up. Pulled a strand in front of her face, looked at it, then looked back at Kitt.

She fished a rubber band from her jacket pocket. Held it up between two fingers.

"You've been slacking." One corner of her mouth twitched. Almost a wink.

Kitt stared at her. Something moving behind those dark eyes—surprise, maybe, or the effort of not reacting to a voice she hadn't heard in two days.

Then she took the elastic. "Turn around."

Peri turned. Felt Kitt's fingers gather her hair. The familiar pull of sections being separated—left, right, center. The pattern starting.

The truck rocked over rough road. Kitt adjusted without pausing. Her hands knew this work in any conditions—kitchen chairs, warehouse benches, the back seat of a truck winding through hills before dawn. The location didn't matter. The hands remembered.

Peri closed her eyes. Let her head move with the gentle pull.

Connor watched in the rearview mirror. Said nothing. But the corner of his mouth shifted.

Over, under, pull. Over, under, pull. The rhythm of it settling into the silence the way a heartbeat settles into a chest. Not fixing anything. Not solving the gas station or the canal or the words that still sat between them like broken glass.

Just this. The one thing that had never needed words.

Kitt secured the tail with the elastic. One last tug to test the hold.

"Done."

Peri's hand came up. Found the braid against her spine. Ran her thumb along it. Tight. Even. Right.

"Thanks."

Kitt turned back to her window. But her shoulders had shifted. Not softened exactly. Just—less locked. Like whatever had loosened one bolt in the tent had loosened another in the truck.

Nobody spoke after that. The cab held four people and enough silence for forty. But it was a different silence now. Not the kind that carried weight. The kind that carried work already done.

The road unwound in the headlamps. Darkness thinning by degrees as they climbed—black to charcoal to the flat gray of a sky deciding whether to commit to morning.

Peri felt the stopwatch pressing against her ribs with every breath. Rise and fall. Rise and fall. Measuring nothing. Counting nothing. Just there, the way a scar was there—healed over but never gone.

But the braid was there too. Tight against her spine. Kitt's hands in her hair like every morning for eight years.

Both things true. Both things hers.

⊙

The bridge appeared through morning mist. Old steel I-beams crossing the track. Rust streaking the girders. The paint had given up a long time ago. Twenty feet above the rails. Maybe twenty-five.

Higher than it had looked on Kitt's diagrams.

Marcus pulled off into a stand of pine below the bridge structure. He'd take the truck to the extraction point, wait for the signal.

The truck stopped. Kitt climbed out first, already scanning the bridge structure above them.

Connor looked back over his shoulder.

"Like I said. Better to be aware of your sister than to apologize all the time."

Peri met his eyes. "But then we wouldn't get to make up." She held his gaze. "That's the important part."

Connor's mouth twitched. He turned and climbed out.

Four of them now. Standing in the trees. Wind through pine branches. Distant birdsong. The faintest glow of dawn outlining the ridge to the east, the rest of the sky still holding onto dark.

Peri looked at the others. Her father checking his gear with that mechanical focus she'd inherited whether she wanted it or not. Connor stretching his shoulders, loose and easy—the only one who looked like he did this every morning. Kitt standing apart, arms crossed, studying the bridge with an engineer's eye. Reading the structure the way Peri read terrain—load points, stress fractures, where the steel was sound and where rust had eaten through.

"Let's move," Kataero said.

They climbed. Ladder rungs slick with morning dew, cold biting through Peri's gloves. Hand over hand, ground dropping away beneath her boots. The height registering in her stomach first—that low pull, gravity reminding her it was still in charge.

She pulled herself over the edge onto the maintenance walkway.

The bridge shifted under her weight. Not much—just enough to feel, a slight give in the steel that said this structure had been standing longer than it should have been. Grating beneath her boots, rusted in patches, the rails barely visible below through the gaps in the dim light. Wind stronger up here, finding the openings in her jacket, pressing cold against her ribs where the stopwatch sat.

View opened up—sky lighter to the east now, a pale band widening along the ridge. Darker overhead. Weather coming.

And there—faint, carried on the wind—a low rumble from somewhere down the grade. Rhythmic. Mechanical. Growing.

The train.

Peri's pulse kicked up. Her hands wanted to move, to check gear, to do something. Energy coiling in her legs, in her fingers. The gray weight cracking. The body remembering what it was for.

Behind her, Kitt made a small sound. Breath catching.

Peri looked back. Kitt stood near the edge, looking down through the grating at the tracks below. Hands gripping the safety rail hard enough to bleach her knuckles. Looking like she'd bite through her own tongue before admitting it.

Peri moved to her. Not close enough to crowd. Close enough to be felt.

"You good?"

"Yeah." Kitt's voice came out tight. "Fine."

She wasn't. But she'd do it anyway. Because that was Kitt's kind of brave—terrified and doing it anyway.

Kataero moved beside Peri. Close. His voice quiet but firm.

"Nothing fancy." Tone that didn't ask, didn't negotiate. "My plan, my rules."

Peri looked at him. First time she'd really met his eyes since the spillway.

"I mean it, Peri. We drop, we execute, we extract. Clean and simple. No improvisation."

She held his gaze. And saw it.

Not anger. Not disappointment.

Fear.

In the set of his jaw. In the lines around his eyes. In the way he held himself—like he was already mourning something that hadn't happened yet.

This was what Connor had been trying to tell her at the fire. This was what the silence in the truck had been carrying. Not punishment. Not withdrawal. Just a father standing on a bridge with his daughters, about to send them onto a moving train, and the last real words between them had been *charity case* and *real daughter* and a sword in the canal.

Her chest ached.

"Understood," she said. And meant it.

Before tomorrow, Peri.

Tomorrow was here.

He weighed that answer. Searching her face for the bright lie she'd built her life around.

Then something shifted in his face. The lines softened. Not all the way—not forgiveness, not resolution. But enough. His hand came up—rough palm cupping her cheek for a moment. Calluses against her skin. Warmth she hadn't earned and he gave anyway.

"Do your thing," he said quietly.

Her eyes burned. She swallowed hard.

The train whistle cut through the morning air. Closer now. Real. The bridge humming under her boots—vibration climbing through steel and grating and into her bones.

Peri turned to face it.

42 | Peri

2191.117 · 05:48

Chapi Loop Overpass | Valcross Junction

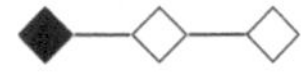

Dark on the bridge. Wind and the smell of wet steel.

Peri stood at the far edge of the overpass—the side facing the grade, where the train would come. Pine trees climbed the slopes on either side of the cut, their tops lost in low cloud. The track disappeared into the dark between them, curving away behind a hillside she couldn't see past.

Somewhere beyond that curve, an engine.

She couldn't see it. Could barely hear it. Just a low vibration in the rails below, felt through the bridge's bones and up through her boots. A suggestion. A promise. Something massive moving toward her through the dark.

She stood there. Hands in her jacket pockets. Stopwatch pressing against her knuckles. The gray weight still on her—sitting heavy in her chest, in her legs, in the space behind her eyes.

Waiting. The thing she was worst at.

Behind her, across the bridge, Kataero's voice carried through the dark. Low. Patient. Teaching.

"Thread it through here. Loop back. Lock the carabiner like this."

She didn't turn. Just listened. His hands on the rope, guiding Kitt through the anchor configuration. The same voice he'd used teaching Peri years ago—the same patience, the same belief that competence was something you built one knot at a time.

Father and daughter. Working together.

She stared into the dark between the pines. The vibration in the rails was stronger now. Or she was imagining it.

"No, look—here." Kataero's voice again. "The load needs to distribute across the beam. Feel where the tension sits."

Kitt's response—too quiet to make out the words. Just her tone. Frustrated. Trying.

Her fingers drummed against the stopwatch.

She couldn't stand here.

Peri crossed the bridge. Not toward Kitt and Kataero—toward Connor, at his anchor point on the opposite rail. Her boots rang on the grating, each step too loud in the quiet.

Connor was already clipped in. Rope secured, harness buckled, everything where it should be. He leaned against the railing with the ease of someone who'd done this when it actually mattered—when the drop was onto enemy positions, not cargo cars.

Peri stopped beside him. Reached for his anchor line without asking. Tested the connection—tugged the carabiner, ran her hand along the rope to the beam, checked where it seated against the steel.

Connor watched her do it. One eyebrow raised. Storm-gray eyes amused in the dark.

"Feel better?" he asked.

"Just checking."

"I was tying knots before your father met your mother."

"And you're old. Old people make mistakes."

The corner of his mouth moved. He said nothing else. Didn't need to.

She crossed back to the train side. Her side. Rope still coiled at her feet, I-beam cold and solid beside her. Not ready for it yet. Hands too restless. Body too loud.

She paced. Six steps one direction, six steps back. Hands out of her pockets. Arms swinging. Letting the restlessness build, letting her body do what her body needed to do before it could do what came next.

Across the bridge, Kataero had moved on to the harness. His voice carrying: "Chest strap first. Then leg loops. Pull here until it's snug—you want it tight but not restrictive."

"I know how a harness works, Dad." Kitt's voice—tighter now. Nerves sharpening her.

"Humor me."

Six steps. Turn. Six steps. Turn.

The engine sound was real now. Distant, muffled by the hillside and the pines. A rhythmic pounding. Pistons. Steam. Something working hard against the grade.

She could feel the gray weight shifting. Not gone. But something was pushing up through it—something that lived in her legs and her lungs and her hands and had been waiting all morning for permission to exist.

She stopped at the railing. Gripped it. Looked out into the dark.

Dawn finding the edges of things. The engine sound filling the valley—that rhythmic pounding echoing off rock and wood, bouncing between the slopes until it seemed to come from everywhere at once.

She breathed. Long and slow. Cold air sharp in her throat.

Her fingers loosened on the railing. Her weight settled into her feet—not shifting anymore, not pacing. Planted. The restlessness still there but gathered now. Concentrated. All the scattered energy of the last hour pressing inward to a single point.

The bridge hummed. Faint tremor building. The train's weight registering through miles of rail and into the steel she stood on.

Her heartbeat found the engine's rhythm without her choosing it. Her pulse and its pulse and the space between them narrowing.

The dark between the pines began to change.

Not dawn. Something warmer. Something moving.

Light.

Warm yellow spilling across the treetops. Painting the hillside in gold. The locomotive's headlamp, still hidden behind the curve but close enough now that its light preceded it—reaching around the hill, finding the pine trunks, the rock face, the steel of the bridge where she stood.

The light touched her face.

And the gray weight broke.

Not gradually. Not in stages. It broke the way ice broke on the canal in spring—one moment holding, the next moment gone, and the current that had been building underneath suddenly free and moving and unstoppable.

⊙

She moved. Not pacing now. Purpose.

Her hands found the rope at her feet. Muscle memory took over—swing the line, let momentum carry it around the beam. Loop catches, wraps, cinches against itself. Carabiner open, rope seated in the gate, lock screwed tight. Three seconds. Clove hitch locked perfect.

She tested it with her full weight, leaning back until the harness pulled against her hips and the rope sang taut. Solid.

Silence from across the bridge.

Then Kataero's voice. Quiet. Measured. Not aimed at Peri.

"That's one way to do that." A pause. "Let's start again."

Kitt's hands on the rope. Kataero beside her. Starting over.

Then she crossed the bridge. One last time. Moving differently now—clean, directed, every step landing exactly where it needed to land.

Connor saw her coming. Straightened. That look—recognition. He'd seen this before.

Kataero looked up from Kitt's harness. His eyes found Peri's face and whatever he saw there made him step back. Gave her room.

Peri went to Kitt.

The train was close. She could feel it in the bridge—the tremor becoming a shudder, steel vibrating hard enough to blur the grating under her boots. The engine sound coming straight for them now, the bend almost cleared, the light blazing brighter.

Her hands found Kitt's harness. Chest strap—hooked two fingers under it, pulled. Snug. Leg loops—tugged each one. Secure. Main connection—grabbed it and pulled hard enough to shift Kitt's weight. Held.

Then the anchor. She tested where the rope seated against the beam, checked the carabiner gate. Load distributed. Lock point seated.

Her hands came up. Cupped Kitt's face. Palms against her cheeks, thumbs at temples. Holding her the way you hold something precious and breakable.

Kitt's eyes were wide. Dark. Kataero's eyes in his daughter's face.

The train came around the hill.

Headlamp blazing. Black smoke laboring skyward. Engine enormous and real and right there—pistons hammering, steam venting, the shriek of metal under strain. Bridge shaking hard enough to feel in her teeth. Rain scattering in the downdraft.

The noise hit like a wall. Swallowed everything.

Peri had to yell.

"RELAX!" Grinning. The Blackwood grin. "THIS IS THE FUN PART!"

She let go of Kitt's face. Stepped backward.

One step. Two.

Her heels found the edge.

Her thumb found the stopwatch. *Click.*

She didn't look back.

⚙

A backflip.

Pure showmanship.

Her body rotated backward through empty air—boots over head, the world spinning. Sky-track-bridge-sky. Rope hissing through the belay device, controlled burn keeping her from freefall. Her braid whipped across her face, weight shifting mid-rotation. Wind caught her, tried to twist her trajectory.

She corrected without thinking. Body and rope and years of training working as one thing.

One full rotation. Clean. Perfect.

Train roof rising to meet her boots.

She landed.

Knees bent, weight distributed. Impact jolted through her legs, her spine—but her body absorbed it. Already part of the train.

Roof vibrated beneath her boots. Alive. Moving.

She unclipped. Carabiner came free and the rope snapped upward, hauled back toward the bridge.

Wind hit her full force—constant pressure from the train's movement, whipping rain into her face. Her shirt snapped and fluttered against her ribs.

She moved toward the front of the cargo car. Her boots found purchase on the wet metal, reading texture through worn soles.

She looked back up at the bridge.

Three figures still there, getting smaller as the train carried her forward. Kitt clipped in at the edge—hesitating. Kataero beside her, perfectly still. Connor ready at his line.

Peri grinned. Raised her hand. Waved.

The bridge disappeared behind a curve.

43 | Kitt

2191.117 · 05:56

Chapi Loop Overpass

"What the actual fuck?"

Peri hit the roof like she'd been born on it. Unclipped. Moved forward. Already waving back, grin bright as a blade.

Kitt stared at the empty space where her sister had been. Train dragged Peri away, second by second, wheel by wheel.

Her pulse hammered in her ears, in her wrists, in the base of her throat. Hands locked on the rope so hard the fibers bit into her palms.

But she couldn't shake the image. Peri's face right before she'd stepped off the bridge—the way she'd looked at Kitt with those eyes, pupils blown wide, black swallowing blue until barely a ring remained.

Sparkling. That was the word.

Like the drop and the moving train and the risk of dying were exactly what she'd been waiting for. Like she was finally, completely alive.

Then that Blackwood smile. And backward into empty air.

How the hell am I supposed to follow that?

"Language." Kataero's voice beside her. Calm. Resigned. This was who Peri was. Always had been.

Connor chuckled low. Shook his head.

"How the hell am I supposed to do that?" Her voice came out strangled.

"You don't," Connor said. "You do it the right way."

⚙

Kataero stepped in front of her. Blocked the train, the drop, everything. Forced her eyes to his.

"Forget Peri." His hands settled on her shoulders. Solid. "Step backward off the bridge. Brake hand here." He closed her fingers around the rope. "Squeeze to slow. Release to drop. Feet first. Bend your knees. I'm right behind you."

She knew the theory. Had practiced on solid ground.

Cargo car slid underneath. Roof slick, moving, indifferent to whether she landed on it or not.

"Now, Kitt. Go."

Her foot found the edge. Radio pack shifted against her spine—twelve pounds of glass and brass molded into a backpack of her own design.

She looked down. Mistake. Her stomach lurched. The gap between her boots and solid surface—fifteen feet and a lifetime.

Throat closing. Hands shaking against the rope.

Fifteen feet. She'd fallen farther during training. Knew the physics. Knew the rope would catch her. Knew the math the way she knew her own name.

But her body didn't care about math. Her body saw the gap and the moving target and screamed at her to step back, to stay on the bridge, to choose the stable reference frame.

Can't—

Kataero's hand on her back. Gentle. Steady. Not pushing. Just there.

"You can do this."

Step.

Free fall. Half a heartbeat of nothing.

Rope snapped taut. Friction screamed through the belay device. She clamped the brake too hard and stalled mid-air—car sliding out from under her, the world swinging.

She let go.

Dropped. Ten feet. Seven. Five.

Impact.

Knees buckled. Spine compressed. Air punched from her lungs. The shock traveled up through her pelvis into her spine—every rib compressed. Vision blurred. For half a second she couldn't breathe, couldn't think, couldn't do anything but feel it radiating through bone.

Her hands scrabbled for purchase, found the roof edge. Metal lip digging into her palms. She held on while the rope yanked her backward and the train dragged her forward. Two forces fighting over her body. She was the failure point between them.

Her right palm lit up. Rope burn. Skin shredding against the weave.

"Unclip! Now!"

Connor was beside her. His hands already reaching for her harness.

"Push and twist."

Fingers shaking, she found the release mechanism. *Click.*

Free. Just the train now, no bridge, no way back up.

Vibration traveled up through her hands, through her knees. Whole car humming with power beneath her. Wind pulling at her—constant pressure, everything moving, no stable reference frame anywhere.

Connor's hand on her shoulder. "Breathe."

She looked at her palm. Raw and red, the weave pattern branded into her skin. Deeper where she'd clamped hardest, the edges white from friction, center weeping. Each heartbeat sent fresh waves of pain up her arm.

"Next time," she rasped, "gloves."

⚙

Kataero dropped behind them.

Controlled descent. Textbook form. He landed, unclipped, crossed the gap between cars like it was pavement. Reached them in seconds.

His hand settled on her shoulder. Brief. Solid.

"You did it."

Not praise. Confirmation. Data point. She was here.

She did it.

Not like Peri. Not with a backflip and a grin and pupils like black suns. With terror and rope burn and knees that buckled wrong and a heart that wouldn't stop hammering.

But she was here.

System held.

⚙

"Forward." Kataero moved past her toward where Peri waited on the car ahead. "Stay low. Test every step."

Peri stood at the front edge of her car. Waiting. That grin still on her face like she'd just proved something only she was keeping score of.

Kitt forced herself to stand. Her legs shook—residual tremor, muscles recovering from sustained load. Train roof uneven beneath her boots: rivet heads, ventilation housings, seams where panels joined. Nothing about this surface was meant to be walked on.

Connor moved ahead of her. Protective positioning. Kataero beside her, ready to catch her if she lost balance.

Each step required conscious thought. Test the surface. Shift weight. Confirm purchase. Move. Her burned palm throbbed with each grip, and the vibration made balance harder. Constant oscillation throwing off her center of gravity.

Her boot found what looked like solid roof. Put weight on it.

The rivet head shifted. Just slightly. Just enough.

Her ankle rolled. Balance gone—she was falling—

Kataero's hand caught her arm. Steadied her. Held until she found her center again.

He didn't say anything. Didn't need to. Just stayed close.

Kitt tested the next step more carefully. And the next. Each one a calculation. Each one a risk assessed and accepted.

She kept moving.

⚙

They reached the gap between cars.

Kitt looked down.

Coupling mechanism. Moving ground beneath. Rails blurring past.

Three feet. Maybe three and a half. Not far—she'd stepped farther getting out of bed. But this wasn't bed. This was two moving platforms with nothing between them but air and consequence. The coupling below, massive and industrial, unforgiving. If she fell into that gap, if her timing was wrong, if her foot slipped on wet metal—

Don't calculate the failure modes. Calculate the success.

Three feet. One step. Physics she understood.

Fear still there. Real and immediate—data her body refused to ignore.

One breath. Deep. Held it.

She stepped across anyway.

44 | Peri

2191.117 · 06:05

Train 47 | Chapi Grade

Kitt reached the front edge of the car. Face pale, hands white-knuckled on the roof edge, but here. She'd made it.

Peri reached across the gap. Hand open. Grinning.

"Told you."

Kitt grabbed her hand, and Peri pulled her across the coupling. Gap disappeared beneath them for a heartbeat—ground blurring past, wheels shrieking against rail—then Kitt's boots found solid metal again. Safe.

Kataero landed behind them. Controlled descent, clean as always, unclipped and moving before Peri could blink. Connor followed seconds later, already scanning ahead.

All four together now. Wind still pulled at them, rain still slicked the roof, but the rappel was done. They were aboard. Committed.

Kataero checked his watch. "Twenty minutes to flat spot."

He looked at Connor. "Engine. Stop the train."

Connor nodded. Turned to Kitt. "C'mon, kid. Stay behind me."

Kitt shot Peri one last look—still breathing hard, something wild still in her eyes—then followed Connor forward. The two of them moving across the rooftop toward the locomotive, already finding rhythm with the train's motion.

Kataero's eyes found Peri's. Brief. No words needed.

Teams split.

Peri turned toward the rear of the train. Toward Car 3.

Kataero fell into step beside her.

⊙

Three cars back. Peri crossed the gaps without hesitation—step, plant, move. Kataero matched pace beside her. Train labored beneath them, steady nine miles per hour up the grade, right on schedule.

Wind and rain and the rhythm of the cars rocking under them. She could feel the train's speed in her legs, in the constant adjustment of balance, the way each step had to account for the surface moving beneath it. Like running on uncertain ground.

Car 3's hatch came up fast. Kataero worked it—three quick motions. Lock gave. He pulled the hatch open.

Darkness below. Oil smell. Metal. Dust.

Peri dropped through first.

Wind cut off. Sound changed—muffled now, just the rumble beneath them and the distant shriek of the locomotive. Air closer down here, warmer, oil and old wood and dust mixing in her lungs. Light came through ventilation slats in long pale bars, the car's interior shifting between shadow and stripe as the train moved.

Labels stenciled across wood: UAD PORT ADAMS — INDUSTRIAL.

Generator components. She checked the manifest numbers against what Kitt had given them—serial codes matched. Everything they came for.

Kataero dropped through behind her. Landed quiet, moved to the opposite wall, checking labels, testing structural integrity with his hands.

They worked in silence. The good kind—not the silence of the truck or the campfire, not the silence that carried weight. Working silence. Two people who knew what they were doing and didn't need to fill the air with proof of it.

Marking crates with quick chalk X's. Kataero finishing one, passing the chalk to Peri without looking, her hand finding it without searching. He moved to the next row, she moved to the one beside it. Six crates total. The rhythm of it clean and simple—mark, move, check, mark. Their paths crossing and uncrossing in the narrow aisle between cargo stacks, each knowing where the other was without needing to look.

The way they'd always worked. Before the spillway. Before everything.

Peri finished marking a crate. Straightened. Let her eyes adjust to the dim light.

"On the bridge," Kataero said. Still working. Tone easy. "With Kitt."

Her shoulders stiffened. The old reflex—bracing for criticism, for the correction.

"You move fast, Peri. Always have." He chalked an X on the next crate. Moved on. "You see a problem and your hands are on it before your head catches up. Sometimes that's the right call. Sometimes it means the people around you never get the chance to find it themselves."

Peri's jaw worked. She hadn't—she didn't—

"But on that bridge, you stopped." He straightened. Looked at her across the dim cargo car. "You checked her harness. You held her face. You stood with her instead of in front of her." His voice stayed even. "That's harder for you. I know that."

His eyes met hers. Steady. The way they'd been her whole life.

"That is who you are, Peri. When you let it be."

Her throat closed. She nodded once and turned back to her work before he could see her face.

They finished the last crate in silence. Just the two of them and the work and the train carrying them forward.

"We'll talk more later."

He held her gaze a moment longer than the job required.

"And Peri—when you figure this out, nothing in this world is going to stop you."

Kataero straightened. Checked his watch. "Fifteen minutes to stop. Let's clear Car 2 before we're stationary. Don't want surprises while Marcus and Seth are exposed."

Peri followed him toward the forward door.

She passed a smaller stack near the wall. Pulled one forward—curiosity, habit, the hands always wanting to know what was there. Read the label: MEDICAL SUPPLIES — VALCROSS CLINIC.

Her hand moved toward the chalk.

"No."

She looked back. Kataero watching her. Not angry. Teaching.

"We could use—"

"Those are going somewhere." He nodded at the label. "Clinic. Town. People waiting for what's in that box." He held her gaze. "Generator parts are insurance cargo—already written off. Nobody misses them. But those?" He pointed. "We take those, someone else goes without."

Peri looked at the crate. At her hand still holding the chalk.

Valcross Clinic. Small town. People in Belfast Mills. People like Emma's family.

Her hand lowered. She set the chalk on top of the crate instead. Stepped back.

Kataero nodded once. Already moving.

She followed.

They stepped onto the catwalk between cars. Wind hit them immediately, the sound rushing back, the world opening up. Ground visible below through the coupling mechanism, rails blurring past. Rain on her face again. Train still climbing.

Ahead: Car 2.

Kataero reached the forward door. Grabbed the handle. Pulled it open.

Five armed men in Continental Authority uniforms stared back at them.

Blackcoats.

Peri's hand reached behind her.

45 | Kitt

2191.117 · 06:06
Train 47

Train roof stretched ahead—car after car climbing toward the locomotive. Connor moved across it like he'd done this a hundred times. Steady. Efficient. Never questioning his footing.

Kitt followed. The procedure she'd built in the last ten minutes was holding—walk the seams, test purchase, commit weight only on structural members. Not fast. Not graceful. But her feet were finding the load paths now, reading rivet spacing and panel overlaps the way her fingers read circuit boards. Each step less calculation, more pattern. The roof was becoming legible.

She didn't try to match Connor's pace. She matched her own.

They reached the front of the train. Locomotive rose ahead, black smoke pouring from its stack. An access ladder ran down the side—metal rungs, slightly rusted, wet from rain.

Connor stopped at the ladder. Looked back. "Stay close. Follow my lead."

Kitt nodded.

He descended. Moving quickly but carefully. Kitt followed, feeling the vibration travel up through the ladder. Stronger here. Closer to the heart of the machine. Radio pack pulling at her shoulders with each rung.

They reached the engine car platform. Narrow grating, barely wide enough for two. Door ahead painted red. Industrial latch. Functional.

Connor's hand found the handle. He looked back at her. "Ready?"

She nodded.

He opened it.

⚙

Three men inside the engine cab. Engineers, focused on their work. One at the throttle, another monitoring gauges, the third checking a logbook.

They looked up as the door opened. Surprise registered first. Then confusion.

Lead engineer stood. "What the hell—"

Connor moved. His hand caught the man's collar, spun him toward the doorway. Engineer stumbled through—nine miles per hour, rain and embankment, survivable—and disappeared into the darkness.

The second engineer lunged for something on the panel. Never reached it. Connor's grip was already there. Same efficiency. Same result.

Gone.

Third engineer looked at Connor. Looked at the open door. Looked back at Connor.

He jumped.

Connor dusted his hands against his trousers and turned back into the cab. No expression. No hesitation. Like he'd just finished clearing dishes after dinner instead of clearing three men off a moving train.

Kitt couldn't move. Empty engine cab stretched in front of her—throttle, brake lever, pressure gauges, systems she'd only seen in technical manuals. Floor vibrated with the engine's rhythm beneath her boots. Everything still running. Everything still moving forward.

And no one at the controls.

Her hands shot up. "Who. Is. Stopping. The. Train?"

Connor glanced at the instrument panel. Glanced out the side window—three figures in the distance, dusting themselves off as they faded into the embankment darkness.

He looked back at her.

Slowly, his hand raised. One finger extended.

Pointed directly at her chest.

Floor tilted. Or maybe that was just her stomach dropping through it.

She looked at the controls. At Connor's expectant face. At the darkness rushing past the windows.

"No." Kitt's feet were already moving. "No no no no no no—how many times, Connor, I'm not that kind of engineer!"

She hit the controls at a run. Her hands found the panel before her brain caught up—dials and gauges clustered across worn metal, levers jutting from the floor, labels rubbed smooth by decades of use.

Unfamiliar. But logical.

Her eyes tracked connections. Steam pressure gauge—needle buried in the red. Speed indicator—nine miles per hour and climbing. Throttle control—staged system, four positions, currently in third. Braking mechanisms—three levers, primary, secondary, emergency, differentiated by handle size and linkage diameter.

Pressure feeds the pistons. Throttle regulates steam flow. Brakes work against the wheels through—

Her hand reached for an unfamiliar gauge. *Wait, what does this—*

Focus, Kitt. Explore later.

But her mind was already racing ahead. Following the logic. Industrial design, standard configuration, just scaled up. Bigger. Heavier. More momentum to control.

Connections revealed themselves. How this lever fed into that valve. How the brake system divided load across all wheels. How the throttle stages corresponded to cylinder pressure. How the steam lines fed from the boiler through the regulator valve to the pistons.

Beautiful.

Her heart slammed against her ribs.

This was what Peri felt on the bridge. That sharp clarity when everything snapped into focus and the system became legible—not with joy, not with that sparkling velocity, but with certainty. Pure, crystalline certainty. The numbers made sense. The system had logic. And she could read it.

Through the forward window, the track curved ahead. Flat clearing visible in the distance—Marcus and Seth waiting with the trucks, counting on her to get this massive machine to the right spot at the right speed.

Getting closer. Fast.

Her hand moved to the throttle control. Felt the detent positions—click, click—pulled back from third to second, reducing steam flow to the cylinders. Train's laboring sound changed pitch—lower, less strained.

Speed gauge needle dropped. Nine miles per hour... eight... seven...

Her other hand reached back for the radio pack. Yanked the velcro patch—glass cells glowed steady blue through the viewing window. Good signal.

"Ground Crew, Tabby. Coming in hot."

But momentum was massive. Hundreds of tons of steel and cargo fighting against the simple act of stopping. Flat clearing approaching fast through the forward window—Marcus and Seth visible now, two small figures beside the trucks, waiting.

She'd overshoot if she didn't engage the brakes.

Her eyes tracked to the braking controls. Three levers. The primary—largest handle, heaviest linkage. Designed for someone with twice her upper body strength and hands that weren't shredded from rope burn.

She gripped the lever. Pulled. The weave pattern branded into her palm caught against the metal surface, raw skin dragging. She worked past the pain. Still nothing. The lever wouldn't budge. Solid as if welded in place. Not seized—just stiff. Decades of thermal cycling, lubricant dried to varnish in the linkage joints.

She adjusted her grip. Hands lower on the handle where the moment arm was longest. Pulled harder. Her arms strained, back muscles engaged. Lever gave maybe an inch, then stopped. Resistance building against her. Not enough.

Come on.

Flat clearing rushed closer through the window.

She looked back at Connor.

Radio crackled. Blue flared bright in her peripheral vision—cells spiking with the incoming signal. Seth's voice, tinny through the speaker. "Acknowledge, Tabby. Visual confirmed. You need to slow that thing down."

"I could use some help, big guy."

Not defeat. Just practical.

Connor moved toward her, but stopped. Stared at her face.

His expression shifted. Recognition. Then concern.

"I know that look," he said quietly.

Kitt blinked. "What?"

"Your eyes." He crossed to the lever, positioned himself beside her. "Seen it before. Colder than hers, but the same."

The words landed somewhere deep. A place she didn't have time to visit.

Connor's hands gripped the lever where hers had been. He planted his feet, solid stance. "Step back."

She did.

Connor pulled. His face set, muscles bunching under his coat. Lever resisting, fighting him with all that built-up mechanical resistance—dried lubricant and thermal distortion concentrated at the breakaway point. A moment of strain—his whole body weight committed to the motion—

CLUNK.

Lever locked into position.

Brakes engaged on every car simultaneously. Metal screamed against metal. Entire train shuddered—a wave of force rippling through hundreds of tons of steel trying to stop all at once.

Kitt grabbed the control panel. Connor braced against the wall. Sound filled everything—brakes fighting inertia, wheels locked and sliding, the whole massive machine protesting its own deceleration.

Floor pitched forward. Her knees buckled but she held on, eyes locked on the speed gauge.

Seven miles per hour... five... three...

Flat clearing ahead. Marcus and Seth's trucks positioned trackside. Close. Too close.

Two miles per hour...

Train crawled. Brakes still engaged, still screaming. Every wheel locked.

One mile per hour...

Then—stopped.

Silence crashed over the engine cab.

Not true silence. Brakes hissed, releasing pressure. Engine ticked as metal cooled unevenly, contracting at different rates. Steam vented somewhere behind them, a soft sustained exhale. But after all that noise, all that force, the stillness felt enormous.

Kitt's legs didn't want to hold her. Her whole body trembling now—adrenaline with nowhere left to go. Hands shaking. Breath coming hard.

But she'd done it.

Stopped a train. Read an unfamiliar system. Trusted the numbers. Trusted herself.

Connor checked the brake lever, made sure it was locked. Checked the gauges, verifying pressure readings. Then he looked at her.

"Good work."

Through the forward window, Marcus and Seth were already moving toward the cargo cars.

Kitt turned toward the door. Her hands still trembling.

46 | Peri

2191.117 · 06:12
Train 47

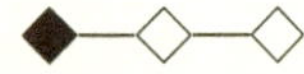

Five armed men in Continental Authority black stood in the doorway of the cargo car.

Blackcoats.

Alert. Positioned. Hands already moving toward weapons.

Peri ducked under Kataero's arm.

Three steps that felt like flight, low and fast, closing the gap before anyone in that car had finished being surprised. Her body reading the doorway and the distance and the half-second before the lead guard's hand reached his holster.

Her fist drove into the lead guard's chest. All her momentum behind it. She felt the impact travel up her arm—the give of him, the breath leaving his body in one hard rush. He folded. Knees hitting the floor, hands grabbing at nothing.

One down.

Second guard's gun clearing leather. Peri's hand found her blade—but Kataero was already there. His strike flashed past her shoulder, catching the guard's wrist. Barrel knocked off-line. She didn't need to look. She knew where his strike would leave the opening. Her blade cleared, pommel driving upward under the guard's jaw. His head snapped back. Hit the floor.

Two.

Third and fourth came together. Coordinated approach—one high, one flanking wide.

Kataero took the flanker without breaking stride. Caught the man's sleeve, redirected his momentum into the metal support beam. Metal rang.

She handled the high approach. Guard's baton already swinging—she stepped inside the arc, too close for the weapon to land with force. Her elbow caught his chin. She hooked his ankle with her boot and he went down hard.

Three. Four.

Not choreographed. Just known. The way her hand found the chalk without searching.

Fifth guard—gray-beard, older, veteran stance. He'd used the seconds wisely. Backed against the far wall, sidearm drawn and leveled. Professional distance. Clear sightline.

"Down. Both of you. Now."

Kataero's hand found Peri's shoulder. Subtle pressure. *Wait.*

Then the train lurched.

Not gentle. Hard. Metal screaming beneath them. Wheels locking, brakes engaging on every car simultaneously. The whole world pitching forward as hundreds of tons of steel fought to stop.

Kitt.

Peri skidded, boots scraping steel, grabbing for a crate. Her right arm slammed into the crate's edge—metal tearing through sleeve and skin beneath. Heat flared up her forearm, sharp and immediate. Blood welling fast, soaking the fabric. Her blade clattered away across the floor, spinning out of reach.

Gray-beard stumbled. Sidearm swinging wide as momentum threw him off-balance.

Kataero hit the deck—but not from the lurch. The third guard, not fully down, had grabbed his ankle as the floor pitched. They tangled, rolling—and then the guard was on top, hands locked around Kataero's throat.

Dad—

Gray-beard recovered. Sidearm coming back up, locking on Peri.

The second guard—jaw already swelling—closed on Kataero from behind. Combat knife drawn. Blade angled for the ribs.

Her father on the ground. Knife coming for his ribs. Everything else gone. Just the next three seconds.

Her left hand found her hip knife. Drew it. Her right arm screaming—blood running down to her wrist, fingers slick—but her right couldn't hold a grip and her left would have to do.

Blade left her hand—

Wobbled.

Caught the knife guard in the thigh anyway. Not where she'd aimed, but deep.

He screamed. Collapsed. Blood spreading dark and fast around the handle.

Kataero got a single breath. Enough.

His elbow cracked into the third guard's temple. Once. Twice. The man went limp.

Kataero surged to his feet. One hand on his ribs, the other striking the nerve cluster at gray-beard's neck before the sidearm could find Peri again. Dropped clean.

Five. Done.

⊙

Silence. Not real silence—the train's brakes still shrieking, metal settling, the knife guard's ragged breathing filling the car. But the silence of threat gone. Motion gone still.

Peri stood there. Breathing hard. Both hands shaking. Not fear. The thing that came after, when the body realized what it had just done and all the adrenaline that had been holding everything together started letting go.

Her right arm throbbed. She looked down at it—sleeve dark and wet, blood still running, the torn fabric sticking to the wound beneath. During the fight it hadn't mattered. Now it was all she could feel. Hot. Pulsing. Deep enough to worry about.

She pressed her left hand against it. Held pressure. Kept breathing.

Kataero tried to push himself upright from where he'd finished gray-beard.

Failed.

He collapsed back against the wall, face blotched with red and purple, bruises forming where fingers had crushed his throat. His breathing was shallow. Wrong. His left arm wrapped around his ribs—instinct, protection, the body guarding what hurt most.

"Dad—"

She was at his side before she'd decided to move. Crouching. Hands under his shoulders, blood from her arm smearing against his jacket.

He reached up.

His palm cupped her cheek.

Warm. Rough. The same hand that had held her face on the bridge. The same calluses. The same steadiness even now, even with his throat purple and his ribs wrong and his breath coming in careful sips.

A nod.

Pat. Pat.

A small, tired exhale. "Good work."

Her eyes burned. She swallowed it down and helped him to his feet, taking his weight against her good side, bracing him as gently as the shaking in her arms would allow.

He stood. Swayed. Found his balance. His fingers flicked—gesture small but clear.

Back to work.

⊙

They secured the guards. Zip ties from Kataero's kit. Weapons cleared. Ammunition pocketed.

Peri moved among them, collecting hardware. Five sidearms, spare magazines, combat knives. Her hands still trembling—fine motor control coming back in stages, the adrenaline crash rolling through her in waves. She found her blade where the lurch had sent it—wedged against a crate near the far wall. Sheathed it against her spine. Weight settling back where it belonged. She pulled gauze from Kataero's kit and cinched it around her own arm, one-handed, teeth pulling the knot tight. Not clean. Functional.

She reached the knife guard. Blood was spreading too fast. Too dark. Pooling on the metal floor, running into the rivets.

Her knife was still buried in his thigh.

She pulled it free. He screamed through clenched teeth—sharp, animal sound that echoed off the metal walls. Blood welled faster.

Her arm pulsed with its own heat as she knelt beside him. She wrapped his wound. Cinched the gauze hard—not gentle, just stopping the bleeding before he lost too much. Her blood and his blood on the same hands now. Same gauze. Same floor.

She wiped her blade clean. Sheathed it.

Gray-beard watched her the entire time. Eyes sharp, calculating even with his hands bound behind his back.

When she finished, he spoke.

"You're fast." A small nod. "Hell of a fight. Been years since I had my ass handed to me like that."

He looked at the bandaged guard. At her bloody hands. Back to her face.

"If you knew what was best for you, you'd kill us."

Peri's hands stilled.

"Probably don't want that on your conscience though." Something like pity crossed his face. "Shame. That's your second mistake."

"What was the first?"

"Stopping this train."

Just the rattle of wheels and the sound of her own breathing.

Gray-beard held her gaze. Not threatening. Warning.

"Whatever you think you're doing here—it won't end the way you hope."

Peri didn't answer. She stood. Wiped her hands on her pants. The blood didn't come off. It never came off that easy.

⚙

Kataero moved to the nearest crate with visible effort, one hand bracing against the wall, the other still wrapped around his ribs. He read the stenciled label: MEDICAL SUPPLIES — VALCROSS CLINIC.

He pulled a pry bar from his belt. Worked the lid. Wood groaned, nails shrieking as they gave. Inside: bandages, surgical tools, medications. All legitimate. All exactly what it should be.

"What kind of medical supplies need a Blackcoat escort?" she asked.

Kataero looked at the secured guards. At the legitimate cargo. At the car they were standing in—Car 2, the one Seth had asked about at the campfire. The one Kataero had called a distraction.

"None," he said.

Outside—muffled through the metal walls—voices. Marcus calling out. Seth responding. Flatbed's engine idling, rough and familiar. Hoist being positioned, chains rattling.

Time to offload.

Kataero moved to the cargo door, each step careful, measured. Grabbed the handle. Pulled it open. Early morning light flooded in, bright enough to make her squint after the dimness of the car. Cool air rushed in, carrying rain and pine and the smell of wet earth.

"Let's work," Kataero said.

They stepped out together. Peri's arm throbbing beneath the gauze. Kataero moving stiffly beside her.

They had a job to finish.

47 | Peri

2191.117 · 06:20

Flat Spot | Valcross Junction

The side door's latch groaned. Peri worked it with her left hand—her right arm burning every time she moved.

Keep moving. Don't stop.

The door rolled open. White. Everything white for a second—morning sun off wet concrete, blinding after the dimness of the car.

Seth and Thomas waited trackside. Flatbed backed up tight to the rail car, A-frame hoist already rigged, slings laid out on concrete still steaming where the rain had met the warming ground. The smell hit her—hot metal, grease, diesel.

Kataero pushed past. His voice came out raw, scraped hollow. "Generator components first. Nothing else matters."

He coughed. Hard. His hand went to his throat where the bruising had started going dark against skin. When he spoke again the words rasped through damaged tissue. "Twenty minutes before someone checks on those guards. If we don't get the dam components off this train, Belfast Mills goes dark."

Twenty minutes. She could feel the edge of the crash waiting—heaviness gathering in her legs, the corners of her vision wanting to soften. Not yet.

Connor was inside, checking crate labels. "Turbine housing. Control systems. Wiring harnesses." He looked up. "Six crates total."

"Six crates in twenty minutes." Carter tested the hoist cable from his position at the controls. "Tight."

"Then move," Kataero said. Another cough tore through him. He braced one hand against the door frame—just for a second, weight shifting like his legs had tried to buckle. Then he was moving again, voice level, like it hadn't happened.

"Dad—" Kitt started forward.

"I'm good." His eyes found Peri. Tracked to her arm where blood was soaking through the gauze. "Go check on your sister."

Kitt's expression hardened. "Peri—"

"I'm fine." Peri was already moving toward the edge. "We've got work."

She jumped down to the flatbed. The impact jarred up through her legs, into her spine. Pain flared bright up her right arm. The pain kept the world focused.

She grabbed chain with her left hand, dragging it toward the nearest lifting point. Everything backward, wrong side, her body adapting around the damage the way it adapted to wind on the rooftop.

Keep moving.

Kitt dropped down beside her a moment later. Field kit in hand. That look on her face—the one that said this conversation wasn't over.

But first, the work.

⊙

Connor and Kataero positioned slings inside the car. Carter ran the hoist. Thomas guided loads as they swung out. Peri and Kitt worked the flatbed—chains through lifting points, ratchet straps cinched tight. Seth oversaw the operation, Marcus on lookout where he could see the road and the rail line both.

First lift: turbine housing.

The crate rose. The hoist cable groaned under the weight. Carter worked the controls faster than safe, the whole frame shuddering.

Out through the door. Swinging. Peri tracked its arc—already moving to where she needed to be.

Down.

THUD.

The flatbed shook under her boots. She was on it before the vibration died—left hand on chain, dragging it toward the lifting point. Her right arm screaming with every jolt, but the screaming was just noise now. Just fuel.

"Peri. Stop."

Kitt's voice. Enough edge to cut.

"We don't have time—"

"You're dripping blood on the equipment." Kitt grabbed her good arm. Fingers digging in. "Stand still."

Peri tried to pull free. The motion sent fire up her right forearm. "I'm fine. The crate needs—"

"You're not fine." Kitt stepped into her space. Close enough that Peri could see the anger and the thing underneath it. "I can't close this wound if you keep moving."

"I wouldn't be bleeding like this if you had been a little easier on the brakes."

Kitt's hands froze on the gauze. Eyes flashing. "You wouldn't be bleeding if you'd told me you were fighting Blackcoats while I was stopping a train."

"Who's got the radio?"

"I do."

Dead stare.

"Oh."

From inside the car, Kataero's rasp: "Enough. Focus."

The same voice that had broken up a thousand arguments at the kitchen table. Same exhaustion underneath it. Different setting. Same fight.

Kitt pulled Peri's sleeve up. The slash was worse than Peri had let herself notice—long, diagonal across her forearm, still seeping. The edges gaped when she moved her wrist. Kitt pressed them together, started applying butterfly closures.

The second crate swung out. Thomas guiding it down.

Peri's whole body pulled toward it. Work waiting. Motion waiting. Her legs wanting to carry her there, her hands wanting something to grab.

She twisted.

The butterfly closure Kitt had just placed tore free. Blood welled up immediately, bright and wrong.

"Goddamn it, Peri!" Kitt threw the useless closure aside. "You're going to bleed out because you can't hold still for ten seconds."

"Just wrap it. Tight. I'll deal with it after."

Kitt's expression said everything. But she grabbed gauze and wrap. Wound it around Peri's forearm hard enough to hurt. Then harder. Pressure wrap—crude, effective, brutal.

Peri felt the tightness bite. Fingers starting to tingle.

"Need to secure the load." She was moving toward the second crate. Left hand on chain, right arm held close, every strap cinched one-handed.

Every jolt up her arm another second she stayed in the work and nowhere else.

⚙

Third and fourth lifts. Control systems marked FRAGILE on every surface. Hoist groaning, sun hot on the back of Peri's neck, sweat mixing with dried blood on her arm.

Connor checked his watch. "Twelve minutes."

Eight minutes left. Two more crates.

Peri's wrapped arm throbbed in time with her heartbeat. Pressure building under the gauze, fingers tingling. Too tight. But the blood had stopped, and that was what mattered right now.

Fifth lift.

The crate swung wide. Carter adjusted before Connor called the angle—years of this, no words needed. Everyone moving faster now, the clock compressing them, squeezing the space between breaths.

Kataero's voice came hoarse and broken from inside the car, calling positions. Each word cost him. Peri could hear him holding together through sheer will.

Then—

The wiring harness tilted. Sling slipping.

"HOLD!"

Everyone froze. The crate hung crooked, swinging, the sling giving another inch.

Carter fought the angle. Degree by degree. Cable screaming.

Seconds stretched. The crate steadied.

Connor's voice, low: "Close one."

Kataero coughed. The sound wet and wrong. "Last crate. Then we go."

⊙

Sixth lift.

Up. Out. Over. Down.

Peri's hands moved without her. Chain in her good hand. Strap. Cinch. Secure. Fingers numb on the ratchet, the left doing everything.

Done.

Connor checked his watch. "Nineteen minutes."

They'd made it. Barely.

And for one second—just one—with the last strap cinched and nothing left to grab, the stillness found her.

Kitt's empty hands on the bridge. The fifteen seconds in the tent. The stranger's voice at the gas station.

She shook it off. Head snapping, shoulders rolling, hands finding the straps she'd already checked. Checking them again.

Not yet. Not here.

Kataero dropped from the car, moving stiff, one hand pressed to his ribs. "Mount up."

Peri counted heads. The number landed before the names did. Six. Should be seven.

She scanned. Kataero at the car door. Connor beside him. Kitt on the flatbed. Carter at the hoist. Thomas by the truck. Marcus on the road.

"Where's Seth?"

Thomas turned, scanning. "He was just here. Helping secure the—"

He stopped.

Peri watched it hit him. Watched it hit Connor. The silence spreading like cold water.

Seth went into the train. Into the cars they weren't supposed to touch.

From inside the open forward door of Car 2, a radio crackled. Static. Then a voice: "Unit Seven-Four, report status."

The guards' radio. Backup checking in.

Kataero's expression went flat. He tried to speak, coughed instead, and when the words finally came they were barely sound: "I'll find him. Get the trucks running."

But Peri was already walking. Toward Car 2.

48 | Peri

2191.117 · 06:28
Flat Spot

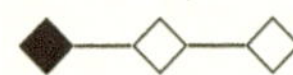

They moved through Car 3 fast. Space felt hollowed out—anchor points where generators had been, chalk marks on the floor, their work erased. Peri's boots echoed against metal. Her right arm hung dead at her side, wrapped fingers beyond feeling. Shakes had started in her shoulders and she couldn't stop them.

Through the cargo door, she could see Thomas and Carter at the flatbed—engines idling, ready to move. Doing their jobs. Waiting.

Through the forward door. Wind cut across the catwalk between cars—brief, sharp, cold enough to make her eyes water. Then into Car 2.

Copper and sweat hit first. Aftermath still hanging in the air.

Guards lay where they'd left them. Five men zip-tied on the floor, wrists behind backs, ankles bound. The youngest—barely older than

Peri—nearest the door, split lip, blood dried brown on his chin. Another's eye had swollen shut. The one Peri had hit first was still curled around his stomach, breathing in shallow sips. The knife guard sat propped against the wall, thigh wrapped in bloody gauze, face pale.

They'd fought hard. Lost harder.

Gray-beard was awake now. Watching like a man counting exits. His eyes tracked Kataero, then Peri, then settled somewhere between them. Waiting.

And Seth.

Deeper in the car, surrounded by opened crates. Medical supplies scattered around his feet: bandages in sterile packaging, surgical instruments still sealed, medications with pharmaceutical labels. Everything legitimate. Routine cargo.

Where he had no business being.

Kataero moved toward him. Voice low, rough—better than right after the fight, but still damaged. Still costing him. "What are you doing in here?"

Seth looked up. His face was wrong—shock mixing with horror. And underneath both, guilt. The guilt of a man who'd found something he couldn't unfind.

"I found something—"

"You were ordered to stay with the offload." Each word controlled, but Peri heard what lived underneath. Fury banked like coals. "You put the mission at risk."

"I know, but—" Seth gestured at the opened crates. "I was checking what else they had. Thought maybe there was something worth—" He stopped. Swallowed. Couldn't finish the sentence with Kataero's eyes on him. "The seams. I found seams in the wall."

"No." Kataero was turning back toward the door. "We're leaving. Now."

Gray-beard laughed. Low. Knowing.

"Smart man. Walk away while you can."

Kataero ignored him.

"Wait."

Kitt's voice cut through. Quiet but certain.

Everyone stopped.

She was just inside the doorway, eyes moving across the car. Not looking at Seth or the supplies. Looking at the space itself. That engineering mind measuring, comparing.

"Something's wrong with this car."

She walked forward slowly. Her hand moved through the air, tracing walls. Working through math only she could see.

"Interior space. It's too small."

She walked toward the front wall, counting steps under her breath. Stopped. Turned back.

"From outside, this car matches Car 3's length. I checked when we were on the roof." Her eyes found each of them. "Inside? Twelve feet short."

Hidden space.

Gray-beard stopped laughing.

Seth pointed to a section of wall, his hand shaking slightly. "There. The seams. You can see them if you look."

Barely visible. Professional work. Deliberate concealment.

Connor moved to it. His fingers traced the hidden join, searching. Found something. Pressed.

Click.

Panel slid aside on oiled rails. Smooth. Well-maintained. A mechanism that got used regularly.

Darkness inside. Smell changed—antiseptic now, sharp and clinical, layered over something stale. Something human.

Peri's eyes adjusted.

A girl.

Young—fifteen maybe. Hard to tell through everything else that was wrong. Strapped to a medical gurney, frame modified with reinforced mounting points. Industrial-grade bindings built into the rails. An IV line running into her arm, clear solution dripping in a rhythm Peri could hear now—soft, steady, mechanical.

The restraints on her wrists and ankles weren't improvised. Medical grade. Designed to hold patients during procedures.

Or prisoners during transport.

Her eyes were closed. Breathing shallow. Sedated.

Peri's wrapped arm throbbed. Her legs wanted to buckle. But something visceral was cutting through exhaustion—a pull that made her step closer instead of back.

Darker complexion. Long dark hair, straight and practical. Too thin—sustained-deprivation thin. Hollows in her cheeks. Prominent bones in her wrists where they pressed against the straps.

Her wrists.

Red. Raw. Abraded skin layered over old scars that had healed and been reopened again and again.

How long had she been fighting these?

"They were moving her like equipment." Kitt's voice came out soft. Horrified.

From the floor, gray-beard spoke again. Quieter now. Mockery gone.

"You should close that panel. Walk away. Forget what you saw."

Connor turned toward him. "Why?"

"Because you don't want what comes next." His eyes steady. Not threatening. Warning. "Whoever you are. Whatever you think you're doing. It ends badly."

"For who?"

"For everyone." He looked at the compartment. At the girl. "You don't understand what you're looking at."

⚙

"Her eyes." Connor had stepped closer to the gurney. His voice had changed—gone tight. "Look at her eyes."

The girl's eyelids fluttered. Opening.

Peri's breath stopped.

Rust. Deep copper-red like oxidized metal. Color of corroded iron, of blood gone dark. Not brown. Not hazel. Not any shade human eyes should be.

They tracked slowly across the compartment, fighting through sedation. Searching. Landing on Peri.

Holding there.

Connor went still. His head tilted slightly—not recognition, but the edge of it. Searching for a reference point and finding nothing. His brow creased.

He looked at Kataero.

Kataero met his gaze. Held it—a small shake of his head. *I don't know either.*

But something lived in both their faces. Not understanding. Not yet. An old shadow stirring—unnamed, unplaceable. Peri could see it but not read it.

The girl's eyes struggled to stay open. Fighting. Losing. Closing again, pulled back under by drugs.

But Peri could still see them. Burned into her vision.

What did they do to you?

"This is what I found," Seth said quietly. "Why I stayed."

The young guard—the one with the split lip—started pulling at his restraints. Panic in his movements now. "You need to leave. You need to leave right now. They track her. They always know where she is. If you don't—"

"Shut up." Gray-beard. Sharp.

But the damage was done. *They track her.*

Kataero moved toward the compartment. His hand reaching for the panel.

"We're leaving."

"No."

Peri's left hand shot out—right arm useless, wrapped tight, fingers dead. Caught the panel before it could close.

Her eyes met his across the unconscious girl.

Warning flickered in his expression. The kind that usually made her step back. Reconsider. Fall in line.

"We can't just leave her."

"We can't take her." Connor stepped forward. Trying to be reasonable. Trying to be the voice she usually listened to. "We don't know who she is. We don't know her medical condition—what she's sedated for, what they're treating. She could be mid-transfer to a facility equipped to help her."

He looked at the IV line. At the drip rate. Measuring what he saw against what he didn't know.

"If we pull that line and we're wrong, she dies in the back of a truck on a logging road. If she's carrying something contagious and we bring it back—"

"Does that look willing to you?"

She gestured at the restraints. At the raw wrists. At the IV dripping sedation into veins that belonged to a child.

"That's not the point—"

"We planned for generators." Kataero's damaged voice cut through. "People are depending on us. Belfast Mills' entire grid depends on what's on that flatbed."

From the floor, gray-beard: "One girl versus an entire community. Listen to him."

Connor checked his watch. "Twenty-two minutes stationary. Backup is coming."

Marcus hovered at the doorway, half in and half out, face tight. "I've got kids at home. I can't bring this back to them—"

Seth, among the opened crates: "There's no angle here. Just heat."

He looked at the gurney. At Peri's hand on the panel. Back to Kataero.

"And since when do we steal people?" Quiet. Not sarcastic. Genuine. "Is that what we do now?"

Voices stacking. Arguments climbing over each other. Reasonable. All of them reasonable.

Connor's logic—the voice that had held her since she was small, the voice that said *before tomorrow* not after, the voice she trusted more than her own. His concern for the girl dressed as caution, and she couldn't tell him he was wrong. Marcus's fear—real, earned, a father who hadn't signed up to become a fugitive. Seth's question sitting in her chest like a stone—the shape of the thing she couldn't answer because he wasn't wrong either. They were about to take an unconscious girl from a train and drive away with her, and the only difference between rescue and theft was what you believed about the people holding the keys. Kataero's command threading through all of it—the same authority from the spillway, from the bridge, from every morning of her life.

And underneath the voices in the room, the ones she carried.

Lin. The stopwatch warm against her hip. She reached for what he would have done and found nothing. Just the absence. Just the space where a father should have been.

Pepper. The hallway. The door closing. The sound of someone leaving because staying was too hard. The pull in Peri's legs right now—the familiar pull, the one that said *run, get out, this isn't yours to carry—*

Kitt's face on the bridge. Empty hands. The shame Peri hadn't seen.

What crown are you competing for, Peregrine?

All of it pressing in. The flow state gone. The high burned off. Nothing left between her and the full weight of it—the voices and the ghosts and the girl with rust-colored eyes and the room full of people telling her to walk away.

She was drowning.

Movement in the compartment.

The girl stirring. Head turning. Fighting sedation with everything she had left—which wasn't much, which was almost nothing, which was just enough.

Eyes opening. Rust catching dim light. Finding Peri through the noise, through the voices, through all of it.

Holding.

Lips moving.

One word. Barely there. More shape than sound—forced through drugged exhaustion, through cracked lips and a throat that hadn't spoken in gods knew how long.

Please.

⊙

Silence.

The arguments stopped. The room stopped. The voices—all of them, inside and out—went quiet.

Just Peri and the girl and the word hanging between them.

She felt it land. Not in her head. In her chest. In the place where the stopwatch usually sat, where the numbers usually lived, where she measured and measured and measured and never found enough.

The measuring stopped.

What rose in its place wasn't loud. Wasn't bright.

Peri's shoulders straightened. Not performance. Not the bright mask she wore when things got hard. Deeper than that. A thing that had been there all along, buried under the times and the comparisons and the running—waiting for a moment when the stopwatch didn't matter and the crown didn't matter and the only thing that mattered was a girl who couldn't save herself asking someone to try.

"Enough."

Her voice cut through the car. Not loud. But it carried weight it hadn't carried before—a gravity that didn't need volume or charm or a Blackwood smile to fill a room.

Peri stepped fully in front of the panel, blocking it with her body.

"We take her."

Kataero opened his mouth—

"I'm not asking." She turned to face him fully. Met his eyes. Held them. "We take her. We get her out. The rest comes after."

Marcus shook his head. "I can't. I'm sorry, but my kids—"

"Then go." Peri's voice held. "The flatbed crew—take the generators. Go home to your families. This doesn't follow you." She looked at him. Made sure he understood. "But she comes with us."

Seth looked between them. Finding no angle that worked for him.

"This is a mistake."

"Maybe." She didn't look at him. "Go or stay. Decide now."

"She's right."

Kitt's voice. Quiet. Absolute.

Everyone turned.

Kitt stood at the compartment's edge. Looking at the girl. At the bindings. At raw wounds layered over old scars.

"This is wrong. We don't leave her."

Kataero looked at his daughters.

Both of them. On the wrong side of every tactical consideration. Choosing a stranger over safety. Choosing conviction over calculation.

He could fight it. Could override them. Could close that panel and walk away and complete the mission and keep them safe.

Do the smart thing.

His expression shifted. Not disappointment. Not anger. She'd seen every version of Kataero's disapproval in her life and this wasn't any of them. A softening around his eyes, his jaw unclenching, a breath released like he'd been holding it for years.

His eyes moved between her and Kitt. Both of them. Standing together.

He exhaled.

"We take her." He straightened. "And we run. Everything changes after this. Everyone understand?"

Meaning clear. No going back. Fugitives now. Hunted.

Gray-beard watched them.

"You have no idea what's coming for you."

He looked at the girl. At Peri's hands reaching for the restraints. Back to Kataero.

Something crossed his face that wasn't mockery. Wasn't anger. Closer to grief.

"Gods help you."

Peri didn't answer. She was moving toward the gurney, good hand reaching for the restraint releases.

The girl's eyes found hers again. Fear and exhaustion and desperate hope underneath—the look of a person who'd almost stopped believing anyone would come.

Still fighting to stay conscious.

"It's okay," Peri said. Soft. Sure. The voice she'd used on Kitt in the alcove at Gate 20. The voice that said *I have you. Nothing bad is going to happen.* "We've got you."

The girl's eyes closed. Trusting. Letting go.

Peri started working the restraints."

49 | Peri

2191.117 · 06:37
Flat Spot

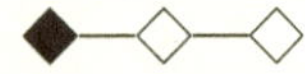

They moved fast. Connor disconnected the IV. Kitt supported the girl's head. Peri lifted with her one good arm—the girl lighter than she should be, bones prominent under hospital gown fabric, ribs pressing through thin material.

Through Car 2. Gray-beard watching them pass. His laughter gone. Pity in its place.

Through the cargo door. Morning sun bright enough to make her squint. Connor below, arms up.

"I've got her."

Peri lowered her down. One-handed. Awkward. Connor's hands catching, taking the weight like it was nothing.

"Everyone to the truck," Kataero said. "Now."

⊙

They gathered by Kataero's truck. The flatbed sat twenty yards away—Thomas and Carter securing the tarp. Seth stood with Marcus near his own vehicle, both watching the family like men waiting to see which way a fire spreads.

Connor wasn't with them.

Peri caught movement at the edge of her vision—Connor at Seth's truck, reaching into the cab. He came out with a rifle. Checked the action. Slung it over his shoulder. Moved to the flatbed. Another rifle from behind the seat. A pistol from the glove box—magazine checked, slide racked, tucked into his waistband.

Then he went to the tool rack bolted along the flatbed's rail. His hands found what they were looking for—a pipe wrench, three feet of forged steel, heavy enough that the muscles in his forearm stood out when he lifted it. He weighed it in his grip. Shifted his hand along the handle until he found the balance point.

He carried everything to Kataero's truck. Laid the rifles in the footwell. Pistol in the center console. The wrench behind the driver's seat, handle up, within reach.

Peri watched him do it. The movements registering but not connecting—like watching someone prepare for a thing she couldn't see yet.

Kataero waited until Connor finished. Then he spoke.

"Seth." His voice was hoarse but sure. Command underneath the damage. "You take the generators home. Marcus, Carter, Thomas—go with them. Everyone who came for the job goes south. Keep things quiet. Don't draw attention."

He paused. Let that land.

"If anyone asks, we split before you opened that compartment. You took the generators, we went north. You don't know why. You don't know where."

His eyes moved to Connor. To Peri. To Kitt.

"The four of us take the girl. Northeast. We stay together until I say otherwise."

Marcus was quiet for a moment. His hands weren't steady.

"My kids, Kat."

"I know."

The silence stretched. Everything they'd built sitting in it.

Then Marcus nodded. Once. Final. That was enough.

Kitt hadn't moved. She was staring at Kataero. Processing. The words catching up to her—*everyone who came for the job goes south*—and the thing that meant for her arriving like a slow-moving train.

"Dad, no."

"I need to go home. The dam—that's my job. Six months of work. The generators are on that flatbed right now. I'm supposed to install them. I'm supposed to finish this."

"The dam will be there when we get back."

"When we—" She stopped. Breath coming harder. Eyes bright and furious. "I stood with you in that car. Like always. Because it was the right thing to do. And now—" Her voice shook. "Now I'm the one who doesn't get to go home. I don't get to do my job. Belfast Mills sits in the dark while we—what? Run?"

The words hit Peri like the train lurch. Chest-first. No bracing for it.

"She made the choice! Not me! I backed her up and now—"

"We stay together. All of us." His voice rose. Sharp. Harder than Peri had ever heard it directed at Kitt. "This is not a discussion."

Kitt recoiled. Physically. Half a step backward, eyes wide—not just from the words but from the tone. He didn't talk to her like that. He never talked to her like that.

"But—"

"Enough."

One word. Final. The word of a man holding together by force and running out of force to do it with. His throat working, the bruises dark against his skin. His eyes not on Kitt's face but past her, scanning the tree line, the road, the distance—reading something she couldn't see.

Kitt's mouth opened. Closed. She looked at Peri—one burning second. Not anger. Not hurt. A decision being made.

Then she turned. Walked to the truck. Opened the rear door on Connor's side. Got in. Pulled the door shut. Firm. Final. The frame settled under the weight of it.

She didn't slam it. That would have been a tantrum. This was worse—controlled. Deliberate. The door of someone who had made a decision about where she stood and who she was willing to sit behind.

Not her father. Not her sister. Connor.

Seth moved forward. Shook Kataero's hand. Then Connor's. Stopped in front of Peri.

"Good luck." Quiet. "You're going to need it."

Not unkind. Just true.

He climbed into his truck. Marcus in the passenger seat. Doors closed. Engine caught. They pulled out without looking back.

Carter started the flatbed. Thomas beside him—they'd made their choice without words, the choice that led home. The engine turned over, coughed, caught.

Both vehicles heading south toward the locks. Dust rising in their wake.

Toward home. Toward the dam Kitt had spent six months building toward. Toward the generators she'd tracked and mapped and fought for. Driving away from her without her.

Peri watched until they disappeared around the bend. The dust settling. The silence filling in where engine noise had been.

⚙

Connor settled the girl in the back seat—middle position, her head lolling against the worn leather. Kitt was behind him, pressed against the far door, arms crossed, face turned toward the window. He checked the rifles in the footwell. Checked the pistol in the console. Then he climbed into the passenger seat. Said nothing. Settled in like a man who'd done this before—ridden into the unknown with weapons within reach and silence behind him.

Peri moved toward the truck.

A hand on her shoulder. Her good one. Heavy.

Kataero.

She turned. Found him looking at her. His face drawn tight—jaw set, eyes hard, the softening from the cargo car gone. Replaced by the calculation she recognized from the briefing, from the campfire, from every moment he'd been reading odds and not sharing them.

"That was the right call," he said.

The words landed. After everything—the spillway, the stopwatch, the silence in the truck, the bridge where he'd cupped her cheek and said *do your thing*—after all of it, her father was standing in front of her and saying she'd made the right call.

Her chest opened. A feeling she hadn't felt in—

"But people could get hurt because of it."

The floor dropped out.

She felt it go—the warmth pulling back from her cheeks, her lips, leaving cold behind. The opening in her chest closing like a fist.

"Sometimes right decisions are the wrong ones."

He held her gaze. Not cruel. Not gentle. Just the truth of it—delivered by a man whose throat was crushed and whose ribs were cracked and who was about to drive his family northeast into a thing he could see and they couldn't.

Then he walked past her. Got in the driver's seat. Closed the door.

Peri stood there.

Morning sun on her face. The clearing empty now except for the stopped train and the tracks running south. The air smelled like diesel and pine and something metallic she realized was her own blood, still seeping through the gauze on her forearm.

What. The. Fuck.

She'd saved a girl. She'd put Marcus's kids at risk. She'd given Kitt's purpose to a flatbed driving south without her. She'd turned her family into fugitives.

All of it true. All of it hers.

Peri opened the rear door behind Kataero. The girl was slumped in the middle. Kitt on the far side behind Connor, pressed against the window. Not looking at her.

Peri climbed in. Settled beside the girl. Closed the door.

The girl's head lolled with the motion, drifting toward Peri's shoulder.

Kitt's voice. Quiet. Not looking away from the window.

"Why is it that when you make a decision, I'm the one who ends up paying for it?"

Peri didn't have an answer.

The silence sat between them. The girl's breathing. The tick of the engine cooling between idle cycles.

Then, quieter:

"Gods, you don't even see it, do you." Not a question. "What this costs anyone but you."

She sat back. Arms crossed. Done.

You travel through the world doing your thing and we all adjust around you.

The gas station. The same truth, three times now. Getting quieter each time. Getting truer.

Kataero started the engine—a low rumble that vibrated through the seat, through her bones.

Connor turned in his seat. Found her eyes.

That look. The one that said: *I see you. I know what's coming. You okay?*

She tried to arrange her face into something reassuring. Felt the muscles fail. She couldn't hold his gaze—looked away, looked at her hands, looked at anything else.

His mouth pressed thin. But he didn't push. Just turned back to the road.

The truck pulled forward. Northeast. Away from the train. Away from Marcus and Seth. Away from the mission they'd planned for months.

Away from home.

⊙

The adrenaline was leaving her.

She could feel it going—draining out through her fingers, her feet, the base of her spine. Not gradually. In waves. Each one pulling more out of her, leaving less behind. Her right arm had stopped being background noise and started screaming—the gauze soaked through, the wound pulsing hot beneath it, each bump in the road sending fire from wrist to elbow. Her shoulders shook. Her hands lay in her lap and she watched them tremble like they belonged to someone else.

The truck hit a rut. Jolted. The girl's head slid sideways, found Peri's shoulder, settled there.

Peri went rigid.

This stranger—this girl with rust eyes and raw wrists and a past they didn't know—using her as an anchor. Trusting her. Leaning into her like Peri was someone worth trusting.

She didn't know what to do with it.

The girl's breathing was shallow. Slow. Still sedated. The faint smell of antiseptic clung to her skin, mixing with something older underneath. Days of it. Weeks.

Peri shifted slightly, trying to ease the pressure on her wrapped forearm where it was pinned between her body and the girl.

The girl just settled deeper. Made a small sound—not quite a word, not quite a whimper. In between.

And stayed.

Outside, trees gave way to open fields. The sun bright and indifferent.

Kitt's reflection caught in the window glass—face closed, eyes fixed on nothing. Her fingers working the crease in her notebook page. Smoothing it. Folding it. Smoothing it again. Six months of relay stations and frequency drift and sleepless nights at the workbench. The generators on a flatbed heading south without her. Belfast Mills waiting for power she'd promised to deliver.

All of it receding behind them at forty miles an hour because Peri had looked at a girl on a gurney and said *we take her.*

Right decision. Wrong one.

Marcus's face. The moment he'd shaken his head. His kids. Eight and ten.

The girl against Peri's shoulder. Trusting.

⊙

Movement. The girl's head turning. Eyes still closed, but working behind them. Fighting toward the surface.

Then—

Two words. Whispered. Barely conscious. Dragged up from somewhere deep.

"Thank you."

The girl settled deeper against her. Breathing evening out. Trusting. Safe. For the first time in however long she'd been restrained and drugged and moved like cargo.

Thank you.

For what?

Her hands wanted to shake. She pressed them flat against her thighs and tried to ground herself in anything that wasn't spinning.

It wasn't working.

No enemy to fight. No crate to mark. No gap to jump. Nothing between her and everything she'd done and everything it was going to cost.

Kitt's reflection in the glass. Arms crossed. Face turned away.

Connor's rifles in the footwell. The wrench behind the seat. Things that meant a violence she wasn't ready to understand.

Kataero's hands on the wheel. The bruises on his throat. The way he'd said *right decisions* and *wrong ones* in the same breath and walked away.

The girl's warmth against her shoulder. Trusting.

All of it pressing down. Pressing in. Deeper than the spillway, deeper than the tent, deeper than eighty-six minutes on a morning that belonged to someone else. No flow to break it. No run to empty it. No performance bright enough to cover it.

Just her. Sitting in the back of a truck. Going nowhere she knew. With nothing left.

The girl warm against her shoulder.

Her hand found the stopwatch. Her thumb found the button.

Click.

50 | Wynne

2191.117 · 17:27

Graphton Station | South of Fort Delvaine

The train slowed as evening light painted the hills gold and amber. Not smooth deceleration—urgent, final. Brakes hissing, the whole car shuddering with the effort of killing momentum.

Through the gaps, Wynne saw buildings. A town spreading through a valley below, industrial architecture clustered around what looked like a mill complex.

The train lurched to a complete stop at the platform.

The junction was small. Just a platform and switching house. But a crowd had gathered near the station building, faces turned toward a glow inside.

Familiar.

Wynne moved closer. Her heart quickened before her mind caught up—the same blue-white pulse she'd stood transfixed by on a hot cobblestone street in Port Madison, barefoot and hungry, a stranger trying to explain radio waves to a girl who'd never left a monastery.

Television.

The box sat mounted in the station waiting area, visible through the windows. Images moving across its surface. She turned to Jaden, who'd stopped beside her.

"This is a television," she said quietly. "These people are somewhere else. The image is here, but they remain there. It sends out pictures and sound from all over the Union—broadcast from towers, carried on radio waves."

The words came out with a warmth that surprised her. She was repeating what a stranger had given her for free on a hot morning when she'd owned nothing but a staff and a pouch of coins no one would take. Passing it forward.

Jaden blinked. Then his expression opened—surprise melting into delight. "Yes. Exactly. And sometimes—" he gestured at the screen, "—they have important things to say."

His tone carried that particular quality he got when someone understood a thing he valued. Like she'd grasped a truth about the world that delighted him.

Wynne smiled. She couldn't help it.

On the screen, a woman in formal dress behind a desk, text beneath her: CONTINENTAL AUTHORITY NEWS SERVICE.

Her voice carried through open doors:

"—incident at Chapi Loop earlier today. Continental Authority officials report a cargo train was stopped and raided by unknown assailants. Valuable electrical generation equipment was stolen, along with restricted medical assets. Authorities are seeking information regarding the attack."

The image changed. A sketch. A young woman—copper hair, sharp features, rendered in charcoal lines that flattened something vital out of whatever face they'd been drawn from.

"Anyone with information regarding this individual is urged to contact local Continental Authority offices immediately. The woman is considered armed and dangerous. Do not approach—"

The image changed back to the newswoman. Wynne watched it the way she'd watched that first broadcast in Port Madison—with wonder at the mechanism, not yet understanding what it carried. The sketch was already fading from her mind. A face she didn't know, in a place she'd never been.

Behind them, Pede appeared at the cargo door, rolling it open. His expression carried bad news.

"End of the line. Can't go any further."

He looked out at the platform. At the crowd. At whatever he could read in the air that she couldn't.

"Security situation ahead. Stopped outside Graphton—whole valley's locked down tight." Pede gestured toward the town below. "Some kind of incident. Don't know details, but the Blackcoats aren't letting anyone through. Including rail."

He looked at them, meaning clear. "Either way, you're off my train. I've got cargo to deliver, and I can't sit here with passengers who aren't supposed to exist."

Jaden pulled out several coins. More than passage would have cost. He offered them to Pede.

"For the trouble. And the discretion."

Pede looked at the coins, then at Jaden. His expression settled—not quite approval, but acknowledgment. He took the money.

Behind him, Al paused in his work. Caught Wynne's eye and raised one hand—not a wave, just recognition. The gesture of a man who remembered a barefoot girl who'd worked until her shoulders burned and figured that was enough to know about a person. Mickie glanced up from his manifest, offered a nod that carried the same quiet weight.

Wynne returned it. These men who'd fed her and taught her and let her ride with them twice now—she might never see them again. The thought arrived without drama. Just recognition. The world kept moving, and the people in it moved with it.

"Stay out of trouble, Order girl," Pede said.

"I'll try."

"Not sure you know how." But there was warmth in his voice.

The train's whistle blew. They watched it pull away—Al and Mickie already back to work before the platform had cleared.

Leaving them stranded.

⌾

Paul scanned the terrain, his body tight with tension. "There." He pointed toward a ridge overlooking the valley. "We can see what we're dealing with from up there."

The path wound through scrub grass and scattered pine. Gentle but steady, and Wynne heard Jaden's breathing labor slightly beside her, his cane finding purchase on the uneven ground. She adjusted her pace without comment. Her shoulder protested the incline—duller now than on the train, but still present, still reminding her of every baton she'd blocked in Hamilton.

The ridge crested, and Graphton spread below them in the evening light.

Maybe two thousand people based on the housing density. But it was the military presence that sharpened Wynne's awareness.

Blackcoats everywhere. Soldiers in dark uniforms standing at intersections, patrolling streets, positioned on rooftops. Heavy weapons visible even at this distance. A perimeter established around the town's center, where a crowd had gathered in the main square.

She read the crowd before she read the soldiers. Shoulders drawn in. Weight back on the heels—the posture of people who wanted to be smaller, who were making themselves less visible without moving. Children held close. Eyes tracking the patrols with the peripheral attention of prey watching predators. Nobody running. Nobody protesting. Just the particular, practiced stillness of a population that had learned how much space authority left them and was staying inside it.

Then the soldiers. Weight forward. Hands on weapons. Scanning intersections with the focused attention of men who expected trouble and were prepared to create it if they didn't find it. Not sentries maintaining order. Occupiers maintaining control.

The difference mattered. She felt it in her stomach before she articulated it in her mind.

"What happened here?" Jaden asked quietly.

Paul's teeth ground. "Nothing good."

They descended toward the outskirts where observers had gathered—people from surrounding areas who'd come to watch, to witness, to try to understand. Wynne, Jaden, and Paul blended into the crowd. Three more travelers caught by the blockade.

Voices carried fragments:

"—arrested fifteen of them—"

"—helping with that rail theft up at Valcross—"

"—union organizers, supposedly—"

"—traitors to the Continental Authority—"

The word *traitors* moved through the crowd like a current. Whispered and spoken and whispered again. Fear underneath it, giving the word weight it didn't deserve.

This didn't feel like justice.

⊙

Paul hung back, his attention less on the military presence and more on scanning their surroundings. His body language shifted—a tension she'd learned to read over the past days. Instinct screaming what his mouth hadn't caught up to yet.

Then Wynne felt it.

Not danger exactly. Adjacent. The particular sensation of being watched by someone who knew how to watch—not casual attention from the crowd, but the focused assessment of a trained eye measuring distance, capability, threat.

She tracked the feeling before she understood it.

A woman stood thirty feet away at the crowd's edge.

Tall. Lean in a way that spoke of years, not youth—muscle pared down to what was essential, nothing wasted. Long black hair pulled back in a practical knot, the white streak framing the left side of her face catching the last of the evening light. Weathered features. And eyes so pale they seemed almost colorless, catching the light like water over stone.

She wore traveler's clothes, dark and practical. But her stance told a different story—weight centered, hands loose at her sides and slightly curled. Not relaxed. Available. The spatial awareness of someone who knew exactly where the nearest three people stood without looking at them.

Wynne knew that stance. Knew it the way she knew her own heartbeat. She'd learned it in a stone chamber from a woman who'd spoken perhaps a hundred words to her in nineteen years.

Order-trained. Absolutely. Unmistakably.

Her heart lifted. Here, in this troubled place full of Blackcoats and fear and whispered accusations—a sister. Someone who'd stood in a circle of Masters and been tested and walked out the other side.

She started forward, staff shifting to the formal carry position Master Thessa had taught—

"Bloody hells."

Paul's voice. Behind her. Low and wrong.

Wynne slowed.

"*Girly.*"

The word stopped her mid-step.

Not generic. Not dismissive. A name. And the way Paul's voice went flat—she'd never heard him sound like that.

The woman's head turned. Those pale eyes swept past Wynne as if she'd ceased to exist, finding Paul through the crowd with the precision of someone who'd been dreading this exact moment. Or waiting for it. Wynne couldn't tell which.

"Paul."

One word. But Wynne heard everything packed inside it—surprise and grim inevitability and something underneath that neither of them wanted named.

Paul moved forward. His body language had changed completely. Not the easy, irritable guide she'd traveled with. Harder. Older. His hand near his gun but not touching it—the posture of a man facing danger that wasn't physical but who'd forgotten how to face any other kind.

They stopped ten feet apart. Wynne stood between them and slightly to the side, close enough to feel what moved in the air. History. The kind that left marks you could see if you knew where to look.

Paul's ribs. The hand that always went there. The old injury remembered.

She looked at the woman. At the hands that could have made that injury. Loose and available at her sides.

"Last we met," the woman said, controlled precision in every syllable, "I left you broken and dying."

Paul's expression didn't change. But behind his eyes—a door opening onto a room he kept locked.

"Still broken." His voice came out flat. Emptied of everything that usually lived in it—the sarcasm, the warmth he hid behind irritation, the protective deflection. All of it stripped away. "Only now I wish I was dead."

The woman's attention shifted. Found Wynne. Assessed her the way one fighter assessed another—not hostile, but thorough. The staff. The bare feet. The way she held her ground without bracing.

"So you're playing protector now?" Directed at Paul, but her eyes stayed on Wynne. "Trying to save this one from becoming like me?"

"Someone should." Paul's voice stayed flat.

"You couldn't save me." A pause that held its own weight. "You won't save her."

She moved then. Not toward Paul—toward Wynne. Deliberate, circling slightly, reading her from multiple angles. Every step precise. Every shift of weight controlled. Movement born from the same stone floors and the same relentless training that lived in Wynne's own body.

Wynne straightened. Found her center—weight settled, breathing even, the staff a familiar line of pressure against her back. She offered the formal greeting Master Thessa had taught, the words carrying the weight of tradition.

"Sister. I am Wynne Kaede, of Port Madison monastery. It honors me to find another warrior of the Order here."

The woman stopped circling.

A micro-expression—fast enough that anyone else would have missed it. But Wynne had spent nineteen years reading Masters who considered visible emotion a failure of discipline. She caught it.

Recognition. And underneath, like a stone at the bottom of a clear stream—grief.

"Elaris Vayne." The grief vanished behind control so practiced it might as well have been architecture. She studied Wynne's stance, her positioning, the specific way she held the carry. "You wear the whites well. Move with proper discipline."

"Thank you." Wynne kept her voice even despite the unease building along her spine. The foundation under Elaris's movement—the same stone floors, the same hands shaping it. "You trained at Port Madison."

Not a question.

"The Order and I walk different paths now." The words closed a door. Locked it. Wynne heard the same guarded finality she'd heard in her own voice during the trial—the sound of someone protecting what remained by refusing to discuss what was lost.

Elaris's gaze narrowed slightly. "How long have you been outside the monastery walls?"

"Weeks. Not quite a month."

"A month." Dark amusement that didn't reach her eyes. "And what has that month taught you?"

The question carried a familiar shape. Testing. The way Masters tested during trials—not seeking information, but measuring the person who answered.

"That the world is more complicated than the monastery prepared me for," Wynne said. "That justice requires investigation. And that people will sacrifice everything for truth, even when the cost falls on them alone."

Elaris was quiet for a moment. Her head tilted—a fraction, barely visible.

"And you still believe those things? Justice. Truth. Sacrifice having meaning?"

"Of course." The words came without hesitation. The same bedrock she'd stood on in the trial chamber, facing Cowe's surgical doubt and Vale's impossible scenarios. It hadn't cracked then. It wouldn't crack now. "These things matter. They're what separate civilization from chaos."

She gestured toward Graphton. The Blackcoats on every corner. The arrests. The crowd's swallowed fear.

"Do you think those people are guilty? That the Continental Authority is pursuing justice down there?"

Wynne looked. Took her time before answering. "I don't know enough to judge."

"Honest." Elaris's expression didn't soften. "But here's what I know. Half those people are innocent. Maybe more. And it won't matter. Because power doesn't answer to justice or truth or any of the words they taught us mattered."

Can you measure fifteen lives here against fifty outside? A hundred?

Master Cowe's voice. From the trial.

"You speak like Master Cowe," Wynne said quietly.

Elaris went still.

Not the controlled stillness she'd been wearing like armor. The sudden absence of movement that comes when someone hears a thing they weren't prepared for. Her pale eyes sharpened, reassessing Wynne from the ground up.

"Elyra trained well." The name came out with weight. With history. A pause that held what Elaris chose not to say. Then: "As did Kaelen Rev, I see."

"Master Rev taught me to hope the world could be better," Wynne said.

"And Master Cowe taught me to calculate what better costs." Elaris's expression shifted. Not warmth. Recognition—the way you recognize a language you once spoke fluently and haven't heard in years. "We'll see which lesson serves you when the world demands you choose."

She glanced at Paul. Something passed between them—private, unresolved, too tangled to read from outside. When she turned back, the recognition was gone. Replaced by something harder.

"I don't think you forgot how to live."

The words left Wynne before she'd planned them. Quiet. Not argument. Observation—offered the way you'd offer water to someone who hadn't asked.

Elaris's mouth opened. Closed.

The pause lasted one beat longer than control should have allowed. A flicker behind those pale eyes—the way a candle gutters when a door opens in another room.

Then it was gone. Sealed away behind architecture that had taken years to build.

"You remind me of someone," Elaris said. Her voice had changed—still hard, but the edge had shifted. Less blade, more warning. "She said things like that. Believed them, too." A beat. "It didn't save her."

She stepped back. The distance between them widened from conversational to formal. To final.

"When your principles collide with the people you love, Wynne Kaede—when being right costs you everything that matters."

She held Wynne's gaze.

"Will you still believe virtue is its own reward?"

Elaris looked at Paul one last time. Whatever she saw there, she kept to herself.

Then she turned and walked into the crowd. Not hurrying. Not looking back. Moving the way the Order taught—centered, aware, alone. The white streak in her dark hair caught the fading light, and then the crowd folded around her and she was gone.

⊙

Paul moved closer. His voice came rough. "You alright?"

"I don't know." Quieter than she'd intended. "Who was she to you?"

Paul looked where Elaris had disappeared. His guard dropped—just for a breath. Long enough to see what he'd been carrying.

"Someone I couldn't save." His mouth worked around the rest of it. "Broken by being right. That's the thing about convictions, girly. Doesn't matter which side you're on. Hold them hard enough, they'll break you or break everyone around you." A pause. "Either way, someone ends up broken."

Wynne looked at Jaden, who'd been silent through all of it. Watching. Processing. His hand on his cane, the analytical mind working behind his eyes.

"We should find somewhere to stay," Jaden said finally. "Figure out how to get through this blockade." A pause. "We're still going to Fort Delvaine."

"Yeah." Wynne gripped her staff tighter, finding her center. "We're still going."

Evening light faded toward dusk. Below, Graphton settled into uneasy night under military occupation.

They'd find a way forward.

⊙

They moved away from the crowd, finding a spot where the observers thinned and the view of Graphton opened below them. Quieter here. Room to think.

Jaden stood at the edge, weight on his cane, staring down at the town. At the Blackcoats on every corner. The perimeter. The power.

"I didn't tell her I was leaving."

Wynne moved to stand beside him.

"My mentor." His voice carried a thing she hadn't heard before. Worry, tangled with guilt. "Shori Ashford. Chief Minister of the Continental Authority." He gestured toward Graphton—the soldiers, the occupation, all of it. "This is her world. Her responsibility. She helped me rebuild after my accident. Guided my research. Protected me when the council wanted to bury my questions about my grandfather."

Somewhere behind them, Paul went still. Turned to study the tree line, suddenly absorbed by the fading light.

Wynne filed that away. Kept her focus on Jaden.

He stared at the soldiers below. At the occupied streets. At the authority his mentor served, expressed as armed men and fearful civilians.

"And I just vanished. With evidence that could destabilize everything she's worked to build."

His throat moved. The guilt was real. The loyalty was real. Whatever his mentor had done for him—the rebuilding, the guidance, the protection—it lived in his voice the way Master Rev lived in Wynne's. You didn't fake that kind of gratitude. You couldn't.

And he'd left without a word. Carrying evidence that might destroy her.

"The people who matter," Wynne said quietly, "will understand why you had to go. Even if you couldn't explain it first."

Jaden turned to look at her. Processing.

Then his shoulders dropped—not fully, but enough. That smile. Sincere, expecting nothing, offering everything.

"Even if I couldn't explain it first," he repeated softly.

Wynne held his gaze a moment too long.

Then looked away. Toward Graphton. Toward the occupied streets below.

Elaris's question followed her still. Followed like a shadow she couldn't outpace.

When your principles collide with the people you love...

She wasn't ready to name what that meant. Not yet.

"Come on," she said. "We've got a blockade to get through."

She started down the slope. Behind her, Jaden's cane found its rhythm on the rocky path.

Paul fell into step behind them both.

"Two broken men and a hopeless idealist walking into a Union hornet's nest of Blackcoats and injustice." His voice had changed. Lighter. Eager. "I forgot how much I missed this."

Korvyn Address

Address to the Continental Council
Seventeenth Day of Autumn, 2156

"One hundred and twenty-nine years ago, our world fractured.

Not by invasion. Not by war. By failure.

The systems that sustained civilization collapsed faster than they could be repaired. Power stations fell silent. Trade routes died. Borders dissolved. Authority did not fall—it evaporated. What remained was hunger, fear, and the certainty that no one was coming to restore what had been lost.

Hamilton endured.

These halls were not built in triumph. They were reclaimed in desperation. Men and women cleared dust from abandoned chambers, repaired walls

RAISED BY AN EARLIER AGE, AND CHOSE CONTINUITY OVER CHAOS. THEY DID NOT INVENT CIVILIZATION ANEW. THEY SALVAGED IT. PRESERVED IT. REFUSED TO LET IT VANISH.

FROM THIS PLACE, THE CONTINENTAL AUTHORITY WAS ESTABLISHED—NOT IN IDEALISM, BUT IN NECESSITY. TO ENSURE THAT THE WORLD DID NOT FALL APART TWICE.

FOR OVER A CENTURY, IT HELD. THROUGH FAMINE. THROUGH DROUGHT. THROUGH DISPUTES THAT THREATENED TO FRACTURE US BACK INTO WARRING PROVINCES. WE ENDURED BECAUSE WE REMEMBERED WHAT COLLAPSE LOOKED LIKE, AND WE REFUSED TO RETURN TO IT.

HAMILTON ENDURED.

THEN CAME THE FEVER.

ROSE FEVER DID NOT DISCRIMINATE. IT TOOK THE YOUNG AND THE OLD, THE POWERFUL AND THE FORGOTTEN. IT EMPTIED CITIES AND FILLED GRAVES. FOR FIVE YEARS, SURVIVAL REPLACED EVERY OTHER AMBITION. IN THAT NARROWING OF PURPOSE, MEASURES WERE TAKEN THAT COULD NOT HAVE BEEN IMAGINED IN CALMER TIMES.

SOME WERE NECESSARY. OTHERS WERE RETAINED.

EMERGENCY POWERS EXPANDED. OVERSIGHT NARROWED. DECISIONS ONCE MADE IN LIGHT WERE MOVED INTO SHADOW. SILENCE BECAME HABIT. SECRECY BECAME POLICY.

HAMILTON ENDURED.

WE NOW STAND IN THE AFTERMATH, FACED WITH THE SAME QUESTION OUR PREDECESSORS UNDERSTOOD ALL TOO WELL: WHETHER AUTHORITY EXISTS TO PRESERVE CIVILIZATION—OR TO CONTROL IT.

THEY GAVE US A CROWN OF DUTY. NOT OF GOLD, BUT OF OBLIGATION. NOT TO RULE, BUT TO PRESERVE. NOT TO COMMAND, BUT TO SERVE.

A CROWN SUCH AS THIS DOES NOT SHINE ON ITS OWN. IT SURVIVES ONLY AS LONG AS THOSE WHO BEAR IT REMEMBER ITS WEIGHT.

HISTORY IS UNAMBIGUOUS. EMPIRES DO NOT FALL ONLY TO ENEMIES AT THEIR GATES. THEY FAIL WHEN CONTROL IS MISTAKEN FOR ORDER, WHEN PROTECTION BECOMES JUSTIFICATION, AND WHEN SILENCE REPLACES RESPONSIBILITY. THEY FAIL NOT THROUGH SUDDEN COLLAPSE, BUT THROUGH GRADUAL NEGLECT—WHEN DUTY IS PERFORMED AS CEREMONY, AND PRINCIPLE BECOMES DECORATION.

I HAVE SERVED THIS AUTHORITY FOR EIGHTEEN YEARS. THIRTEEN IN UNIFORM. FIVE IN THIS CHAMBER. I HAVE DEFENDED OUR BORDERS AGAINST FORCES THAT WOULD GLADLY SEE US FRACTURED AGAIN. I KNOW THE COST OF VIGILANCE. I KNOW THE NECESSITY OF STRENGTH.

I ALSO KNOW THE DANGER OF FORGETTING WHY THAT STRENGTH EXISTS.

I SEEK NO OFFICE, NO MONUMENT, NO LEGACY. I ASK ONLY THAT WHAT WAS ENTRUSTED TO US BE CARRIED WITH CARE.

BECAUSE THE FEVER HAS PASSED.

BUT WHAT IT REVEALED HAS NOT.

AND IF WE ALLOW DUTY TO BECOME ORNAMENT, AND AUTHORITY TO BECOME POSSESSION, THIS CHAMBER WILL ENDURE LONG AFTER THE PRINCIPLES IT WAS MEANT TO GUARD HAVE WILTED AWAY.

THREE TIMES, THE WORLD TRIED TO BREAK US.

HAMILTON ENDURED.

BUT SURVIVAL IS NOT INTEGRITY. ENDURANCE IS NOT HONOR.

WHAT THIS CHAMBER DOES NEXT WILL DETERMINE WHETHER HAMILTON ENDURES—OR MERELY CONTINUES."

Renik Korvyn
Minister of War

(Transcribed and preserved in the Archives of Valdris Promontory. Select passages inscribed in the Grand Rotunda by order of Chief Minister Aldric Vance, 2158.)

Author's Note

2026.073 · 21:52

Kasson, MN | United States

I finally did it. I finally brought Peri, Kitt, and Wynne's world to life.

This has been quite a journey. Not an easy one — but one worth taking.

This world started thirty years ago. Maybe longer. Indiana, of all places — hard to remember I ever lived there. But if I'm honest, it reaches further back still. To my teenage years, reading comic books, designing games on the Apple IIe, trying my hand at being a comic book artist by sketching characters that were appealing... mostly to a teenage boy. Those ideas never left, only matured. My twin brother worked on the guts of our games while I added the cosmetics, the flair, the world. Who would have thought I'd still be building after all this time.

If you've read the dedication, you already know — the characters came from the people I love. Most authors hide the people they care about in their books. I'm no different. In time, you'll find Megan, my wife Kris.

You'll find my grandson Oliver. You've already met Winslow — Wynne — and a few others buried in these pages. I take inspiration from everywhere I see it.

The title came to me in church, and the timing felt like a small miracle.

I'm a member of South Zumbro Lutheran Church, south of Kasson. We have two wonderful pastors, Pete and Jeff. Jeff is a football coach, and this particular service was about athletes chasing crowns that really mean nothing. First Corinthians 9:25 — "Everyone who competes in the games goes into strict training. They do it to get a crown that will not last, but we do it to get a crown that will last forever."

The perishable crown. A temporary reward. That became my template for Peri.

Once I understood what I was doing, the novel took off. I had a path to follow, characters worth exploring, and a world I wanted to feel real. What started as an adventure novel about a thief trying to do good turned into a character study of what happens when you start measuring the wrong things. When you start running from the thoughts in your own mind.

Peri is not perfect. None of these characters are. But she's fascinating.

She's going to change this world.

Thank you for making it this far.

JT Baldwin
Builder of Worlds

CONTINENTAL AUTHORITY

Administrative Reference Index

Territorial Distribution Approved

ETHSHELM Primary steel production center during the pre-Silence industrial era. Received raw ore via the Kyjorh Canal system from mining operations in the Blackiron Hills. Current operational status: Limited capacity. Restoration efforts ongoing.

LACKCOATS Common parlance for uniformed personnel of the Continental Authority enforcement division. Official designation: Continental Security Services. Responsible for infrastructure protection, territorial compliance, and transport security operations.

(LAC)KIRON HILLS Mountain range in the Kyjorh region, historically significant for mineral extraction operations. Rich deposits of iron ore supplied Bethshelm foundries via the canal system prior to 2027. Also referenced as the Kyjorh Mountains in regional documentation.

CAD HAMILTON Capital Administrative District. Seat of the Continental Authority and location of Valdris Promontory, the governmental complex housing the Continental Council chambers. Established as permanent capital in 2054 following ratification of the Continental Charter.

CHIEF MINISTER Highest executive office of the Continental Authority. Presides over the Continental Council and holds final authority on matters of territorial governance, infrastructure allocation, and security operations. Current officeholder: **Shori Ashford** (appointed 2183).

CONTINENTAL AUTHORITY Governing body of the unified territories (**Union**), established 2054. Formed in response to the infrastructural collapse following the Silence of 2027. Responsible for territorial coordination, resource distribution, trade regulation, and civil order across all administered districts.

CONTINENTAL COUNCIL Legislative and advisory body composed of appointed Ministers representing key governmental functions: War, Internal Affairs, Infrastructure, Agriculture, Trade, and Territorial Coordination. Convenes in the Grand Rotunda of Valdris Promontory.

GATE 20 (HAMMISON LOCK) Southern lock of the Kyjorh Canal system. Critical junction connecting the canal network to central distribution routes. Inoperable since 2027. Restoration designated as priority infrastructure initiative under current administration. Reopening projected to restore full north-south commercial transit.

GATE 31 (KIRON HILLS LOCK) Northern lock of the Kyjorh Canal system, situated in the Blackiron Hills region. Primary transit point between mining territories and the canal network. *[See Administrative Circular 2191-0042]*

HAMMISON CORRIDOR Major north-south transit route connecting agricultural northern provinces to central distribution networks. Partial operational capacity since 2187. Full restoration scheduled pending completion of Gate 20 lock system repairs.

JULIAN DATE SYSTEM Standard calendrical notation adopted by the Continental Authority for administrative uniformity. Format: YEAR.DAY (e.g., 2191.117 = 117th day of year 2191). Eliminates regional calendar variations inherited from pre-Silence systems.

KYJORH CANAL SYSTEM Pre-Silence logistical network connecting the Blackiron Hills mining operations to Bethshelm steel production facilities. Comprised of thirty-seven primary locks, the Kyjorh Dam, and associated reservoir infrastructure. Collapsed following the Silence of 2027. Restoration efforts represent one of the Continental Authority's most significant infrastructure initiatives.

KYJORH DAM AND RESERVOIR Water management system supporting the Kyjorh Canal. Structural integrity compromised following the Silence due to maintenance failure and material decay. Full reservoir capacity pending downstream lock restoration.

SCRAPPERS Colloquial term for unaffiliated individuals or groups operating outside sanctioned trade and labor networks. Often associated with salvage operations, unlicensed transport, and gray-market resource distribution. Status: Non-compliant. See also: *Infrastructure Reclamation Protocols*.

THE SILENCE (2027) Systemic technological failure resulting in the collapse of global digital infrastructure. Cause: Unknown. Effects: Immediate cessation of electronic communication, data storage, and networked systems worldwide. Precipitated the Reconstruction Era and eventual formation of the Continental Authority.

WESTREACH TERRITORIES Frontier region along the western border of Continental Authority jurisdiction. Characterized by limited infrastructure, sparse population centers, and ongoing territorial disputes. Subject to periodic security operations and resource assessment surveys.

Reference Index compiled for administrative use. Unauthorized reproduction prohibited. For updated territorial designations, consult your district coordinator.

– | Aerin

2191.117 · 21:14
Chapi Grade

Field lights. Generators. The hum of equipment she didn't need to identify.

Aerin stepped out of the vehicle and walked. The night air tasted like ozone around her—faint, familiar, the way it tasted before a storm that wasn't coming.

Bodies moved around her. Blackcoats. Forensics. Communications officers speaking into equipment. None of it mattered.

Jin followed. She didn't need to check. He was always where he should be.

The mobile command unit sat at the center of the staging area. Riveted steel chassis with thick armored plating, antenna mast bolted to the roof, light spilling from an open bay door. Voices inside—someone giving a report, someone asking questions, someone laughing.

She entered. The laughter stopped.

Faces turned. An officer with a stylus. Another with a clipboard. Recognition immediate.

"Where is he?"

The officer pointed toward the back.

She moved through the partition. Jin stayed at the threshold.

Gray-beard sat at a folding table. Bandage on his neck. Hands flat on the surface. Across from him, another officer—notes, questions, the same information asked six different ways.

Irrelevant.

"Out."

The officer hesitated. Aerin looked at him. He left.

Aerin sat. Close. No space for evasion.

"Agent Revalis."

"Sergeant Matthews." She waited.

"We were outmatched."

"Five guards. Two unknowns."

"Trained." He didn't look away. "An older male, knew exactly where to hit. The girl moved before any of us could register what was happening."

"Military?"

"No."

"Territorial?"

"No."

"Western provinces? Rival interests?"

"No."

Aerin studied him.

"Enhanced?"

"No." He shook his head. "Just people. Living day to day."

Ordinary people had taken her target.

The inefficiency of it was almost interesting.

"The girl," Aerin said. "Describe her."

"Early twenties. Copper hair. Blue eyes. Fast." He paused. "Could have killed us. Didn't."

"Didn't."

"Bandaged my man's leg after she put a knife through it." He shifted. "I warned her. Twice. Told her to walk away."

"She didn't listen."

"No."

"Name?"

Matthews paused. "The older one called her... Peri."

Peri.

The name filed itself away. Indexed. Retrievable.

"Direction?"

"We were tied up in the car. Couldn't get a visual. But it sounded like they split—one group heading north, the other possibly south."

"How long ago?"

"Thirteen hours. Give or take." Matthews straightened. "I called a perimeter blockade as soon as we were freed and had a working radio. Put blockades on all roads surrounding the area."

Thirteen hours. Perimeter already in place.

"My men are ready to mobilize," Matthews said. Lower now. Leaning forward. "As soon as we get a direction confirmed, we can have units—"

"Your men failed. The asset was your responsibility."

Aerin stood.

"That girl had a chance to do the smart thing."

Matthews's voice carried behind her. "I warned her. Told her what was coming. She didn't listen."

The door closed behind her.

Jin straightened at the threshold, falling into step.

"Agent Revalis."

A voice from the far side of the bay. Not nervous—professional. Controlled enough to interrupt without being asked.

Aerin stopped.

A woman stood at a field terminal. MERIDIAN portable unit—amber glow against phosphor screen. Mechanical keys. Rotary dials.

"We had a hit on the northeast quadrant." Her hand rested on the terminal casing. "T-23 heading north. Broward County. Mile marker 14. Logged at 10:47."

Northeast. T-23. Eleven hours ago.

"Dispatched units?"

"Two squadrons deployed. Combing probable routes north of the marker."

Aerin stepped in front of the terminal. The woman moved aside without being asked.

Her fingers found the keyboard. The display shifted—authorization codes rendered as dashes across the phosphor, then mapping data tracing routes from their current position. The last was a query for a name. Peri. She keyed it. Waited.

The query transmitted. Silence. Then the response crawled across the screen, character by character.

QUERY NOT FOUND.

Aerin held one command key and cleared the display. Restrictions restored.

Name tag. Russell. Late thirties. Sharp features. No wasted expression.

She'd reported data. Not interpretations. Hadn't flinched. Hadn't looked away.

Russell went into a different file. The kind she kept closer.

Aerin left.

Jin fell into step beside her. Through the staging area. Past the lights and the officers.

At the perimeter's edge, she stopped.

Northeast stretched into darkness. Distance that didn't matter.

Peri.

The air cracked. Faint at first—like a hand across wool in winter. The hair on her arms lifting, settling. Then stronger. A low hum she felt before she heard it, rising from the steel at her wrists, her collarbone, her throat. Warming against skin. The ozone sharpened—not the faint taste from before but close now, real, climbing from the metal buried beneath mahogany like heat off a charging coil.

Her vision shifted. Edges hardening. The dark peeling back—tree lines resolving, road grades sharpening, distance collapsing into detail that had no business being visible at this range.

Gold bled through everything. Warm and steady, like amber catching light from the inside.

Jin was at the vehicle. Waiting.

"Northeast," she said.

Jin drove.

Also by JT Baldwin

BLOOD & STEEL UNIVERSE

Found on Amazon

⚙

Forged in Blood & Steel — Volume 1 Short stories from the world of the Continental Authority. Seeds of rebellion, glimpses of monsters, and the ordinary people caught between.

The Palisade Journals — Complete Collection Five novellas spanning decades of conspiracy, corruption, and resistance. The foundation of everything that comes after. *(Also available as individual volumes)*

Wilted Crowns — Ironforged Book One You are here.

⚙

Coming Soon

Empty Throne — Ironforged Book Two The hunt begins.

www.ingramcontent.com/pod-product-compliance
Lightning Source LLC
LaVergne TN
LVHW050912080826
845145LV00001B/61

* 9 7 8 1 9 6 8 9 2 3 2 2 8 *